NICOLE TAYLOR

The Case Against Her

This book was professionally typeset on Reedsy.
Find out more at reedsy.com

For my love

Contents

1

Chapter 1

The precinct was humming with activity; detectives carted nervous suspects in and out of interrogation rooms as pens scribbled across endless case notes. The phones on the rows of desks seemed to be constantly ringing and the noise was giving Laura a headache. She rubbed her temples irritably, trying to lessen the throbbing that was building in her head. A high turnover of cases lately meant stacks of paperwork and she had barely scratched the surface.

A coffee mug inscribed with the words 'I'm nicer after coffee', was dropped onto her desk, rattling her from her thoughts. "Last day of freedom Carlsson." Kyle leaned over her desk, his distinct cheeky smirk plastered on his face as he ran his hand through his light brown hair. He touched and played with his hair more than any woman would, constantly making sure it parted perfectly to the side. She wasn't in the mood to deal with his antics today, not that she was on any other day, but today especially she decided she wasn't going to engage. Instead, she picked up the mug of steaming hot coffee and took a sip, her tongue uniting with the caffeine in utter bliss.

"Foster and I have bets on how long it takes for you to request a new partner. I've got three days."

Laura opened her vivid green eyes only to roll them at Kyle, "No one can be as bad as Miller." She jerked her thumb toward the empty desk beside her. Coffee cup rings littered its surface from the previous resident. Just one of his annoying quirks that had irked Laura to no end.

"Captain told you who it is yet?"

Laura shook her head. "They're coming in this afternoon. Apparently, it's an inter-state transfer."

"Please let it be a woman." Kyle looked toward the ceiling and placed his hands together in mock prayer.

"You're gross."

"What? Work's so busy at the moment I don't have time to date." Kyle frowned. His big blue eyes pleading like a child's.

"Like I said, gross. No new detective is going to sleep with you." Laura hoped anyway, women had a tendency to do stupid things when it came to Kyle.

"Well whoever it is will probably be in and out in a week and then I'll have another possible option," he winked.

"Don't get your hopes up. I have a good feeling about this one." Laura turned back to her paperwork, hoping that this time she was right.

Coming back from lunch Laura noticed the Captain's door was shut. She could hear voices behind the frosted glass and could only assume her new partner was inside. She sat back down at her desk and began sifting through the slightly smaller pile of paperwork. After a few minutes the Captain's door opened and the grey-haired man smiled in her direction.

"Carlsson, come in and meet your new partner." He held the door open, his large frame almost completely filling the space. Though she could still see the framed newspaper clippings of all his most noteworthy cases, Laura guessed barely an inch of wall in that office was still visible. He even had a clipping from his very first week on the job, the Fairhope Gazette had run a story after he caught a bag snatcher in action on the main thoroughfare in town. Laura couldn't help but chuckle that this was the article he chose for his desk, rather than the hundred other more high profile cases. Laura had come to realise, you could take the cop out of the South, you just couldn't take the South out of the cop.

As she moved past the Captain, she noticed a woman sitting in a chair with her back to them. Her dark hair was tied up in a long ponytail that waved down her white blouse. The sight provoked a sense of nostalgia, though Laura quickly quashed it. More than one person could wear that hairstyle, she hated that all these years later certain things still triggered her. She closed her eyes and pushed away that thought as she entered the room.

"Detective, this is Detective Isabella Medina. Your new partner."

Butterflies instantly swirled in Laura's stomach and her heart thundered in her chest. The stunning woman with her familiar chocolate brown eyes stood up and turned towards her, a nervous smile on her lips. She was overrun with nostalgia, the feeling so powerful she wasn't quite sure if this moment was real or not. She tried to relax her facial features as she stared into the chocolate eyes. That damn sparkle was still there, she cursed. Isabella reached out her hand and Laura briefly hesitated before stepping forward and shaking it firmly. Her hand was warm, she could almost feel those slender fingers trailing along the side of her face. She blushed slightly at the thought and dropped the woman's hand.

"It's good to see you Laura," she blushed, her eyes drifting from hers to the floor.

Laura nodded simply and tried to produce a polite smile for the Captain's sake, but she couldn't quite make it happen. She felt like someone was squeezing the air out of her chest. It didn't help that Isabella had only gotten more beautiful in the time since they had seen one another. Her jawline and cheekbones were far more angular, her lips even fuller with age.

"You two know each other?" The Captain asked surprised.

Laura looked up, thankful the other detective hadn't caught her staring. Isabella opened her mouth to say something, but Laura promptly cut her off. "We went to high school together." Laura said, playing down the complex relationship they had once shared. Isabella's eyebrows furrowed, and Laura thought she looked hurt. But like the brilliant actress Laura had come to know her as, her features soon returned to those of the charming girl next door. Polite, unreadable, and devastatingly beautiful.

"Great! You two should get along nicely then." The Captain smiled happily at Laura. His brown eyes were so expressive, she could see the glimmer of hope that this partnership would last. She had always enjoyed proving the man wrong and she was sure this time would be no exception.

"Definitely," Isabella turned to Laura once more with a friendly smile, but she averted her eyes.

"Carlsson, seeing you two already know each other, why don't you give Medina a tour." Laura nodded at the Captain and stepped back out into the hallway. She felt Isabella step out behind her as the Captain's door shut behind them.

"Look Laura—"

Laura pointed toward the vacant desk beside her, Isabella's eyes falling on the rings and rings of coffee stains, her mouth turning down distastefully. "That will be your desk, the drawers are already filled with spare notepads and pens." Laura pointed to a staircase at the end of the room, "If you go up the stairs and turn right, you'll find HR, they will issue you with a laptop." She pointed toward the far end of the room where there were three large windows, covered with venetian blinds. "Those are the interview rooms. We generally have free reign, but detectives from other precincts do occasionally use them, like today."

She turned again to her right, avoiding eye contact with the other detective. The majority of light coming into the office was from the bright fluorescent tubes above their heads. The light above Laura's desk had been flickering for weeks now. After multiple ignored emails to maintenance, she was about ready to change it herself. She stood by her desk and pointed across the hallway, "Behind that door is the break room. There are a few vending machines and a coffee machine, as well as a fridge if you want to bring in your own meals."

She turned back to the few desks surrounding theirs, most filled with pictures of partners and kids, coffee mugs that read 'world's greatest Dad', or trinkets people had bought in Thailand or Bali. Laura's on the other hand featured none of those things. She had a few simple mementos, her laptop, her phone, a clock and her signed baseball. She had always despised clutter and didn't believe in advertising her private life on her desk. She motioned widely with her arms, "All of these desks belong to the homicide squad, if people aren't at their desks they're out on cases or getting in a wink of sleep."

She was breathing heavily now; the nerves had caused her to talk incredibly fast and she was still so overwhelmed with the whole situation.

"Who's the new recruit?" For once Laura was grateful for one of Kyle's interruptions. He ran his eyes over Isabella's figure before the woman turned around to look at him. He flashed her one of his most charming smiles and smoothed his tie down his broad chest as he approached her.

"Isabella Medina," she held out her hand to Kyle and he slowly shook it, staring deeply into her eyes as he did. That dazzling smile, widening even further. Laura rolled her eyes and crossed her arms.

"Lovely to meet you Detective Medina. Detective Kyle Reynolds at your service." Isabella dropped her hand forcefully from his tight grip, but smiled politely. Laura had to stifle a chuckle. Kyle's approach usually went one of two ways; women were completely charmed by him or they were repulsed. Laura sensed that for Isabella, it was the latter.

"Laura's just giving me the tour."

"First name basis already, huh?" Kyle smirked and raised his eyebrows at Laura suggestively. Thankfully Isabella hadn't seemed to notice and Laura rolled her eyes at him for the millionth time today.

"Actually, Reynolds? Do you want to finish giving Medina the tour? I've got some things to do."

"Sure!" Kyle exclaimed excitedly. As soon as the words left his lips Laura turned on her heel and stalked down the hallway. Isabella's dejected chocolate eyes watched her disappear.

After work was Laura's favourite time to work out. The precinct gym bustled in the mornings, everyone looking to start their day with a hit of endorphins. Laura preferred the distraction at the end of the day, she left her emotions in that gym at the end of every shift. Each punch to a bag, each kilometre on the treadmill, every weight successfully deadlifted helped erase the faces of the victims she was trying to get justice for. Until she woke up the next morning, those were the first faces she always saw. Sweat was dripping down her back, but today only one face was plastered in her mind as she pounded the bag. Chocolate eyes and long dark hair haunted her heart, the pain pulsating in her chest felt just as fresh as it had all those years before.

5

* * *

One of Laura's gloves deflected off the bag and collided with something hard. "Sorry I didn't see−" Laura looked up and met those same chocolate eyes staring at her.

"I probably deserved that." Isabella rubbed at her now bruised shoulder and then fidgeted nervously with her hands as she looked down at the mats. Laura ignored the comment and ripped off her gloves, very conscious of the sweat dripping down her body. She walked past Isabella to the side of the gym and grabbed a towel from inside her bag, wiping herself down. She looked back towards Isabella and noticed the woman's eyes on her legs, she looked up when she felt Laura's gaze.

"Laura, please let me just say this," Isabella paused and looked up into Laura's emerald eyes, breath escaping her mouth as the indignant irises connected with her own. "I know me being here is a huge shock to you."

"Isn't it for you?" Laura shot back without thinking.

"Um," Isabella shifted her weight between her feet, "I'd actually heard you were working homicide at the 34th." Laura was surprised to hear this, but she kept her face neutral and let the woman continue. "Cate mentioned it." Laura nodded now, that made sense. It was an unstated rule between Cate and herself to never mention Isabella, but it seemed that wasn't the case between the other two friends, and she wasn't sure how she felt about that.

"I don't really know what to say except I'm sorry. I'm sorry for everything that happened back then, I really am, and I'm sorry it's taken me so long to apologise to you." She looked up at Laura again and she could tell Isabella was finding it hard to find the right words. "I had no idea we would end up here and I really didn't mean to ambush you. I was just hoping..." Isabella's sentence died on her lips as Laura picked up her drink bottle and brought it to her mouth. The sleeve of her jumper slipped back revealing a small tattoo of a baseball bat. Laura noticed Isabella's eyes on her tattoo as she pulled down her sleeve, the black ink disappearing beneath the fabric.

Isabella took a deep breath to steady herself. "I was just hoping we could try and put the past behind us and start fresh." Her shoulders were slumped as she finally raised her eyes to stare into Laura's.

Laura could feel the tears prickling at the back of her eyes, she cleared her throat, trying her best to sound authoritative. "Look this has all been a pretty huge surprise and I'm still processing to be honest. Everything that happened, happened a long time ago and we're not the same people anymore. I have no idea who you are, and you have no idea who I am." She could tell her words stung Isabella, the detective trying not to flinch under her gaze. "The Captain gave you a glowing recommendation, so I'm going to hold on to that. I think we can both be professional about this, don't you?"

"I do."

"Great. I'll see you first thing tomorrow Iss-" Laura noticed the slight change in Isabella's features as she nearly said it, the other detective looking hopeful. But she managed to cut herself off before she did. God damn force of habit, she cursed internally. Instead she simply mumbled, "Isabella." She grabbed her bag and without another look in the detective's direction, walked out of the gym.

* * *

"Morning," Isabella smiled brightly as she walked into the office, provoking a flinch from Laura. She had barely slept at all the night before and she still hadn't had her coffee.

"Morning sunshine," Kyle winked, leaning back in his chair across from Laura, his hands resting behind his head to show off his biceps. She could see the glint of his smirk in her peripherals. She took a deep breath to calm herself, as the air rushed in through her nose she was engulfed by the familiar sweet floral scent of daisies. The smell provoked so many conflicting feelings; adoration, angst, and confusion all at once. She heard Isabella stop beside her, something heavy was dropped onto her new desk, keys rattled as they were placed on the wood and she could feel brown eyes on the back of her head.

"Hey." Laura could tell this softer greeting was specifically aimed at her, she felt her muscles tense and her mouth become dry. She didn't want to spark any suspicions by ignoring her in front of Kyle, but she was never very good at faking her feelings.

"Hi," Laura looked at Isabella briefly before turning back to her paperwork. She immediately wished she hadn't looked up when she saw what Isabella was wearing. The detective's tight black pants accentuated her curves, a light denim blouse slightly tucked in at the front. Her dark hair fell on either side of her face in perfect waves, she looked beautiful. Footsteps echoed down the hall as she looked up to see Jordan walking towards them from the break room. He had a short buzz cut and a stubbly black beard that faded perfectly into his brown skin. He put his coffee mug down on the desk across from Isabella and offered her a sweet smile.

"Hi there, I'm Jordan Foster." His demeanour was warm and his southern drawl was even more inviting.

"Isabella Medina," she shook his hand and smiled brightly. Laura could tell Isabella felt far more relaxed in the Southern man's presence than in his partner's.

"What no coffee for me this morning Foster?" She looked up at Jordan, a sarcastic pout on her lips.

"Sorry Carlsson, I don't have three sets of hands." He motioned to himself, Isabella and then back to her. She scoffed in response and turned back to her paperwork. Great, now Isabella was even robbing her of her morning fix. "Reynolds said you're from Miami?"

"Yes, originally. For the last two years I was working narcotics down there and before that I was a beat cop in West Hollywood."

"Why did you want to transfer here?" Kyle probed, Laura looked up briefly from her paperwork and glared at him.

"Just wanted a new challenge and my sister was moving here for college so I thought it was a good opportunity to make the move," Isabella smiled. Laura was intrigued to know more but she was careful not to show any signs of interest.

"So what's the dirt on Carlsson?" Isabella blushed slightly, looking down at Laura. "What was she like back in the day? Let me guess, school stoner?

8

Slutty cheerleader?" Without thinking Laura grabbed the vintage baseball on her desk off its stand and threw it with force at Kyle. She hadn't really intended it to be that hard, but the groan it elicited from Kyle when it hit his stomach gave her more pleasure than she would normally care to admit. Isabella had to bite her lip to hide her smirk.

"Jesus Carlsson. Were you a bloody pitcher in school?" He groaned as he cradled his stomach, his brows crinkled in pain.

"Next time it's my gun," Laura threatened playfully before walking over to retrieve the ball. She dusted it off on her pants and carefully placed it back on its stand. Jordan rolled his eyes and shook his head at Isabella, the look saying 'yes these two were crazy, and yes this was their normal.'

"But seriously Medina, I'm dying to hear about teenage Carlsson?" He pleaded.

She cleared her throat nervously, clearly pondering before the words began flowing swiftly. "Well, there was practically no sport she wasn't good at. Everyone always picked her first for their team, even the boys, and she couldn't handle losing." Laura's eyes were focused on her paperwork, but all of her concentration was channelled into listening to every word the detective said.

"Sounds about right," Jordan chuckled, though Isabella wasn't disturbed by the interruption as she continued rattling on.

"But she wasn't just a jock, she was one of the smartest in our grade. I probably would've failed half my subjects without her. She was the most determined person I'd ever met." Laura couldn't stop the slight blush creeping across her skin. She risked a glance up at Jordan and Kyle who were eyeing Isabella intently, swept up in her description. "And... she was charming. In the sweetest way. One compliment from Laura and everyone swooned, particularly when she looked at you with those incredible emerald eyes." Her cheeks flushed as she looked up at the detectives surrounding her.

As soon as Isabella mentioned her eyes, Laura's heart began racing in her chest. She didn't dare look up in case her flushed cheeks betrayed her. She couldn't help but feel the description of her was incredibly overstated, but she was flattered nonetheless. She felt butterflies churning in her stomach briefly before she thought back on everything that had happened and the butterflies disappeared, replaced instead with an ache in her chest.

"Wow."

"Yeah wow," Kyle smirked, and Laura could feel his eyes burning a hole in the back of her head.

"So are you married? Single?" Jordan pressed.

"I'm single." Laura's eyes lifted of their own accord, immediately searching for Isabella's ring finger. Sure enough, it was empty. Her phone buzzed beside her and she scrambled to answer it.

"Carlsson." She nodded to herself as she listened to the voice on the other side of the line, the other detectives watching her intently. "Be right there." Laura stood up and grabbed her badge and keys from on top of her desk.

"Murder?" Jordan asked.

"Yep."

"Can we come?" Kyle asked eagerly.

"Nope." Laura turned around and began walking towards the elevator, "You two have paperwork to do." Isabella looked towards Laura unsure of what to do. Jordan clicked to get her attention. She looked at him and he frantically waved his hands, shooing her towards the elevator. She grabbed her badge and ran for the doors just before they closed. Laura was annoyed, but intrigued when she managed to slip inside, she was used to leaving her partners behind.

Laura stalked toward the crime scene with Isabella scurrying along behind her. Tape cordoned off three grand terrace houses in an expensive street downtown. Patrol officers were on guard to keep the prying neighbours away. A temporary marquee had already been put up on the sidewalk to shield the deceased. As they approached Laura noticed Parker was hovering over a woman's body on the ground. Her glasses perched on the end of her nose in concentration, her long black hair tied up in a bun.

"Parker, what have you got?" Laura asked.

"Caucasian female in her late thirties–" Parker looked up towards Laura as Isabella ducked under the police tape. Her jaw practically hit the floor as she saw the new detective moving towards them. Laura had been so overwhelmed by her sudden arrival that she had completely forgotten to warn Parker. Something she deeply regretted now seeing Parker's reaction and anticipating the awkward moment about to play out. Isabella approached slowly as Parker gradually composed herself and managed to stand up.

"Hey Parker." Isabella waved, stepping up behind Laura. Parker didn't utter a word of response, her expression a mix of shock and anger, Isabella's eyes drifted down to the ground.

Laura couldn't handle the tension, particularly with the rest of the forensic team moving about around them. "You knew that I was getting a new partner Parker?" The medical examiner simply nodded. "Well," Laura pointed to Isabella and Parker let out a small gasp. Her cheeks blushed and she wished her friend would find her composure quickly.

Parker looked at Laura for a brief second, a flurry of emotions being exchanged between them in just one glance. She looked at Isabella again and this time her face was blank, her usual warm disposition replaced with slight hostility. "Welcome to the team I guess."

"Thank you." The detective's tone was soft but she made sure to keep eye contact with Parker as she said it.

"The body?" Laura prodded.

"Yes, as I was saying...caucasian female in her late thirties. She suffered blunt force trauma to the head when she hit the ground, completely fracturing her skull. From the force of the impact and the trajectory of the body it seems she fell from a height of several metres." Parker turned to point at the terrace house just behind them with a balcony on the third story. "Most probably from that balcony."

"Do—" the detective's asked at once, each stopping to look at the other awkwardly.

"Do you have a time of death?" Laura was slightly annoyed when Isabella stole the words straight from her mouth, but a small part of her was also impressed. She wasn't easily intimidated. Parker hesitated slightly before addressing the newcomer.

"I'll have to get her body back to the lab before I can tell you any more, but based on lividity I would estimate the time of death to be between twelve and two am this morning."

"Great." Laura spoke up before Isabella could take the lead again. "Thanks Parker." She turned away from her best friend and ducked back under the police tape, headed for the terrace house behind them, Isabella hurrying after her.

* * *

Laura sat down at her desk and sighed, re-reading over all of the statements they had just taken. She yawned and ran a hand through her long wavy blonde hair, the lack of any sleep the night before weighing down on her. Her phone buzzed beside her and she saw a text message from Parker.

Parker: OMG Laura! Thanks for the warning. I practically choked on my tonsils when I saw her. Need details ASAP!!!!

Laura: My place 8pm?

Parker: I'll be there.

Laura was startled when a mug of steaming coffee was placed down on her desk. She looked up and saw the familiar chocolate eyes gazing down at her. "Figured you needed that." Isabella shrugged and sat down at her desk, beginning to unpack various objects from inside her box.

"Thanks." Laura could tell Isabella was trying extra hard to get into her good graces. She just wasn't sure yet of her motive. She took a sip of her coffee and was surprised when she tasted a small ounce of sugar. She had always taken her coffee black with one sugar. She just didn't expect that after all these years Isabella still remembered that.

"So are you thinking the husband?" Laura looked up from the statements and looked over at Isabella as she placed a photo frame on her desk. It looked to be a photo of her and Savannah, but it was hard to reconcile the young girl she once knew for the young woman smiling in the photo.

"It's looking that way, but we don't know anywhere near enough yet to make any conclusions." Laura reproached, Isabella simply nodded.

"So Parker went to medical school hey? I never would have seen that happening." Isabella laughed. "I guess I always expected her to end up in the arts." Laura nodded slightly, her heart ignoring her brain when it came to acknowledging Isabella. "If anyone was going to do medicine, I always thought it would be you." Laura's eyes flitted upwards and connected with Isabella's, she could see the curiosity in her features.

"Well, things change," she said. Her fingers absentmindedly trailing her wrist.

"They do."

2

Chapter 2

As the ball soared over the net she ran forward to spike it, her hands connecting at just the right spot with enough force to send the ball back toward an open space in the opposing team's side. The other team had no chance defending a hit like that and Laura's team cheered the point.

As she waited for the other team to serve she looked over to a group of girls giggling on the side lines. It was always the same three girls who seemed to get out of whatever sport they were doing and instead made up silly games on the side lines. Laura rolled her eyes, they were so immature. Frowning in her disapproval she somehow couldn't manage to pull her eyes away from the loudest of the group, Isabella. Her enigmatic smile and boisterous laughter were captivating. The whistle blew, "Point for red," the coach yelled. Laura looked down at her feet to see the ball had landed just in front of her, the rest of her team now glaring rather than celebrating her. She cursed under her breath and glared one last time toward the girls. Bloody Isabella.

She stood outside the Biology classroom nervously, waiting to see if any familiar faces turned up. She saw Cate approaching her with a friendly smile. She was a shorter girl, with auburn hair and a warm personality. They weren't exactly friends, but they had classes together before and Cate was always friendly. "Hey, I'm so glad you're in this class. I was worried I wasn't going to know anyone," she smiled warmly.

"Me too," Laura smiled back, some of her apprehension draining away.

Parker bounced over towards them on the balls of her feet, her black tights accentuating her dancer's physique. "Cate, thank god. I was so worried about who I'd be paired with for labs." Parker grabbed her chest as if a huge weight had been lifted off.

"Same! You know Laura right?"

"Hey," Parker gave her a small wave and friendly smile in acknowledgement.

They turned to enter the room as a rush of footsteps pumped down the corridor behind them. Laura turned around to see Isabella running in their direction. She threw her arms around Cate's neck and the short girl chuckled as she turned around to see who was embracing her.

"I'm so happy you're in this class!" Isabella chirped to Cate, a huge grin plastering her face. Laura had no idea the two even knew each other. She knew they definitely weren't close friends, so the enthusiastic hug seemed a bit much. "We can be lab buddies!" Laura instantly sighed and rolled her eyes, a feeling of dread taking over as she realised she was going to be forced to interact with the girl. She could just see their lab results going downhill already.

Isabella gave Parker a polite wave, her eyes then focused on Laura and her lips formed a spectacular smile that caused her eyes to sparkle. Butterflies immediately rose in Laura's stomach, though her brain couldn't quite conclude why.

* * *

The doorbell rang and Laura ran from the couch to answer it. As she opened the door she saw Parker standing on her doorstep, a tub of Ben and Jerry's chocolate fudge brownie ice cream in her hands. Laura couldn't help but laugh when she saw that. "I thought ice cream was only prescribed immediately after the heartbreak?"

"I figured there might be some new cracks to patch," Parker shrugged. Laura sighed and opened the door, Parker had always been very perceptive. They walked into Laura's modern kitchen, fitted with stainless steel benches and appliances. Laura grabbed two spoons out of a drawer and handed one to Parker. After they had consumed half the tub of ice cream, Parker finally spoke up. "So...how did this even happen?"

"I have no idea," Laura admitted. "Did you know she was a detective?"

Parker shook her head. "Her socials are all private, but I've never really gone looking. I said she was dead to me that day and I meant it." Laura couldn't help but smile slightly at her best friend's resolute loyalty.

Laura began telling Parker about the weeks leading up to Isabella's arrival and the Captain's descriptions of a promising detective from Miami who would be joining their team. She told her about her near heart attack when she saw Isabella sitting in his office afterwards and their subsequent conversations since. Parker waited until she finished to finally speak, words taking a few moments to present themselves to her.

"Jeez. It's just so bizarre. So, she knew you worked at the 34th?" Laura nodded. "Girls got balls I'll give her that," Parker chuckled. "Did she know she was going to be partnering with you?"

"I doubt it. Her balls couldn't be that big."

"So, she really called you charming?" Laura blushed when Parker brought up Isabella's description of her past self, and simply nodded in response. "Seriously? What is this woman's deal?"

"It's so confusing."

"After everything that happened, I just don't understand why on earth she would want to work with you. Her own feelings, or lack thereof aside, she has to know you hate her. So why put herself through that?"

"I don't know."

When Laura woke up the next morning she swore furiously when she saw the time on her clock. She was late to work. Her lack of sleep, in combination with all the wine her and Parker had drunk the night before, had messed with her body clock. She grabbed the first clothes she could find along with her make-up bag and ran out the front door.

As the elevator doors opened, she heard laughter emanating from the desks. Kyle, Jordan, and Isabella were all standing around and watching something on Jordan's phone. As Laura approached Kyle turned away from the video and gave her the one up. "Decided to grace us with your presence today after all Carlsson?"

"Bite me Reynolds." She quipped. Kyle smirked and offered her a suggestive look. Isabella looked over her shoulder subtly as the two detectives exchanged banter, her eyebrows furrowing inquisitively at their flirtation.

"Give me a time and place boss."

"You're disgusting."

The video ended and Isabella turned to Jordan with an endearing smile. "He's so cute Foster. Definitely going to be a handful that one," she chuckled. Laura's heart leapt at the sound that had caused her so many butterflies in the past. She knew what content the videos must have contained. Jordan was obsessed with his year-old son, Andre. He constantly brought in adorable videos of the baby running amuck around their apartment.

"Hey Carlsson, rough night?" Jordan pointed to Laura's white blouse.

"No, why?" Laura looked down and noticed she was wearing a lacy red bra underneath her white blouse. The top was completely see-through. Jordan and Kyle burst into laughter, her cheeks flushing red. Great.

"Here." She looked up as Isabella shrugged off her black blazer and handed it to her. "I was hot anyway." She hesitated for a second before deciding she had no other option but to accept. She couldn't deal with Jordan and Kyle's snarky comments for the rest of the day and she definitely couldn't go out in the field with a see-through blouse.

"Thanks," she said, before sliding her arms into the blazer. It was still toasty warm from its previous occupant.

"You're welcome." Isabella picked up one of the two coffee mugs on her desk and handed it to Laura. "It should still be warm."

"Oh," Laura took the mug, taken aback by the gesture, "thanks."

A little while later Laura headed to the morgue for an update. She pushed the double doors open, Isabella running after her to avoid being hit when the doors swung shut again. Parker was leaning over Alicia Pickett's body, the name of the woman they now knew had fallen to her death outside her terrace home. She was a successful corporate lawyer who had lived full-time with her publican husband twenty years her senior and part-time with his twenty-year-old daughter. Parker had done a good job suturing the woman's head wounds, but she was still barely recognisable. As they approached the table

Isabella hung slightly back.

"Hey Parker."

"Hey," Parker looked up and smiled at Laura. She looked over Laura's shoulder at Isabella and the smile vanished.

"Hey," Isabella smiled, Parker just nodded at the detective's greeting and focused her attention towards Laura.

"Nice blazer," she said, looking Laura up and down. "I'll definitely be borrowing that one." Laura blushed in embarrassment.

"It's actually Isabella's." Parker looked shocked as she said it, but Laura wasn't about to make things more awkward by explaining why she was wearing Isabella's blazer.

"You can definitely borrow it," Isabella smiled warmly.

"Uh, thanks," Parker said awkwardly, shooting Laura a glare.

"So what have you got?" Laura swiftly manoeuvred the conversation back to their investigation. Parker lifted up the white sheet exposing the woman's abdomen. There was a mix of purple and blue bruises all over her body, but there was a clear concentration of yellow bruising on her stomach. Parker pointed to the blue and purple bruises.

"These bruises here are a day or two old, so we can conclude that they were caused upon impact with the sidewalk." She pointed to the concentration of yellow bruising on the woman's stomach. "These bruises are four or five days old, so she had these well before her death. There's more of the same on her back. And here..." Parker pointed to the woman's wrist where there were yellow bruises in a striped pattern. "There's a clear handprint in these bruises."

"Well then I guess we're paying Mr Pickett another visit."

An hour later they were exiting the Pickett residence again, having taken another statement from Mr Pickett. He vehemently denied ever having laid a hand on Mrs Pickett and couldn't account for what might have caused the bruises. When Laura became firmer with him, he immediately declined to answer any more questions until his lawyer was present. They stepped back onto the sidewalk and Laura sighed in frustration.

"We need to talk to the daughter," Isabella said firmly, but Laura merely rolled her eyes.

"He just refused to talk to us unless his lawyer was present, there's no way he's letting us talk to his daughter."

"So we don't ask permission then." Laura looked at Isabella confused. "There was a photo on the hall stand of her wearing a Delta Gamma sorority shirt. Why don't we take a trip to NYU?" As they made their way towards the campus Isabella pulled out her phone and began typing.

"Who are you texting?" Laura asked sceptically.

"Our tour guide."

They pulled up at the north end of the campus and made their way over to a park bench where Isabella instructed they would meet their guide. A few moments later Laura heard an excited voice calling from behind them, "Bella!" Turning around she saw a young woman running towards them. She had the same slender figure as Isabella, the same dark hair and goofy smile. Laura instantly knew who it was, Savannah.

"Hey Sav," Isabella wrapped her sister in a hug as Laura watched on awkwardly. She was happy to see the sisters were just as close as they always had been. There was a dull ache in her chest though as she looked at the young woman, the last time she had seen her she had been a young girl. She had completely missed her growing up and that hurt her more than she thought it would. "You remember Laura right?"

"Of course," Savannah smiled brightly and turned towards Laura wrapping her in a tight hug, "Hi Laura." Laura relaxed into the hug, her chest filling with warmth as the young woman clung to her tightly. She hadn't realised she had been holding her breath up until then, but Savannah welcoming her like family felt right. It reminded her of home.

"Hey Sav."

"It's so good to see you!" Savannah stepped back and looked Laura up and down, "Someone got exceptionally hotter." Laura's cheeks flushed bright red and she laughed. The bold little girl she had known was still in there.

"What about you, I bet all the guys and girls swoon over you." Savannah just shrugged and smiled.

"Uh please, I don't want to hear about that," Isabella chuckled.

"Shut up Bella," Savannah shot back. Laura couldn't help but smile at their sibling banter, it was so easy to slip right back to where they'd been ten years ago. Only now Savannah could actually keep up. "Come on. I'll take you to this sorority."

They patiently waited out the front of the sorority, letting Savannah go to the door and enquire about the Pickett girl for them. They didn't want to spook her. When the girl from the photos exited the sorority, Savannah led her down to the lawn and Isabella and Laura both flashed her their badges and asked if they could ask her some questions.

The girl appeared nervous, but tried to mask that fact with a brisk nonchalance she was most definitely not pulling off. They sat down on the front steps of the house and began asking her about her relationship to the victim, her relationship with her father and the goings on in the house. Laura noticed she fiddled with the rings on her fingers the entire time and stuttered over quite a few answers. When they brought up the bruises on the victim's arms the girl shrugged and claimed she had no idea about them. They finished taking her statement before thanking her and giving her their cards to call them if she remembered anything further.

"How did you go?" Savannah asked.

"Not sure yet. We have to go back to the precinct and go over the other witnesses' statements to start piecing together a story." Savannah nodded. "Thank you so much for your help though," Laura smiled.

"You're welcome. Now you can thank me by taking me out for coffee." Laura looked down at her watch and peered back towards their cruiser.

"Sorry Sav, we really should be getting back," Isabella apologised.

"Don't be annoying Bella, it's five thirty. The traffic going back downtown will be terrible. You can spare half an hour." Isabella shot her a playful glare. The way she spoke to her sometimes it was like she was the older sibling. "Good. It's settled."

"Great," Laura added stiffly. She was nervous about having coffee with the two sisters, but a part of her was desperate to know more about this Savannah. If she happened to reveal some insights about Isabella as well, she was happy to write that off as an added bonus.

The coffee shop on campus was packed with students. Tables overflowed with multiple coffee cups, textbooks and laptops as college kids frantically crammed for classes with little to no sleep. A group got up from a table towards the back just as they entered and Savannah bolted to secure it. Laura settled in a seat beside her and studied the menu on the board above the cashier.

"What do you guys want? I'll go up and get it," Isabella offered.

"I'll just have a black coffee with-"

"One sugar," Isabella interrupted her and chuckled. "You know they do make over twenty different coffees here, are you sure you don't want to branch out?"

Laura shook her head and had to bite her gums to stop herself from reciprocating Isabella's brilliant smile. "Creature of habit."

"I'll have an Iced Caramel Macchiato with an extra shot of espresso." Isabella raised her eyebrows at her sister's order. "I have a test tomorrow and I was at a party all of last night. I really need to stay awake." Isabella rolled her eyes and huffed. "Don't give me that look Bella, I can multitask." With a shake of her head, Isabella disappeared to join the long line waiting to place orders. Laura knew she was in trouble the moment Savannah's brown eyes fell on her. There was a look of inquisition in them and her wry smile was certainly revealing.

"So? What have you been doing with yourself Carlsson?"

"Wouldn't you like to know Medina," Laura quipped back, resting forwards on her elbows and matching Savannah's smirk.

"I would. With that hot body, I bet you've got many a story to tell," Savannah gave her a cheeky wink and leant back in her seat.

"I should've guessed this was how you were going to turn out. You were always too sassy for your own good," Laura dodged, outwardly appearing calm, though truthfully, she was nervous of what Savannah might ask.

"Well, I had some super sassy role models when I was younger." Savannah's smile faded slightly and her tone softened. Her expression became one much more akin to the little girl she had known. Laura's own smile faltered. She hadn't often considered what life must have been like for Savannah when everything she knew changed.

"I never had the chance to chat to you back then and say goodbye. I'm sorry Sav," Laura said sincerely, looking the young woman directly in the eyes so she knew she meant it. "It all must have been so confusing for you."

"Yeah it was, it was hard. I missed you a lot in those early days, I didn't understand what happened," Savannah's voice cracked and she took a deep breath. "But I know it wasn't *your* fault." Laura nodded sedately, it was hard for her to imagine little eight-year-old Savannah scared and upset after so much change. She wondered how often Savannah had asked after her, wondered if she was going to come by to watch a movie or take them on walks. "Isabella cried for a solid six months when we moved to Cali."

Laura's eyebrows furrowed as she imagined Isabella being upset about the move. She had been so confident and sure at the time. She had insisted it had been what she had wanted, so she could hardly imagine that Savannah was remembering things correctly. "You were young, maybe she was a bit homesick in the beginning. I'm sure the new house and husband made her very happy." Savannah chuckled darkly.

"God no. There was no house! We lived in a tiny one-bedroom apartment in Berkeley for years. Isabella worked two jobs on top of college just to keep us afloat." Laura looked at Savannah again confused.

"I thought Isabella married Mitch?"

"Oh she did. But after a few months we were lucky to ever see him. He was so wrapped up in the college lifestyle, I think he was ashamed with it all really. The apartment, being married at eighteen, having to look after a kid. I don't think the reality of it all quite stacked up." Laura nodded considering all of this. She wasn't surprised at all that Mitch had turned out to be a douchebag. Laura had always gotten that vibe from him. Hearing about how rough their life had been she couldn't help but feel sympathetic toward Isabella. She had been just a kid herself at the time and she had to look after Savannah as well.

"I don't think she's even been in love since..."

"Here you go." Savannah was cut off as Isabella returned to the table, setting their coffees down in front of them. Laura looked up into Isabella's eyes as she smiled warmly, after everything Savannah had just told her, she found herself offering her own smile back.

The three women caught up on everything Savannah had been doing for the last few years. She had arrived in New York a month ago to start her first semester of college and Isabella had decided to move with her. They managed to avoid any topics of conversation around Laura or Isabella's lives and instead focused on Savannah.

Savannah had them in fits of laughter as she imitated her highly strung professors and joked about the flurry of moronic frat boys on campus. It felt good for Laura to laugh with the sisters again, it almost felt like no time had passed. If one good thing had come from everything, it was the young independent woman sitting across from her. Looking at Savannah Laura felt a sense of pride at how well she had grown up.

"So, remember that night when you guys had your junior prom and you made out at the top of the stairs?" Laura almost choked on her coffee when the words left Savannah's mouth as she thought back to that night nearly twelve years ago. "Yeah, I wasn't sleeping," Savannah laughed casually.

* * *

"Isabella!" Laura yelled as she skipped over to their group, enveloping Isabella in a tight hug. Ordinarily Laura wouldn't be caught dead skipping through the playground, but Isabella brought her silly side out. Isabella's freezing fingers caused her to shiver as they wrapped around her waist. "Gosh you're freezing!"

"Sorry," Isabella shrugged, turning around so her back was to Laura and wrapping her oversized tracksuit jacket around them both. Laura's smile only grew in response.

"How was the test?" Cate asked as Laura and Isabella shuffled closer to their friends.

"I don't know, I think it went ok."

"Just ok, pfft! You nailed it and you know it," Parker smiled.

"Laura, you're too modest," Cate shook her head and she blushed, a feeling of warmth gathering in her chest as she looked at her friends, feeling incredibly grateful.

The bell rang way too quickly for Laura's liking and they began moving towards their Biology class. She shed her jacket and handed it over to Isabella, she smiled brightly in thanks. "Did you guys hear what happened to Ainsley the other day?" Parker asked them as they walked.

"No, what?" Cate asked.

"She got expelled."

"Ainsley Young? Seriously? Why?" Laura was dumbfounded. Ainsley was incredibly respectful and studious and she couldn't understand how someone like that would ever get expelled.

"Well you know how she's gay right?" Cate, Isabella and Laura all shook their heads.

"She got caught kissing her girlfriend in the carpark after school, and the Dean said she was encouraging homosexuality and so they expelled her." Their school was an incredibly prestigious Catholic Private School and anything remotely un-Catholic was frowned upon. Laura's mouth went dry and her palms turned clammy.

"That's absolute crap. This school is so fucked up!" All three girls looked at Cate shocked. She never swore and she was sure to be at mass every Sunday, but here she was getting fired up about Ainsley Young being expelled. Laura liked her all the more for it and all three girls nodded their agreement.

"Isabella!" One of the boys from Mitch's soccer team came running up behind them and interrupted their conversation. He handed her a note before winking at her and running back off the way he came.

"What's that about?" Cate asked as they walked into the classroom and sat down at their desk.

"Open it, open it," Parker urged.

Isabella slowly peeled the sticky tape from the note and opened it. In messy scrawl were the words 'Will you be my date to the prom? - Mitch'. Isabella looked up at Laura, but she was staring out the window.

"Bella!" Cate jumped up and down excitedly. The sudden excitement brought Laura's focus back to the group and she saw all the girls hovering over a note on the desk. She picked it up and read over the words, her stomach lurched when she reached the end.

"You're going to say yes right Bella?" Parker urged.

"I don't know…" she trailed off, trying to catch a glimpse of Laura's emerald eyes.

"He's super cute. You guys would make the cutest couple! Don't you think Laura?" Parker looked over at her friend. Laura looked up and plastered a smile on her face, trying to look as convincing as possible.

"For sure. You guys would look great together." She said convincingly, Ainsley Young's face still dancing in her head. Isabella looked down at the table as the words left Laura's mouth. She took a few moments before she raised her eyes and smiled.

"I guess I'm going to prom with Mitch." Cate and Parker both yelped in excitement and pulled her into a hug.

The hall was beautifully decorated with draping silver fabric and hanging gold stars. Most of their classmates were already on the dance floor, the tables surrounding it merely holding discarded jackets and purses. As soon as they entered the hall Parker grabbed Laura's wrists and dragged her to the dance floor. Laura had decided to ignore Isabella and Mitch and have a good time with her friends. The DJ continued to drop hit after hit and Laura found she was actually enjoying herself, swept up in the bass of the music and swaying her hips rhythmically to the beat. Isabella watched her best friends dancing around crazily in the middle of the dance floor, their laughter echoing around the hall. They didn't care at all what anyone else thought, they were having the time of their lives.

Mitch practically had two left feet, the two of them were continuously stepping on each other's toes before Isabella finally gave up and dragged Mitch to get a drink. He pulled her towards his group of friends, the boys all crowding around a metal flask that one of them had snuck in. Isabella declined a swig and sat down at a vacant table.

The familiar tune of synthesisers and percussion coursed through the speaker as Isabella sat morosely at the table. Laura looked up when she heard the tune, spinning around the dancefloor and searching the crowd. When she spotted the sparkling brown eyes, she rushed over to Isabella's table. "It's our song!" She yelled excitedly, grabbing Isabella's hand and interlacing their fingers before she *dragged her onto the dance floor.*

"It's murder on the dancefloor, you'd better not steal the groove…" Sophie Ellis–Bextor's hit song blasted through the speakers.

Laura began twirling Isabella around in circles as she sung the lyrics back to her, never breaking eye contact. Isabella was in a fit of giggles the whole time as they danced and jumped around, not paying any attention to what anyone else was doing and just focusing on each other. When the song ended, she pulled Isabella into a tight hug as a slow song began emanating from the speakers. Isabella pressed her lips against Laura's ear, "You make me really happy."

Laura pulled back from the hug and looked into Isabella's chocolate eyes, her cheeks flushed as the girl gave her a shy smile and Laura tried to take in what she just said. They were always so playful with one another that Laura had been taken aback by the sincerity and adoration in Isabella's voice.

"Can we have this dance?" Mitch interrupted, Laura shooting him the death stare as he and his intoxicated friend Jud sidled up to them. Mitch grabbed a hold of Isabella's hand and pulled her towards him. Laura's fingers reluctantly let go of Isabella's as Jud's hands closed around her waist. Laura spent the entire song searching for Isabella's eyes, but Mitch had pulled her in so close that it was impossible to see. Laura's dance partner had taken advantage of her distraction and was freely running his hands up and down the back of her dress.

As the song ended the intoxicated boy leant in and closed his lips around Laura's. Completely repulsed Laura shoved Jud as hard as she could and he toppled over onto the floor with a loud thud, causing their classmates to all look at her. "You're disgusting, don't you dare touch me!" She looked to her left for Isabella but saw Mitch watching on, on his own. Cate was standing just to the left of him holding her boyfriend Jack's hand, looking angrily at the scene. Laura caught her eye, a clear question in her stare, and Cate pointed towards the parking lot.

Laura stormed out through the doors and looked across the empty parking lot for her best friend, but it was so dark she could hardly see. "Isabella!" she shouted into the darkness, her own voice echoing back to her in the silence. They were only a couple of minutes walk from the Medina's house, so Laura figured that's where she would go. Taking off her wedges Laura began running towards the house.

As she turned onto Isabella's street, Laura caught sight of the girl running up ahead and she picked up her pace. She disappeared behind her door and just moments later Laura crossed the porch and ran inside, not bothering to knock. She heard footsteps on the stairs and ran up after Isabella, grabbing her wrist as they reached the top and turning her around to face her. "Issi?" Laura asked, concerned when she saw the tears streaming down her face. "What's wrong?"

Isabella simply shook her head and didn't answer, keeping her eyes focused on the floor. "I'm worried Issi, what happened?" She gently raised her fingers underneath Isabella's chin and tilted the girl's head so she was forced to meet Laura's eyes. "You can tell me anything."

"You kissed him." Her words came out as barely a whisper and more tears began trailing down her cheeks.

"What?" Laura was completely shocked for a moment as she tried to process Isabella's words. "Issi, I didn't kiss him," she reassured the girl, whose eyes had once again returned to the floor. "He kissed me and the second I realised what happened I shoved him away from me." Isabella was still looking at the floor and not acknowledging what Laura had said. In her own moment of bravery Laura decided to speak up. "He wasn't the person I wanted to kiss tonight."

Isabella blinked her eyes to try and fight back the tears. "Who was?" she asked tentatively as she looked up into the green eyes that were full of concern. As she asked her question the tension in Laura's body seemed to withdraw and the concern in her eyes faded to utter adoration.

"You." Without thinking Laura stepped forward, gently cupping Isabella's face in her hands as she pressed their lips together in a tender kiss. It only took a second for Isabella to begin reciprocating, as Laura captured Isabella's bottom lip in between her own. When Laura pulled away, she watched as Isabella's chocolate eyes slowly fluttered open. She was relieved to see a huge smile stretched across her face, her tears had vanished as her eyes sparkled up at Laura.

* * *

Laura looked at Savannah in complete and utter shock. She had no idea Savannah ever knew anything about what was going on between herself and

Isabella, aside from their friendship. Laura risked a glance at Isabella and was surprised to see her still smiling happily. As they were leaving Savannah wrapped Laura into a tight hug and made her promise that they would catch up properly soon. A request that Laura couldn't help but agree to as the sisters then embraced one another.

They got back into the car and drove the majority of the ride in silence. As they pulled up out the front of the precinct Isabella cleared her throat and turned to Laura. "Sorry about before. Savannah doesn't know when to keep her mouth shut," she smiled shyly, Laura's cheeks flushing at the not-so-subtle reminder of their first kiss. "She always adored you."

3

Chapter 3

Laura stuck the last witness photo up on the whiteboard and took a few steps back to take it all in. Mr Pickett's piercing dark eyes were staring back at her from his photo. An involuntary shiver ran up her spine as she thought about the yellow bruises covering his wife's body. Footsteps echoed down the hall behind her. She turned around to see Isabella approaching with two steaming mugs. The detective handed her a coffee and turned her attention towards the board.

"Thanks," Laura said, lifting the mug to her lips and taking a sip.

"I see I've been replaced as your official barista," Jordan raised his eyebrows and smiled as he approached the two women and looked up at the board.

"It's probably for the best. You can't make coffee for shit," Laura returned Jordan's smile. He rolled his eyes and huffed, Isabella letting out a small chuckle at the interaction.

"I thought you said she was charming Medina?" Isabella bit her lip to hide her smile and shrugged as Jordan shook his head.

"She's *only* charming when she wants to sleep with you." Kyle smirked as he sidled up beside Isabella, causing her to blush at the implication.

"Well then how would *you* even know Reynolds?" Laura glared playfully back at him as Jordan made a sizzling noise with his mouth. "Now what do we know?" Laura turned back to the white board and her demeanour instantly changed.

"Reynolds and I took statements from the neighbours and they all attested to hearing frequent arguments in the house between Mr and Mrs Pickett."

"We also spoke to the maid and she admitted to seeing Mr Pickett be violent towards Mrs Pickett in the past." Laura nodded as she took in the information, these statements all but confirmed her suspicions of Mr Pickett.

"Did forensics pick up on anything else during their sweep?" Isabella interjected.

"There were scuff marks all along the tiles and the paint was chipped along the railing where someone pushed her," Kyle answered.

"They also found this," Jordan walked over to his desk and picked up a plastic bag with evidence inside and held it up to the inquiring detectives. "I was about to take it to the lab for testing."

"What is that?" Laura and Isabella echoed one another, Laura shifting uncomfortably.

"That is a King of Denmark butt," Jordan said referring to the cigar in the bag.

"Didn't Mr Pickett say he never went out on that balcony?" Isabella asked.

"Yep," Laura answered her. "And yet I saw those same cigars on his desk... I think it's time we brought him in."

* * *

"I'm not saying anything until my lawyer gets here." The balding man sitting in front of Laura was sweating profusely as her green eyes pierced into his. They were both sat across from one another at a table in one of the interrogation rooms. Isabella was standing up against the wall, Laura had decided on this positioning as an emotional tactic. She wanted to create distance between herself and Isabella in order for the 'good cop, bad cop' relationship to work.

"That's fine. Though your lawyer is only going to be delaying the inevitable." Laura was trying to bait the man to tell them what they wanted before his counsel arrived and shut him up. "We have sworn statements from your neighbours and your maid that you were physically abusive towards your wife, Mr Pickett."

"That's ridiculous," the man stuttered nervously. Laura removed a photo from the folder on her desk and placed it in front of him. The photo clearly showed yellow bruises in the shape of a hand on Mrs Pickett's wrists.

"Now if we do a handprint analysis I highly suspect that *you* are going to be a match for these bruises." The man looked towards the door and kept his mouth shut. When he didn't answer, Laura decided to go with another tact. "You said you don't use the balcony your wife was pushed from, correct?"

"Yes," he confirmed resolutely.

"How long do you think it's been since you used that balcony?"

"I don't know…" he appeared to be struggling as he cast his mind back. "Maybe two years ago."

"Then why did our forensic team find one of your cigar butts on the balcony?" He looked surprised and didn't answer. As they had planned, Isabella now moved forward in preparation for her role as 'good cop'.

"The cigar butt is in the lab for DNA testing as we speak Mr Pickett. Your best defence now is the truth." Unlike Laura's strong tone, Isabella spoke softly. Trying to appear as though she were on his side.

"I can't explain it," the man pleaded, looking up into Isabella's chocolate eyes. "I haven't been out there." Laura's phone began buzzing in her pocket and she tapped on Isabella's shoulder for her to follow. They exited the room and stepped into the observation area behind them, looking at Mr Pickett through the glass. Parker's name flashed on the screen and Laura put her on speaker.

"Have you got something Parker?"

"Yes. I've just gotten Mrs Pickett's toxicology reports back. We found a cocktail of substances in her system. She had a blood alcohol rating of 0.09 and we found traces of whiskey and Zoloft."

"Zoloft?" Isabella questioned, beginning to rifle through the papers in her folder.

"Yes, Zoloft. It's an anti-depressant medication. In large doses it can cause severe drowsiness," Parker explained.

"Well, that explains how someone was able to force her over the balcony," Laura concluded, looking back over her shoulder at Mr Pickett in the interrogation room.

"There was a purchase on the housekeeper's credit card five days ago for Zoloft," Isabella handed Laura the credit card statement.

"Mr Pickett has some explaining to do."

After hanging up on Parker the two women spoke about their next plan of action before re-entering the interrogation room. This time Laura stood back as Isabella took the chair opposite the suspect. "Was your wife a big drinker Mr Pickett?" The man looked confused by Isabella's line of questioning.

"Not particularly. She had a glass of whiskey every night before bed, but that was it."

"Are you a whiskey drinker Mr Pickett?"

"No. I don't like spirits." He reached for the glass of water on the table and took a sip, the pressure clearly getting to him.

"A publican that doesn't like spirits?" Isabella questioned sceptically.

"I sell the stuff; doesn't mean I like it."

"Who has access to the spirits in your house?" Laura probed.

"Everyone with a key. The maid, housekeeper, my wife, my daughter," he rattled off, clearly not understanding the relevance of this line of questioning.

"Was your wife on any medications?" Isabella sat down slowly next to Laura, trying to appear casual.

"She had tablets for her blood pressure. That's all I know of." He answered, more sweat beginning to bead at the top of his forehead. Isabella was determined not to yield.

"How about yourself?"

"Nope. Fit as a fiddle."

Isabella placed the credit card statement with the highlighted purchase of Zoloft in front of the suspect. "Can you explain then why your housekeeper filled a prescription for Zoloft?" The man looked even more confused. There didn't seem to be anything at all sinister with the purchase to him.

"Our housekeeper sometimes picks things up for my daughter as well. That's her prescription."

Laura kept her face expressionless as she looked into the man's eyes. He seemed to be telling the truth. Isabella stood up and thanked the man before exiting the room, Laura following closely after her.

"I have to say, I didn't see that coming," Isabella said, staring up at Laura.

"We don't know anything for sure. But if it was the daughter that drugged Mrs Pickett. We need to establish a motive."

* * *

The sky outside was dark and the usual hum of activity in the office had died down in the last few hours. Just the four detectives were left pouring over statements and evidence from their case.

"Their financials just came through," Isabella held up a wad of paper from her desk. "I think you're going to want to see this." Kyle, Jordan and Laura all got up from their desks and walked over to study the papers in front of them. After a few minutes Laura finally spoke up.

"That's our motive." All three detectives nodded and smiled at one another relieved. Jordan tried stifling a yawn, all four of them were absolutely exhausted from the last few days.

"We'll bring her in first thing in the morning. Everyone should go home and get some rest; it's going to be a big day tomorrow," Laura ordered, putting on her coat.

"Anyone up for a drink?" Kyle suggested

"Not tonight," Laura said, grabbing her handbag from underneath her desk and packing up some case notes to bring home. Isabella walked over towards the elevators to switch off the printer, as the doors opened, she looked up surprised. A stunning brunette woman with legs that seemed to go on forever, stepped out of the elevator. Her light brown hair was slicked perfectly back into a tight bun. She wore a pencil skirt and matching blazer, with Louis Vuitton pumps.

"Can I help you?" Isabella asked confused, patting down her dishevelled hair as she looked at the woman's flawless countenance.

"I'm looking for Laura Carlsson?" The woman looked down the hall and noticed Laura standing by her desk. She smiled at Isabella and continued walking past her, Isabella following swiftly behind.

Laura looked up as she heard footsteps approaching, her green eyes settling on the beautiful woman walking towards her. Her face broke into a wide smile, her eyes went from tired to adoring in just one glance.

"Hey babe," the brunette woman smiled at Laura and grabbed her neck, pulling her in for a quick kiss. Isabella's cheeks flushed as she watched their intimate exchange.

"Hey," Laura smiled back, slightly dazed.

"Ready to go?"

"Definitely," Laura smiled and took the woman's hand in hers, interlacing their fingers. Isabella's eyes drifting from their interlaced hands to Laura's enchanted smile.

"Hey Rachel," Jordan came walking over and pulled her into a tight hug, as Laura continued clinging to her hand.

"Hey Jordan. How's Andre?"

"He's good. Growing up *way* too fast!"

Rachel chuckled, "I bet."

"Laura's refusing to join us for a drink, can I tempt you?" Jordan smiled charmingly at the woman.

"Not tonight. I've got to be in court early tomorrow."

"For the Westin case?" Jordan asked, Isabella watching on intrigued.

"Yeah. They want to hear an independent ME's perspective on the injuries." Isabella seemed to deflate when she realised Laura's girlfriend was a doctor, her shoulders drooped and she leant back against Laura's desk.

Rachel sensed Isabella's presence behind her and turned around to face her. "I'm sorry, I didn't introduce myself. I'm Rachel Cavanaugh. Laura's girlfriend." She reached out her hand to shake Isabella's.

"Isabella Medina. I'm Laura's new partner," Isabella held out her own hand reluctantly, her eyes drifting to Laura nervously. Laura could tell she was probably waiting to see Rachel's reaction to her name, but Laura knew there wouldn't be one. She hadn't talked much about her past with her girlfriend.

"Nice to meet you." Isabella appeared shocked as Rachel's demeanour remained friendly, no sign of recognition.

"Alright, let's get you home babe." Rachel smiled up at Laura as she wrapped her arm around the woman with the striking green eyes.

"Think about that drink for next time, Rach," Kyle urged. "You've got to share her with us sometime," he joked.

"Nope. She's all mine." Rachel pulled a cheesy smile at Kyle as the two women said goodbye to them all and walked towards the elevator. Isabella watched on, still frozen on the spot as the doors began closing and Rachel leant in to place a kiss on Laura's lips.

* * *

"NYPD open up!" Laura shouted as she knocked on Chloe Pickett's sorority door. Isabella was standing behind her, her hand lingering above the gun strapped to her waist, just in case. A young college girl opened the door. Her hair fluffy with sleep as she rubbed at her eyes.

"Yes?" She asked, confused.

Laura flashed the girl her badge. "Detective Carlsson NYPD, is Chloe Pickett home?" The girl nodded and led them into the sorority and up the stairs to Chloe's bedroom. She looked worried as she disappeared down the hall and the two detectives knocked on the door. Chloe's face turned white as she opened the door and saw the two detectives staring back at her.

"We have a few more questions Miss Pickett," Laura pushed past the girl and into her bedroom. Her closet doors were wide open and Laura caught sight of hangers and hangers of designer clothing. Isabella walked over to the dresser, noticing a bag of ice discarded on the top. She turned back around to the girl and raised her eyebrows.

"That...that's not mine. Some guy left it here after a party." Isabella just raised her eyebrows once again and gave Chloe a look to tell her she wasn't buying it.

"Do you smoke Chloe?" Laura interrupted. Chloe was practically shaking at this point.

35

"Occasionally. Generally, only when I'm drinking," she admitted.

"How about cigars Chloe, do you smoke cigars?" Chloe turned her attention towards Isabella, the clogs clearly turning in her head.

"No." She shook her head, but the frantic shaking of her hands betrayed her.

"So, you've never smoked one of your father's cigars?"

"No," she said, quieter this time and less resolute.

"Then tell me, why did we find your DNA on a cigar at your step-mother's crime scene?" Chloe looked absolutely petrified now as Laura stood above her, arms crossed.

"Ok I smoked it. I don't understand what the big deal is." Chloe shrugged, trying to appear nonchalant as her chest became redder and redder.

"The big deal is, that, that cigar places you at the murder scene," Isabella's voice grew stronger now, angrier. She was trying to rattle her.

"How does a college student afford all of these designer clothes?" Laura ran her hands over the garments in the girl's closet. Dior, Channel, Gucci, all the big brands were there.

"I have a trust fund."

"Had a trust fund," Laura corrected her. "You emptied it." Chloe swallowed, clearly surprised by the amount they knew. "What did your step-mother say when you asked her for money?"

"I didn't ask her for money," she tried to deny the allegation, but Laura could tell her confidence was waning.

"Your housekeeper has confirmed you did. And that your step-mother refused."

"How long have you known about the divorce?" Isabella asked her. She looked completely rattled now, as it was becoming harder for her to deny the allegations.

"Wh-what divorce?"

"Your father already told us you knew they were getting divorced," Isabella refuted, not giving Chloe a chance to formulate another lie. "You knew your father was in debt and when you found out about the divorce, there would be no money to pay off your own debts. Unless...your step-mother died before the divorce was processed."

Laura picked up a packet of Zoloft from her nightstand and waved it at Chloe. "You and your father were drowning in debt and your step-mother was leaving, leaving you and your father with nothing. You went over there that night, knowing full well that your step-mother has a glass of whiskey before bed each night and so you dissolved the Zoloft in her drink. When she came out onto the balcony to scold you for smoking, she was already drowsy. You pushed her over the edge. Didn't you Chloe?" Tears began streaming down her face and she buried her head in her hands.

"Didn't you?" Laura raised her voice now and Chloe jumped, looking up into the piercing green eyes.

"I owe some bad people money ok. She refused to give it to me. They were going to hurt me. I didn't see another option."

Isabella stepped forward now and unclipped her handcuffs from her belt. "Chloe Pickett we are placing you under arrest for the murder of Alicia Pickett." She lifted Chloe off the bed and handcuffed her hands behind her back. "You have the right to remain silent. Anything you say can and will be used against you in a court of law. You have the right to have an attorney. If you cannot afford one, one will be appointed to you by the court."

* * *

"Wee, ooo, wee, ooo, wee, ooo, wee, ooo "

"Savannah, shh. Laura's trying to drive," Isabella scolded her younger sister from the front seat as a police car sped past them. There was a trivia night at their high school and Laura and Isabella had been tasked with babysitting duties.

"Where is this place Alex?" Laura asked, looking at her younger brother in the rear-view mirror. His brown hair sat messily over his eyebrows, his eyes fixed on his phone as he continued texting. Laura's youngest sibling, Ellie, nudged him. She was the mini version of Laura when it came to looks, just not personality.

"Um...not much further. It's right next to the mall." When they were about a block away from the mall, Alex told Laura they could pull over.

"What? Embarrassed to be seen with us Alex?" Laura playfully glared at him *as he opened his door. Alex just rolled his eyes and jumped out.*

"Keep it PG-13 for the kiddies ok?" He winked at Isabella and slammed his door, running off into the darkness. Isabella's jaw dropped and she stared at Laura in complete shock. Laura returned her bewildered look, her cheeks blushing red. Not wanting to create any more suspicion with Ellie watching on in the back, Laura looked back towards the road and headed towards Isabella's house.

As they walked inside Isabella pointed Ellie towards the DVD cabinet and told the two younger girls to pick a movie. When they were happily distracted browsing the titles, Isabella dragged Laura upstairs to her bedroom. The door had barely shut when Isabella turned on Laura.

"You told Alex?"

"No I didn't tell him!" Laura protested. "Who knows what he was going on about." Laura tried to reassure Isabella and herself in the one statement. But she couldn't think of any other reason for Alex's joke, other than that he knew the truth.

"He winked at me Laura! He knows." Isabella's hands dropped from her hair and hit hard against her thighs.

"Well I didn't tell him. I don't know how he would've found out," Laura said defensively, taking a seat on the bed as she watched Isabella pace nervously. She knew he had made a habit of going through her messages in the past, she was almost certain that's what he had done.

"This is bad Laura."

"Don't freak out ok? This is Alex. He's not going to tell anyone. I have way too much dirt on him for that." Laura smirked and Isabella shot her another anxious look. Laura grabbed her hand and pulled her into a tight hug, resting her chin on Isabella's head. "Trust me Issi. I'll talk to him."

Isabella sighed and pulled away from the hug, clearly still stressed about their situation. "I don't want to lose you," she confessed. Her brown eyes darted to the ground insecurely.

"You won't. I won't let that happen." Laura pulled Isabella in and placed a soft kiss on her lips.

* * *

Laura and Isabella sat at their desks, finishing some paperwork on the first case they had closed together. As much as Laura didn't want to admit it. They made a great team, they always had. The elevator doors opened, and Kyle and Jordan rushed towards them. Huge grins plastered on their faces.

"Case closed!" Kyle held up a high-five to Isabella and she reciprocated, as Jordan did the same to Laura. "How does it feel ladies?"

"Like an innocent woman was murdered and this is hardly cause for celebration." Kyle pouted at Laura's answer, and she smiled back. She couldn't resist pushing his buttons.

"I think this calls for celebratory drinks...Medina, Carlsson. We're going out!"

"Reynolds, I'm tired," Laura protested, her shoulders slumping and her lips knitting together in a pout. Isabella watching on with hopeful eyes.

"No excuses Carlsson," Jordan pushed back. "You're going to go home, gussy up and I'll pick you up in an hour." Laura went to protest again, but Jordan held a finger to his lips. "Everyone's got the day off tomorrow, suck it up!"

"Yeah plus, we have a new team member that hasn't properly been inducted. Prepare for a full interrogation tonight, Medina," Jordan winked at Isabella suggestively and the detective rolled her eyes and smiled back.

Laura contemplated the night she had envisioned spending, a glass of red wine, curled up in blankets on the lounge watching trashy reality television. It was her kind of perfect night, but then on the other hand, there were other temptations to going out. To much excitement and raucous applause from Kyle, she stood up and mumbled an 'ok'.

An hour later Isabella was knocking on Laura's door to pick her up. When the door swung open Laura practically gaped when she took in Isabella on her doorstep, eliciting a small smile from the detective. Isabella was wearing a black leather skirt and white blouse, her lips painted in a dark red shade.

Laura was wearing high waisted black leather pants and high heel boots with a black mid drift that showed off an inch of skin. She had darkened the makeup around her eyes to accentuate the green.

Laura hated to admit it, but she liked the look of lust in Isabella's eyes.

She herself was trying her best not to stare, but it was difficult. She could feel the tension rolling between the two of them. Isabella's sheer top didn't leave much to the imagination and Laura was having to force herself to meet her eyes. Laura finally broke the tension with a chuckle as she looked at her watch, it was five minutes past. "I thought I was on time." Isabella felt her pulse race, it was the first genuine interaction they had had since she had arrived.

"Sorry, Jordan asked me to come up and get you. He was quite antsy to get going." Isabella smiled insecurely.

"Don't be," Laura shrugged off her apology, her eyes running over Isabella's outfit again. "You look great," Laura smiled genuinely as Isabella's face lit up, her eyes practically sparkling.

4

Chapter 4

"A karaoke bar, really?" Laura looked right at Kyle as they entered the dingy bar, knowing full well who would be responsible for the venue choice. The bar was packed with a mix of rowdy wall street types, college girls and older men who Laura thought looked like gangsters.

"Oh come on Carlsson, you need to loosen up a little." He stepped behind Laura and began massaging her shoulders, she slapped his hands away just as fast. "Always with the violence," he playfully scolded her before she rolled her eyes.

Jordan made a bee line for an open booth close to the front of the stage, as the other three headed for the bar. Isabella and Laura took out their purses, but Kyle quickly shook his head. "First round's on me."

They both thanked him before making their way towards the booth. Isabella slid in next to Jordan, leaving the seat next to Laura open for Kyle. A few minutes later Kyle turned up to their table with a tray of shots, "TEQUILA!" Kyle took extra care to roll each syllable off his tongue as he placed the tray down in the middle of the table and clambered into the booth beside Laura.

He then began handing them out, insisting they each take one. Jordan unwillingly took the shot before informing them all that he wasn't drinking. Kyle tried to insist but Jordan shook his head, informing them of his imminent death if the car wasn't home for his wife's morning yoga class.

The other three detectives all clinked their shots together, before throwing them back. When Laura's empty shot glass hit the table, she grabbed the unwanted shot in Jordan's hand and downed that as well. "Carlsson's not messing around tonight," Jordan laughed.

"If I'm going to be singing later, I'm going to need to be drunk."

After a few more rounds of tequila, the four colleagues settled into a comfortable conversation. Isabella was eager to learn more about the other detectives and was firing off a series of questions at them while the others added in their own questions throughout.

"So, all three of you seriously studied criminal justice?" Kyle asked surprised, as the three other detectives all nodded their heads. "Well, aren't you all gold star detectives."

"Why? What did you study?" Laura asked and Kyle blushed slightly before taking a sip from his beer.

"I don't want to say." Jordan laughed and Kyle's eyes grew wide. "Don't you dare tell them!" Jordan was laughing even harder now as he saw the panic in Kyle's eyes.

"Come on Jordan, reveal?" Isabella pleaded playfully.

"Jordan," Kyle pleaded, in his most sincere tone. "I'll do all of your paperwork for a week."

"That's not even worth it," Jordan laughed. "He studied Graphic Design." The detective revealed, causing a raucous of laughter from Isabella and Laura.

"I was young, and it was the degree with the hottest chicks ok," Kyle justified, still blushing. Trying to deflect the attention from himself, he shot a question at Isabella. "Where did you go to school Medina?"

"Berkley," she replied modestly, the reminder causing Laura to take a large swig of her beer.

"Another bloody genius on the team." Kyle rolled his eyes at his colleagues.

"I had a lot of help," Isabella justified, looking over at Laura. She could feel Isabella's eyes on her, but pretended instead to be reading the alcohol content on her beer. "So... how did you meet your wife, Foster?"

"We were high school sweethearts. I was on the football team, and she was a cheerleader. I was so shy and awkward at school, she ended up having to ask me out. She's still filthy I didn't pick up on all her hints," he chuckled. "We had our first kiss at the Junior Prom-"Jordan was interrupted as Laura began coughing and spluttering on her drink. Isabella's eyes shot up to meet hers and both of them blushed before looking away.

"You good Carlsson?" Kyle laughed. "First time drinking is it?"

"Sorry, went down the wrong way," Laura lied. "I'm going to grab another drink." Laura slid out of the booth and stalked towards the bar, taking deep breaths to try and calm her nerves.

The karaoke bar had gotten a lot busier now and some tone-deaf suits were on stage giving a terrible rendition of 'Stayin' Alive' by The Bee Gees. As Laura stood waiting at the bar, she felt someone's gaze on her. She looked to her left and saw a tall man, with greasy black hair in his late thirties eyeballing her. She quickly looked away and turned back to the bar to try and get the bartender's attention.

"Hey there," the man leant up against the bar next to her and she had to stop herself from gagging when she smelt the garlic on his breath. "Can I buy you a drink?"

"I'm fine thanks." Laura kept her gaze on the bartender, not wanting to pay the man the slightest bit of attention.

"Oh come on, just one drink?" He drawled, clearly he had, had quite a few already.

"No thank you," she replied curtly once more.

"Come on baby-"

Their conversation was interrupted as Isabella stepped up to the bar, purposely placing herself between Laura and the older man. The man's garlic odour masked by Isabella's daisy perfume. Laura couldn't help but move closer to the woman to take it in, she loved that smell. It was distinctly Isabella.

"Hey, did you get your drink?" Isabella turned towards Laura, completely blocking out the sleazy man next to her.

"Not yet."

Isabella nodded and looked towards the bartender who was serving people at the opposite end of the bar. She sighed and turned back towards Laura, shamelessly running her eyes over Laura's naked abs.

"You always did look good in black." Butterflies murmured in Laura's stomach from the compliment. Was Isabella really flirting with her? Isabella leant further over the bar and flashed her brilliant smile at the bartender who then instantly walked over to take their order. Laura couldn't help but roll her eyes. Typical. Isabella always caught people's attention. She took a few deep breaths to calm her nerves and decided Isabella's compliment was purely due to intoxication.

"Wow darling, you are stunning!" Laura couldn't help but be annoyed when the sleazy man from before started hitting on Isabella this time. But she looked unfazed and kept her back to him, instead smiling warmly back at Laura. Her eyes were doing that sparkling thing that made Laura's knees weak and she couldn't help but smile back. After being ignored by both women the man had wandered around behind them, so they were forced to acknowledge him.

"Damn...you girls are sexy. Can I buy you ladies a drink?"

"No." Isabella and Laura both shot back angrily. Once again their synchronicity in speech and emotion were frightening Laura thought. Their drinks arrived and they eagerly left the bar and returned to the booth, leaving behind the sleazy man and his disgusting scent.

As they arrived at the booth Kyle and Jordan were just getting up. "Prepare for the best serenade of your lives ladies." Kyle winked at them, as he and Jordan headed for the stage. Laura and Isabella both laughed as they slid into the booth next to each other so that they could see the stage. Isabella's arm grazing hers as she did so, eliciting small goose bumps.

Jordan and Kyle each grabbed their microphones, and the crowd began cheering as the piano rang out. Isabella and Laura instantly turned to look at one another as they recognised the song. Vanessa Carlton's 'A Thousand Miles' blasted through the speakers and they both laughed as Kyle and Jordan started singing the lyrics.

"Do you remember when we learnt the actions to this from White Chicks?" Isabella asked.

"Remember? I still know the moves," Laura laughed, forcing a grin from

Isabella. They laughed and sung along for the rest of the song. When Jordan and Kyle finished, they earned huge cheers from the intoxicated crowd, before another duo took the stage.

"Excellent song choice!" Isabella commended the men as they returned to the booth.

"Yeah, who knew you could sing Jordan," Laura complimented.

"Thank you," Jordan smiled happily, taking a sip of water.

"Hey, what about me?" Kyle pouted.

"Definitely don't quit your day job," Laura chuckled.

"Ouch. Let's see you do better Carlsson, you guys are up next." Laura's chest reddened and she took another long sip from her cocktail.

"What are we singing?" Isabella asked excitedly. Laura cursed internally, she was one of those people that was always excited about anything.

"Laura's favourite song," Jordan chimed in.

"Which is?" Laura stared at the two detectives sceptically trying to think what they might have chosen as her 'favourite song'.

"You'll find out," Kyle winked.

The song ended and it was their turn to take the stage. Despite the alcohol Laura was still really nervous. Isabella gave her a warm smile before grabbing her hand and dragging her up to the stage. Laura's mouth went dry as she looked out on the crowd watching them. Kyle and Jordan, both gave her a big thumbs up.

The song began playing and the familiar synthesisers and percussion rang out before the lyrics for Sophie Ellis-Bextor's 'Murder on the Dancefloor' appeared on the screen. Laura could feel her cheeks burning and she didn't dare look to her left to see Isabella's reaction. The boys were right, as camp as it was now given her profession, it was her favourite song. It had been for a long time; she just had no idea they knew that. She definitely didn't like Isabella knowing that all these years later it still meant a lot to her.

The lyrics came on and both women started singing into the mic, Laura risked a look at Isabella and her initial embarrassment was washed away as she saw Isabella grinning back at her. Both women lost themselves in the music, it was like they were sixteen again. They were practically shouting the whole song as they bounced around on the stage. The moment Laura had looked at Isabella the crowd had faded away and she lost herself in the sparkling chocolate eyes.

The song ended and the bar erupted into applause. Laura and Isabella were giddy with laughter after their performance, Isabella took the chance and pulled Laura into a hug. Laura was surprised initially, but happily reciprocated. They were still smiling stupidly when they fell back into the booth.

"Talk about chemistry, you guys killed it up there," Kyle smiled at them, causing both women to blush.

"Thanks. What even made you choose that song?"

"Anytime we've been out, as soon as that song comes on, you're always bolting for the dance floor." Laura blushed again as Isabella's smile widened.

Half an hour later the bar had given up on karaoke and instead the stage had transformed into a dance floor. Isabella, Laura and Jordan were watching on as Kyle was trying out his best moves on a group of young women that looked college age. They were all laughing when they saw him break out the sprinkler.

Jordan shook his head and looked over at Isabella with excited eyes. "Come on Medina, you can show me some moves."

"You're on."

Jordan held out his hand to Isabella and led her up onto the dance floor. Unlike Kyle, Jordan could actually dance and was twirling Isabella around to the beat. Laura couldn't tear her eyes away from the detective as she rolled her hips and ran her hands through her hair. Laura's cheeks were heating up as she thought about Isabella's hands running over her skin.

When the next song began playing, Isabella came bounding off the stage and grabbed Laura's hand dragging her up to dance. Jordan played their shield for the next few songs, being a barrier for them for the hordes of sleazy men that kept trying to dance up against them.

Whitney Houston's 'I Wanna Dance with Somebody' began playing next and their intoxication made both Laura and Isabella squeal in delight. Jordan took his chance and excused himself for the bathroom, as both women began screaming the lyrics of the song. Isabella grabbed a hold of Laura's hand and began twirling her around the dance floor.

As they danced a group behind them kept stumbling over the dancefloor, pushing Laura so that her body was pressed up against Isabella's. Her forearm was resting against the wall beside Isabella's head, the detective's hand placed on her waist. Laura sensed that familiar sexual tension rolling between them as Isabella's chest heaved against her own.

It felt like her skin was on fire where Isabella was pressed against her. The brown eyes were staring up at her lips and she was struggling to breathe. Laura leant in towards her, her eyes fluttering closed. She could feel Isabella's warm breath against her skin as she wet her lips.

Yells pierced through the music and Laura pulled away when she recognised the voice, Kyle. She began shoving her way through the dancers as more shouts came from the front of the stage.

"Laura!" Isabella was yelling after her, unsure of what was happening.

As Laura broke through the crowd, she saw two large men holding on to Kyle's arms. The sleazy man that had hit on them earlier at the bar, sucker punched Kyle, eliciting another loud moan. Blood was pouring from his nose and it looked as though his lip was split. If the men behind him weren't holding him up, Laura was sure he would have been on the floor. The sleazy man raised his fist once again and Laura jumped in front of Kyle before he could hit him. The man had already swung at this point, and he had thrown so much weight behind his fist that it was too late to stop it. The man's closed fist connected with Laura's jaw and she fell, out cold onto the floor.

Isabella scrambled through the crowd, she jumped off the stage and grabbed the sleazy man's wrist, yanking it behind his back. The man yelled as she pulled, twisting his shoulder. She kicked out his legs at the knees and slammed him face first into the floor, her slender body resting on his back.

Kyle was shouting Laura's name over the blasting music as Jordan came sprinting towards them. The lights turned on and the music was cut as Jordan wrestled one of the men off Kyle. A few other men from around the dance floor suddenly rushed in to help and managed to free Kyle from the large man's grip. Isabella called to one of them to take over for her and once he was resting on the man's back, she leapt off and ran to Laura.

Laura's eyes were closed and there was blood dripping from a cut on her lip. Isabella carefully rolled her onto her back and pulled her head into her lap as the bar's bouncers moved around them to assist with the culprits. "Laura, can you hear me?" Isabella squeezed Laura's hand and her eyelashes fluttered open to reveal the dazzling green eyes. She was disorientated and clearly in pain, her eyes were circling without intent, clearly dazed.

After a few moments she began coming to, Isabella could see the panic forming in her eyes. "Kyle?" Laura tried to sit up, but Isabella swiftly pushed her back down again. She looked to her left and saw Jordan holding on to a severely battered Kyle. His face was swollen, but surprisingly he was still conscious. "He's alright. You got to him just in time," Isabella reassured her. Relief washed over Laura's face as she heard her friend was ok.

"You scared me for a minute there." Isabella looked down at the green-eyed woman, stroking the sides of her face soothingly.

Half an hour later the four detectives were walking into the emergency waiting room, Isabella and Jordan both supporting Kyle's weight as Laura walked on ahead. As she got to the reception desk, she flashed her badge and asked to see Cate Hanly. Jordan and Isabella lowered Kyle into a vacant chair in the waiting room, his head slipping to rest against the wall.

"You should really sit down Laura," Isabella suggested, the detective still quite shaky on her feet.

"No I'm fine," she said, pushing past Isabella and heading towards Kyle.

"Kyle? Keep your eyes open ok, the nurse is coming." Kyle nodded slightly, one of his eyes had practically swollen shut. Laura grabbed a hold of his hand and stroked the back of it as she stared at the doors that led through to the clinic.

A few moments later the doors burst open and Cate came rushing towards them wearing pink scrubs and pushing a wheelchair. She had matured a lot since high school, fine lines around her eyes, but still the same warm features, and flushed pink cheeks.

"Laura, what happened?" She asked concerned, squatting down to examine Kyle.

"There was a bar fight. Two guys were holding him back as another one punched him. I think maybe he might have some broken ribs. He's been complaining of chest pain."

"They also knocked Laura out," Jordan added, making sure she would be examined too.

"Alright come through and we can take a proper look at you both." Cate ushered them all through the open doors, Jordan helping to lower Kyle into the wheelchair. She led Laura to a bed just inside and ordered her to lie down, whilst she pushed Kyle further down the hall. Jordan followed after Kyle, leaving Isabella to look after Laura. She laid back on the bed, wincing slightly as her head hit the pillow.

"Are you ok?" Isabella closed the curtain behind them and sat down on the bed by Laura's feet. A nasty bruise was already forming on Laura's jaw and her lip had swelled up around the cut.

"Fine," Laura said curtly. "My heads just throbbing." The curtains opened abruptly as Cate stepped inside and her eyes fell on the woman perched on the end of Laura's bed.

"Isabella?" Cate asked shocked, clearly not having noticed her amongst all the chaos.

"Hey Cate," Isabella smiled warmly.

"Uh, hey," Cate said confused, but turned her attention back to Laura. "So, ah, what happened to you?" She asked.

"She got sucker punched. She was knocked out for around a minute," Isabella answered, Laura's eyes still closed.

"Gosh Laura," Cate shook her head.

"She was just complaining of a headache," Isabella informed her.

"Laur, can you open your eyes for a minute? I just need to ask you some questions." Laura's eyes fluttered open, though they were slightly glazed and bloodshot. She felt like she had been hit by a truck, both physically and emotionally.

"Isabella said you have a headache?" Laura nodded. "Are you feeling nauseous or dizzy?" Laura shook her head, though that wasn't the complete truth. She definitely did feel nauseous, though she knew that wasn't a symptom of the headache. "What about before you got punched, can you remember the rest of the night?" Laura's eyes found Isabella's before she could stop herself. The other detective was smiling gently at her, her chocolate eyes full of concern.

"No I don't really remember much." She lied, playing with the starchy sheets. "I'm pretty sure there was singing at some point." She risked a glance toward Isabella, the detective letting out an almost inaudible sigh as her body looked to deflate at the end of her mattress.

"Ok, I think you've got a concussion," Cate concluded. "Can you get someone to come and pick you up?" Laura nodded and felt around in her purse for her phone, but in her haste she knocked it to the floor.

Isabella stood up and bent down to retrieve it. "Here Laura, I'll do it. Who do you want me to call?"

"Can you call Rachel?" Laura asked. Guilt swimming in her stomach as she asked after her girlfriend. Isabella simply nodded, emotionless, and left the room to make the call.

Nearly an hour later they heard Rachel's frantic voice on the other side of the curtain as she called her girlfriend's name. Isabella sighed and stepped out from behind the curtain, waving to a panicked Rachel.

"She's in here." Rachel rushed past Isabella and straight to Laura. Her green eyes fluttered open as Rachel took her hand.

"Oh baby," Rachel cooed, running her fingers lightly over Laura's swollen jaw. Isabella shifted uncomfortably in the corner, as Rachel lightly kissed Laura's forehead. The kisses only making Laura feel even more guilty for the kiss she had nearly shared with the woman now watching on from the corner.

"I'm alright Rach," Laura squeezed her girlfriend's hand to comfort her. The adrenaline had worn off once she had laid down and now all she could feel was her throbbing headache and the promise of a deep sleep pressuring her eyelids.

"If you're not getting hurt at work, it's bars now? What are we going to do with you Laura Carlsson?"

"You could kiss me," Laura suggested with a weak smile, trying to erase her feelings of guilt. Rachel smiled and leant forwards, lightly pressing her lips to Laura's. Laura noticed Isabella look away and pretend to adjust the curtains.

"Come on," Rachel broke her inner monologue. "Let's get you home." The older woman propped Laura up in the bed and Isabella moved closer to help support her. Cate slipped back inside the curtains as Isabella and Rachel managed to get Laura's arms around their shoulders.

"Here, I've got her discharge papers," Cate handed a piece of paper to Rachel.

"Thank you so much Cate, we really appreciate it. We'll have to organise dinner soon with Kevin?" Rachel suggested, causing Laura to smile. Her girlfriend was always so thoughtful in that way. Cate's husband Kevin was a firefighter and so between his and Cate's schedules they always had difficulty nailing down a date for dinner, but it was always like no time had passed once they did.

"Sounds great."

"How's Kyle?" Laura asked, her expression changing to one of deep concern. As much as they bantered back and forth between one another, he was still one of her best friends and she hated the idea of him being hurt.

"He's pretty banged up. Two fractured ribs and a swollen face, he was lucky there were no fractures to his nose or jaw. He should be discharged sometime tomorrow."

Laura sighed in relief. "Thanks Cate."

"Don't mention it."

As soon as Laura was in the front seat, her head rested against the window and she closed her eyes and drifted off to sleep. Rachel had offered to drive Isabella home as a thank you for looking after Laura and the detective had been too tired to resist.

"I'm glad Laura has you for a partner," Rachel caught Isabella's eye in the rear-view mirror as she addressed her. "She's had a rough year and it's good to see her settling down. She doesn't trust people easily, but it's clear she trusts you." Isabella shifted uncomfortably in her seat, but smiled at the compliment nonetheless. Rachel continued rattling on like Isabella and her were old friends.

"She's a hard nut to crack you know. She's always bottling up all of her emotions and it's so hard to know what she's thinking." Isabella nodded along as Rachel spoke, gazing out at the dark streets as they drove. "She's had a hard life I know that. With everything that happened when she was younger, there's a lot of trauma there." Isabella eyes refocused on the rear-view mirror when she said this.

"Laura never likes to talk about her past, she struggles to trust people. But I know there was someone. Parker has sort of implied it before…" Isabella's eyes were bearing into the mirror now, unable to look away. "And I don't know that she's ever really got over it. It's like she gave away her heart all those years ago and she's never really gotten it back." Tears started prickling in Isabella's eyes as she spoke.

"You knew each other all those years ago…" Rachel looked up to meet her gaze once again as Isabella blinked away her tears. "Do you remember who it was?"

Isabella shook her head, "No idea."

5

Chapter 5

"Hey, how's the trial going?" Parker asked as Laura sat down at the table opposite Cate. It was a few days into the prolific murder trial regarding a wall street executive and Laura was already exhausted. She had agreed to meet up with Cate and Parker at their favourite sushi restaurant to fill Cate in on the whole Isabella situation. The three best friends generally caught up every two weeks for dinner, but they had missed the last few due to their busy schedules.

"Draining. I honestly have no clue how they manage to make court room dramas look exciting." On the contrary, this case had so far been days of the defence and prosecuting attorneys arguing back and forth over what evidence would be allowed to be discussed.

"Ain't that the truth," Parker nodded in agreement. Laura knew she had been to her fair share of trials since becoming a Medical Examiner as well.

"How's Kevin doing? Parker said he had an accident at work?" She had always adored Kevin, he always put Cate first. She had a lot in common with Kevin, they both risked their lives on a day-to-day basis and that made relationships difficult.

"I swear that man is in the wrong field of work. He's the biggest klutz I know. He tore two ligaments in his ankle jumping off the back of the truck," Cate rolled her eyes, causing Parker and Laura to chuckle. "It's just lucky we get good medical through the hospital."

"Rough," Parker nodded. "Ok I can't wait any longer, what the hell happened the other night?"

Laura sighed, contemplating exactly what she was going to tell her friends. Looking into their eyes she knew her chances of successfully lying to them were slim. But she decided she was going to attempt to be vague anyway. "Well basically Kyle hit on this woman at the club, who happened to be the fiancé of an Italian mobster also at the bar..." both women looked alarmed, but not surprised, this wasn't the first Kyle tale Laura had shared.

"So anyway, by the time I heard Kyle shouting two men had his arms pinned behind his back and the main mobster was throwing punches. Kyle was barely conscious at that point and when I saw the guy lining up another punch, I jumped in front of him before he could hit Kyle again." Laura ran her fingers over the purple bruise on her jaw. "He knocked me out before I had a chance to react."

"Jeez Laur," Cate said, shaking her head. As much as she was surrounded by injury and death day to day, Laura knew she struggled hearing about the dangers her loved ones often faced.

"Where were Isabella and Jordan at this point?" Parker asked, her tone conveying her confusion as to why the other detectives hadn't intervened.

"From what Kyle told me, apparently Isabella tackled the mobster that punched me straight afterwards and pinned him down."

"Wow. I never would have seen Isabella as a cop. I mean you were surprising enough. It's just so hard to imagine her tackling some huge guy," Cate laughed. Even Laura could recognise the image of slender Isabella tackling a burly mobster to the floor was comical.

"Well, it happened. That's when Jordan apparently got back from the bathroom and he and some other guys in the club tackled the men holding onto Kyle. Next thing I know I'm coming to in Isabella's lap." Parker and Cate both exchanged a glance, though Laura didn't quite catch their expressions.

"Wait a minute, did you say you remembered hearing Kyle shout for help?" Cate asked sceptically. Laura blushed, she could be a terrible liar sometimes and this time she'd been caught out.

"Don't be mad, but I may have lied about having a concussion," Laura admitted sheepishly, her heart beating faster in her chest.

"Why would you even do that Laura?" Laura just shrugged and didn't answer, shrinking slightly under the intense gaze of her two oldest friends.

"Cate, who else was in the room when Laura lied about being concussed?" Parker asked, glaring at Laura.

"Isabella."

"Spill!" Parker said forcefully and Laura groaned internally, it was frustrating how well they could read her sometimes.

Laura ran her hand through her wavy hair and sighed. Her heart was racing and her palms were sweating as she stared into their eyes. "Right before the fight...Isabella and I nearly kissed." Cate and Parker both gasped.

"What the hell Laura?" Parker demanded furiously.

"Do you not remember what she did to you? Ten years of therapy still haven't fixed you, don't tell me you're going to open yourself up to that heartbreak all over again?" Laura was taken aback. Cate wasn't usually that blunt, but she understood her tough love was coming from a good place.

"I know. It was just a weird night, ok? The guys picked our song for karaoke; and we had this really fun duet, and all these old feelings started swirling around. Did I mention I was really drunk?"

"Laura," Parker breathed shaking her head.

"That's why I lied about the concussion. I thought if Isabella thought I didn't remember anything, then it could all just go away."

"What about Rachel?" Cate asked, Laura could sense the judgement in her tone and she felt a pang of guilt that she had barely considered Rachel in everything that had happened.

"I know. Nothing happened, ok? For a moment I was eighteen again. That's all it was, a weird feeling of nostalgia." By this point Laura wasn't sure if it was her friends she was trying to convince or herself.

"Are you sure?" Parker asked, raising her eyebrows. Laura felt like she was being cross examined.

"Yes. I care about Rachel. A lot! She's so incredible, she's intelligent, kind, loyal...I don't want to do anything to jeopardise us." As the words left her mouth Laura really thought about how true they were. Her girlfriend had been nothing but supportive of her and she never left Laura contemplating the authenticity of her feelings. With Rachel, Laura always knew where she stood.

"Do you love her?" Cate pushed.

"Isabella?" Laura asked confused.

"No, Rachel?" Parker rolled her eyes again; it was clear she was struggling to believe Laura had moved on.

"Oh...I don't know. I don't just throw those words around," Laura tried justifying herself. She knew Rachel was perfect for her. There was just always something holding her back.

"Do you still love Isabella?"

"No." Laura hesitated for just a fraction of a second, causing Cate to shoot Parker a knowing look. "No, after what she did, I should hate her. But... I still have to work with her."

"What are you going to do then?"

"No more personal connections. Going forward, it will be purely professional."

Cate and Parker both gave each other the look that said they highly doubted any sort of relationship between Isabella and Laura could be anything but personal.

* * *

Laura was nervous as she stepped into the lift to head upstairs. The court case had dragged out for a few weeks and aside from a few texts here and there, she hadn't spoken to Isabella since that night at the bar.

Laura stepped out of the lift and began walking down the hall, her heart beating rapidly in her chest. Jordan was typing away on his laptop as Isabella sat down at her desk with two coffee mugs. It was a gesture Laura had become accustomed to in the last few months, but she had decided she needed to implement some boundaries.

"Morning," Laura's voice came out raspy as she greeted her colleagues, dropping her keys and handbag on to her desk.

"Welcome back," Isabella smiled brightly, but Laura didn't look towards her.

"Thanks." She made sure to keep her eyes down and not look at the other detective. She could see Isabella shifting uncomfortably in her peripherals.

"How was it?" Jordan asked, looking up from his laptop.

"Good. It's still going, but I'm not required in court anymore. The prosecution have built a strong case so I think the jury will return a guilty verdict."

"That's great," Jordan nodded happily. "Just need Kyle back and the A team will be back together."

Laura smiled and took a seat, sighing as she did so. She felt exhausted already, she knew it was her anxiety weighing on her. She made a mental note to force herself to the gym in the evening. As much as she didn't feel like it, she knew it would make her feel better.

"I made you a coffee," Isabella stood up and placed the steaming mug on her desk. She put her hand on Laura's shoulder as she did so, and without thinking Laura flinched. She looked up in time to see Isabella's cheeks flush at her response and she took a step back. Laura could see the confusion in her eyes, the hurt. But she knew she had to do this, to protect herself.

She reached behind her handbag and held up a styrofoam coffee cup in response. "I already had one, all yours." She pushed the mug back towards Isabella and then opened up her laptop. Isabella picked up the mug slowly, staring for a few minutes at Laura's back, before walking off towards the break room.

* * *

"Hey strangers," Kyle came walking towards the detectives with a huge smirk plastered on his face. It had been a month now since the incident and things had been relatively quiet in the precinct. Laura had done her best in the last week to avoid any significant interactions with Isabella and the other detective had obliged and given her, her space.

"Hey partner," Jordan sprung to his feet and grabbed Kyle's hand, bringing him in for a quick hug. Kyle grimaced slightly as Jordan slapped a hand across his back. The swelling around his face was all gone now, but there was still some bruising and signs of abrasions here and there.

"The man's got fractured ribs Foster, take it easy," Laura scolded Jordan when she saw Kyle wince.

"That's alright, I'm tough," he winked at her as Isabella approached him and pulled him in for a hug.

"Thanks for the flowers Medina," Kyle said as she pulled back from the hug. Laura was surprised to hear Isabella had sent Kyle flowers, she hadn't even thought to do that. "My Mum was ecstatic when she came over and saw them, she thought I had a girlfriend." All of the detectives laughed.

"Hell hasn't frozen over yet," Laura mocked him. In all the years she had known him, Kyle had never once had a girlfriend. He usually always capped his dates at the one-month mark, preferring to live the bachelor lifestyle.

"I missed you too Carlsson," Kyle smiled and took a seat at his desk opposite her.

"Remember that time your mother thought Carlsson was your girlfriend?" Kyle shuddered at the thought and Laura reached across her desk to lightly slap him as Jordan rocked in his chair from laughter.

"Your taste's not that good," Laura joked.

"Why would she even think you guys were dating?" Isabella asked.

"Probably because they were passed out in bed together," Jordan laughed and Laura noticed the shock on Isabella's face. Kyle shook his hands when he saw her expression.

"Not like that," Kyle said shaking his head. "We used to wingman and woman for each other before Laura got herself wifed up." Isabella raised her eyebrows and nodded, sitting down at her desk and shuffling some papers.

"Yeah I don't know which of the two of you is the bigger stud," Jordan scratched the side of his head like he was thinking. Isabella spoke up before she could stop herself.

"Laura? A stud?" Again, Laura noticed the tone of surprise. It had been a long time since they had known one another, and Laura knew she was very different now to the girl Isabella had known. Plus, it was Isabella's fault she had never settled down before now, she just wasn't going to say it.

"Oh yeah," Jordan confirmed. "I thought I'd never met a bigger flirt than Reynolds in my life, but Carlsson gives him a run for his money."

"Yeah alright Jordan, just because you've been off the market since high school, suddenly the rest of us are whores," Laura rolled her eyes, trying to make out that Jordan was exaggerating her dating history. She really hadn't slept with that many people, she just enjoyed causally flirting. It kept her mind off other things.

"No, I didn't say anything about Isabella," Jordan smirked and Laura grabbed the baseball off her desk, ready to peg it at Jordan.

The Captain's door opened and their squabble was interrupted. Laura placed the baseball back on her desk, as the grey-haired man stepped outside. He looked straight at Kyle, "Welcome back Reynolds. How are you feeling?"

"Good, thank you Sir."

"Good to hear. I still don't want you out in the field until you're back to a hundred percent. So light duties for you until then." Kyle looked like he was about to protest until he saw the Captain's firm expression and just nodded instead. "There's been a homicide in China Town, Carlsson, Medina, you should both head down there now."

"Actually Captain, I've got a bit of paperwork here that I really need to finish. Do you mind Foster?" Laura turned to look at Jordan.

"Not at all," Jordan said excitedly. Laura knew he had been holed up in the office the last few weeks and he was desperate to get out.

"Alright it's settled. Foster and Medina, get going."

"No problem." Medina mumbled. Though Laura knew, it was definitely a problem.

* * *

"Hey Laur," Cate smiled as Laura approached their usual hang out by the studios. Cate's back was leaning up against Jack's chest as the couple sat against the brick wall. Jack was planting soft kisses on Cate's neck and she kept chuckling and telling him to stop.

"Hey," Laura smiled back, looking to Parker who was clutching a biology textbook in her hands and scribbling down notes on a pad of paper. "Where's Issi?" Ordinarily Isabella would be the first person to greet her.

"Think she's with Mitch," Cate shrugged and Laura felt the familiar pang of jealousy rising in her chest. Isabella had been spending more time with Mitch to ensure no one got suspicious about their relationship. Parker looked up from her notes and gave Laura a sweet smile.

"Want to go for a walk Laura?" The green-eyed girl nodded and the two best friends began walking towards the oval. As they approached the oval the pair noticed a big group surrounding the soccer goals. They decided to head over to see what the commotion was all about and blended in to the back of the crowd. Mitch and one of the other boys from the soccer team were both in competition over who could do the most chin ups on the soccer goals.

After a dozen or so chin ups the other boy dropped down and the crowd cheered Mitch, moving in to embrace him. Laura's heart rate accelerated as she saw Isabella step up to give him a hug, a big smile on her face. The boys from Mitch's team all started chanting 'Kiss, kiss, kiss, kiss, kiss!'. Isabella's cheeks flushed red and Mitch leant in and placed a kiss on her lips. Laura looked away, she couldn't handle it, she felt like she was going to be sick.

"Laura?" Laura picked up the tone of concern in Parker's voice, she obviously wasn't doing a great job of concealing her emotions. Her eyes were prickling with tears and she was blinking furiously to get rid of them. She didn't care what Parker was thinking at that point, all she could think about was the terrible pain shooting through her chest. She was taking deep breaths and looking out at the opposite side of the oval. "Want to keep walking?" Parker suggested.

"Laura!" Another sharp pain shot through her chest as she heard Isabella yell from somewhere behind her. She could hear running footsteps and sharp intakes of breath behind her, but she didn't turn around. "Hey Parker."

"Um, hey."

"Laura, want to go for a walk?" Isabella asked, Laura turned around to look at her, the panic visible in her eyes. Laura just wasn't sure if she was ready to absolve that fear for her

"I think Cate wanted me to help her with some...homework. You good Laura?"

Parker asked, already starting to take steps backwards towards the studios. Laura nodded and gave her a smile, though that smile was dropped as she looked at Isabella and turned around.

"Laura?" Laura looked down, her arms folded. "Laura...Laura I'm sorry. I didn't want to kiss him. He just kissed me, I wasn't paying attention." Laura checked around them to make sure no one was listening, but they were standing at a deserted end of the oval. She could see Mitch in the distance jumping around and laughing with his friends. She felt Isabella slide her hand into her own and lace their fingers together. "You know I'm only hanging out with him to protect us; the kiss was never a part of the plan."

"I don't know, kind of seems to me like you have feelings for him," Laura said coolly, as though she was just coming to that realisation herself.

"Laura," Isabella stood in front of her, forcing her to look at her as she spoke. "I only have eyes for you, no one else," Isabella asserted. "How could I when you are the most perfect person I have ever met. There is no one else I want to be with." Laura's chest filled with warmth at her reassurance and she gave a small smile in response.

"Do you promise?" She asked softly. Isabella let out a sigh of relief.

"Pinky promise."

* * *

A ball of paper hit Laura's head for the zillionth time that morning and she couldn't ignore it any longer, the frustration inside her had built up to boiling point.

"Are you five Reynolds?" She lifted up one of the small paper balls he had been blowing at her all morning through a straw. "One more and I swear I'll break your ribs all over again." Kyle smirked at Laura's reaction. He had persisted with annoying her for over an hour, she knew she was giving in to what he wanted, but she couldn't take it any longer.

"I'm bored," Kyle sulked.

"Well then you can help me with my paperwork." She began rifling through the pile of folders on her desk, looking for something to give him.

"Why didn't you go with Medina this morning?" He inquired.

"You heard why. I have paperwork to do."

"But you never turn down the chance to go out into the field." Laura's heart rate had sped up at his line of questioning.

"Well, there's a first time for everything," Laura sighed, trying again to focus on the documents in front of her.

"Did something happen between you and Medina at the club?"

"What?" Laura asked completely bewildered by his question.

"Look I may have been off my rocker, but I saw the way she was looking at you when you were unconscious."

"Don't be ridiculous. Just because I'm gay, doesn't mean you get to sexualise all of my friendships-"

"Don't you dare try shutting me up by playing the gay card Carlsson. I know what I saw." Laura's cheeks flushed, and she rested her head on her hand to try and hide it. "Did you two ever date back in the day?"

"No," Laura spat at him, her cheeks flushing an even darker crimson. Kyle just smirked in response and picked up a folder from her desk, she knew he had gotten his answer.

6

Chapter 6

"Thanks Tom. This morning we are here in the 34th Precinct morgue with Medical Examiner Doctor Parker Hill." They all stood crowded around the television in the break room, Kyle chowing down on a bagel as the camera panned towards Parker and the reporter held out his microphone towards her. She began showing the reporter around the morgue and highlighting the different work areas and different tools that a coroner used.

"We know how popular forensic science has become in television shows and podcasts. Have you had many cases where your evidence has clinched the case?"

"As we know these days to see a conviction the forensic evidence is everything, circumstantial evidence is not enough to secure a conviction. It's a team effort we have a fantastic team of crime scene investigators, police and detectives that work together to achieve the good results," Parker smiled, adjusting her glasses nervously.

"Aww shucks," Kyle chuckled, the rest of them laughing too.

"And why do you think it's a great career path for high schoolers interested in science and medicine?"

"Being a medical examiner is definitely not an easy job. It never could be when you're dealing with death on a day-to-day basis. Unlike being a surgeon, or a GP, your patients can't be treated or saved from illnesses or injuries. It is your job instead to find out exactly how and why your victim died and bring that closure to the victim's families, which is extremely rewarding. And you get to do that whilst working as part of a team of extraordinary crime solvers."

"Thank you very much Dr Hill for that interesting insight, Tom, back to you."

"Thanks Phil. To breaking news now, reports out of New York University indicate multiple shooters have opened fire on the University campus with witnesses indicating that a possible hostage situation is now taking place inside the arts building. More on that as the scene unfolds..."

Before anyone could speak Isabella was racing out the break room doors, Laura dashing after her, nerves flaring in her stomach. Isabella grabbed Laura's keys off her desk and bolted for the elevator. As she stepped inside, Laura thundered in after her seeing the absolute terror on Isabella's face. She grabbed Isabella's hand, that was enclosed around the keys, and tried to pry them from her grip. Isabella pulled her hand back firmly and glared at Laura. Laura shook her head.

"Issi," she said softly, her green eyes piercing into Isabella's. "Let me drive."

* * *

Laura slammed the car door and chased after Isabella as she ran toward her house.

"You know I'm faster than you", Laura shouted as she gained on Isabella on the stairs, managing to grab at her legs, Isabella squealed and giggled as she wriggled free. She clambered into Laura's room and slammed the door.

"Hey! Let me in," Laura banged on the door, puffing from all the exertion.

"Nah uh," Isabella teased from the other side.

"I'm pretty sure what you really mean, is you're dying to let me in..."

"Am I?"

"Yes."

"I don't let losers in the door," Isabella teased.

"I'm not a loser, it wasn't a fair race." Laura leant her head on the door, she

could feel the vibrations of Isabella's body leaning against the other side.

"Yes it was, you've got longer legs, I evened the odds."

"Mmm but you always tell me you love my legs," Laura flirted back, hoping this would entice Isabella to open the door.

"You're right, I do love your legs."

"You know what I love?"

"What?"

"Your smile, your cute little belly button, the wispy bits of your hair that always creep out despite how many times you've tucked them back." The door cracked open, Isabella standing behind it biting her lip, her cheeks slightly blushed.

"You're so charming Laura Carlsson."

"Only with you." Laura mumbled before stepping forward and crashing her lips into Isabella's. She ran her fingers through Isabella's hair, taking in the sweet smell of her shampoo.

The back of Isabella's legs hit Laura's mattress and she wrapped her arms around Laura's neck as they fell on top it. Laura rolled onto her back and pulled Isabella so that she was straddling her hips.

As Isabella leant into the kiss, Laura lightly pushed her back. Isabella pulled back, panic in her eyes as she attempted to catch her breath. Laura raised her hand to Isabella's face and began stroking her cheek to reassure her.

"Hey, it's ok." She saw Isabella take a deep breath. "I just had to stop now or I wouldn't have been able to stop at all." Isabella frowned at her and Laura sat up, resting her back against the bed head.

"Why do we need to stop?" Isabella asked confused.

"I want it to be special," Laura admitted shyly, instantly turning a deep shade of crimson. Isabella slid forward into Laura's lap and brushed a strand of hair out of her face.

"Me too," Isabella smiled, her eyes sparkling down into Laura's.

"Is it ok that we wait then?" Laura asked anxiously. Isabella smiled and grabbed a hold of Laura's hands.

"Of course."

"Don't get me wrong. I want to...you know. But I don't want to rush this Issi," Laura pointed to herself and then Isabella. "Me and you. I want to do this right."

Isabella smiled once again as she looked into those piercing green eyes. "Who knew Laura Carlsson was such a romantic?"

"You do," Laura said quickly. "You're the only person that needs to know." Laura smiled as a big grin spread across Isabella's face. It was her favourite thing.

The front door slammed downstairs and Laura and Isabella heard footsteps running up the stairs. Laura looked at Isabella with complete and utter panic written all over her face. Alex's voice called down the hallway. "It's just me! I'll be in my room...with headphones on!" He shouted loudly. Both girls burst into laughter, their initial panic washing away.

* * *

Laura flicked the lights on in their cruiser as they went speeding downtown. Her hands were holding on so tightly to the wheel that her knuckles were bone white. Her nerves and sheer panic were only just overpowered by her churning fury.

"Come on, come on Sav, pick up!" Isabella was holding her cell phone desperately to her ear. It was the fifth time already she had tried calling her younger sister and Laura could tell her nerves were peaking. She answered finally, deafening silence on the other end.

"Savannah?" Isabella called into the cell as she switched it to speaker.

"Bella?" Savannah whispered, Laura could hear the terror in her voice.

"Savannah, tell me you're not in the arts building?" Isabella pleaded, her voice cracking.

"I'm on the fourth floor Bella. I'm scared." Savannah was whimpering quietly on the other end, Laura's heart ached at the sound.

"Listen to me Sav, it's going to be ok. Have you seen the shooters?"

"No, but we've heard gunshots. A lot of them. I think they're getting closer Bella." Savannah was crying even louder now and Laura could tell this was increasing Isabella's panic.

"Shh, shh Sav. I need you to stay quiet. Are you hidden?"

"We're hiding under some desks, but there's not much cover."

"What room are you in?"

66

"Four hundred and elev-" A gunshot rung out through the phone and interrupted Savannah. The young woman fell silent. Isabella lowered her voice even more now, Laura could tell she was trying her hardest to sound calm.

"Sav, stay calm ok and stay quiet. Hide the best that you can. Laura and I are coming ok. We're com-"

More gunshots rung through the phone and it sounded like glass was shattering in the vicinity. They heard a shout and the line went dead. A sob escaped Isabella's lips as she dropped the cell phone into her lap. Laura felt like she was going to throw up, but she tried as best as she could to hide it. Reaching across the seat she took hold of one of Isabella's hands in her own. The detective held on tightly and Laura could feel the tremors running up her body.

"It's going to be alright. You need to calm down ok?" Laura glanced away from the road for a second to meet Isabella's chocolate eyes. Trying to calm her down with one of her piercing stares. "We won't be able to help her unless you try to calm down. Take some deep breaths ok?"

Isabella started breathing deeply as more tears fell from her face. Laura squeezed her hand again and held on tightly. She was racing at a dangerous speed through the streets of Manhattan, but she didn't care. They had to get there as fast as they could. This was Savannah.

Laura pulled up at the north end of the campus where the police had already set up their base. There was police tape cordoning off the area and guard rails were placed around the surrounding streets to keep back the crowd. The SWAT team had already arrived and were stationed around the square, their guns trained towards the arts building. A police chopper was flying overhead and when Laura looked up at the surrounding buildings, she could see snipers already in place.

Isabella's door slammed shut and she went running towards the tactical van. Laura chased after her, watching as two patrol men grabbed a hold of a panicked Isabella. Laura ran to them and removed her badge and flashed it at the men.

"Detective Carlsson homicide, this is Detective Medina. We need to get inside."

"No one's allowed through Detective," one of the patrol men said, shaking his head. Isabella was getting increasingly frustrated and Laura was worried she was going to charge straight on into the arts building.

"Who's in charge here?" As she said it Laura recognised the Police Commander exiting the van, he was a large stocky man with a thick moustache. She had worked with him before at the 21st.

"Excuse me, Inspector Coleman?" The Commander looked towards her and began approaching the women, a look of recognition sparking on his face. "I'm sorry sir, my name's Detective Carlsson-"

"I remember you Detective," the Commander said firmly. Clearly torn as to whether this was a conversation worth his time in a moment where time was of the essence.

"This is my partner Detective Medina," Laura introduced. "Her sister is inside the building. We were just on the phone to her, but we lost connection. She was on the fourth floor in the arts building and from what we could tell, the shooters were on that floor."

"How long ago was this?" The Commander seemed interested now.

"Five minutes ago." Laura answered and the Commander nodded his head.

"Thank you for the information, Detective." The Commander said, beginning to turn away.

"Excuse me sir, can you tell me how many shooters there are?"

"As far as we've been able to confirm, two. I'm sorry, I have to go." Laura grabbed a hold of the man's shoulder, forcing him to look at her.

"What's your plan of action? Are you going to send in SWAT?"

The Commander sighed, clearly annoyed now that Laura was taking up so much of his time. "Not at this stage Detective. We have no clue what the situation in the building is. Now I'm sorry, I have to go. I hope your sister is ok Detective Medina."

Isabella looked frantic as the man walked away and Laura pulled her back towards their car. Isabella was struggling against her grip. "Laura let go. I need to get inside," Isabella whispered angrily.

"I know. We're going to get inside Isabella. I just need to call Foster first."

Laura spent the next few minutes in frantic discussion with Jordan, whilst Isabella paced desperately up and down the length of the car. Jordan was an alumnus of NYU and had worked as a janitor at the school during his time there, so he knew the campus better than anyone. When Laura had told him of their plan to sneak into the arts building Jordan immediately refused to tell her anything. Laura then argued that it was better for all of them if he helped them, with or without his help, they would be going in.

That turned things around real fast, Jordan began shouting directions down the phone. Apparently, there was an intricate set of tunnels beneath the buildings that had once been used to move mail across the campus, but were now one of the best kept secrets in New York. Jordan texted the women a map of the buildings and instructed them to head behind the square to the back streets and enter through the architecture building. Once inside he instructed them on how to reach the basement and from there, how to access the tunnels.

"Foster, I'm going to put my phone on speaker now and leave it in my pocket so that you can hear what's going on. Under absolutely no circumstances are you to say a word, ok? We can't have any noise whatsoever once we're inside," Laura instructed, taking a deep breath. "If something goes wrong, I need you to feed this line back to Commander Coleman from the 21st. He's in charge down here."

"Ok Carlsson no problem. Good luck you guys. Stay safe."

"Thanks," Laura muttered, unable to fully take in his words at this point. "Radio silence from here on out." She tucked the phone into her back pocket and continued walking.

A few minutes later Laura and Isabella had successfully managed to sneak into the architecture building and were in the process of locating the tunnel door within the basement. They located the door in the far corner of the room, but Laura sighed in frustration when she saw the padlock attached to it. She frantically scanned the room, but couldn't see what she was after, until her eyes landed on Isabella. The woman was wearing a thick jacket and Laura knew it was perfect for what she needed.

"Give me your jacket?"

"What?" Isabella asked confused.

"Jacket now!" Laura whisper yelled. Isabella shrugged it off and handed it to her. Laura began unholstering her gun from her waist and balled the jacket up as a silencer. Holding the jacket over the gun, Laura pointed it at the padlock and fired. The padlock cracked down the middle and Laura pulled the door open, scrambling down into darkness.

She brought the map up on her phone, as Isabella used her own phone as a torch. A hundred or so metres down they located the door Jordan had indicated. Laura took a deep breath before looking at Isabella with her piercing green eyes.

"Are you ready?"

Isabella just nodded and turned off the torch, placing the phone back in her pocket as Laura did the same. Both women pulled out their guns and Laura nodded at Isabella before pushing the door open slowly. They entered a dark basement full of old furniture and discarded books, as she breathed in she could smell mildew in the air. Her eyes fell on a door at the far end of the room and she motioned for Isabella to follow. They crept towards it slowly, Isabella reaching for the handle and pulling the door open slightly. They stopped and listened. Silence.

It was dark inside the building; the police had cut the power so that the only light that was coming into the staircase was from the skylights a few stories up. Laura motioned for Isabella to open the door further and she stepped inside first, treading as lightly as she could. They began walking up the first flight of stairs, their guns trained upwards. When they reached the ground floor Laura motioned for Isabella to open the door.

"But she's on the fourth-"

"We need to quickly check each floor to make sure the shooters are both on the fourth. We don't want any surprises," Laura whispered back and Isabella nodded.

When Isabella opened the door, Laura poked her head into the foyer to have a look, keeping her body concealed in the staircase. There were bags and laptops scattered over the floor and a long trail of blood that led behind the reception desk, the sight causing Laura to shudder. The red and blue lights of the police cars were just visible through the entrance doors. Not wanting to be seen by the police outside, Laura did one last scan of the area and ducked back into the staircase, shaking her head so Isabella got the message to keep moving.

When they stepped onto the first-floor corridor, they were met by almost complete darkness. The blinds in the surrounding rooms were all drawn and there was glass littered all over the floor. More discarded items were scattered over the floors, and more frighteningly drops of blood. They moved through the classrooms as quickly as possible, checking for signs of life, but again there were none.

Laura poked her head inside one of the classrooms and her eyes fell on a grizzly scene. Two bodies lay on the floor inside, surrounded by pools of blood. Laura's stomach churned when she saw them. There was too much blood for either person to still be alive. She pulled Isabella away before she could look inside, not wanting her to think the worst for Savannah. "Come on, this floor's empty," she whispered before stepping back into the staircase. They did the same thing when they came to level two, with the same result. Anyone that had been on these floors, wasn't anymore.

As they stepped onto the third-floor corridor, something felt different. Laura's heart rate sped up as she sensed people moving about in the opposite classroom. She turned to face Isabella and held up her hand to tell the detective to listen. They heard glass crunching under someone's feet and whispering. Raising their guns, both women began walking towards the door, crouching down so that whoever was inside wouldn't be able to see them through the windows. When they got to the door Isabella began standing up, Laura grabbed her shoulder and mouthed 'stay down'.

Laura slowly slid to a standing position alongside the door and peered through a slit in the blind. Inside she could see two boys and a girl huddled closely together. The boy in the middle was grimacing and biting down on his lip, when Laura looked closer, she saw a large patch of blood on his thigh. It was clear he was badly injured and his friends were trying their best to support his weight.

She looked around the rest of the corridor, listening for any other movement. When she was met with silence, she slid her badge off her belt and decided to lead with that. She motioned to Isabella that there were people inside and to wait ten seconds before coming in after her. Isabella nodded from her crouched position.

Laura slowly turned the door handle and stepped inside. The teenagers saw the movement out of the corner of their eyes and all looked up at her in horror. Laura was holding up her gun in one hand and her badge in the other. She raised a finger to her mouth, and the students nodded. She clipped her badge back on her belt and began walking slowly forwards, trying to avoid stepping on any glass.

"I'm detective Carlsson from the NYPD," she informed the students in a whisper, as they stared back, terrified. She watched as their eyes flickered to the door and she knew that Isabella must now be entering the room. "This is my partner Detective Medina. We're here to help," she reassured them.

Looking down at the boy's leg she noticed a bullet was lodged in his thigh and blood was steadily dripping from the wound. Laura's eyes darted around the room and she picked up a pair of scissors resting on the table next to her and began cutting off her sleeve at the shoulder. The material of her sweater was stretchy, perfect for a bandage. She slid her arm out of the material and turned towards the boy.

"We need to stop the bleeding. I'm going to tie this around the wound, try not to make any noise." The boy nodded and Laura fastened the black material tightly around his thigh, causing him to flinch and grimace, but he held his tongue. He was very white and from the amount of blood already on his jeans, Laura knew he was in a lot of trouble. She signalled for the teens to stay put and motioned for Isabella, leading her back to the door.

"He's going to die if we don't get them out," Laura whispered. A conflicted look crossed Isabella's face and Laura knew what she was thinking. Laura was thinking the same thing. Savannah. "I know," Laura reassured her, rubbing her arm. "But we can't leave these kids here." Isabella looked down as she thought over what Laura was saying. "Isabella, I need you to lead these kids down to the tunnels and out to safety ok?" Isabella looked up at her confused. "I'm going to go to the fourth floor and get Savannah."

"No. She's my sister, I'll go."

"Isabella you're not focused. You're too emotional. Right now, I'm Savannah's best bet." Isabella's eyes connected with Laura's and she could see the fear pouring out of them, but she also saw the understanding.

"I can't lose her Laura," Isabella said, fighting back the prickling in her eyes.

"You won't Issi, I promise. I'm going to get her," Laura whispered, squeezing Isabella's hand one last time before she walked back to address the teenagers. "Ok come on. We're going to get you guys out of here."

Isabella walked ahead of the students as they supported their injured friend, her gun held tightly in her hand. Laura opened the classroom door, her gun trained on the corridor. They took slow steps ensuring not to step on any glass as they went. When they got back into the staircase, Laura held a finger to her lips. Isabella was staring up at the fourth floor and Laura knew she didn't want to leave.

"Are you going to be ok?" Laura whispered so that only Isabella could hear her. She nodded once and looked into Laura's piercing green eyes, a look that told Laura she was scared it might be for the last time. Isabella grabbed a hold of her free hand.

"You have to come back to me Laura," she pleaded, Laura's heart leaping at her words. She didn't want to think about the possibly of this being their last conversation.

"I will, I promise," Laura whispered

"Pinky promise?" Isabella asked and Laura could see the tears in her eyes now as she said those words.

"Pinky promise." She gave Isabella a small smile, her eyes lingering as she tried to savour the moment. She turned around to face the stairs, silently moving up towards the fourth floor without another look back.

7

Chapter 7

Laura turned the door handle as quietly as she could, opening it just enough to allow her to peek into the corridor. The first thing she noticed was the pool of sunlight illuminating the corridor from further down the hall. It reflected beautifully against the fragments of glass it surrounded, casting light shadows against the ceiling. The second thing she noticed was the sound of crushing glass under foot. Lots of feet.

"Arms up!" A voice shouted fiercely, though Laura could detect a nervous quiver in his tone. The sound made her heart race, she had no idea what weapons the shooters were armed with or what situation she was walking into. All she knew was that she couldn't leave Savannah there.

Taking a deep breath Laura slowly stepped into the corridor, carefully shutting the door behind her. She looked for the number of the classroom beside her and saw the symbols '401' next to the door. Crouching down, she crossed further down to the other side of the corridor, careful to avoid the shards of glass, not wanting to give away her position. More numbers appeared on doors, '402' and then '404'. An overwhelming dread gnawed at her insides as she realised the voice was coming from somewhere near room 411.

She took a deep breath and continued slinking forwards in her crouched position, she hugged the wall tightly as she snuck a look at the classroom. Her eyes fell on the number '411'. The beautiful sunlight that streamed in through the windows was being obscured by the most chilling shadows. The shooter had his gun pointed at the students as they stood arms raised against the windows. It was a common tactic used to disrupt snipers. From what Laura could tell as she caught small glimpses of his face as he turned about the room, he looked to be college age himself. Her eyes searched the part of the room unobscured for the young woman with the dark brown eyes, but she couldn't see Savannah anywhere.

"Hey!" A voice yelled and the slender shooter moved into the centre of the room, a handgun held tightly in his right hand. He was sweating profusely, his curly dark hair a mop of moisture. "I said no phones!" His skinny arm reached out, grabbing a man from the window and dragging him to the floor.

He grabbed the phone out of the terrified man's hand and through it to the floor. Pointing his handgun at it, he fired, the sound ricocheting around the room. Several students screamed. The shooter began pacing back and forth behind the man. Laura sensed he was losing control. The boy on the floor was shaking like a ragdoll, his sobs echoed by the students watching on. Laura stared into his face, his light brown hair and pale skin, his green eyes, he looked just like Alex.

"What I say goes, you hear me!" The shooter yelled, his hand shaking as he pointed the gun at the students, daring one of them to step forward from the windows. He lowered the gun so that it was resting against the man's head. Laura saw a shiver pass up his body, his sobs halting as he waited for the shot. Laura's eyes widened in horror, her foot carrying her forward before her mind had caught up.

She took a deep breath and stepped out from behind the wall, her gun trained on the shooter. "Wait!" The shooter flinched, jumping backwards and nearly tipping over a desk as he raised his own weapon towards her. "Easy," Laura warned him as she took tentative steps towards the room, entering through the open door. The man on his knees was sobbing loudly, realising he had just escaped death for the time being. "I'm a Detective and I assure you if you try anything, I will get off a shot before you can blink."

The man didn't say anything, she watched droplets of sweat pooling on the stands of his curls. His eyes were darting frantically in their sockets, she could see the clogs ticking over in his head. Her eyes momentarily flickered behind, connecting with a pair of familiar chocolate eyes. Savannah was lightly sobbing, her hands raised above her head. She shook her head pleadingly at Laura. She looked away at once, not wanting to draw his attention to Savannah.

"Put your gun down," a harsh voice called from the doorway. In her peripherals she saw another larger man entering the room, his rifle trained on the back of her head. Laura heard Savannah release a panicked sob and her mouth went dry. This was going to be it for her. The man moved to her side, a nauseating stench permeating from his sweat stained t-shirt. He jabbed the rifle in her back, nudging her forward, "On your knees," he spat harshly in her ear as he pried the gun from her hand.

She dropped to her knees beside the sobbing man. A million memories trickling through her mind as she kneeled waiting to die. It was true what people said about your life flashing before your eyes right before you died. As the man lifted his rifle, all she was a vintage Babe Ruth baseball. The hairs on the back of her neck stood up as she felt the revolver come to rest on the crown of her head. She closed her eyes in anticipation, a sudden wave of calm radiating through her body.

The sound of the shot was louder than anything she had ever heard, it seemed to echo in her ears as she waited for the darkness to take her. Instead she felt someone fall against her, their limp body hitting the floor with a thump. She opened her eyes and looked towards the second shooter, the more slender man. He began firing off rounds towards the doorway, she heard a pained yelp from behind her, which she recognised as Isabella's. Panic rose in her chest and she scrambled to grab her gun off the floor. The shooter was still aiming at the doorway as Laura lifted her gun and fired a shot straight at his chest. The boy fell limp to the floor, his head crunching horribly with a desk as he fell.

"Isabella!" She scambled from the room and out the door. The detective was crouched down in the corridor, blood dripping from her shoulder as Laura skidded to a stop in front of her and dropped to her knees.

"I'm ok. It's just a shard of glass," Isabella reassured her. Laura let out a long sigh of relief. She felt like it was the first breath she had taken in the last five minutes.

"Bella!" Savannah came barrelling out of the classroom and dove into Isabella's lap sobbing. The older sister wrapped her arms around her and they both cried. Laura slid down the wall next to Isabella, taking deep breaths as the SWAT team burst through the staircase door. They had their guns raised and torches shining as they moved through the corridor and into the classroom, shouting as they went.

"Carlsson? Laura?" A voice broke her out of her daze and she saw Jordan crouched down in front of her wearing a bullet proof vest. "Are you alright?" Laura just nodded and wiped away a stray tear that had made its way down her cheek. Jordan helped her to her feet and pulled her in for a tight hug. "You're a crazy son of a bitch Carlsson," Jordan chuckled lightly and Laura gave him a small smile.

As they walked out through the entrance doors, they were greeted by more police officers and a line of paramedics waiting to treat the injured. Isabella and Savannah were swept away by a pair of emergency responders as Jordan led her over to Police Commander Coleman.

"That was a completely reckless and idiotic move Detective and if things had played out differently you might not even be standing here right now," the Commander declared angrily. Laura was nodding along as he spoke, but she wasn't really taking in what he was saying. She was too busy searching the surrounding crowd for the Medina sisters. "You're lucky I'm not taking your badge right here Carlsson. Foster connected us to your phone so we were able to listen to the scene unfolding." He put his hands on his hips and looked down at her contemplating. "You did good work in there."

"Thank you, sir." She barely made eye contact with the stoutly man, her eyes still scanning the crowd. He continued to stare, but didn't open his mouth to say anymore. She took at as her que and stalked away to search for Isabella and Savannah. She waded through distraught students hugging one another and sobbing uncontrollably, she made a point not to look too closely at their faces. She didn't want to see the pain reflected back.

She noticed a paramedic hand Savannah a blanket and a bottle of water, he was talking to her softly, trying to her calm her down. Next to them was an open ambulance and Laura could see Isabella being treated inside. The paramedic used tweezers to delicately remove a shard of glass from the wound, she saw Isabella's face contort as she got closer.

"Fuck." She smiled as Isabella cursed. It wasn't often it happened and it always looked unnatural when it did. Isabella noticed her walking towards them, she smiled warmly and her eyes radiated their familiar sparkle. Laura couldn't help the surge in her chest when she saw that smile. An hour ago, she wasn't sure if she would ever see it again. "Hey," Laura smiled nervously and Isabella bit her lip when she saw the detective blushing.

"Hey." She smiled back, as the paramedic wrapped an adhesive bandage over her cut. "I didn't get to thank you in there…" Laura waved her hand and shrugged like it was nothing as the paramedic stood up and left the cab. "No Laura, don't do that." Laura raised her eyebrows at Isabella in confusion. "Don't act like what you did in there was anything short of amazing. You saved so many lives. You saved Savannah's life-"

"And you saved mine," Laura smiled, stepping up into the cab and taking a seat next to Isabella on the bed.

"I don't really even remember what happened in there. All I remember was seeing you kneeling on the floor with a gun to your head-" Isabella's voice cracked and Laura took her hand. "I thought, I thought I was too late." Tears were running down Isabella's face and Laura ran her fingers across her check to wipe them away.

"I'm here Isabella. We're all here," she reassured her. "You were right on time." As the words left Laura's mouth, she couldn't help but feel they had a greater meaning. Her life had completely changed the moment Isabella had walked into the 34th and back into her heart.

Everyone was exhausted once they had finally finished being questioned. Jordan offered to drive them all home, but Laura refused, telling him to go straight home to his own family. She knew Bri would be anxiously waiting for him. Isabella climbed into the front seat of the cruiser with Savannah in the back. A soft buzzing began emanating from the middle console, Isabella looked down, Rachael's name was flashing on the screen. Laura glanced at the screen, then held down the button to turn it off.

"Let's get you guys home hey?" Laura caught Savannah's tired and scared eyes in the rear-view mirror.

"Bella, I don't want to go back to your apartment tonight," Savannah pleaded. "It's awful there." Laura raised her eyebrows, Isabella had made a few comments about her apartment being dingy, but she didn't realise it was that bad.

"I guess we can check into a hotel for the night."

"Don't be ridiculous," Laura interjected as she pulled the car onto the street. "You guys will stay at mine." Isabella and Savannah both smiled. Laura took that as a 'yes' and drove on to her apartment without another word.

Once they were inside Laura pointed them towards the guest bedroom, handing each of them a towel and some spare pyjamas. Half an hour later Laura found herself sitting on her long modular lounge, stifling a yawn she picked up the remote and turned on her large flat screen TV. She was met with the image of Police Commander Coleman outside of the arts building at NYU.

"So far, we can confirm five fatalities, including the two suspects, with at least six other people currently being treated for injuries," Coleman said sorrowfully.

"Can you confirm that the shooters were taken down by the SWAT team?" A reporter asked

"I can confirm that a small tactical team was sent inside the building and were successfully able to take down the shooters," Coleman answered. Laura shook her head, at least with this version of events she would get to keep her job. She heard the soft padding of footsteps behind her and turned off the TV. Isabella came walking into the room and sat down on the lounge beside her. Her hair was still wet from the shower, her face free of any makeup, she looked far younger, more like the girl Laura had once known.

Isabella bit her lip in that cute flirtatious way she always used to. Laura smiled sweetly back and shuffled closer to her on the lounge. Even in her sweatpants and hoodie, Laura still felt Isabella was breath taking. As they stared into one another eye's a rolling tension passing between them, Laura heard another pair of feet padding down the hall. Savannah appeared in the doorway and walked straight towards the lounge, sitting down next to Laura and curling in to rest on her shoulder.

"When I said I wanted a proper catch up Laura, this wasn't exactly what I had in mind," Savannah smiled, provoking smiles from Laura and Isabella. It was exactly the kind of light-hearted joke they needed to table the awful tension they had been holding onto all day. Laura turned and flicked on a movie, within half an hour, Savannah and Laura were both fast asleep. As she doze her head slid further down the lounge, coming to rest on Isabella's shoulder. She smiled and lightly stroked Laura's hair and she listened to her steady breathing. A sharp knock on the door startled Isabella. She gently stroked Laura's cheek to wake her up. The dazzling green eyes fluttered open and stared back into her own. Laura smiled up at Isabella, lifting her head off her shoulder and yawning.

"Door," Isabella mouthed and pointed to the front door. Laura nodded and slid slowly off the couch, careful not to wake Savannah who was still fast asleep. As Laura began opening the door, it was pushed by someone on the other side and Rachel clambered into her arms. Laura stumbled back a few steps as the woman clung on tightly to her neck, she let out a small chuckle.

"Rach," she whispered, not being able to help a small smile.

"Laura Carlsson-" Rachel yelled at her before Laura cupped a hand over her mouth and pointed to the sleeping girl on the couch. Rachel looked over to the couch, her eyes landing on Isabella who was staring back. Isabella smiled at her awkwardly, before turning away.

"Let's go outside," Laura whispered, ushering her into the hall.

Once the door was shut Rachel began again. "What the hell Laura I thought you were dead!" Rachel cried exasperated, tears falling down her cheeks. "When I couldn't get you on your cell I called Jordan and he said you had been at the shooting but you were ok. But that was hours ago. I've been calling and calling."

Laura reached forward and pulled Rachel into a hug, wiping away her tears with one of her hands. "I'm sorry, Rach. My phone died," Laura lied. "I didn't mean to scare you."

"Why were you even there Laura?"

"Isabella's sister Savannah goes to NYU and she was in the building when the shooters entered, so we...we went to get her out," Laura shrugged like it was no big deal, as Rachel stared at her sceptically. Laura could see the thoughts ticking over in her head.

"God, I wish you weren't so reckless Laura. I swear you're going to send me to an early grave." Rachel shook her head.

"I'm sorry," Laura repeated, grabbing Rachel's chin so that she was looking into her eyes. "But I'm ok, Savannah's ok, Jordan and Isabella are both fine," Laura added in Jordan's name at the last minute to prevent further hurt. "We're all alright. That's the important thing." Rachel nodded and gave Laura a small smile.

"I love you Laura Carlsson." Rachel stared up into the dazzling green eyes, Laura trying her best to keep her shock from them. They had never said those words before and Laura wasn't sure she was ready to say them now. Instead she smiled and grabbed Rachel's neck, pulling her in for a soft kiss.

Isabella and Savannah ended up staying at Laura's apartment for another few days as they all recovered from the trauma of the shooting. The death toll had remained at five in the subsequent days, and the other victims were in stable conditions. Laura was particularly relieved to learn that the injured student Isabella had led out, was going to make a full recovery.

The Captain had called the day before to tell Laura she and Isabella were both being awarded a Medal of Honour and Jordan a Medal of Valour for their efforts. He had a disgruntled tone as he told her, Laura knew he was angry about them disregarding protocols. She was sure he had, had to deal with a lecture from Coleman. But she supposed the medals helped protect the fabricated story that was being fed to the media. She didn't want any sort of award for that day. She didn't feel she deserved one. Leaving the arts building with her own life, Savannah's, and Isabella's, was all the reward she wanted.

Kyle was absolutely filthy when he found out. He still had trouble moving freely with his fractured ribs, and Jordan had decided that two of his friends in mortal danger was two too many. She had called Jordan earlier that morning, apparently Kyle was still ignoring him. The three women spent a lot of time watching trash TV and playing board games. Laura repeatedly kicked both of their asses at Scrabble until Savannah refused to play anymore. They ate copious amounts of junk food and sung loudly to nineties hits. After the horrors they had witnessed in the arts building, it felt good to laugh. At least for a little while.

Isabella showed off her culinary skills in the kitchen each night, preparing an array of Mexican dishes for Savannah and Laura to sample. Laura happily played sous chef, though cooking definitely wasn't her forte. Naturally Savannah didn't offer to lift a finger, but was their harshest critic when sampling the food. She felt like they were all making up for lost time over those few days and she learnt so many new things about both of the sisters. It was strange how tragedy brought people together, at least it had this time.

When they opted to spend time on their own, Savannah usually hogged the TV remote. Isabella raided Laura's well stocked library and lost herself in different worlds, Laura looking over occasionally to study the various expressions that crossed her face as she read. Laura on the other hand sat in the corner of the lounge room by the window and painted. She painted anything and everything to distract herself from her thoughts. Fields of yellow daisies, cobbled and narrow roman streets and chocolate brown eyes. When Savannah came up behind her and acknowledged her painting, Laura looked up startled. She hadn't been aware that she was painting them.

"Well aren't those eyes all warm and sparkly?" she said, leaning over Laura's shoulder. Isabella put her book down and wandered over to examine the painting as well. "And whose eyes might they be?" Savannah asked, cocking an eyebrow. Laura could tell what she was getting at, she hadn't even been consciously painting them. She tried to hide the nervous stutter in her voice as she answered her.

"Only the sassiest girl I know," Laura teased, trying to imply they were Savannah's.

"I wouldn't describe Isabella as sassy," Savannah smirked, taking a bite of her apple and returning to the lounge. At least the shooting hadn't broken her spirit, Laura thought as she flushed red. Isabella just studied the painting, ignoring her sister's comment.

"It's really good Laura. You're really talented," she smiled, her eyes far more vivid in life than they could ever been on paper. "I mean, you always were. It's seriously annoying how talented you are." Laura's cheeks blushed even harder at Isabella's compliment.

"And they say I'm charming," Laura chuckled and rolled her eyes, trying to diffuse the tension between them.

She hadn't been expecting the ache that was left in her chest when Savannah and Isabella went home. Her apartment felt so empty without them. The two women had enough energy and personality between them to fill the whole of Manhattan. She was nervous of the thoughts that might now return without their distraction.

She looked at her watch, Rachel would be there any minute. The two women hadn't spoken very much in the days after the shooting whilst she recovered, but she now welcomed the company. Though she felt the anxiety of Rachel's confession weighing on her. Would she be expecting an 'I love you' back? The doorbell rang and Laura rushed to open it, greeting her girlfriend with a warm smile. Rachel looked gorgeous. Her hair was loosely braded and she was wearing a strapless black dress that accentuated her curves perfectly. Laura's smile widened when she saw the bottle of rosé she was grasping, she could do with some liquid courage.

"Hey baby," Rachel smiled, her voice sultry, it sent an inadvertent shiver up Laura's spine. She stepped forward and pulled the brunette woman in for a deep kiss, trying to wash away any insecurity she might be feeling after the other night. When Laura broke away from the kiss, she smiled and looked up into the deep blue eyes.

"Hey beautiful. Come on in." Laura led Rachel into the dining room where the she had set the table with a few candles and a vase of white orchids.

"Aw babe, this is really sweet." Rachel smiled at Laura's romantic gesture. "Thank you." They enjoyed a few glasses of rosé as they devoured their chinese take away, Rachel careful not to ask too many questions about the shooting. When they got to the end of the meal, there was a few moments of silence, Rachel's fingers tapping anxiously on her empty wine glass.

"Something on your mind Rach?"

"Mmm maybe..." the brunette woman admitted shyly.

"Do you want to tell me what it is?" Laura inquired as Rachel reached for some more rosé.

"I've just been thinking... you risked your life going into that building for Isabella's sister. That's a pretty big deal..." she took a sip from her wine and peered up at Laura tentatively. At Laura's lack of response, she seemed to gain more confidence. "It's been ten years since you've seen either of them. Like you barely even know them anymore." Laura shrugged and looked down at the table, fiddling with a crumb on her placemat. "You must have been pretty close all those years ago to risk your life like that? You're reckless, but not that reckless." Laura sighed when she realised what her girlfriend was getting at.

"We were close. Me, Isabella, Parker, Cate, we were all best friends. Their families were like my family," Laura stated apathetically.

"Then why did you stay friends with all the other girls and not Isabella?" Rachel pushed.

"I don't know Rach. We had a falling out. People change and we just went other ways with our lives," Laura uttered, slightly more abruptly than she meant to.

"So, you two never dated?" Rachel was straight to the point now, she could tell Laura was being evasive. Laura looked into her blue eyes for a moment and considered whether or not she should tell her girlfriend the truth.

"I mean... you could barely even call it that at eighteen." Rachel just nodded like she had confirmed all of her suspicions. Her shoulders slumped slightly and her face drooped, Laura reached across the table and grabbed a hold of her hands, squeezing them with her own. "That was ten years ago Rach. We're just friends now. I care about you and I like where things are going with us and I don't want anything to jeopardise that." Rachel smiled as she looked into the piercing green eyes that were so irresistible. She leant forward across the table to plant a tender kiss on Laura's lips.

8

Chapter 8

"Are you sure you don't want to come?" Laura asked as she slipped on her black leather boots. Turning to face the mirror to see how they looked with her light denim jeans. She tucked and untucked her white blouse, eventually deciding to leave it tucked in.

"Yes I'm sure. I want you to go have fun with your friends." Rachel smiled, wrapping her arms around Laura's neck. "Damn my girlfriend is sexy." Laura smiled as Rachel ran her eyes over her outfit, her eyes lingering on the black lace bra that was peeping out from underneath her linen blouse. She had also paid extra care to her eye makeup, choosing a darker eyeshadow so her green eyes would pop.

"Thanks, gorgeous." Laura leaned in and kissed Rachel softly on the lips. Rachel grabbed the back of her neck and pulled her in closer, deepening the kiss as her hand snuck inside Laura's blouse. Her fingers traced the outline of the lacy bra as she pushed her hips into Laura's. Goosebumps rose on Laura's forearms as the touch, she felt herself leaning further into the kiss.

"What was that for?" Laura laughed as Rachel pulled away, adjusting Laura's shirt so it didn't look crinkled.

"So you don't forget about me tonight." Rachel fiddled with Laura's long hair, her eyes purposely avoiding the green ones.

"Not going to happen." Laura smiled and planted a kiss on her cheek, quite determined to mean it. Despite the whirlwind of feelings Isabella was churning inside her, she wasn't going to act on them. She was resolute that whatever was going on with her and Isabella, it was just going to be a friendship.

"Good, because as soon as you get home, I'm ripping you out of that bra." Rachel bit her lip suggestively and Laura felt heat rushing to her cheeks.

"Sounds like a plan." She leant in and kissed Rachel's cheek. Closing her apartment door behind her she took a deep breath to steady herself. It had been a decade between drinks, she just hoped everyone would remember their table manners.

* * *

Laura rang the doorbell and heard the thud of feet running down the stairs. A huge smile erupted across Isabella's face as she opened the door. Laura noticed she was wearing a new summer dress, covered in small sunflowers with her usual white converse sneakers. Her long hair cascaded down her shoulders in light curls. She looked down at her own outfit, a band tee and a pair of ripped denim shorts and wondered if she should have gone out and bought a new outfit too.

"You look stunning," Laura breathed, running her eyes over Isabella's dress.

"Ditto," Isabella grinned back, biting her lip.

"Come on, we've got places to be."

They drove towards the beach and Laura pulled over as they came to a fish and chip shop on the main street. She ran inside and picked up a large parcel of hot chips with a couple of scallops. The smell was incredible, it engulfed the entire car eliciting a grumble from Isabella's stomach. They drove for a few more minutes before pulling into a car spot with a magnificent view of the beach. Laura opened the boot of her hatchback to reveal a cosy picnic set up with fluffy pink blankets and oversized pillows.

"Wow," was all Isabella could say when she saw all the effort Laura had gone to. Laura leant forward and flicked a switch and the back of the car was illuminated with fairy lights. Isabella's eyes opened wide as she took it all in.

"Come, come. Sit down." Laura pulled Isabella into the back. They settled in amongst the pillows, Isabella cuddling in to Laura's chest as she watched the

rolling waves crash against the sand. Laura was alternating feeding Isabella a chip and then herself, when she kipped the order and had two in a row, Isabella whacked her on the arm. Laura chuckled and poked her tongue out, giving Isabella two in a row next. Laura immersed herself in every word Isabella spoke. It didn't matter what she spoke about, the passion with which she talked about cooking, philosophy and music just endeared Laura all the more.

"What are you smirking about?" Laura asked, looking at Isabella, the sparkle of the fairy lights reflecting in her eyes.

"Nothing, just something Parker said earlier."

"What was that?" Laura pried.

"She said she's never seen you happier." Laura smiled, there was some definite truth to that statement.

"I've never been happier."

"Really?

"Of course. You make me the happiest version of myself." Isabella blushed at Laura's words. She was staring into Laura's eyes with such intensity, it was hard for her to keep eye contact.

"Such a charmer," Isabella shook her head. "This is the perfect date."

They left the beach feeling extremely giddy and joyful. They blasted the radio in the car on the way home, singing at the top of their lungs with their raspy voices and giggling incessantly. Laura didn't want it to end as she pulled into Isabella's driveway. Her heart beat erratically as she stared into the brown eyes.

"This was the best date ever," Isabella sighed happily.

"It was," Laura agreed, leaning forward and resting her head on Isabella's forehead.

"I don't want it to end," Isabella whispered gloomily.

"Me neither," Laura kissed Isabella's forehead then turned to open her door.

"Where are you-"

"Stay there," Laura called over her shoulder as she ran to Isabella's door and opened it. She offered her hand to Isabella. "Miss Medina." Isabelle fought back a grin as she took her hand.

"So chivalrous." Laura shrugged and smiled back. "You really are going all out with all the date clichés," Isabella laughed, causing Laura to pout playfully.

"Don't worry, you're blowing them all out of the water." Laura grinned and leant in for a sweet kiss, her lips tickling from Isabella's touch.

Glass shattered somewhere inside the house and they broke away. Isabella looked panicked as she grabbed the door handle and ran inside, Laura chasing after her. They made their way to the kitchen and found Samuel Medina clutching a bleeding hand. A broken whiskey glass on the counter. *"Dad?"* Isabella's voice was laced with concern. Samuel's shirt was laced with sweat, Laura noticed his eyes appears glazed and bloodshot.

"I'm alright Bella," the man said softly.

"No you're not, you're bleeding." Isabella picked up a tea towel and wrapped it around his hand.

"I'm fine." Once his hand was wrapped up he reached for the half empty whisky bottle on the kitchen counter. Isabella stepped in front of him and pushed it further behind her.

"Give me the bottle Bella!" He yelled angrily, Laura flinched, looking nervously toward Isabella.

"No, you've had enough." Isabella shook her head, her jaw set, arms folded across her chest. Laura had never seen Samuel like this, his cheeks flushed a darker shade of red as he tried to reach past Isabella and grab the bottle, but she stayed put.

"GIVE IT TO ME!"

"NO!" Isabella shouted back with such ferocity, Laura's heart raced in her chest. Samuel pushed his daughter as he tried to grab the bottle from the bench, Laura stepping forward slightly, wondering if she should intervene. She was so scared. As they wrestled, the bottle slid off the bench and smashed to the floor, the shatter causing Laura to flinch.

"No," Samuel cried, sinking to the floor amongst the broken glass and spilt whiskey. He held his head in his hands and began to cry. Tears were streaming down Isabella's face as she looked down on her father. The smell of the spirits filled the room, stinging Laura's nostrils.

"Come on Issi." Laura grabbed Isabella's wrist, her own hands shaking. They turned and retreated up the stairs to Isabella's bedroom. Laura pulled her onto the bed and wrapped her arms around her. Isabella let the tears run mercilessly

now, soaking Laura's shirt.

"It's going to be alright." Laura soothed, running her hand over Isabella's back in light circles. Though she really wasn't sure that, that was true. "I'm here for you."

* * *

When Laura arrived at the trendy Manhattan sushi restaurant she was ushered towards a table at the back, where Parker and Cate were already seated. The restaurant was busy, though the price of dishes did gain you a few extra inches between tables than was often granted in the city. It was always a bug bear of Cate's when they went to a restaurant so noisy, she had to shout to be heard across the table. Laura had to hide a smirk, Cate was the one person who needn't worry about being heard. Her speaking voice was close enough to a shout already.

"Damn, you look gorgeous Laur." Parker remarked, the tone of surprise not going undetected.

"What like I don't normally?"

"I mean, you do, it's just you've gone to more effort than normal." Cate added hesitantly, appearing to decide halfway through her commentary that maybe she shouldn't have chimed in after all.

"Good to see you're keeping tabs on my outfits, I'll remember this." Laura tried to be light hearted in the delivery, but it came across far more defensive than she wanted. She knew what they were implying, that she had dressed up for Isabella. She tried to tell herself that wasn't the case, but she had gone out and bought the blouse and the bra the day before.

"Ok just quickly before Isabella gets here," Cate whispered to them. "Let's keep things nice and civil and give her a chance ok? We all know what she did and it was terrible, but we're going to try and cut her some slack. That was ten years ago, she had her reasons. Let's just get to know her as she is now."

"I have been doing that Cate?" Laura looked at her quizzically, quite frustrated with the lecture. She was the one who had been partnered with

Isabella for weeks now and the one who should be holding on to the most resentment.

"Yes, sorry Laura, that speech really was for Parker."

"Hey!" Parker rolled her eyes as the waiter arrived to take their drink orders. Cate and Parker ordered sodas, Laura a whiskey. She felt she needed a stiff drink to ease the excited nerves coursing through her veins.

"Hey." Laura looked up to see Isabella standing awkwardly at the end of the table. Her gold hoop earrings were giving serious 90s vibes, especially combined with her messy bun. Laura was glad she had put an effort into her own outfit when her eyes wandered over Isabella's white dress, the straps fell off her shoulders accentuating her tanned skin. Laura was completely beguiled.

"Hey Bella, you look great." Cate smiled from the top end of the table. Isabella sat down in the chair next to her, her eyes flitting nervously toward Parker.

"Thanks Cate." Laura gave her a warm, reassuring smile and Isabella smiled widely back. Laura got the sense she was still getting used to her not being outwardly hostile. Silence fell around the table for a brief moment. Laura looked at Cate to lead the conversation, Cate was staring at Isabella with a friendly smile, Parker was suddenly very interested in the chopsticks on top of her napkin and Isabella just looked uncomfortable.

"So, how's everything going after the shooting?" Laura and Cate both looked at each other surprised as Parker was the first one to break the silence, albeit somewhat reluctantly. The words did sound strained as they left her lips, her eyes struggling to maintain contact with Isabella's. Laura could sense Isabella relax a bit more, just to know Parker was going to be speaking to her.

"Yeah ok, I suppose I'm coping about as well as anyone. The precinct has offered us psych's to talk to, I had my first session this week and that was really helpful." Isabella nodded, her eyes slightly glazed. "I thought it might be easier, being a cop and going through something like this, you think that maybe you're more acclimatised to this sort of thing, but you're not."

Isabella shook her head and Laura could tell she was fighting back tears.

They hadn't talked about the shooting at all in the three days they spent together afterwards. All of them had tried to put on a brave face for one another. But each night they had gone to bed, Laura was haunted by the sobs that emanated from the Medina's room. She wasn't sure which sister, the sounds were coming from, maybe it had been both of them, but they were chilling.

"I just wish we could've done more," Isabella sighed and looked down at her hands dismally. "Three innocent lives lost." The day had taken a far bigger toll on Laura's psyche, than she cared to admit. She had seen some awful things in her career as a homicide detective, but the shooting had felt far more personal. She had been there and experienced the events. Removing herself emotionally from the graphic images she had seen wasn't as easy as it normally was.

She had barely slept the last two nights from the nightmares. She kept seeing the two bodies inside the classroom surrounded in pools of blood. The frightened young man shaking next to her, that would almost definitely have been murdered if it weren't for her, and Savannah's terrified brown eyes. Those were particularly haunting. She wanted to protect those innocent eyes from the cruelty of the world. Though she couldn't even protect herself. Anytime she closed her eyes, she could feel the shooter's rifle on the back of her head, just waiting to end it all.

"You did plenty," Cate said softly, breaking Laura from her reverie. "More than anyone could ever expect."

"We were really happy to hear that Savannah was ok," Parker offered cordially, smiling at Isabella this time. Laura noticed a small smile appear on Isabella's lips in response.

"All thanks to Laura," Isabella said humbly. "I never would have made it very far inside if she hadn't come with me." Isabella glanced at Laura and she offered her a small smile, still feeling rattled by her own thoughts.

"You guys are so brave," Parker said shaking her head. "If I heard gunshots, I don't care whose inside, I'm running the other way." They all laughed, breaking the tension that had built up. Cate reached across the table and placed her hand on top of Isabella's.

"Laura told us how you saved her neck in there. We're just so thankful you got there when you did."

"Me too," Isabella smiled, biting her lip once again. Laura noticed Isabella's body appear to deflate as she let out a breath she had been holding onto since arriving.

"You should've brought Savannah to dinner. I'm dying to see her all grown up. Laura hasn't stopped going on about her." Parker laughed, changing the tone of the conversation once again.

"She's definitely sassy, that's for sure." Isabella laughed. "Um, but she'll be at the memorial tomorrow night. So, you'll see her then." Cate and Parker both nodded and gave a small smile. None of the women were looking forward to going. It still felt too raw. But Laura knew it was the right thing to do, she needed to be there to honour the victim's, it might even provide some closure.

* * *

Laura and Rachel were handed a candle as they entered Washington Square Park. Thousands of other flickering lights moved silently around them like ghosts. People were gathered in small groups, comforting one another. It was starkly quiet. The bustling of the city traffic reverberated around the square, the rustle of the leaves louder than the movements of thousands of bodies.

Three large posters were propped up around the centre fountain. Thousands of bouquets laid beneath them. Laura eyes connected with the eyes of a girl on one of the posters and she immediately looked down at her feet. She wasn't ready to see their faces. The images of their lifeless bodies still haunted her. The girl's eyes were full of hope and life and Laura didn't want to see those eyes and think about their deaths. She felt Rachel's fingers interlace with her own, and she looked to her girlfriend.

"Whatever you need, I'm here." Rachel smiled softly, her eyes full of concern. "Shall we go and lay this bouquet?" Rachel motioned to the bouquet of white lilies in her arm. Laura looked down again. Rachel had picked them up on her way home from work so they could lay them down at the memorial. It was a beautiful gesture, thoughtful. Rachel just didn't know about the white lilies and Laura didn't feel like telling her.

"Uh, I'm just not sure that I want to go up there just yet. Would you mind?"

"Of course." Rachel squeezed her hand, her eyes falling on someone behind Laura. She gave a smile and a nod and turned around, making her way through the crowd.

"I still hate white lilies." Laura smiled and turned around. Isabella was standing behind her wearing jeans and a long black coat. Laura could see the concern and nerves in her eyes as she held on tightly to her own hands.

"Me too." The words came out as barely a whisper, her voice cracking slightly. Isabella stepped forward and wrapped her arms around Laura. She melted into the embrace, her face resting in the warmth of Isabella's neck. She could smell the familiar daisy scent as Isabella's arms wrapped tightly around her. She had forgotten how comforting her hugs were. She felt completely enveloped, safe.

"Hey Laur." Laura opened her eyes and saw Savannah now standing beside Isabella. Her eyes were glassy, her cheeks still stained with shed tears. Laura didn't want to break the hug, she didn't feel ready for it. She opened one of her arms and pulled Savannah in instead, Isabella wrapping one of her own arms around her sister.

"How are you doing?"

"Ok." Savannah's voice came out muffled as she spoke into Laura's shoulder. "How are you?"

"Ok."

"Hey guys." Parker's voice spoke softly from behind them. Laura slowly detached from the hug and turned around. Parker was holding on to Cate's hand, the nurse had tears slowly running down her cheeks. Kevin was on the other side gripping onto his wife. Laura stepped forward and hugged Parker as Cate hugged Isabella and then Savannah. It felt nice to have the support of her best friends on a night like this. They had always shown up for her whenever she needed them over the years. But for some reason, it was Isabella's hug she craved the most.

"How you doing Kev?"

"I'm alright." He smiled back at Laura's greeting, his big arm still tightly wrapped around Cate. He was over six foot four and was well built, though he always wore a goofy smile, his long wavy hair falling nearly to his shoulders.

A young girl climbed up on the stage beneath the arch and began strumming on an acoustic guitar. She dedicated the song to the arts students of NYU and began singing a soft folk song. Everyone in the park turned to face the stage, their arms wrapping around their loved ones. Isabella squeezed in beside Laura and wrapped her arm around her back, Parker on her other side. They stood and listened in silence to the music, their candles inside their cups glittering in front of them.

After a few songs Laura saw Rachel moving through the crowd towards them, Kyle, Jordan and his wife Bri following behind. It was nice to have them there. Bri wrapped her up in the tightest hug and gave her a warm smile. Even Kyle simply gave her a hug, no fist bump or silly banter. Laura noticed Rachel ensured she and Kyle squeezed in between her and Isabella as they turned again to watch the stage. She couldn't help feeling slightly annoyed by this, which she knew was the wrong emotion.

She slipped her arm inside Rachel's jacket and pulled her closer be her waist. Rachel looked up at her and smiled brightly, resting her head on Laura's shoulder. Laura's eyes wandered over to Isabella's, she was holding Savannah and staring at the stage, her eyes briefly connecting with Laura's before flickering away again.

After the musician's set, a minute of silence was led by one of the students. Then followed numerous speeches by friends and family of the victim's, students and teachers who had been inside the building that day. Laura found herself building up walls inside her head and attempting to compartmentalise like she did at work. The speeches were heart breaking and raw, tears slipping from her eyes as one of the victims' little sister's read out lines from his favourite picture book. Laura could hear Savannah's soft sobs just next to her, Isabella holding on to her tight and whispering words of comfort. The speeches finished up and the music began playing again, the crowd slowly beginning to disperse.

"We're thinking of you guys." Bri hugged Laura tightly again, promising to drop off some lasagne later in the week. Laura smiled gratefully and squeezed her tightly once more.

"Sorry we have to go," Jordan apologised. "Andre's at my Mum's place and Bri doesn't like leaving him there overnight."

"That's totally fine, I completely understand. I'll probably be heading off shortly. Thank you for coming."

"Of course." Jordan gave her a kiss on the cheek and he and Bri disappeared into the crowd. Cate was chatting to Rachel, and Parker was making small talk with the sisters. Kyle wrapped his arm around her and sighed.

"A walk?" He asked, linking his arm with hers.

"That sounds good." Laura breathed, glad to have Kyle's arm to hold onto. They meandered through the different groups, most of them students. She could hear memories being exchanged, some laughter interspersed now with tears.

"You doing ok Laura?"

After a few moments pause she answered. "Yeah...I'm doing ok." Laura deliberately elongated the last two syllables.

"You know I shot a guy my first year on the job."

"Really? I didn't know that." Laura was surprised this was the first she was hearing of it.

"Not exactly something to brag about," Kyle chuckled darkly. "A woman had made a call, her boyfriend was abusing her, he was threatening to kill her and he had a knife. I'd only been on the job about six months." Laura tried imagining a young, hesitant Kyle with skinny arms. It was hard to picture. "I was with one other cop, Dave Richardson, he was an older bloke." Kyle was staring across the park in that glazed over way people do when reliving a memory.

"We got to this old run-down apartment block in Harlem. You could hear the screams from outside, so could the people from inside. But none of them did anything. We ran inside with our guns drawn, the door was locked. I remember my heart going about a million miles an hour.

"We yelled for them to open the door, but of course they didn't. Richardson told me to stand back as he kicked down the door. They were standing there in the living area, the woman's night dress was covered in blood, he'd already stabbed her." Laura gritted her teeth picturing the scene. Domestic violence was the biggest issue facing the force, just no one spoke about it. She had come across similar scenes in her own career.

"He was holding the knife to her throat, threating to cut it. I remember Richardson edging inside and trying to calmly talk the guy down. I was hardly keeping hold of my gun, I could see it shaking violently in my hands." Laura could feel the tremors in Kyle's arm now as he spoke, his voice was breathless.

"The man was getting more and more agitated and pressing the knife further into her throat, blood was trickling down. The man wasn't paying me much attention, I think he could tell I was green, so he had his eyes fixed on Richardson. He was begging the man to let her go, we could both see how much blood she was losing, she could barely stay on her feet. And quite soon after, she couldn't at all. She passed out and he couldn't keep a hold of her, she dropped to the ground and he lunged forward. I don't even remember firing. But somehow I got a shot off and it hit him in the stomach." Laura squeezed his hand as the emotion in his voice became thicker.

"What happened then?"

"He collapsed. Richardson started CPR on his girlfriend and I detained him as we waited for the ambulance. But she was dead when they arrived. She had lost too much blood."

"And the man?"

"He lived, he's still in prison." His face was white as a sheet, his eyes resentful. "I still see her face in my dreams at night, still remember every detail of that funeral. It's the close ones that hit you harder."

"Sorry that happened Kyle."

"I'm sorry too. But that's why we do what we do right? Not to save everyone, no one can do that, but to save as many as we can." Laura nodded, looking back out across the park at the mourners. He was right, but they both knew accepting that as the truth was the hardest part.

"Alex." The name left her lips almost imperceptibly. When the man turned his head towards her, she saw the slightly darker colour of his hair, the lips thinner and the nose just a bit wider. She stopped dead and blinked rapidly as he came into focus. As her eyes focused on him, he seemed to sense her gaze and looked towards her. His face dropped and all of the colour vanished from his cheeks as he saw her. He looked just as anxious as she felt.

"Laura, you ok?" Kyle asked concerned. He followed Laura's intense gaze to the young man now approaching.

"Hi." The man looked nervous as he stared into Laura's eyes. "I don't know if you remember me—"

"I remember you," Laura's tone was robotic, her stomach a contortion of knots.

"Oh. Well, I never got to thank you for what you did that day," he shifted uncomfortably, looking down at his feet. "You saved my life. Thank you."

"You're welcome," Laura replied, desperately trying to block out the flood of memories trying to break through.

"Drew!" Someone called from behind him. He looked over his shoulder towards a young woman waving at him.

"I've got to go." Drew looked back towards Laura and offered one last small smile. "Thank you again." Laura just smiled and watched him disappear. Kyle wrapped his arm around her back and gave her a squeeze.

"Ready to head back?" Laura nodded and Kyle turned them back towards their group, the crowd far thinner now than it had been half an hour ago. They were all still huddled in the same spot they left them, chatting away. Savannah and Parker seemed to be getting along really well, just like they had done years ago.

"Hey, we were wondering where you guys got to," Rachel smiled and held out her hand. "I'll take her back now." She joked. Laura let go of Kyle's arm and turned to look at him.

"Thanks for the walk." But her eyes really said 'thanks for the talk'. Kyle smiled back, without, for what may be the first time ever, any hint of sarcasm.

"Any time." Kyle walked over to Kevin and began chatting as Rachel pulled her into a hug. She held her tightly, Laura's eyes falling again on Isabella standing behind them. The brunette woman met her eyes and smiled. Rachel pulled away from the hug as Laura noticed her glance back at Isabella before refocusing her attention.

"I love you Laura Carlsson." She said sweetly, though a little loudly for the moment. Laura was sure that was intentional. She couldn't help her eyes once again flitting to Isabella's. The brown eyes seemed to dim when they connected and Isabella looked away. "Laur?"

"Anyone want to share an Uber?" Kevin asked, breaking the tension and allowing Laura to remove herself from the situation.

"That would be great," she chimed in, not allowing anyone else to jump in first. She figured company would be a good distraction. They hugged Kyle, Parker, Savannah and Isabella. Laura lingering for just a second longer on the last hug.

Cate, Laura and Rachel squeezed into the backseat, letting Kevin have the front. Rachel was focused on the window, paying her no attention when Laura placed a hand on her knee.

"How many stops?" The driver asked the car before setting off.

"Tw—"

"Three," Rachel chimed in over the top of her. Laura sighed, her head falling back against the headrest.

9

Chapter 9

"So I understand you're here Detective, as you were involved in the shooting at NYU, is that correct?" Laura nodded stiffly and looked at the room surrounding her. It was very sterile, with cold LED lights and white washed walls. A desk sat in the corner of the room with a laptop, a few folders full of files and a photo of a young family. Two oversized armchairs were placed in the middle of the room, now occupying Laura and the psychologist. Laura shifted uncomfortably as she looked up at the inspirational posters around the room, offering helpful advice for anxiety and depression.

Therapy made her nervous. She'd always refused it after big cases in the past, but this time the Captain had been insistent for both her and Isabella. Therapy had always held a negative connotation in her family.

"I'd like to ask you a bit about it if that's ok?" Laura finally made eye contact with the psychologist who was offering her a warm smile. Purely because of the woman's profession Laura took her gentle tone and warm smiles as an act of sympathy. Sympathy to her meant that in the giver's eyes you were vulnerable. A trait she had promised herself she would never be again.

"Sure. I'm just here to clock in my hour and leave." Laura's tone was almost aggressive as she spoke. She could see the psychologist was slightly taken aback.

"I understand Detective, not everyone agrees with counselling or therapy

99

or whatever you would like to call this. I know that you are here because you have to be, not because you want to be. But try and think of this as any other conversation. I'm not going to write any notes, I'm simply here to listen and respond to your answers with questions." Laura sighed and nodded.

"Why don't we start with how you ended up involved in the shooting?" The woman leant back in her chair, giving Laura a serious look. Ever since the shooting she had closed her mind off to the memories of that day. Opening up those flood gates once again felt like self-sabotage. Laura relayed the events of the morning as impassively as she could, the psychologist offering her encouraging nods as she did so.

"So you didn't question your partner on wanting to go to the scene of the shooting?"

"No."

"You didn't think that maybe seeing as her sister was inside the building, that she was too emotionally distraught to be involved in the operation?"

"I did think that," Laura answered bitterly, getting annoyed with her judgemental questioning.

"I'm not judging you Detective. I am just trying to understand why you followed your colleague's lead when she was clearly emotionally compromised?"

"Because I could understand how she felt. If that was my brother or sister, I would've done the same thing."

"Why did you go to the fourth floor yourself Detective? Why not let your partner go?"

"Like you said, she was emotionally compromised and not in the right frame of mind to do so. Someone had to get the teenage students to safety, so only one of us could go." Laura crossed her arms over her chest and met the woman's gaze with her piercing green eyes. The psychologist looked somewhat uncomfortable at the Detective's intimidating glare.

"What's your relationship to Detective Medina?"

"We're partners," Laura answered stiffly, trying her best to be evasive. "Though I'm not sure how that is relevant. I thought this session was about me?"

"It is. Just humour me." The woman smiled at her. "How long have you been partners?"

"A few weeks." The psychologist looked surprised at her answer.

"Only a few weeks?"

"Yes." Laura could tell the woman knew there was more to it than that. Rather than going back and forth for another few minutes, she decided to end the mystery. "Before that, we were friends at school."

"Uh, so you've known each other most of your life then?"

"Sort of. We hadn't seen each other in ten years until a few weeks ago."

"How come?"

"We had a falling out," Laura answered, becoming irritated now. Talking about the shooting was one thing, but dabbling in her personal life was off limits.

"What was it about?"

"I thought we were here to talk about the shooting?"

"We are Detective. I am just trying to understand the relationships at work." Laura let out a frustrated sigh and glanced down at her watch. 10am. Her hour was up. She promptly stood up and offered the woman a phony smile.

"Well Doc, that's all I've got time for today—"

"Wait, Detective—" Laura gave the woman a wave as she grabbed her coat and beanie and closed the door behind her.

She stepped out into the cool New York air, thrusting her hands into her pockets as she turned towards home. It was a long walk and ordinarily she would use the subway, but today she felt like she needed it. The psychologist had tried to rattle her with all of her little insinuations. She was meant to be there to talk about the shooting, not to analyse her past and present relationships. She had felt completely exposed in that room, like the psychologist could almost predict what she was thinking. In her head she was fantasising about walking into the Captain's office on Monday morning and refusing any further appointments.

The autumn breeze whipped up the bronze leaves that littered the kerb as she walked. She covered her eyes to shelter from the debris, as she crossed the road into the park on her way to her apartment. There was a line of people right in the middle where she needed to go. She could tell by their dishevelled and dirty clothing that many of them were homeless. As she looked towards the front of the line, she noticed several people walking away with pots of soup and cups of steaming hot coffee.

It warmed her heart to see people rallying to help those in need. As she got closer to the crowd she attempted to cut across the line, her eyes closing in on a familiar figure at the front. Isabella. The brown eyed woman was working the coffee pot, pouring steaming coffees for the homeless of Manhattan on her day off. Laura's heart fluttered at the sight. She contemplated fading into the trees and continuing on her walk home. Without really noticing it though, she began moving forwards in the line.

"Could I please get one black coffee with—"

"One sugar," Isabella interrupted her automatically. She looked up, clearly shocked to see Laura standing before her, but smiling nonetheless. Her cheeks were rosy from the breeze, a small leaf clinging to the strands of her windswept hair. She looked younger in this setting, more like the Isabella Laura had known.

"Don't worry, I'm paying." Laura smiled warmly back and gave Isabella some change.

"What are you doing here?"

"Out for a walk," Laura lied easily. "What are you doing here?"

"I volunteer here," Isabella answered softly.

"Oh," Laura said, leaving space for Isabella to continue speaking.

"I've got this Bella, go chat to your friend." A teenage girl with pink hair and dark eye makeup stepped forward and offered to take over for Isabella. Isabella thanked her and moved out from behind the table, motioning for Laura to join her on a nearby park bench.

"So what is all this?" Laura asked.

"It's called YOTS. Youth Off the Streets. It's a national organisation that helps troubled youth struggling with drug addiction, homelessness, criminal history and mental illness. Part of what they do is getting the youth involved in the community through food drives like this. Some of these kids do it as part of their probationary community service. I've been volunteering with them for the past six years. First in Cali and now here."

"Oh," was all Laura could think to say once again. These past ten years she had attempted to build this less than perfect image of Isabella in her head, but the detective was hell bent on erasing that. Laura took a sip from her coffee to ease the awkward silence. It was instant coffee and it sure tasted like it. Laura had to fight a grimace as the bitter liquid touched her tongue.

"I know, it's not the best coffee," Isabella attempted to apologise, noticing Laura's slight grimace.

"No, no. It's, it's good," Laura lied. Isabella rolled her eyes and grinned at Laura.

"So, what did that guy say to you last night?" Isabella asked cautiously, watching Laura's smile fade from her lips. "Kyle told me about it on the way home."

"Right..." Laura was caught off guard by Isabella's question. "He just thanked me for saving his life." Isabella nodded and looked out across the park, watching the little kids running around on the nearby playground, their scarfs flapping in the wind.

"I can't believe you risked your life for him," Isabella said, surprising Laura once again. She looked at her quizzically, she had never told her about saving the man. Isabella caught her confused gaze. "I read your statement," she answered. Laura nodded. It wasn't surprising that Isabella had been through the police file for that day. Ordinarily she would have too, but she wasn't quite ready for that.

"I feel like I would've done it for anyone, but he looked just like—"

"Alex?" Isabella answered. Laura stared at her again completely bewildered. It sometimes felt like Isabella knew her better than she knew herself.

"Yeah," Laura agreed, turning her attention back to the park. The two women sitting in silence for a moment as they watched the line growing smaller. Laura's phone buzzed in her pocket. "Carlsson." Laura nodded as she listened to the voice on the other end of the phone. "We'll be right there." She hung up and looked at Isabella with a stern expression. "There was a murder in the square last night. They've just found a body."

Laura and Isabella left the park, making a detour past Laura's house to change and pick up the cruiser. They then headed for Washington Square Park. There were workers in high vis dismantling fences and cleaning up rubbish. There was a large tow truck beside the container toilets waiting to cart them away. Isabella flashed her badge at the patrol cops that were safeguarding the square, they lifted the tape and let the detectives pass under. They walked inside the women's toilets and found Parker inside the disabled cubicle, standing over a woman's body.

"Hey Parker," Laura greeted the ME, with a sombre tone. Parker looked exhausted from the night before.

"Hi Laura, Isabella," she nodded. The shooting paired with the last few nights of bonding had softened her. Parker acknowledging Isabella at work was a big step forward. Laura crouched down to survey the body. The woman was young, probably in her early twenties with light blonde hair and a slim figure. Her eyes were closed, something that would have been done after she died. There was blood pooled around an incision in her abdomen. The most interesting part about the scene though, was the foreign emerald object on her chest. A green dollar bill was stuck with blood to the victim's chest. Laura immediately believed it to be a calling card.

"What can you tell us?" Isabella asked as she ran her eyes over the body.

"Based on lividity, she was likely killed in the early hours of this morning."

"What can you tell us about cause of death?" Laura leaned closer to get a better look at the wound, careful to avoid the nearly dry pool of blood at her feet.

"Just based on the injuries I can see, it looks like she was killed by a stab wound to the kidney. By the force of the incision and the amount of blood, she would have been dead within a few minutes. A wound of that depth, I'd say it wasn't your run of the mill pocket knife, this looks more like a hunting knife." Laura nodded her thanks and turned to a man dusting for prints on the cubicle door.

"Have forensics found anything?" Laura enquired.

"Nothing so far Detective," he shook his head, his hair stiff with gel. "This was a high traffic bathroom last night so the crime scene could be littered with thousands of different finger prints and DNA profiles." Isabella and Laura both nodded and turned back towards the body. Isabella pointed to the dollar bill on the victim's chest.

"What do you make of this Carlsson?"

"It looks like a calling card to me."

"That's what I was thinking," Isabella agreed solemnly. "Was there any ID found on the body?"

"No," the man shook his head, moving towards the mirrors to begin dusting there.

"The bastard might have taken it as a memento," Laura huffed, standing up and running her hand through her wavy hair.

"Are you thinking we've got a serial killer on our hands?" Parker asked.

"I don't want to jump to any conclusions," Laura said, trying to ease Parker's anxiety. "But based on what my gut's telling me, I don't think this is last victim we find staged like this." Parker looked thoughtful as she looked back down at the body.

"Thanks Parker, let us know if you find anything else of note from the autopsy." Isabella smiled warmly. Laura noticed the smile grew even wider once Parker had returned it.

"Will do."

* * *

They had rifled through hours and hours of CCTV footage trying to identify the young woman and her possible killer. Laura lifted her second coffee of the day to her lips and took a big gulp. It was also the second coffee today made by Isabella, but this one was much better than the first. The lift chimed open and Jordan and Kyle exited. They were both wearing casual clothes, jeans and T-shirts. After all it was meant to be their day off. If Laura had learnt anything since joining the homicide squad though, it was that murder never rests.

"Yo, yo, yo," Jordan smiled cheerily. He, like Isabella, was always upbeat.

"Don't we get a day off in this place Carlsson?" Kyle winked at her. She just gave him a sarcastic glare and went back to trawling footage.

"Did you guys find anything at missing persons?" Isabella asked.

"Nope, nothing. There's been no missing persons reported in the last twenty-four hours matching her description." Laura sighed, disappointed. So far, they had absolutely nothing to go off.

"Find anything on the CCTV?"

"Nada," Isabella answered resting back in her seat. Jordan just nodded and sat down on the edge of his desk. "How was Andre when you picked him up?"

"Absolutely feral," Jordan shook his head. "Just one of the very reasons Bri dislikes my mother. She pumps him full of sugar. Kid smiles and she gives him anything he wants. Took us half the night to try and get him to sleep."

"See, this is why I'll never have kids. I need a solid eight hours to look this good," Kyle grabbed his jaw and turned his face side to side for them all to examine.

"I've got something," Laura interrupted, causing the detectives to jump up and crowd around her laptop. As they watched they saw the young woman walking past the fountain, the crowd having largely dispersed by this time. She looked unsteady on her feet as she wandered towards the toilets. The cameras lost sight of her as she walked beneath the trees towards the cubicles. No one else entered the frame during that time.

"Dammit!" Laura slammed her fist against the desk, causing Isabella to jump.

Jordan's phone buzzed and he picked it up. "Foster?" He was silent for a few moments as the other detectives watched him. He hung up and looked directly at Laura.

"What?"

"Someone just lodged a missing person's report matching our victim."

Informing a victim's family about their loved one's death, had always been the worst part of the job. It was terrible delivering that news and watching their families heart break. A wound Laura knew would never fully repair.

They still hadn't established a clear motive for the murder. The woman had gone to the memorial with some college friends, they became separated at some point during the night and they assumed she had made her way back to the dorms. The next day when she still hadn't arrived home, they had called her parents. Neither her friends nor her parents could think of any possible reason someone would want to kill her. She was just a sophomore in college and was loved by everyone. She had no debts, she didn't take drugs, she barely drank. All of these things contributed to the lack of motive and therefore pointed more and more to a potential random homicide.

"Parker?" Isabella stopped typing and watched as Laura took the phone call. "We'll be right there." Laura nodded towards Isabella and without a word the two stood up and began walking towards the morgue. They entered the chilled space to find Parker leaning over the woman's pale body.

"What did you find?"

"Interestingly, we found traces of Rophynol in her system." The way she said 'interestingly' left Laura confused.

"Why interestingly?" Isabella asked, taking the question straight out of Laura's mouth.

"Rophynol is the date rape drug and there is no trace of sexual abuse."

"So the killer merely used it to make her drowsy, making it easier for him to kill her without a struggle." Laura concluded, Parker nodding her head.

"In that case the killer had to have interacted with her before entering the bathroom in order to slip her the drug," Isabella added.

"Pretty bloody bold going after someone at a memorial right?" Parker questioned, slightly bewildered. "You've got to be pretty arrogant to think you can kill someone in public like that."

"Well his arrogance has paid off...so far." Laura was anxious to ensure it wouldn't again. They headed back upstairs and Laura opened her case notes, sifting through the details they knew so far. Foster and Reynolds were out in the field interviewing students who had attended the memorial. The more she thought about the case, the more troubling the case appeared.

"I saw Ellie's in town," Isabella smiled, taking a seat at her desk, half a sandwich clasped in her hand.

"What?" Laura was taken off guard. One, that Ellie would be in New York and two, that Isabella would know about it. The brunette's face dropped at her tone and she looked confused.

"Oh...sorry. I thought you knew," Isabella said softly, her eyebrow furrowed as she surveyed Laura.

"Nope."

"Well I'd love to see her. Do you think she'll drop by?"

"No Isabella I don't!" Laura spat back at her with certain fury. Isabella leant back in her chair, she looked startled. "Look Isabella...Ellie and I don't speak. We haven't really spoken in a long time. So, no I don't think she'll be dropping by," Laura huffed.

"I'll go make us a coffee," Isabella almost whispered it as she stood up and left. Laura felt a rush of guilt when she watched Isabella disappearing into the break room. She couldn't control her anger when it came to Ellie, but she didn't mean to take it out on Isabella. The whole thing with Ellie was just too painful for her to deal with. She promptly stood up, grabbing her keys and stormed towards the exit of the precinct.

10

Chapter 10

The scent of daisies filled her nostrils, as Isabella's perfect lips trailed up her jaw to her lips, applying soft kisses between her moans. The metallic taste of blood licked at her tongue as she bit down on her lip. She begged her throat not to release the scream that was residing there. Isabella was imprinted on her every sense. Laura collapsed onto her body, their damp skin clinging together as they caught their breath. She nuzzled her face into her open neck, her nose searching for that irresistible scent. But she could no longer smell it. The daisies were gone. She opened her eyes and was met with a pair of luminous blue ones. Disappointment washed over. The eyes weren't chocolate brown, nor were they sparkling.

"Mmm that was hot," Rachel husked, leaning down and applying a soft kiss to Laura's forehead. Laura smiled weakly in response, unable to fight the longing anxiety churning inside her. Rachel slid out from underneath her and began getting dressed. She pulled a fresh pair of lingerie out of one of Laura's drawers and slipped them on. Laura's mind wondered what they might look like on tanner skin, darker hair. She could almost smell the daisies. She did up the final button of her blouse and walked over to the bed, leaning down to seal their lips in a kiss.

"I'm off to work, call me later?"

"Of course," Laura smiled. Rachel was the only woman that had ever made her feel anything apart from pure lust. Before Rachel, she never would have played into any of those petty relationship vices. She had pretty much sworn off relationships altogether. But the brunette woman had been persuasive and she quickly fell for her wiles, intelligence and kind heart.

"Bye baby," Rachel blew her a kiss and walked out the bedroom door. She threw her face into her pillow and pressed it down so as to muffle the sound as she screamed. The doorbell rung and she sighed frustrated. She wasn't in the mood to deal with anyone. Grumbling, she stood up in search of clothes. Her black panties laid discarded at the end of the bed, her grey hoodie on her armchair. She threw both on and headed for the door.

As she opened the door, her heart leapt in her chest as the sparkling chocolate eyes stared back at her. Her cheeks flushed red, she prayed Isabella couldn't read minds. Isabella's eyes cast over her wild and ruffled hair and then lowered to her bare legs. Isabella swallowed, her eyes lingering a little too long on Laura's thighs.

"Isabella," Laura's husky voice forced her to look back up as she bit her lip. "What do you want?"

"I wanted to apologise for yesterday. I didn't know about Ellie. I really didn't want to upset you," she said awkwardly, looking down at the ground. Laura sighed and opened the door wider, inviting Isabella in. They settled on the couch, Isabella keeping her eyes deliberately on Laura's face. "I just wanted to let you know, that if you wanted to talk about it, about Ellie, that I'm here." Laura nodded and began fiddling with the strings on her hoodie. "Look Laura, I'd like to think that we're friends..." she lingered on the word 'friends', leaving it open as a sort of question. Her chocolate eyes looked so vulnerable as she stared at Laura.

"We are friends Isabella..." Isabella's facial expressions softened. "The Ellie thing is just a really long and complicated story and I don't want to bother you with it."

"It wouldn't bother me, but ok," Isabella agreed, clearly not wanting to push the issue.

The doorbell rang again and Laura looked towards the door confused. For the second time today she was completely shocked when she opened it. Standing on her doorstep was the last person she ever expected to see there.

Ellie.

"Hey sis, miss me?" Ellie smirked sarcastically. Laura's heart rate accelerated as she saw her scarily thin sister's bitter expression. Seeing Ellie's red and dilated eyes Laura knew she was on something.

"Ellie...what are you doing here?" Laura's voice came out shaky, nervous. She was usually so confident and firm. But when it came to her family, she became a shell of her normal self.

"Are you going to let me in or what?" Ellie huffed, crossing her arms over her chest.

"I don't think that's a good idea..."

"Are you serious right now?!" Ellie's voice ricocheted off the walls. Laura's eyes wandered around the hall to make sure none of her neighbours were roused.

"Don't shout at me Ellie..." Laura spat, matching her tone, though much quieter. "You have no right to just show up here."

"Whatever, I need your help." Her tone was arrogant and resolute. She seemed to know Laura wouldn't refuse her.

"What the hell have you done now?" Laura asked through gritted teeth, her fists clenched at her side.

"Let me in and I'll tell you," Ellie tried to push the door open but Laura blocked her path. Their bodies were only inches apart now and both of them were seething. Isabella slid off the lounge and slowly crept up behind Laura, grabbing a hold of one of her hands. Laura flinched. Relaxing only when she realised it was Isabella. Her partner gently pulled her back inside, opening the door for Ellie.

"Let her in Laur," Isabella said softly, trying to calm Laura down. Ellie's eyes fell on her and widened in shock. Her eyes drifted to their entwined hands and Laura was suddenly very conscious of her provocative state.

Anger rippled across Ellie's face as her dark eyes pierced into Laura's. "What is that bitch doing here?" She spat incredulously.

Isabella left as soon as Ellie entered, Laura apologised for her behaviour but Isabella wasn't having any of it, she waved her off and left gracefully. Ellie wasn't offering any of her own apologies, though Laura understood why. She sighed and turned towards the lounge where Ellie had made herself quite comfortable, her sister glaring at her.

"Jesus Ellie—" her phone began buzzing in her pocket, she sighed and closed her eyes and answered. "Carlsson." Jordan's deep voice came through the other end.

"We need you at the precinct. We've got another body. Carlsson..." Jordan trailed off hesitantly. "There's a dollar bill on the girl's chest."

* * *

"You look like hell," Jordan commented as he handed Laura a mug of coffee. He was still wearing his gym clothes after his morning workout. The office was quiet, still too early for the bulk of the staff to be in. It was just barely light outside after all.

"Thanks a lot," Laura grumbled as she yawned.

"You look like you haven't slept," Jordan said frowning.

"I haven't. This case is kicking my ass," Laura sighed as she flipped through the folder containing the photos from yesterday's grizzly scene. Another dead girl was found with a dollar bill on her chest. Like the girl before her, she was in her early twenties, had blonde hair and died as a result of a singular stab wound to the kidney. She had been found inside a club bathroom, once again a public place and once again the bathroom was covered in fingerprints and DNA. "But that's not why I couldn't sleep. Ellie came by yesterday."

"Your sister?" Jordan asked surprised. She had only briefly mentioned her younger sister over the years. Particularly whenever Ellie bulldozed back into her life looking for help with some sort of trouble.

"Yeah."

"What did she want this time?"

"My help, of course. She got done for possession once again. She's actually facing gaol this time around." Laura leant back in her chair and ran her fingers through her hair, trying to massage the tension that had built up in her head.

"Morning!" Laura was surprised when she heard Isabella's chipper voice call out from behind her. She checked her watch in disbelief, Isabella was much earlier than normal. Her daisy perfume flooded Laura's nose and despite her tiredness and anguish, she couldn't help but notice how beautiful the detective looked. Her wide smile took up half of her face, her warm energy quenching some of the despair that had built up in Laura's chest.

"Morning," Jordan and Laura both replied together.

"You're in early," Jordan commented, clearly also surprised by Isabella's punctuality.

"Savannah woke me up at the crack of dawn," Isabella rolled her eyes. "Someone went out partying last night and can't hold her liquor." Isabella shook her head disapprovingly, causing both Jordan and Laura to let out a chuckle. Her eyes fell on Laura and she frowned with concern, "Are you ok Laura? Carlsson?" Isabella corrected.

"Yeah," Laura answered, her tone unconvincing. Laura picked up her coffee and took a long sip.

"How did things go with Ellie?" Jordan raised his eyebrows at Laura, clearly wondering how Isabella already knew.

"Well, she got done again for possession and this time she's looking at gaol time."

"I'm sorry."

"Don't be. I kind of want her to go. It might finally wake her up a bit."

"No you don't " Jordan said disapprovingly. He was right, it was definitely the anger talking.

"I just don't know what to do anymore," Laura shook her head, resting it in her hands as she leant her elbows on her desk. Isabella placed a hand her shoulder and gave it a reassuring squeeze. The sound of high heels tapped their way down the hall. Laura felt Isabella's hand fall from her shoulder.

"Laura!" Laura leant up off her desk and looked over to see Rachel approaching, somewhat irritated. "So you are ok?" Her hand rested on her hip, a belt wrapping around the waist of her grey dress.

"Yes," Laura answered, raising her eyebrows in confusion. Rachel hadn't bothered to acknowledge Jordan and Isabella's presence, which surprised

Laura as she was usually very friendly. The pair stood watching somewhat awkwardly.

"You never called me yesterday like you said you would," Rachel pouted, her voice almost a whine.

"Sorry, Ellie showed up on my doorstep."

"Oh," Rachel said, sitting down on Laura's desk. Her knees were almost against Laura's chest. Laura looked awkwardly at the other detectives and shifted her chair backward. "What did she want?"

"Me to get her out of another drug charge," Laura shrugged. After having explained it three times now, the words had lost their feeling.

"Laura, you can't help her again," Rachel said irritated. "She's a money draining junkie and a selfish brat. It's time to let her lay in her own bed." Laura felt her blood boil. She had always whinged about Ellie's antics over the years to Rachel, but the woman had generally been supportive.

"That's my sister you're talking about Rachel, be careful," Laura warned. Jordan pulled a face at Isabella as if to say 'awkward', but still neither of them left. They were too transfixed by the argument.

"I know baby," Rachel said, grabbing one of Laura's shoulders. "But it's not like you're close. She just uses you, she doesn't respect you. You don't need someone like that in your life."

"So what, I'm supposed to just cut her out of my life and forget about her? I don't give up on people Rachel." She saw Isabella flinch in her peripherals, she knew it probably sounded like a dig.

"I'm not saying give up on her—"

"Yes you are," Laura cut her off, seething. "She hasn't had an easy life. This isn't all her fault. As much as I might dislike who she is now, she's still my baby sister and I love her."

"Ok, I'm sorry," Rachel stood back up and was looking down at Laura guiltily. Laura couldn't even look at her she was so angry. "I'll call you later ok?" Laura just nodded without making eye contact. Rachel leant down to place a kiss on Laura's forehead, but she didn't react. The tapping of Rachel's heels faded down the corridor, Laura's eyes still fixed at a point somewhere in the distance.

Isabella broke the awkward silence that was hanging over the three colleagues. "If you need help with Ellie Laura, I know a good lawyer in Manhattan. I'm sure I could get her a good deal, he's one of the best."

"Why?" Laura asked bluntly, her sister had been a total bitch to Isabella yesterday after all.

"Because Laura, she's family," Isabella almost whispered nervously.

"Thanks Iss—"

"Whaddup bitches!" Kyle yelled as he approached them, cutting off Laura. "Check it out, no more brace!" He said excitedly, pointing to his free arm.

* * *

"You little shit!" Laura yelled, loud enough that Isabella could hear it from outside her front door. Isabella let herself in and walked towards the lounge room.

"Hey guys!" Isabella said excitedly as she stepped into the living room. Laura and Alex barely even acknowledging her, both totally transfixed by their game. Ellie however shot up from the opposite lounge to envelope her in a hug.

"Bella, come sit with me." Ellie was holding onto her so tightly that she practically wrestled her onto the opposing lounge.

"You're done Laur," Alex threatened as he sent a blue shell her way.

"No, no, no, no!" The shell hit Laura, and Alex's cart went flying past her as he chuckled menacingly. "Bastard!"

"Snooze you lose," he smirked.

"Are they always like this?" Isabella asked Ellie amidst laughter.

"Yep," Ellie sighed rolling her eyes.

They were on their last lap now and the tension between the two of them was palpable. Alex started arrogantly singing Queen's 'We Are the Champions' as he was approaching the finish line, Laura sitting back in third now. Laura was furious, she was extremely competitive and couldn't handle being goaded. Abruptly, she slapped the remote out of Alex's hand, causing his cart to halt and the second-place cart to cross the line in first instead.

"You bitch!" Alex exclaimed angrily and Isabella placed her hands over a laughing Ellie's ears.

"That'll teach you to be a cocky asshole," Laura frowned, shoving Alex in the shoulder. He was just about to shove her back when Astrid Carlsson walked into the room.

"Hey! Cut it out," she warned and Alex just glared back at Laura as she poked her tongue out. "Hi Isabella." Astrid's voice was somewhat strained as she greeted her.

"Hi Astrid."

"Ellie, come on. Homework," their mother gestured behind her and Ellie got up off the lounge, the two disappearing down the hall.

"Want a game Bella?" Alex asked, a devilish look in his eyes. It was clear to Laura that he viewed Isabella as an easy opponent. Isabella moved her hand, subtly shaking the keys in it, trying to catch Laura's attention.

"Nah that's ok. Thanks anyways Alex." He shrugged and started a solo game.

"Wait?" Laura questioned, standing up off the couch. The rattling keys had, had the desired effect. "Why do you have your Dad's keys?" Isabella grinned bashfully. "Did you get your license?!" Isabella nodded and Laura practically crash tackled her onto the lounge in excitement.

"Get a room," Alex grumbled, earning paranoid 'shh's' from both girls.

"Wanna go for a drive?"

"Hell yeah! OMG I'm so excited for you," Laura clapped, a huge grin on her face. Isabella couldn't help but return it.

They ran out into the driveway and buckled themselves in the car. Laura felt somewhat strange being in the passenger seat for a change, she was so used to always driving. "I'm going to miss being your personal chauffeur," Laura admitted shyly.

"Well now we can take turns," Isabella smiled back.

"Ok," Laura agreed happily.

"Ice-cream?"

"Yes!"

They drove the back streets into town singing along to the radio with their windows down. They pulled up at a set of lights, in the main strip of town, the music humming around them. On the other side of the intersection Cate and Parker were stopped, the two girls on their way home from dance practice.

"Ohhh, is that Isabella and Laura?" Cate asked somewhat unnecessarily. She had already worked that out for herself.

"Yeah," Parker said excitedly.

"Isabella must have gotten her license."

"Beep them so they see us," Parker suggested. As Cate was placing her hand in the middle of the steering wheel, they watched Laura lean her head towards Isabella. The two girls exchanged a kiss before returning to their singing. All of the colour practically drained from Cate's face as she watched the exchange and her hand fell off the steering wheel.

"OMG." The lights turned green and Isabella drove off, but Cate was frozen. The line of cars behind her beeped at them mercilessly.

* * *

Laura trotted towards the park halfway between her house and the psychologist's office. It was the third Saturday in a row now that she had stopped by the food drive to grab a coffee. Laura couldn't even stand the taste of the coffee, it was the woman with the chocolate brown eyes she craved. Despite her appointment, her Saturday morning ritual had quickly become her favourite.

Isabella's warm breath was coming out in clouds as it mingled with the frosty morning air. She looked down to pour another cup of steaming hot coffee for the line of people waiting. She nearly dropped the cup when she handed it to the man in front of her, her eyes continually wandering to the back of the line.

"Looking for someone," Isabella jumped, nearly spilling hot coffee everywhere as Laura's husky voice whispered against her ear.

"Jesus Laura," Isabella breathed, grabbing her chest. Laura playfully smirked and Isabella smiled back. Laura was wearing her same black beanic and combat boots, a long coat wrapped around her. Isabella's blue jeans were stained with chocolate powder, her long hair tucked into the back of her hoodie.

The girl with the pink hair had spotted Laura amongst the crowd and had brought her into the staff section to see Isabella. Like the Saturdays before she offered to replace Isabella so that she could take her morning break with Laura. Isabella handed her last coffee to Laura. She smiled and dropped a few dollars in the jar, the two then making their way over to their park bench.

Laura wasn't sure what it was about this particular setting, but here she felt less vulnerable. She felt confident enough to let her well-fortified walls down and talk about real things. She was enjoying getting to know this version of Isabella again.

"So I contacted the lawyer I mentioned the other day, I got Ellie an appointment with him on Monday," Isabella smiled, watching as Laura took a sip from the bitter coffee. Laura smiled through gritted teeth as it washed over her tongue.

"That's amazing. Thank you so much, I really appreciate it," she said sincerely, brushing Isabella's hand with her own briefly as a thanks.

"You're welcome," Isabella smiled happily, clearly relieved to be helping. "Have you spoken to Ellie since the other day?"

"Once. She rang me two nights ago for an 'update'," Laura made air quotation marks. "These last few years it's like she's a whole different person. I feel like I lost my little sister." Laura shook her head sadly.

"You haven't lost her Laura. She's still the same Ellie, she's just hurting," Isabella reassured her, reaching out to place a comforting hand on her knee. A cool gust of wind caused Isabella to shiver.

"Here," Laura stood up and shrugged off her coat, handing it to Isabella. Isabella looked delighted at the gesture as she smiled 'thanks' and pulled on Laura's warm coat. Her smile faltered as the arm of Laura's jumper rode up revealing her tattoo.

"You don't have to answer this, but what happened with you and Ellie?" Laura's green eyes shot down to the ground at her question and she began playing with the coffee cup in her hands. Her heart was racing. She wasn't sure that she wanted to have this conversation, but after a few moments she began speaking.

"She blames me. For the accident," Isabella's jaw fell open. Laura could see her shifting uncomfortably, her mind ticking over.

"Wh-what?" Isabella asked in disbelief. Laura just shrugged as if to say 'she couldn't blame her'. "Laura listen to me, it's not your fault ok? It was an, an accident," Isabella stumbled, staring into Laura's eyes. It felt nice to hear those words, though it didn't ease the guilt Laura still felt.

"Can we talk about something else?"

"Sure," Isabella practically whispered. "How's Rachel?" Laura knew she was referring to the fight they had, had in the precinct.

"Fine. I mean I guess I can't really blame her for her reaction to all of this. She doesn't even know Ellie, she just knows all the awful things I've told her about her. I mean how bad does that make me look?"

"You need to stop beating yourself up. You're doing the best you can," Isabella reassured her. "So Rachel and Ellie haven't actually met?"

Laura shook her head. "I hadn't seen Ellie for a year until just the other day. Rachel and I have only been together like nine months."

"How did you guys meet?"

"Through Parker actually. The two of them went to college together and then got jobs together in the coroner's office and she introduced us one night. It took Rachel months to get up the courage to ask me out," Laura chuckled at the memory. "I wasn't the most approachable person back then I guess." Laura looked up and noticed Isabella was looking out towards the playground somewhat awkwardly. She realised that confiding in her ex-girlfriend about her current girlfriend probably wasn't the most considerate thing to do.

"So what time's Ellie's meeting with the lawyer on Monday?" Laura asked, swiftly changing the topic.

"Eleven," Isabella answered, rummaging through her bag for something. "Here, give her this. This is the card with the address and his number and everything." Laura's eyebrows scrunched together as she read the name on the card.

"Davis?" Laura asked, looking down at the name 'Martin Davis' on the card. Even though it wasn't Mitch's name, she felt her blood beginning to boil in her veins.

"Yeah," Isabella answered awkwardly, her cheeks turning a deep shade of crimson. "He's Mitch's father."

"Oh."

"I still see him from time to time. He and I always got along so well. But he's the only Davis I still hear from," Isabella added, trying to reassure Laura.

"Ok."

"I hope this doesn't change anything Laura. He's a really great lawyer and I know he could really help Ellie and that's all I want."

Laura nodded, she felt slightly nauseous, but she forced a smile. "Thank you. I really do appreciate this."

Isabella sighed with relief. "You're welcome."

A few minutes of comfortable silence followed as they both stared off towards the playground. Laura was pensive as she took another sip from her coffee. Isabella nearly laughed as she watched Laura try to prevent a grimace as she swallowed harshly.

"You're different from before." Isabella raised her eyebrows in confusion.

"How so?"

"I don't know, just...different," Laura answered vaguely. "But then at the same time you're exactly the same."

"I'm not that scared kid anymore Laura," she whispered. Laura knew exactly what event Isabella was referencing. She looked into the warm chocolate eyes that exuded so much adoration and vulnerability in that moment and she thought seriously to herself for the first time. Could she finally believe her?

11

Chapter 11

It had been a few weeks since the last attack by the serial murderer. They had nicknamed him the 'Washington Killer', in reference to the dollar bills hr left behind on the girl's chests. They couldn't officially call him a serial killer yet because he still only had two victims, but the signs were there. They hadn't released any information regarding the specifics of the murders to the media yet, they didn't want to create a panic. Laura was standing in front of the murder board processing all of the information they knew so far about the killer, which wasn't much.

He definitely had a type, both girls were in their early twenties, blonde and attractive. It was evident that there must be some motive behind how he chose his victim's. He was also very methodical in dosing his victim's with roofies before killing them, ensuring by the time he attacked them, they wouldn't be in a state to fight back. This also lessened the likelihood of the victim's extracting the killer's DNA through defensive scratches.

The one thing the evidence agreed upon was that the killer was most likely male. Both girls were killed in the same way, one stab wound to the kidney. Delivering that blow required a lot of upper body strength. The fact that both girls had been murdered in public places also indicated premeditation. He had to have scoped out each location before the murders in order not to be discovered in the act.

"Hey sexy," Kyle smirked, taking a seat as his desk.

"You got laid didn't you?" Laura asked, returning his smirk. She could always tell with Kyle, there was an overly chipper and arrogant air about him.

"You betcha! Doc gave me the all-clear yesterday," Kyle hummed proudly.

"So naturally you slept with the first girl you stumbled across," Laura rolled her eyes.

"Not the first, jeez Carlsson I'm not that desperate. The second. And before you ask, she was a dancer with the New York ballet. I swear I've never had better sex in my life!"

"You're just saying that because you haven't gotten any in weeks!"

"Whatever. What about you Carlsson? Is Rachel the best sex of your life?"

* * *

Laura was sat on her bed reading To Kill a Mockingbird for the millionth time. She had read the same page over and over, her mind continually wondering to Isabella. After a few minutes she gave up and decided to text her girlfriend.

Laura (4.15pm): Hey, how's your day going?

When half an hour had passed and Laura still hadn't heard anything, she mumbled 'fuck it' and snatched her keys from her desk. Within a few minutes she was pulling into Isabella's driveway, it was drizzling outside and the sky was already dark with thick clouds. Isabella's front door was slightly ajar and her heart leapt in panic. She ducked out into the rain and ran inside. She ran to the living room and found Samuel passed out on the lounge a bottle of whisky on the coffee table beside him. Laura rolled her eyes and ran to the stairs, taking them two at a time as she made her way to the second floor.

"Isabella? Savannah?" No answer. She checked both of their rooms, but both were empty. She noticed Isabella's phone sitting atop her bedside table. She clicked the home button and saw her unread message flash on the screen. A loud clap of thunder rung out over her head, causing her to jump. Shit. The open door could only mean Isabella was out there somewhere in the middle of a storm.

Laura drove around town aimlessly, trying to think where an upset Isabella might go. She was leaning forwards, almost touching the steering wheel as she squinted through the windshield, trying to see the road over the bucketing rain. Something inside her told her to check the beach. She pulled into the deserted carpark and looked through her windshield, desperately trying to search the sand for any sign of Isabella. She was about to start reversing back out when she spotted a small dark shape sitting down on the sand.

"Isabella!" Laura yelled as she threw her door open and ran down the beach. Her clothes were already soaked through by the heavy rain, but she didn't care. Isabella was gazing out amongst the waves, crying to herself silently. Lightning cracked in sky around them, an shiver running up Laura's spine as she ran.

"Issi!" Isabella looked over her shoulder and saw a panicked Laura running towards her. She stood up as Laura crashed into her, enveloping her in a frantic hug. "Come on. It's not safe out here," Laura whispered into her ear, wrapping an arm around her shoulder.

She pulled Isabella towards her car, rubbing her arm soothingly as they walked. She opened the boot of her hatchback and the two girls huddled underneath. "You're soaked to the bone Issi," Laura murmured as Isabella shivered uncontrollably. Her tears now frozen on her face. "We've got to get you out of these clothes."

Laura grabbed the zip of Isabella's hoodie and began pulling it off, followed by her tank top and shorts, leaving Isabella shivering in her crop top and underwear. Laura then stripped off her own drenched clothes and piled them on the floor.

"Let's get out of here." Laura grabbed Isabella's hand and tried to pull her towards the front of the car, but Isabella refused, shaking her head.

"Not yet. Can you just hold me?" Isabella asked softly.

Laura nodded and climbed into the boot pushing down the backseats as Isabella climbed in beside her. She kept pillows and blankets permanently in the back in case they ever decided to go on a spontaneous picnic. Even the fairy lights remained up, from their date. Isabella laid down on the fluffy blue blanket and arranged the pillows as Laura flicked on the fairy lights. The sound of the rain pounding down on the car was deafening, but all Laura could hear was the sound of her heart beating in her ears.

She laid down next to Isabella on the pillows and pulled her head onto her chest. "Are you ok?" Laura asked tentatively, massaging her hands in Isabella's wet *hair.*

"I am now," Isabella breathed softly against Laura's neck, causing a flutter of butterflies to surge in her stomach. Isabella began placing soft kisses up the length of her neck, each one sending an electric shiver up Laura's spine. Their cold skin was heating up by the second as Laura pulled Isabella down by the back of her neck to plant a strong kiss on her lips. Isabella responded by pulling at the straps of Laura's crop top.

"Issi...we said we'd wait," Laura protested, but Isabella continued to plant wet kisses up her jaw, over her cheeks and on the tip of her nose. "I want it to be special." Isabella stopped abruptly and stared down at her intently. Her eyes were sparkling, she was looking at Laura with an almost unfathomable adoration.

"It will be special Laura. It's you and me. We don't need to overthink this." Isabella stroked Laura's cheek tenderly with her thumb. Laura smiled, a warmth pulsating from her chest and spreading throughout her entire body. She had no idea it was possible to be this happy. "I want you Laur. I care about you so much and I trust you."

Laura's cheeks flushed, a wide smile taking over her face as she tried to quash her feelings of bashfulness. "I care about you too Issi, more than anyone." She knew she not only cared for her, but she loved her. She loved her more than she had ever loved anyone before, but she held onto that. Smiling, Isabella leant down and kissed her. Their teeth unintentionally scraped together as they both smiled widely.

* * *

"Carlsson?"

"Hmm?" Laura blinked rapidly at an intrigued Kyle.

"Just having a little naughty day dream about your girlfriend?" Laura laughed cynically, trying to hide her obvious embarrassment about being caught out.

"Something like that," she mumbled. He didn't say past or present girlfriend, so it technically wasn't lying.

Laura looked up to see Isabella walking towards them, her boots tapping rhythmically on the floors. She was wearing a pair of high waisted black pants with military style buttons running down from the waist, that accentuated her wide hips perfectly. Laura's skin felt clammy at the sight, her heart accelerating as Isabella came closer. Her mind flashing back to boot of that hatchback.

"Damn Isabella," Kyle broke the awkward silence that had fallen over them, causing Laura to look up and meet Isabella's chocolate eyes. "Now that I'm back in action, how about we call it a night?" He winked at her, stepping closer to stand beside Laura, just a few inches from Isabella.

"In your dreams Reynolds," Isabella fired back harshly.

"I don't know about my dreams, but maybe Carl—" Laura hit Kyle in the ribs, shutting him up.

"Let me just get changed," Laura smiled, finally pulling herself together. "In fact, why don't you help me decide on an outfit?" Laura grabbed a hold of Isabella's wrist and pulled her towards the stairs and up to the female locker room. She couldn't stand witnessing anyone flirt with Isabella, even if it was someone as unthreatening as Kyle. The sound of Kyle's wolf whistling faded away as they ascended the stairs. Laura opened up her locker and started unbuttoning her blouse from behind the door.

"So, what are the options?"

"Oh," Laura popped her head out from behind the door, her eyebrows raised. "Umm...I actually only brought one outfit. I just wanted to save you from Reynolds."

Isabella chuckled. "Not all heroes wear capes."

"This one wears a gun," Laura winked popping her head out once again, only this time her blouse was undone giving Isabella a perfect view of her lacy black bra. Isabella's eyes wandered lustfully over the lace. Laura kicked off her shoes and unbuttoned her pants, slowly pulling them down to reveal a matching pair of panties. She was very conscious of the fact Isabella's eyes were on her body as she changed, and she liked the feeling.

Laura pulled on a white turtle neck top and a black spaghetti strap dress to go over the top. She then slipped her feet into a pair of high black stilettos and finished the outfit off with a long black coat. She kept her hair tied back in a slick pony tail. As she stood up to face Isabella, the chocolate eyes were still hovering around her legs.

She cleared her throat and Isabella's eyes shot up, a red blush spreading across her cheeks. Laura flashed her one of her classic charming smiles with its usual hint of mischief. She stepped forward so that their faces were inches from one another. Isabella looked shocked for a moment, her teeth holding on to her bottom lip. Laura reached forward, she could see the anticipation written all over Isabella's face. Then she bent down and picked up her keys from the bench beside them, grazing Isabella's thigh as she did so.

"Ready?" She asked with that same smirk. She could see the frustration in Isabella's eyes as she nodded. She herself felt frustrated, the tension was dizzying. Temptation was crippling every nerve in her body as she picked up her purse and turned towards the door.

Half an hour later their cab was pulling up in front of the Thai restaurant. Now that the awkward tension between the old friends had mostly dissipated, Laura had decided to invite Isabella to their fortnightly catch ups. She could tell Isabella was still nervous though as they stepped out of the cab.

Isabella hesitated as they entered, fiddling with her jacket in the foyer. Laura simply gave her a wide smile and gently rested her fingertips on Isabella's lower back, guiding her to their usual table. Once they took off their coats and sat down Laura could see Isabella relax again as they fell into easy and casual conversation with their friends. But what didn't disappear was the tension she felt rolling between them anytime their legs brushed one another under the table or their shoulders rubbed together.

"Have you guys done your Christmas shopping yet? I'm like halfway done, but I'm starting to panic that I'm not going to finish it all."

"Cate, Christmas is still three weeks away," Parker rolled her eyes. Cate always seemed to panic about the most superficial things.

"I know. But I look forward to it all year. I like seeing people's faces when I give them their gifts. Speaking of, I already put everyone's names in a bag for secret Santa..." Cate said as she dug around in her handbag. Laura noticed Isabella looking around the room awkwardly and realised she forgot to invite her.

"Do you and Savannah have any plans for Christmas?" Laura asked, drawing Isabella's eyes back to her.

"Not really, we were just going to have lunch at my place," Isabella blushed uncomfortably.

"I meant to ask you a few weeks ago, but Parker, Cate and Kevin, Jordan and Bri, and Kyle are all coming to my place for Christmas. We sort of do it every year. Do you and Savannah want to come?" Isabella's face broke into a delighted smile.

"We'd love to! I don't even have to ask Savannah, I know the answer," Isabella laughed.

"Great! Luckily for you Laura, I already put their names in the secret Santa." Laura pretended to wipe imaginary sweat off her brow and Isabella chuckled.

"Ladies first," Cate offered Isabella the bag of names.

"As opposed to what?" Parker scoffed as she pointed to herself and then Laura. "Pimps and hoes?"

"Hey! Why are you the pimp and I'm the hoe?" Laura pouted.

"You know why," Parker smirked.

"Whatever. You're the single one." Laura crossed her arms indignantly causing Isabella to smirk as she unravelled the name on her piece of paper. Kyle.

Cate passed the bag to Laura next and she pulled out a piece of paper, unravelling it to reveal the name. Isabella. Fate you fickle thing Laura thought to herself smiling.

"What are the rules?" Isabella asked.

"Fifty dollar limit, other than that, go nuts!"

A few hours later Laura and Isabella shared a cab on their way back to Isabella's house. Isabella fiddled with the keys at her door, continually looking over her shoulder at Laura. When she did finally get the door open, she ducked inside, almost shutting the door behind her.

Laura was confused. "Everything alright?" She called, slowly pushing the door open.

She was surprised, as she stepped inside, to see just how small and rundown Isabella's apartment actually was. She had heard a few comments here and there from Savannah and Isabella herself, but she didn't expect this. She knew Isabella was earning decent enough money at the precinct to be living in much better conditions than this, it was dispiriting. Her eyes darted between the mould stains on the ceiling to the dark stains on the carpet. The latter making her want to swaddle herself in anti-bacterial wipes before she proceeded any further. It was clear Isabella had tried her best to make the place homely with some nice décor and bedding, but the apartment still felt claustrophobic and grungy.

She tried to keep her concern for Isabella's living conditions from her face and just smiled warmly back at Isabella, who was clearly uncomfortable having her in her space. Isabella began rummaging through some papers on her coffee table, trying to find her notes.

Laura walked over to sit down on Isabella's bed and noticed To Kill A Mockingbird sitting on her pillow. She couldn't help but smile. "You're reading my favourite book." Isabella blushed as Laura smiled up at her.

"It's my favourite book too."

"Since when?"

"Since ages ago. It had an impact." Laura smiled happily back at her, thrilled to have influenced her taste in literature.

"Is that so?"

* * *

It had all happened within the space of an hour. Laura got the call that a body had been discovered inside a dark corner of a casino night club in Atlantic City and now her and Isabella were speeding on their way down there late in the evening. The body was of a young, attractive, blonde woman. Like the two others before, she had a dollar bill on her chest. There were three bodies now. They officially had a serial killer on their hands, and he was on the move.

The Captain ordered Laura and Isabella to head down and liaise with the New Jersey detectives handling the case. They were to gather any evidence they could to bring back to New York. Once again Kyle had whinged and moaned about missing out, but the Captain had silenced him with one of his intimidating glares. Despite his little tantrum, Kyle still wasn't the most distressed person when it came to the trip. Rachel had practically stared daggers at Isabella when they showed up at Laura's apartment to pack her stuff.

Rachel hadn't been about to let her leave without first marking her territory. She practically attacked Laura as they went to leave the apartment, forcefully sticking her tongue down Laura's throat as Isabella was forced to watch. It was clear to her what her girlfriend was doing, and while she couldn't blame her, she was making things uncomfortable. She reciprocated nonetheless and tried to reassure Rachel with the kiss.

Despite the late hour, their road trip was actually rather enjoyable. Laura had insisted on driving, which Isabella had been happy about as it meant she could play DJ. They had always bonded over their love of music and today wasn't any different. Isabella was picking songs they had listened to as teenagers creating a mood of nostalgia as they both sang along. Isabella's phone buzzed as Laura's husky voice rang out around the car.

Savannah (10.23pm): How's the road trip going? No making out at any red lights?

Isabella (10.25pm): I wish. Instead I got to watch Rachel and Laura make out. Fun times!

Savannah (10.26pm): That's alright, she's just sent her off horny on a trip with her ex-girlfriend.

Isabella (10.27pm): HA!

Savannah (10.28pm): Just keep your heart's safe ok.

Isabella (10.29pm): What do you mean?

Savannah (10.32pm): That I know there's no one more capable in both of your lives to completely destroy the other one.

"Are you ok?" Laura turned to look at Isabella concerned; the detective had turned completely white.

"Oh, yeah. Savannah was just checking to make sure neither of us had fallen asleep at the wheel," Isabella laughed casually, but Laura could tell she was upset. She decided to let it go and turned her attention back the road.

"Well you can tell Savannah to go to sleep because I would never fall asleep with you in the car," Laura said protectively. Isabella blushed and a genuine smile spread across her face. Laura reciprocated, glad that she had managed to cheer her up from whatever had upset her.

Savannah (10.36pm): Sorry, that sounded dramatic. I'm just worried about you.

Isabella (10.38pm): It's fine, you know I have no intention of hurting Laura ever again and as for me...you can't break something that's already broken.

As they entered the outskirts of the city, Isabella left her playlist on shuffle and gazed out the window as 'Murder on the Dancefloor' came on and both women looked at each other and smiled.

"Tune!" Isabella squealed.

"Such a banger, best dance song EVER!" Laura clapped the steering wheel excitedly. "I Wanna Dance with Somebody a close second." Isabella nodded.

"Though I don't think Jordan would agree with you." Isabella chuckled. Laura's mind wandered back to the night at the Karaoke bar, Jordan had scurried off to the bathroom when the song had started playing.

"I've never seen someone more enthusiastic about going to the bathroom," Laura laughed as she concentrated on the road in front of her. They were in the heart of the city now, not far from their hotel. Laura could feel Isabella staring at her. In her peripherals she could see Isabella looked confused, mad even.

"We're here," Laura sighed in relief as they pulled up in front of their hotel. "I'm officially exhausted." Laura headed inside to check-in as Isabella unpacked the car.

It was after midnight and the hotel lobby was completely empty apart from a few hotel staff. When Isabella walked into the lobby carrying the rest of her and Laura's bags, she could hear raised voices coming from the reception desk.

"This is absolutely ridiculous! Just three hours ago I called to book two rooms and now you're telling me you're fully booked!"

"I'm sorry miss Carlsson, there must have been a glitch in our system—"

Laura cut her off before she could continue apologising, her quick temper on full display.

"That doesn't solve our problem though, does it?" Laura spat back.

"Laur," Isabella comforted, placing a hand very carefully on her shoulder and pulling Laura backwards. "Calm down ok," she said softly, as angry tremors ran through Laura's body. "What's the problem?" Isabella asked, directing her question towards the frightened woman behind the desk.

"Our system has made a double booking and now the second bedroom you had requested is occupied and there is only one room booked under your name."

"Oh," Isabella said, clearly now understanding Laura's rush of anger. "Is it a twin room?"

"It's a queen ma'am," the woman admitted warily, her eyes flitting nervously to Laura who was still shaking in anger.

"And there's no other rooms available at all?"

"We're fully booked I'm sorry," the woman apologised genuinely, still looking incredibly nervous.

"Well you weren't this eve—"

Isabella cut her off before she could continue. "That's fine. Could we have the key please?" The woman quickly handed Isabella two key cards. She dragged a disgruntled Laura away before she could abuse the receptionist again. As the lift doors closed, Isabella peaked through her long dark hair at Laura. Laura's anger was slowly subsiding, she was taking deep breaths to calm herself.

"I see you've still got your famous temper." Laura just huffed in response and stormed off towards their room as soon as the lift doors opened.

When they entered the room Laura flicked on the lights and a bed was illuminated in the centre of the room. So much for a queen Laura scoffed to herself, the bed looked far more like a double to her. She was going to be forced to endure a tension filled night with Isabella. A night breathing in her smell, listening to her steady breathing and feeling the warmth of her body radiate beside her, but not being able to touch her.

It was now well past midnight as Laura lay on the bed in a pair of shorts and a tank top. She was scrolling through the messages on her phone as she heard the bathroom door open. She looked up and saw Isabella peeping at her through a small slit.

"Can you close your eyes for a minute?"

"Why?"

"Because I didn't know that we would end up sharing a room and so I packed...not the best pyjamas," Isabella said nervously and Laura immediately burst out into laughter. She was laughing so hard that her body was convulsing on the bed and she actually began struggling to breathe.

"Laurrrraaaa," Isabella pleaded with her cutely. She was clearly very insecure about whatever it was she was wearing. Laura gradually composed herself and leant back up again against the bedhead.

"Ok, ok. My eyes are closed," she said closing them. She had to bite her lip to stop the smirk threatening tenancy on her lips.

She heard the door slide open and the sound of Isabella's light footsteps running across the bedroom. When she felt the comforter being pulled up, she couldn't restrain herself any longer and decided to have a quick peek. She regretted it when she saw what Isabella was wearing. A lacy white tank top and booty shorts. Her pyjamas combined with her windswept hair made her look incredibly sexy. A shiver ran up Laura's spine as she closed her eyes again.

"Can I open my eyes yet?" Laura asked sarcastically.

"Yes."

Laura looked to her side, Isabella was lying down on the pillow, the white sheet of the bed pulled right up underneath her neck. She was looking up at Laura sheepishly. Laura looked at her and smiled playfully, remembering Isabella's past aversion to lingerie. She clearly recalled Isabella saying one time that lingerie was 'just a male invention to objectify women'. She chuckled at the memory, Isabella slapping her across the shoulder.

"Ow."

"Don't laugh at me," Isabella scolded her angrily.

"I'm not, I'm not. I'm laughing at past Isabella."

"Why?"

Laura lifted up the covers and slid herself down in the bed so that her head was resting on the pillow next to Isabella. She looked up at the ceiling as she tried to channel her best Isabella impersonation. "'Lingerie is just a male invention to objectify women'," Laura chuckled. This time Isabella hit her even harder across the shoulder.

"Ouch!"

"I told you to close your eyes," Isabella said grumpily.

"Oh come on, you know me. Someone tells me to do something, and I do the complete opposite." Isabella tried her hardest to fight a smile but she couldn't.

"You're such a child." Laura decided to ignore her pathetic scold and hit her with a question instead.

"So who'd you buy them for anyway?" Laura asked, unable to stop herself.

"No one, I bought them for me." Isabella blushed.

Laura scoffed as if she didn't believe her. "No one buys lingerie just for themselves."

"Well I did."

Laura laughed again as Isabella crossed her arms over her chest, an annoyed pout on her lips.

"Okey doke."

"So you're telling me you don't wear lingerie?" Isabella rolled her eyes. Laura knew Isabella had seen her black lacy underwear in the locker room a few days before.

"Sometimes. But I don't rely on it. A girl once told me my body was 'beautiful all on its own'," Laura smirked as she looked into Isabella's chocolate eyes, again directly quoting one of her rants from ten years ago. Laura could see the surprise in Isabella's eyes as she said it. She usually avoided bringing up memories from the past, but she was enjoying the flirtatious banter.

"Sounds like a wise girl," Isabella smiled back and Laura just shrugged. Isabella rolled her eyes once more and turned over on her side so her back was facing Laura. Through the gap in the tight sheet Laura's eyes fell on the transparent white lace. The set really did look beautiful. Isabella flicked off the lamp beside her bed and the lingerie disappeared into darkness, causing Laura to let out a sigh.

"Night Laur."

"Night Issi."

It had taken Laura a long time to finally fall asleep. Her mind was filled with inappropriate thoughts of Isabella in her lacy white pyjamas. The fact that Isabella was inches away from her, the smell of her hypnotising perfume permeating around them, didn't exactly help. But eventually as she listened to the calming repetition of Isabella's breathing, she had dozed off.

It felt like she had just fallen asleep when she was startled awake by muffled yells and thrashing beside her. She instinctively reached for the gun on her night stand when she heard Isabella mumble once again.

"Please no..." she was begging, a pained tone to her voice. "Please don't hurt her." Isabella's arms and legs were thrashing around in the bed and colliding with Laura's body, but she felt frozen as she lay there listening to Isabella's nightmare, her own heart thrashing in her chest.

She was sure she could picture exactly what Isabella was dreaming about, she had the exact same dreams every night and she had to stop herself from reaching out and scooping Isabella into her arms. She had no choice but to lay there and listen to the beautiful woman with the chocolate brown eyes live out her nightmares. After a while she couldn't take it anymore and she picked up her phone to see multiple messages from Parker, Kyle and Jordan.

She replied to Jordan first letting him know that they had arrived at the hotel and apologising for not replying sooner. Parker's messages however, were not so subtly prying as to the nature of their sudden trip and clearly fishing to find out any details about her and Isabella. She knew Parker was worried about her, but she continually reassured her she needn't be. Now that Isabella and her were just friends again, she was safe. She texted back telling Parker it was all business and nothing more. Laura didn't even bother replying to Kyle's message, the minute she saw the GIF he sent of two rabbits going at it she decided she was freezing him out right there and then.

12

Chapter 12

As Laura stepped into the lobby, she was surprised to see that Isabella wasn't in the breakfast hall at all, but instead engaged in an animated conversation with the receptionist. The two women were laughing heartily over something Isabella had just said. Typical, Laura thought. Isabella could make anyone love her in two seconds, that's why she always played good cop in their interrogations.

As Laura approached the women, she couldn't help but be annoyed. It felt like Isabella was contradicting her. Isabella glanced up at Laura and smiled brightly, waving her over. Laura saw the receptionist stiffen as she approached, which amused her slightly. Her phone buzzed and she held up a finger to Isabella.

"Hey Rach." She smiled, Isabella rolled her eyes as she heard who it was. "It's been less than twelve hours," Laura laughed. The receptionist had gone to serve another customer as Isabella focused on Laura. "You're being ridiculous," Laura smiled. "I miss you too Rach, I'll talk to you later." Laura shook her head playfully as Rachel flirted with her on the other line. "Bye." She hung up the phone and turned to Isabella, the detective staring off dazedly into the distance.

"Medina?"

"Hmph?"

"Ready to go? We can grab breakfast on the way." Isabella just nodded and followed Laura out the doors.

The trip to the morgue had been as expected, the victim Kelly Fields, was a blonde, nineteen-year-old waitress from Atlantic City out for a night on the town with her friends. She had wandered off when she started feeling dizzy and they didn't see her again until an hour later when other club goers found her dead in a dark corner of the Casino. Just like the other victims she had been dosed with roofies and had died as a result of a singular stab wound to her kidney.

They spent the rest of the day talking with various squadrons in the New Jersey police. They met with the homicide squad that had taken on the case and then the forensic team that had gone over the crime scene. Like the other murders there was no known witnesses, but Laura couldn't shake the feeling that this time around, someone must have seen the murderer. It was too crowded and he would have had to have been lingering near the bar in order to dose the woman. After successfully convincing Isabella that their best bet would be to head to the club to talk to possible witnesses, they decided to head back to the hotel to recuperate before the long night ahead.

An hour later Laura found herself wandering through the hotel in her search for the pool.

Isabella had grabbed her swimmers when they got back and said she was going to do some laps, but that had been a while ago now. Laura was bored in the hotel room, she decided she wouldn't mind seeing the pool, or the woman in it.

She snuck inside the door and took a seat beside Isabella's towel, watching the woman glide across the pool as she freestyled from one end to the next, flipping her petite body over quickly in a tumble turn at each end.

BESTIES <3 (Group chat)

Cate (4.00pm): So...what's new?

Parks (4.01pm): Nothin'.

Laura rolled her eyes as she watched her best friends' quick responses. She knew whatever was coming was staged. Cate had clearly lined this up, Parker was never that quick at replying.

Cate (4.03pm): So no one's shared a bed with an old flame lately...?

Laur (4.04pm): Subtle. Nice work.

Laura shook her head, Isabella had obviously already mentioned to Cate the whole sleeping situation. Just great. She wasn't going to hear the end of this now.

Parks (4.05pm): Seriously Laur? What the hell?!

Laur (4.06pm): What? I didn't have a choice, they double booked us.

Laur (4.06pm): Don't say anything to Rachel, Parker! She's tripping as it is.

Parks (4.08pm): I won't. But she's kind of upset about this trip Laur. She keeps asking me questions about Bella that I keep dodging.

Laur (4.09pm): Oh god.

Parks (4.10pm): I kind of may have mentioned a while ago, when she asked me, that you were madly in love with Isabella and she broke your heart.

Laur (4.11pm): What the actual fuck Parker!!

Cate (4.12pm): Ditto.

Parks (4.12pm): I didn't say it was Bella specifically! I just said there was a girl. But I think she's starting to put the dots together...

Laur (4.13pm): Great, just great! Fucking great best friend, you are Parker. All of that stuff was private.

Parks (4.14pm): I'm sorry Laura!!! How the hell was I supposed to know Isabella was going to end up being your partner?! I never thought we'd see her again!

Cate (4.15pm): Laura chill. Parker didn't mean any harm, she was being a good friend to Rachel by telling her that. You were pretty difficult before you two started going out.

Laur (4.16pm): Hit me while I'm down why don't you Cate!

Laura threw her phone back down beside her and picked up her copy of To Kill a Mockingbird as she tried to drown out her best friends irritating commentary.

"Where are you up to?"

"What?" Laura looked up startled. Isabella was looking down at her, her long wet hair cascading down her back, stopping just above her waist. Laura's eyes drifted over her glistening skin, her black one-piece swimming costume taunting her. It was definitely not built for aerodynamics, a lengthy slit ran down the front, the back completely open. Laura decided she liked it all the more that way.

"Can you pass me my towel?" She asked, biting down on her lip.

"Su-sure," Laura said, scrambling to shut her book and pass the towel over to Isabella. Isabella stifled a laugh as Laura practically fell off her lounge chair.

"So now I've got you reading To Kill a Mockingbird?"

"No, I got you onto it."

"In the beginning yeah. But you're reading it now, because you saw that I was reading it." Isabella began drying herself slowly, taking extra care to dry her chest, dabbing it continually. Laura couldn't look away.

"Maybe I just felt like reading it again all on my own."

"Just admit it, I'm the shepherd and you're the sheep." Isabella bent down to dry her legs, Laura staring unashamedly. She didn't have it in herself to argue back, it was taking all of her will power not to take Isabella back to their hotel room right now.

A few hours later they were standing out the front of the casino club. Laura's arm was wrapped around Isabella's waist as she supported her weight. A man at the bar downstairs had bought them a round of shots and when Laura had said she wasn't drinking Isabella had downed all of them in quick succession. She supposed it was the time frame, or Isabella's small frame, but the detective was awfully tipsy. Though technically they weren't on duty, Laura couldn't help but be mad at the irresponsibility. She had never seen Isabella drink like that before. It was a little too reminiscent of her father.

As they approached the door Laura could see the attractive female hostess eyeing them sceptically. It was clear she was weighing up whether or not to allow them entrance due to Isabella's intoxicated state. Laura decided it was time for some of her 'irresistible Carlsson charm'. First rule, hit them with a disarming compliment.

"Wow," Laura said as she approached, running her piercing eyes over the woman's body seductively. "You are incredibly beautiful."

The hostess blushed heavily and Laura flashed her one of her most charming smiles. It wasn't like it was hard to flirt with the woman. She had an incredible body, with long toned legs and cleavage that was popping out of her silky dress. The woman's eyes ran up the length of Laura's tight white dress.

"Oh, um, thank you."

"But I bet you already knew that. That's why you're on the door right, to seduce men and women to come inside?"

"Oh, uh..."

Laura smirked at the affect she was having on the woman. Her confidence and blunt approach always caught her 'victims' off guard and left them even more curious about her. Isabella mumbled something incoherently drawing the woman's gaze and Laura cussed inwardly. She stepped forward slightly, so that she was only inches away from the woman, looking directly into her eyes. She knew her green eyes had a certain effect on women and she used it.

"Your dress really isn't fair on us mere mortals," Laura whispered in her ear. "I really need to drown out my desires." The woman let out a sexy laugh as Laura pulled back and gazed into her eyes again. She could see the lust in her irises as she removed a card from the folder she was holding and handed it to Laura. The name 'Lily Suarev' was written on the card, below the title 'exotic dancer' and a phone number. Laura wasn't surprised, she was beautiful.

"I get off at three, maybe we can work on those desires then," she said as she bit her lip playfully.

"Sounds like a date, Lily," Laura smiled back, elated that she had managed to get them inside in spite of Isabella.

Laura supported Isabella in-between club goers as house music thrummed around them. Bodies were pressed closely together as people jammed to the music or made out in dark corners. Laura noticed a few eager eyes watching Isabella around the room. Laura had to admit, she looked incredible. Her dark hair was styled in a casual wave and she had on a long sleeve, short, black dress. It had the same effect on Laura as her lacy white pyjamas. She was glad she had a goal to distract her.

"You were flirting with her, why were you flirting with her?" Isabella said in an accusatory tone as they arrived at the bar.

"Someone's finally come to again," Laura rolled her eyes, disregarding Isabella's comment, as she pushed her into a bar seat.

"That woman gave you her number," Isabella's tone was harsh and Laura didn't appreciate the attitude.

"So? I'm never going to call her. I needed her to allow drunk you into the club."

"Oh," Isabella said, her voice coming across soft and innocent like a child's. "But you never flirt with me." Isabella's tone was so dejected that Laura couldn't help but frown.

"Can I get you ladies a drink?" The young male bartender interrupted them and Laura sighed in relief, worried where Isabella's low inhibitions were about to take them.

"Jack and coke please."

When the bartender returned with her drink, Laura placed her fingers on his wrist and slowly ran them up his hand to grab the glass. The boy looked to be in his early twenties, immature, and inexperienced. And like she predicted, her small gesture had excited him. She could practically see the lust exuding from his eyes as they fell on her semi-exposed chest. Men were so easy.

"What brings you ladies to town?" He asked with a charming smirk.

"How do you know we're not locals?" Laura asked playfully as she returned his smirk.

"I'd remember you two," he winked and Laura smiled. It was all too easy.

"We're actually just here for the night, we had a photo shoot today." A forensic photo shoot, Laura laughed to herself.

"Can't say I'm surprised," the young man smiled charmingly. "You're both flawless." Isabella chuckled and Laura nudged her under the bar to shut up.

"Thank you handsome," Laura gazed deeply into his eyes with her emerald ones, the man was practically drooling. "One of the girls from our agency was actually killed here a few nights ago, so we came to drown our sorrows."

The bartender's face turned sombre and he reached across the bar to place a comforting hand over Laura's. The New Jersey PD hadn't had much luck when they questioned the club staff. The casino had all of their employees sign extensive non-disclosure agreements to stop any bad publicity.

"I'm sorry to hear that. I was actually on that night, I served your friend. She was really beautiful."

"She was. Everyone adored her, some a little too much."

"What do you mean?"

"Well she'd sort of been having issues with this guy, he kept hanging around and following her everywhere."

"What did he look like? There was this weird guy at the bar drooling all over her the other night."

"Um I'm not too sure. What did the guy at the bar look like?"

"Young, probably early twenties. Floppy brown hair, relatively tall. Had a backpack on I think." Already the bartender had revealed so much more than he had been willing to share with the Jersey detectives.

"What made you think he was drooling over her?"

"He kept asking her and asking her if he could buy her a drink, even after she said no he still persisted. But she said yes eventually, I think she was sort of enjoying his persistence."

"Right. Did you get his name?"

"No. But while we're on the topic, what's your name beautiful? I'd love to buy you a drink."

"It's Michelle," Laura smiled back at him. She figured they'd gotten all the information they were going to get from the club. They now had a possible description of the offender that they could cross check against any CCTV.

"So how about that drink?"

"Give me one second, bathroom," Laura apologised and flashed him one last disarming smile before she grabbed Isabella and began manoeuvring their way to the door. As they got closer, Laura felt a hand close around her wrist. She was just about to yell at whoever had grabbed her when she looked up to see Lily smiling at her.

"I never got your name?"

"It's Michelle," Laura smiled back, trying to think of a way she could lose Lily as well. The girl was obviously persistent.

"Laur—" Isabella began to mumble, Laura poking her in the ribs to shut her up. When Isabella didn't fall over at her touch, Laura let go of her waist and allowed her to stand on her own.

"That's a beautiful name." Lily smiled, running a finger over Laura's exposed thigh.

"Hey gorgeous," a man sidled up to Isabella, forcing her to look to her side, away from Laura and Lily.

"Uh, hi," Isabella managed to get out. The reappearance of Lily was sobering her up a lot faster.

"Baby, why don't you come dance with me." The way he phrased it really wasn't a question. His strong hands grabbed tightly onto Isabella's hips as he attempted to drag her towards the dance floor.

"No, take your hands off me," Isabella protested, but with the loud music the man paid no attention and wrapped his arm around her waist. Her usual strength diminished with the alcohol as she shoved against his grip. He had managed to drag her a few steps when he suddenly went flying forwards and an enraged Laura appeared beside her.

"Don't fucking touch her," she yelled at him, her eyes menacing as the man regained his balance and stepped right up to Laura's face.

"You're lucky there's witnesses here, I've got no qualms in hitting a bitch." Laura's body was reverberating with anger.

"And I've got no reservations in handing your ass to you. Stay the fuck away from us." Laura thrust her knee forward and hit the man in the groin, he arched over in pain and looked up at her with glassy eyes.

"Bitch," he groaned, doubling over. "You're fucking crazy!"

"Yep," Laura turned and grabbed Isabella's hand. "Come on, let's go."

"Michelle!" They heard Lily's desperate voice call from behind them but Laura just ignored it and stormed out of the club, dragging Isabella along with her.

The taxi ride and the elevator ride up to their hotel room were filled with an awkward silence. You could cut the tension between the two detectives with a knife. When the lift doors opened Laura practically bolted out of them, leaving Isabella trailing behind. Laura was sitting on the edge of the bed taking off her stilettos as Isabella entered the room. Her eyes purposefully avoiding the other detective's.

"Laura I'm sorry." Laura didn't answer her. "Honestly, I thought me being tipsy would actually help the investigation. You're not the most subtle when it comes to questioning people and I thought if I were drunk, no one would think we were cops."

"That's the dumbest thing I've ever heard, and I am too subtle," Laura spat, her now dark eyes finally flashing up to meet Isabella's.

"It's not dumb, it's a tactic. Just like you and your flirting," Isabella rolled her eyes.

"That's a useful tactic. You being drunk isn't. Who knows what could've happened with that guy tonight. You were in no condition to fend anyone off," Laura said angrily, taking deep breaths to try and calm herself down.

Isabella walked over to the edge of the bed and positioned herself in front of Laura's legs, placing her hands on Laura's shoulders. "Lucky you came and sorted him out then," Isabella smiled, Laura's expression softening.

"Isabella—"

Isabella turned around so her back was facing Laura. "Undo me please." Laura obeyed and pulled the zip down, Isabella's lacy red underwear peeping out. Isabella shimmied out of the dress making sure to stick out her butt, so that it was practically in Laura's face.

"Isabella, what are you doing?" Laura's voice trembled, a mixture of fear and desire.

"Nothing."

"Yeah ok Mrs Robinson," Laura said, raising a sceptical eyebrow as her eyes ran over Isabella's tanned body, just her most intimate parts covered by the lacy underwear.

"What so you can flirt with Lily, but you can't flirt with me?" Isabella asked again, this time looking hurt.

"Isabella—" Laura went to protest, but again she was cut off as Isabella pushed her further back on the bed and climbed onto her lap so that she was straddling her thighs.

"Why Laura? Am I not as sexy as these other women?"

"No."

"Do you really hate me that much?"

"No Isabella—"

Isabella swept her hair to one side, completely exposing the skin of her neck to Laura as she placed her hands on Laura's waist. Laura saw Isabella staring at her lips and her own eyes flicked down to Isabella's. She remembered every perfect kiss they had shared. Isabella licked her lips and closed her eyes as she leaned forward. Laura found herself mimicking Isabella's actions as she felt Isabella's warm breath on her skin.

"I don't love you Laura. I never loved you."

Laura pulled back suddenly before their lips could touch and Isabella's chocolate eyes flashed open in horror. "I-I'm sorry. I-I didn't mean—"

"You're drunk Isabella, go to sleep." Laura said harshly, rolling Isabella off her lap and leaving her in the bed as she retreated to the bathroom.

Laura spent what felt like hours in the cold shower trying to wash away whatever it was that had just happened. She had let herself get carried away with Isabella's wiles. She couldn't do that again. Isabella was just after sex, that was it. She was trying to seduce Laura and then she would just end up leaving her like before.

When she finally exited the bathroom, Isabella was fast asleep. She climbed into the bed beside her and tried to calm her thoughts. After a tortuous hour of tossing and turning, her eyes began giving in to the fatigue and fluttering closed.

"No, wait don't!" Isabella yelled.

Laura's eyes shot open as Isabella thrashed around, kicking Laura in the shins. Laura cursed and grabbed her phone, moving to the edge of the bed to escape anymore secondary attacks. When she turned her phone back on it lit up with a million messages, mostly still from the group chat conversation from earlier. She decided not to open them, it would just make her feel even more guilty about what had almost happened.

She instead opened Instagram and left a flirty comment on her beautiful girlfriend's most recent post. She was all dressed up in her winter coat with a cute beanie, drinking a coffee in Central Park. Coffee. Isabella. Dammit.

"Don't touch her!" Isabella yelled again and Laura was sure that any minute there would be angry knocks on the door from other hotel guests.

She didn't want to wake Isabella, she didn't feel like speaking with her. But she didn't want to get kicked out of the hotel either. Sighing, she put down her phone and moved back up to her spot in the bed, getting ready to tap Isabella's shoulder.

"LAURA!" Isabella screamed and tears were streaming down her face as she thrashed around in the bed.

Laura was shocked as she looked down at Isabella. She had just assumed Isabella's nightmares from the shooting revolved around herself and Savannah. Her heart ached when she realised how upset Isabella was with whatever might be happening to her.

"Isabella," she whispered softly, shaking the woman's shoulder. Isabella thrashed around again and sobbed even harder.

"La-Laura," she cried again.

Watching her cry like that was breaking Laura's heart. She stopped trying to shake Isabella's shoulder and instead sat up against the headboard. She grabbed Isabella by her shoulders and pulled her up into her lap, wrapping her arms around her. The thrashing continued for a while before Laura felt her own eyelids slipping closed.

"Laura?" Isabella stared up at her confused, blinking sleepily in the early morning light. Laura still had her wrapped in a tight embrace, herself hardly having slept.

"I'm here," Laura answered softly and placed a gentle kiss on the top of Isabella's head. "Go back to sleep."

Isabella sighed contentedly and pulled Laura down so that both of their heads were resting on the pillow. Laura listened as Isabella's breaths slowed and became rhythmic once more, her own eyes fluttering closed.

* * *

Laura was at the reception desk handling their bill as Isabella arrived downstairs. Laura was dressed in one of her usual tight pantsuits that was equally sexy and intimidating. When she turned around Isabella gave her a warm smile, but Laura instead averted her gaze. Things looked differently to her now in the fresh light of day.

"Morning," Isabella smiled brightly as Laura approached.

"You ready?" Isabella just nodded and Laura stalked off towards the valet.

Isabella piled her luggage in the back of the cruiser and then looked towards Laura, the detective's gaze focused on something in the distance.

"What is it?"

"Just a man, he almost..." Laura paused, a pensive look on her face. "Doesn't matter."

They both climbed into the cruiser and Laura flicked on the radio, an overwhelming silence filling the car.

13

Chapter 13

"Merry Christmas Laur!" Savannah squealed as she threw herself into Laura's arms, causing her to stumble back a step.

"Merry Christmas Sav," she returned, squeezing Savannah one last time before she darted off to greet the rest of the guests.

"Merry Christmas Laura," Isabella smiled, her chocolate eyes sparkling up at Laura.

Laura had been avoiding Isabella all week after what had happened in Atlantic City, but she couldn't revoke their Christmas invite, that would have been cruel.

"Merry Christmas Isabella," Laura tried her best to return the warm smile and even reached out with one arm to give Isabella a half hug.

"Medina, you made it!" Kyle mumbled as he chewed the remainder of his pig in a blanket.

"You know, it surprises me more and more each day that you've never had a girlfriend Reynolds," Isabella smiled sarcastically.

"My Mum says the exact same thing," Kyle winked back before pulling her into a side hug. Laura disappeared back into the lounge room as Isabella walked over to the Christmas tree and placed her Secret Santa gift beneath it.

"Isabella," Isabella smiled as Jordan called from behind her. He was standing beside Laura's large couch holding an excitable Andre is his hands. "Come, I want to introduce you," Jordan smiled proudly, bouncing the little boy on his hip and blowing him raspberries. Andre had rosy cheeks and a captivating toothy grin.

Jordan ruffled his tight buzz curls, he was completely amused with the gold chain around Jordan's neck. "And this little man is Andre."

"Wow Jordan he's more adorable in person, if that's even possible," Isabella cooed as she took hold of one of the boy's tiny hands.

Savannah joined them, pulling silly faces at Andre as Jordan handed him over to Isabella for a nurse. The detective smiling happily as she placed Andre on her hip. Laura had zoned out of her conversation with Cate as she watched Isabella interacting with Andre. Her knitted white dress, adorned with a red Santa hat, made her look insanely cute. The little boy was just as enthused by Isabella, playing with her long wavy hair as he tried to reach her hat.

"Laura?" Cate asked, pulling her attention back to their conversation.

"I'm sorry, what?"

"You're as bad as Kevin I tell you, the attention span of a goldfish," she laughed rolling her eyes.

"Hey!" Laura heard Kevin protest from his spot on the couch next to Kyle.

"Or maybe it's the conversation that's lacking," Parker teased as she walked up behind Cate and wrapped her arms around the woman's waist, hugging her from behind.

"Whatever. You try talking to her then, I assure you she'll lose interest in about two seconds." Cate said as she looked at Laura, the detective once again staring across the room at Isabella.

"Alright, watch me," Parker smirked, loving the challenge. "So Laura...I heard Jordan's getting promoted to Captain." Nothing registered on Laura's face as she continued staring off into the distance, unaware that Parker was even speaking. "Clearly the wrong tact," Parker mumbled to Cate before a wicked smile flashed across her face. "Kyle and Isabella had sex."

"What?" Laura practically shouted, a horrified look spreading across her face as she looked at Parker. Everyone in the room all turned their attention towards Laura curiously.

"Just kidding, I'm not pregnant!" Parker joked, shouting so that whole room heard as they all laughed and went back to their own conversations. "Sorry," Parker said far softer this time. "A joke."

"Hilarious."

"Secret Santa time?" Cate asked as she sat down on the lounge, clapping to get everyone's attention. "Everyone grab a seat!" She called, waving everyone to the lounge. Bri came bustling in from the hall after putting Andre down to sleep. "Seeing as Isabella's wearing the Santa hat, I think she should play Santa Claus." The rest of the group all murmured statements of agreement as Isabella sighed, got up from the lounge and walked over to the tree.

She picked up a present wrapped in brown wrapping paper and adorned with red and green bows, reading the name off the top. "Cate." Cate smiled happily as Isabella handed her the present and she unwrapped a 'nurses shapes' cookie cutter with cutters in the shapes of crosses, needles and bedpans.

"OMG I LOVE IT!" Cate clapped happily causing everyone to laugh.

"Of course you do my darling," Kevin smiled, as he leant in to place a tender kiss on his wife's lips.

Laura was endeared by their relationship. She was so happy that Cate had found someone that made her incredibly happy and gave just as much to the relationship as she did. After her terrible break up with Jack, Kevin was the perfect person for her to end up with.

After a few more people opened their presents Isabella lifted her own present from under the tree and handed it to Kyle. He began unwrapping and Jordan burst into laughter, quickly joined by Laura and then the rest of the room. Kyle stared at the box with mock anger, 'Realistic Inflatable Sex Doll' written across the top and sides.

"Fuck you all. Just because I'm single! I can assure you I still would've gotten laid more than all the rest of—" he pointed at them all individually in emphasis, stopping when he got to Laura. "Well, maybe not Carlsson..."

"Oh fuck off Reynolds," Laura said as she threw a cushion at him from the other side of the lounge.

"So Laura's a slut? Noted," Savannah chuckled as she looked at Laura, her cheeks turning red.

"He's exaggerating Sav," Laura tried to assure her, but Kyle's scoff detracted from her efforts.

"I thought you had a girlfriend?" Savannah asked, still somewhat confused.

"I do. She's working."

"Shame," Savannah said sarcastically, grinning up at Isabella. Isabella glared back, a look that said I'll deal with you later.

Isabella handed out the last few gifts until there was only one left under the tree. Her own. It wasn't just one gift either, but a bunch of gifts individually wrapped and grouped together with ribbon. Each gift was labelled with a number.

"Ok seriously? What happened to a fifty dollar limit?" Parker asked as she saw all the presents in Isabella's arm.

"Just because there's more than one, doesn't mean it's more expensive than fifty dollars," Cate countered.

Isabella unwrapped the irregular shaped first gift an array of chocolate bars falling out. Laura had picked out all of her old favourites, she knew Isabella was a sucker for chocolate.

"Chocolate, good start," Savannah nodded.

Gift number two was soft and squishy. She pulled out a brown teddy, dressed in a pink t-shirt. A typed note dangling from around the toy's neck. It read 'a snuggle buddy to keep the nightmares at bay'. Isabella's eyes flickered up to Laura's, but Laura just smiled casually as if she had no clue who the gift giver was.

Isabella then unwrapped gift number three, Laura held her breath knowing it was a risky choice. The wrapping contained Isabella's all-time favourite movie, 'Life is Beautiful'. The Italian film had been Isabella's mother's favourite, Laura knew how special it was to her. Isabella blinked back tears as she turned the DVD over in her hands.

"Ugh I hate subtitles," Kyle moaned as he picked up the DVD.

"Lucky it's not you that's going to be watching it then," Isabella shot back as Jordan made a sizzling noise with his mouth, causing everyone in the room to all chuckle.

The last present was labelled number four. She slowly unwrapped the present her own brown eyes staring back at her on canvas. The eyes formed the centre of a larger painting. Laura had used all black paint except for the eyes which were a warm chocolate brown. Laura had taken inspiration from a polaroid picture they had taken by the beach on their first date.

Laura had kept the picture in her underwear drawer ever since she had taken it. For some reason she had never been able to bring herself to get rid of it. It had been her favourite photo for the longest time, the happy expression on Isabella's face made her smile every time she looked at it. Isabella's warm chocolate eyes wandered across the room and connected with her own and she saw that damn sparkle in them that she adored so much. She couldn't help but smile back.

"You know Laur it's called 'secret' Santa for a reason," Parker scolded as her eyes looked over the painting.

"What?" Laura tried to appear oblivious, but failed miserably. "Why do you assume it's me?"

"I swear you're the worst liar I've ever met and that's saying something next to this one," Parker nudged Cate playfully.

"Hey!" Cate objected as Kevin ruffled her hair affectionately.

"It's true babe."

"Still, low blow," Cate sulked.

"I had no idea you were this talented Carlsson. Been holding out on me, have you?" Kyle winked.

"In more ways than one," Laura teased back.

A few drinks later and the Christmas ham was out of the oven, they were all seated around Laura's large dining table to enjoy the feast of delectable dishes on offer. The volume of noise only increased as dinner progressed. More and more wine was consumed around the table, leaving everyone but Cate slightly tipsy. The noise was so loud they almost missed the tapping of someone at the door.

"Expecting someone Laura?" Jordan asked quizzically.

"No," Laura shook her head confused. "Unless Rachel's gotten off early."

Laura got up from her seat to answer as everyone else returned to their conversations.

She was taken completely by surprise when she opened the door to find Ellie on her doorstep. She looked tired, albeit still pretty, dressed in a long black coat with a sparkly gold dress and black heels beneath. Her eyes weren't their usual colour of cold defiance, instead they were more pleading, desperate. Laura's heart dropped as she took in the vulnerability she saw before her. No matter what Ellie had done in the past, she was still her baby sister.

"Laur please," she begged. "I don't have anywhere else to go."

Maybe it was the happiness of a day spent among friends or the fact that it was Christmas, but Laura had no will to resist. She simply sighed and opened the door further so that her little sister could enter.

"Merry Christmas Ellie."

"Merry Christmas Laur," she smiled weakly as she leant forward and gave Laura a quick hug.

Laura led her sister back through the living room to the dining area, everyone falling silent as they saw Ellie walking in behind her. Laura motioned to the spare seat between herself and Kyle and Ellie sat down.

"Ellie everyone, everyone Ellie," Laura introduced as she poured her sister a glass of wine.

"Thanks. Hi everyone," she smiled. Laura noticed her eyes didn't look bloodshot for once.

Ellie began chatting to Kyle and the table returned to normal chatter. Laura felt multiple eyes fixed on her, but she ignored them and continued her conversation with Bri. She felt relieved that Ellie was able to sit down and be civilised. Maybe she was beginning to change.

"Isabella and Laura weren't 'friends' in high school. They dated." Ellie corrected Kyle loud enough for the table to hear. Laura was sure she had jinxed herself.

Kyle's face opened into a wide grin, his long-held suspicions confirmed. Laura's heart rate picked up as she anticipated what might be about to happen.

"Is that right Carlsson?" Kyle asked playfully, all eyes around the table falling on her. She didn't even hesitate this time, there was no point in denying it now thanks to Ellie. She would just try and quash the conversation before it got any further.

"Yes, we dated. Happy now?"

"Very," Kyle smirked. "I've got a few questions."

"Shoot," Ellie offered as Laura kicked her underneath the table. Everyone seemed to be paralyzed by the conversation. Most of all Isabella. One could mistake her for being parched, the way she was downing her wine.

"We were friends first, we dated for a short time. It was a high school relationship, there really aren't any juicy details." Laura said sternly trying to end the conversation there.

Spurred on by the alcohol and his lowered inhibitions, Kyle continued to press undeterred. "Who dumped who?"

"Isabella dumped Laura," Ellie jumped in, relishing telling the captive audience all the grizzly details. "She decided she was straight after all and left her for the biggest jock in their year. Not that you could blame her, Mitch was a definite catch!"

Laura felt nauseous. Her cheeks were red with humiliation and she was ready to bury herself under the table.

"Ellie, that's enough," Parker warned protectively.

Ellie ignored Parker's warning and instead continued. "Of course Laura was completely in love with Isabella, she had practically picked out the schools their kids were going to go to. But no, the bitch ripped her heart out and then stomped on it for good measure."

"Ellie!" Cate shouted from across the table. If looks could kill, Ellie surely would have been dead. Instead she just smirked. The rest of the table looking at the usually quiet Cate in shock. Even Kyle now looked to regret his choices.

Laura rose from her seat and all eyes fell on her. She was pale, her hands shaky. She gave the table her best smile as she picked up the empty wine bottle in front of her.

"More wine?" She asked, walking away towards the kitchen before anyone could even reply.

Isabella stood up to follow her, but Savannah held her arm and made her stay. "Not yet Bella, give her a minute. I'll go." Savannah stood up and walked over to Ellie's chair. "I'm not surprised Laura cut you out of her life Ellie. You're a selfish bitch and no one wants you here," Savannah glared before storming off towards the kitchen. Ellie stood at the same time and moved off towards the bedrooms.

"My bad," Kyle apologised to the table. "I'll deal with it." He got up and followed her, leaving everyone else in an awkward silence.

"Anyone like a cookie?" Kevin finally broke the tension surrounding them all as he offered a plate of cookies he had made. Everyone smiled and chuckled lightly, a few people taking a cookie.

Laura heard footsteps entering into the kitchen, she turned around to see Savannah, her expression sympathetic. She blinked furiously so Savannah wouldn't see her damp eyes.

"Are you ok Laur?" Savannah asked tentatively.

"Of course Sav, I'm fine," Laura reassured her, offering her a warm smile.

"Ellie was just trying to defend you. In her own messed up way." Laura was surprised by Savannah's assessment of the situation. She knew that's what Ellie was doing, but the way she did it had only hurt Laura and she was sure Isabella too.

"I know."

"I would've done the same for Isabella. In fact, I am." Savannah said, prompting Laura to raise an eyebrow in confusion. "Look I know I was only young when you guys were together, but I think I've heard about you every day since you weren't." Laura shifted uncomfortably, she didn't want to be going into this with Savannah. "I'm not justifying what my sister did, what she did was awful. She had her reasons, she needs to tell you those. But she was an idiot, she broke your heart. But don't think yours was the only one. As much as your heart was broken by what she did, hers was shattered."

Laura looked down at the floor as she tried to process all of the information she had just been given. Isabella heartbroken? Surely not. What possible reasons could she have then for ending it if they were different from what Laura knew?

"The painting turned out really good," Savannah interjected, pulling Laura's thoughts back to the present.

"Thanks."

"Isabella's right, it's not fair how talented you are."

"Well it's not fair how wise you are," Laura laughed, breaking the tension as she pulled Savannah into a hug. "God I missed you Sav."

"I missed you too Laur," Savannah agreed, resting her head on Laura's shoulder.

"How are the nightmares? Are you still seeing that counsellor at school?"

"Yeah once a week. They've been getting better, I think it's really helping."

"Good, I'm glad."

"Bella says it's helped her too. She's really been working through a lot. Not just the shooting but a lot of stuff from a long time ago. I think she's finally making peace with some things."

"Well...that's great," Laura offered, unsure of what she should say.

"How about you?"

Laura just shrugged. She hadn't been all that open with her psychologist, yet another one of her protective measures. She didn't like rehashing the past, it just brought up old feelings that she had fought hard to suppress.

"Yeah good," Laura lied, giving Savannah's shoulders one last squeeze before they disentangled from one another.

"Ready to join the fun?"

Laura just nodded and followed her back out into the dining area.

"Yay more wine!" Parker clapped, standing up from her chair and embracing Laura in a hug. No one else said anything, they just smiled and continued their conversations, trying not to make Laura feel any more uncomfortable.

"Love you," Parker whispered into her ear as she took the wine and sat back down at the table. Feeling brave, Laura walked to the other end of the table and sat down next to Isabella.

"Hey," Laura said softly, so the other end of the table couldn't hear them.

"Hey," Isabella returned shyly.

"Cate did you see my Christmas present?" Parker asked obnoxiously loud.

"Um, no?" Cate looked at her confused.

"Oh you've got to see it, guys, shall we?" Parker asked, motioning to the lounge room, making it perfectly clear to everyone that she was clearing the room for Laura and Isabella. Everyone got up and left leaving Laura and Isabella alone.

"I'm sorry about Ellie," Laura apologised, the room now empty. "If it helps, most of the time she hates me."

"You don't need to apologise," Isabella said softly, looking down at her lap. "Everything she said was right."

"Maybe...but that was a long time ago. I've moved on."

"Even so, I've been wanting to apologise to you properly ever since I've gotten here." Laura shifted uncomfortably in her seat under Isabella's gaze, but she kept her eye contact. "I can never expect you to forgive me for what I did, I know it was totally unforgivable. I was just so scared and I panicked and I threw away the best thing that ever happened to me. Not a day has gone by since then that I haven't regretted it—"

"Laura?" Rachel's voice called from the lounge room, the sound of footsteps approaching them. Laura's palms began sweating and she felt a small bit of guilt trickling away in her stomach. She stood up from her chair as Rachel came walking towards them.

"Merry Christmas baby!" The brunette woman pulled Laura in for a passionate kiss. Laura wrapped her arms around her girlfriend's waist, Isabella standing up to leave. So many things left unsaid.

After a few more hours of laughter and drinks all of the guests were gone, except Isabella, Savannah and Parker. Ellie had excused herself to one of the guest rooms before allowing her sister to say no. Laura had finished cleaning up in the kitchen when she entered the lounge room to find Savannah and Parker passed out on the lounge. The two had entertained everyone with a thrilling game of eggnog pong which saw both women get absolutely sloshed within the space of half an hour. Isabella was watching a Christmas film on the lounge as Rachel had excused herself to shower.

"Are you sure you don't want to stay?" Laura asked Isabella, seeing how inebriated Savannah was, she was worried about them getting home safely.

Though with Parker and Ellie now crashing, there really wasn't much space left.

"No, thanks. I should get her home," Isabella smiled warmly.

"Let me help you to a cab," Laura offered, throwing one of Savannah's arms over her shoulder, Isabella taking hold of the other arm. After a few minutes of struggling they had successfully managed to place Savannah in the cab.

The cold wind swept Isabella's long hair into her face as they shivered on the pavement. Laura leant forward, gently tucking a loose strand of hair behind one of her ears.

"Thanks," Isabella whispered, her warm breath tingling against Laura's lips.

"Thank you for the apology. It meant a lot to me," Laura said sincerely, not once breaking their gaze.

"I meant what I said Laura. If I could go back in time and take it all back I would. I would never hurt you like that again," Isabella said earnestly.

Laura nodded and looked down at the floor as the taxi driver beeped at them to hurry. Laura stepped forward and pressed her warm lips against Isabella's cheek in a gentle kiss, lingering for a second.

"Goodnight Issi," she whispered as she turned on her heel and walked back inside the building.

"Goodnight Laur," Isabella whispered into the night, her fingers clutching at the spot of the kiss.

14

Chapter 14

"Morning Carlsson," Jordan smiled as he sat down at his desk. "How was the rest of your break?"

"If you can even call it a break, honestly I'd rather be at work than at home with Ellie," Laura rolled her eyes as she thought back on the previous painful two days with her entitled younger sister.

"What's this about Ellie?" Kyle entered the conversation, a smirk on his face.

"Nothing, just that she's a brat."

"Oh I don't know, I thought she was fun," Kyle grinned at Laura, a flirtatious look in his eyes.

"No! Don't you even think about it," Laura threatened, causing Jordan to chuckle.

"Come on Foster, help a brother out," Kyle pleaded.

"Nah bro, you're on your own. Carlsson would beat your ass! Besides, it's bro code. Family members and exes are strictly off limits."

"Shit, wish I'd known that before I slept with Medina the other night," Kyle joked, winking at Laura. The detective's green eyes bored into his furiously. Jordan stood from his chair, trying to deescalate the situation before Laura well and truly blew a gasket. He grabbed Kyle by the shoulder and began guiding him toward the lifts.

"Come on Reynolds, let's check if digital forensics have that footage for us," Jordan suggested as the lift doors opened and Isabella stepped out holding two coffees.

"Ah Medina!" Kyle smirked cheerily, scanning around him to make sure none of his superiors were in the vicinity. "Tell me, how is Carlsson in the sack?"

Isabella's jaw dropped at the question, Jordan leant forward to steady her hands before she dropped the tray of coffees she was holding. Laura simply turned around to glare at Kyle, looking back to her paperwork once she saw Isabella's flushed expression.

"Can't be that great if you dumped her right?" Kyle smirked once again, casting a look back at Laura when he heard her chair scrape against the floor as she stood up.

"I, uh…" Isabella stumbled, clearly overwhelmed and uncomfortable with this entire conversation. Sensing the imminent danger from Laura's approach, Jordan once again intervened.

"He's just kidding Medina. We know who you are now, we're not worried about the past. I am however worried about the present, Reynolds let's go. Carlsson's two seconds away from kicking your ass." Kyle looked over his shoulder to see a furious Laura approaching and decided to heed Jordan's advice, bolting towards the elevator, Jordan following after him.

"Morning. Sorry about that," Isabella said, looking down at the floor as Laura approached.

"Reynolds is a dick. Don't worry about it. Apparently, he now wants to sleep with Ellie. He'll be lucky if he makes it through the day with his appendage attached."

Isabella smiled, handing Laura her coffee as she took a sip from her own.

A little while later Kyle and Jordan returned, both bearing serious expressions and holding up a USB. "You guys are going to want to see this," Jordan informed them. Passing Laura the USB as she earnestly plugged it into her laptop.

The digital forensic team had blown up the footage from outside the night club in Atlantic City. Based on the bartender's clothing description they found a man on the CCTV that was a match. Only problem was, he was facing away from the cameras and the image was heavily pixelated. As they watched, the footage gradually zoomed. As Laura squinted at the blurry image, she could just make out an outline of branding on the man's backpack.

"What does that say?" Isabella asked, squinting her eyes and rotating her head to the side to try and read it.

"Shred Fitness," Jordan clarified.

"How can you even read that?" Laura asked, not able to make out any lettering.

"I can't, but I recognise the logo I think." He pointed to a black fuzzy shape in the middle of a lime green circle. "If I'm right, that's a set of dumbbells. And then that black fuzzy bit beneath it must say Shred Fitness."

"If you say so," Laura was unconvinced, but it was the best lead they had.

"I did a trial there a few months back, the lime green stands out." Jordan shrugged. "Luckily it's a boutique gym, as far as I'm aware there's only one and it's in Greenwich Village."

"Such a gym whore. Just pick one already and stick to it," Kyle teased.

"Alright, as soon as you pick one woman and stick to her."

Kyle rolled his eyes, ignoring the comment.

"It's worth a shot," Laura said, ignoring their banter. "Ready Medina?"

"Actually," Isabella hesitated. "I can't. I've got an appointment I need to be at in half an hour."

Laura looked at Isabella questioningly, it was unlike Isabella to withhold information, but it was none of her business to pry. "Ok...we'll see you later then?"

"Definitely," Isabella nodded.

"Looks like you guys get to come now." Laura picked up her keys. She was not looking forward to the next few hours stuck in close proximity to Kyle.

"I call shotgun!"

"Dammit," Kyle cursed, Isabella laughing as the three detectives disappeared into the lift.

* * *

Isabella lay in bed, unwilling to open her eyes. The ache in her chest was so extreme it was hard to breathe. Her cheeks were stained with tears as she sat up. She pulled her t-shirt up to her nose. Her mother had brought the lucky Irish souvenir back from Europe after a backpacking trip many moons ago. Despite having been through the wash millions of times, she still smelt her mother on it.

She rolled herself out of bed, her heart hammering in her chest as she made her way to the kitchen. It was the anniversary of her mother's death. Two years on her grief felt just as immense as it had the day her mother left them. Her battle with bowel cancer had been relatively short compared to some. The cancer didn't disappear and then come back years later like it did for many people. She was diagnosed, sought treatment and a few months later she was dead.

She began pulling out some eggs and bacon from the fridge. Her mother used to make a special breakfast for them every Sunday. As much as she wanted to roll up in the foetal position and cry all day, she knew her mum wouldn't want that. Her mum always told them when she left, she didn't want them to grieve for her. She said she couldn't bear watching over them and seeing them cry. Instead, she made them promise her that they would celebrate life and remember the good times. Isabella had worked very hard every day to maintain that promise. Her father on the other hand had broken his almost immediately.

As she stirred the scrambled eggs around the pan she tried to conjure up all of the happiest memories she had, had with her mum. Like their obsession with seeing old films at the moonlight cinema and eating copious amounts of ice cream. Her love of reading was completely born from her mother. Isabella would rest her head on her mother's lap as she read to her. Stories of mythical swords and creatures, of tremendous loss and victory and of great love. The kind of love that consumed your whole heart. She had always thought of that love as fiction, a lovely dream, but not reality. That was until Laura.

After her mother passed away Laura had come along and taken the fractured pieces of her heart and made them whole again. She wondered what her mother would think of Laura. Surely she would love her? Would she be worried she were a girl? Isabella doubted it. If she saw how Isabella loved, surely she wouldn't worry about the who. Her mother was a hopeless romantic after all. She only ever had eyes for Samuel. They had gotten together so young, now that she was gone, he wasn't sure how to live without her.

Savannah's shrill scream interrupted her thoughts. She dropped the pan on the stove and bolted towards the stairs as her father began yelling incoherently. There was a loud crash as glass shattered, her sister's sobs ensuing.

She burst through the door of her father's bedroom, horror gripped her tightly as she took in the scene. Her baby sister was curled on the floor clinging to her tiny foot as blood dripped steadily from her skin. She noticed a smashed whiskey bottle beside her, the smell completely overpowering. Her father tried to crouch down beside Savannah and console her, but as he reached out to touch his youngest daughter she screamed and flinched away from him. His eyes looked bloodshot, his shirt soaked in sweat.

"Don't you dare touch her! Get away from her!"

Samuel looked shocked by her fury. He stumbled backwards into the bed, his eyes still fixed remorsefully on Savannah. Isabella ran to the bathroom and grabbed a towel, wrapping it tightly around Savannah's injured foot.

"We're all hurting, you didn't die when Mum did. You're still here. If you keep going like this, not only will you have lost Mum, but you will lose us as well," Isabella threatened, tears once again glistening in her eyes. "You're on your last chance now. This is it for you."

She lifted Savannah up into her arms and carried her carefully down the stairs, her back straining from the weight. She placed Savannah on the kitchen bench, turning off the stove as she reached for her phone. After two rings Laura picked up.

"Hey Issi," Laura said cheerily, Isabella could practically see her smile through the phone.

"Can you come and get me and Savannah?" Isabella asked frantically.

"What's wrong?" Laura asked worriedly, Isabella could hear the sound of her keys rattling in the background and her footsteps hammering down the stairs.

"She's trodden on glass and her foot is bleeding. I need to get her to the hospital."

"I'm on my way."

Isabella and Laura sat anxiously in the waiting room, a nurse having taken Savannah away to patch her wound. Isabella was furiously biting her nails, her eyes glazed as she anxiously awaited her sister's return. She had barely said two words to Laura since they arrived at the hospital.

"Ms Medina?"

"Yes," Isabella confirmed as she looked up into the eyes of the nurse approaching them.

"My name is Elizabeth. I'm the nurse in charge of child welfare at the hospital. Savannah is your sister, isn't she?" Isabella just nodded her head in response.

"Are your parents here?"

"No, my father wasn't home," Isabella lied, trying her best not to alarm the nurse.

"Can you tell me how your sister was injured?"

"My sister pulled a towel off the bench and knocked down a bottle of whiskey from the counter," Isabella knew she couldn't lie about the alcohol as Savannah wreaked of the awful substance. She just had to make the situation sound completely innocent. "The bottle smashed on the floor and she stepped on the glass."

"Ok. You're sure that's what happened?" The nurse probed.

"Yes," Isabella answered confidently, the nurse just nodded.

"Ok, well the nurse is just finishing up her stitches. We will be able to discharge her very shortly. Your father will need to come into the hospital when he gets home to sign off on all of this."

"I'll tell him. Thank you," Isabella smiled lightly, though it didn't reach her eyes.

"Not a problem sweetie. You did the right thing rushing her in here," the nurse smiled warmly.

Isabella sighed deeply and slumped down in her chair, resting her head in her hands. Laura placed her hand on Isabella's back and began tracing comforting circles around it.

"She didn't knock the bottle off the counter, did she?" Laura asked knowingly.

"No," Isabella answered.

"It's going to be alright Issi. She'll be alright."

"Will she?" Isabella asked disturbed. "I don't think it will. What if something like this happens again and they take her away?" A sharp sob emanated from

Isabella's lips and Laura pulled her into her chest.

"They won't Issi. Nothing's going to happen to Savannah. We won't let it." *Isabella's warm tears were soaking into Laura's shirt as she held her tight.*

"I can't lose her Laura. She's all I have left."

"You won't lose her Issi. I promise." Laura squeezed. "And she's not all you have left, I'm here too."

"Pinky promise?"

"Pinky promise," Laura confirmed, leaning down to place a tender kiss on Isabella's temple.

* * *

Isabella checked the time on her phone, she was becoming more and more nervous as the minutes rolled by.

"She's got five minutes," Martin Davis said firmly, as he looked down at his own watch. "If she doesn't show up before then, there's nothing I can do."

"She'll be here," Isabella confirmed resolutely, sounding far more confident than she actually felt. She really wasn't sure what Ellie would do. She knew the youngest Carlsson didn't want to go to gaol. She wasn't that naive. She wasn't the type of woman that would survive gaol and Isabella was sure she knew that.

As they stood waiting outside the courthouse, Isabella noticed Martin had all of the same nervous tics as Mitch. He was fiddling continuously with the wedding ring on his left finger, something Mitch had repeatedly done. That was when he'd actually been wearing it, which was rare. He also paced back and forth in the same spot, a habit that had irritated Isabella to no end in the few years they had lived together. Looking back on it, she wasn't sure how she had lasted that long. She could barely think of one tic of Laura's that irritated her.

"Sorry I'm late, my cab driver took a wrong turn," Ellie said breathlessly as she ran up the last few steps.

Isabella looked Ellie up and down, despite being slightly dishevelled from her sprint, she looked nice. Better than Isabella had seen her in recent times. She had a far healthier glow now that she was sober. Her black and white dress complimented her pale skin, the blazer adding a level of sophistication Isabella was surprised she could achieve. Looking closer she recognised it to be one of Laura's.

"Well at least you made it. Now let's go," Martin said, clearly irritated as he walked through the doors, leaving the two women on their own.

"I didn't know you were coming," Ellie said confused, as she surveyed Isabella.

"I thought you could do with the support. I know you didn't tell Laura about today," Isabella offered as warmly as she could. She hoped that one of these days she was going to get through to Ellie.

"Oh," Ellie seemed taken aback. Her cheeks blushed and her eyes fell to the floor. "That's actually really nice of you."

"Ellie," Isabella said softly, stepping forward so Ellie would meet her eyes. "Despite what you may think, I care about Laura a lot and I care about you. I'm trying to make up for my mistakes. You guys are family to me."

"I appreciate that," Ellie smiled shyly, all her previous bravado gone.

"Now come quickly before the judge decides to throw you in gaol," Isabella joked, holding out her hand for Ellie. She gratefully took it and they walked into the courthouse hand in hand.

Half an hour later they were exiting the courthouse, the judge having rejected a gaol sentence after some great arguments from Martin, instead Ellie received a hundred hours of community service.

"Thank you so much Martin, I really appreciate your help," Isabella said sincerely.

"Yes, thank you so much Mr Davis. I don't know how to repay you." The man smiled warmly at Ellie.

"You're welcome Ms Carlsson. I would do anything for my favourite daughter in law." Isabella smiled warmly and gave the man a hug. He made her promise to come over for dinner soon before he began descending the stairs.

"Daughter in law?" Ellie asked, looking down at Isabella's bare ring finger.

"Once upon a time. It was a naive mistake."

Ellie nodded, looking down the steps towards the bustling street. "Look I'm sorry for embarrassing you at Christmas. I guess I have a problem with dwelling on the past and I should give you the benefit of the doubt. I really appreciate all your help with this."

"Thank you, I appreciate the apology. And don't mention it, as I said you guys are practically family."

"Can I at least buy you an ice cream to say thanks?" Ellie asked innocently, causing Isabella to chuckle.

"Are you buying me the ice cream or is Laura?"

Ellie smirked at the question. "Well technically Laura..." Isabella shook her head and smiled. "I really need to get a job."

"Can't help you there," Isabella said, linking her arm with Ellie's as they descended the stairs. "But about that community service..."

* * *

The receptionist at Shred Fitness was just as you would expect him to be. Big, burly and had a Colgate smile. His eyes zeroed in on the small bit of cleavage that was showing from the white blouse Laura was wearing. That was until she flashed her badge in his face, then his eyes quickly met hers and his perfect smile faltered.

"Detective Carlsson NYPD, this is Detective Reynolds and Detective Foster. Do you have a few minutes to answer some questions?"

The detectives laid out the photos from the CCTV vision, hoping he might be able to identify the man by his clothes. "Sorry, I don't recognise him," the receptionist offered whilst shaking his head. Seeing as it was dark and the footage was heavily pixelated, it wasn't exactly surprising.

"Joe!" He called out into the gym. Several gym goers glared at him in the mirrors as they lifted their dumbbells. Another large man, wearing a Shred Fitness t-shirt, approached them with an inquisitive look. "These Detectives from the NYPD want to know if we recognise this guy." Joe leant down to look at the photos, studying them intently for a few moments.

"Mmm nah, don't think so." Joe shook his head.

"Just take another look for a minute," Jordan insisted. "Look at the shoes, the jacket, his cap...The red kicks and purple cap. They're unusual."

"Yeah maybe..." Joe considered. "I suppose the cap looks a bit like a Lakers cap. There was this one dude that used to come in a lot in Lakers gear, could maybe be him I guess."

"What's the name?" Kyle asked.

"Not sure about the guy in the CCTV, but I know the guy he would spot with sometimes. Greg something..." he clicked his fingers. "AJ get up the name Greg in the system." AJ typed away at the computer and a long list of Greg's trailed down the screen. Joe grabbed the mouse and began scrolling, his eyes scanning. "Blant, Greg Blant, pretty sure that's the guy."

* * *

"Hey," Parker called from the couch, startling Laura as she entered her apartment.

"Jesus Parks, you almost gave me a heart attack," Laura complained as she made her way into the living room. Parker was sat in the middle of the lounge wrapped up in one of Laura's fluffy throw blankets and munching on a bowl of buttery popcorn. "I would say make yourself at home but..."

"Well, you did give me a key," Parker smiled, tearing her eyes away from the screen for a second to look at Laura. "Your house is closer to work than mine and you always have food," Parker shrugged. "Plus, I still haven't heard what went down between you and Bella on Christmas Day." Laura groaned and flung herself down on the lounge next to Parker, taking a handful of popcorn from her bowl. "But first, how was work?"

"Yeah it was good. We might actually be making headway on the Washington Killer. We have the details of someone who could potentially identify him."

"Wow Laura that's huge!"

"I know."

"If you cracked this case, I swear the Mayor would just about give you the key to the city. People are up in arms about this one. The media loves this guy for some reason."

"I know it's been getting a lot of publicity. The Captain's been on our back, pressure from higher ups."

"Makes sense." Parker offered the bowl of popcorn towards Laura and then turned to face her, a mischievous smile spreading across her face. "So, Bella?"

Laura just sighed and started the story from the very beginning. Parker took a hold of her hand as she became breathless.

"So when I sat down at the dining table after my conversation with Savannah, I apologised to Isabella for Ellie's behaviour."

"Really?" Parker asked shocked.

"Uh, yeah," Laura answered, sheepishly. She knew Parker was wary of her getting heartbroken again. "I mean it was totally uncalled for. I was embarrassed. I can't imagine how embarrassing that would've been for Isabella in front of all of you plus Kyle and Jordan."

"Well yeah, she did seem to attempt to have the table cloth swallow her whole," Parker laughed.

"Well anyways, she wouldn't let me apologise. She said she deserved all of what Ellie had said and then she apologised. Like properly apologised for everything that happened." Parker's jaw dropped at the confession.

"Did she give you any reasons for why she did it?"

"Well...no. But she might have if Rachel hadn't interrupted us to kiss me," Laura rolled her eyes.

"You're complaining that your beautiful girlfriend wanted to kiss you on Christmas Day?" Laura blushed slightly at the intimation.

"No?"

"Laura..." Parker whined.

"What I can't help it ok? All these old feelings have cropped back up again and new ones have sprouted," Laura complained.

"A farming analogy, really?" Parker teased.

"Mocking me, really? I'm clearly frazzled at the minute Parks."

"Clearly."

"It's just, all those things I used to love about her are still there. She's like the warmest person I've ever met, she makes everyone feel comfortable. Her smile is probably the most perfect thing I've ever seen and the way her eyes sparkle when she looks at me, it's just…"

"Well no, I can't say I've been on the receiving end of Isabella's sparkly eyes."

"One minute she's totally adorable and cute and the next she's the sexiest woman in the room. The willpower it takes to keep my hands off her sometimes…I never knew I had it in me. Not to mention she's incredibly intelligent, the way her mind works Parker, I think she's probably as good a detective as me."

"No!" Parker exclaimed in mocking.

"She's still that same girl I fell in love with, only better somehow. She's so incredibly selfless how she volunteers with disadvantaged youth and the homeless, it's amazing. I don't think I've met anyone quite as brave either, to come back to face us all after everything and somehow manage to wiggle her way back in." Laura shook her head like she couldn't believe the balls on the woman. She was in a total state of admiration.

"How she could possibly still be single I have no idea…"

"Mmm I might," Parker smirked.

"What do you mean?" Laura asked, finally stopping for a breath.

"Clearly she came here for you Laur. It's totally obvious to everyone but you. I mean come on, moving to New York, coincidentally ending up working at the 34th, and partnering with you. No. That's one too many coincidences if you ask me."

"Really?" Laura asked intrigued, she hadn't really thought about it like that before. But when displayed in front of her, it was quite embarrassing she hadn't considered it.

"Yes Laura, come on. Aren't you the all-star detective?" Laura rolled her eyes. "I guess it's lucky for her then that you feel the same way."

"Wait a minute, we don't know for sure that she has feelings for me. Like genuine feelings outside of the obvious physical attraction."

"Ok…let's say we don't know she has feelings for you," Parker sighed.

THE CASE AGAINST HER

"What if she did? What if she admitted those feelings to you? What would you do?"

Laura didn't answer her as a contemplative look took over her features. After a drawn-out pause, she opened her mouth to speak. "I don't know... Rachel—"

"Laura you can't stay with someone out of guilt. Do you love Rachel?" Laura didn't answer. "Can you forgive Isabella?"

15

Chapter 15

"I'm back," Laura called, dropping her keys in the bowl on the hall stand as she made to climb the stairs to her bedroom.

"Laura! Can you come here a second?" Her mother called from the kitchen, her tone peaking Laura's anxiety slightly. She shrugged it off and walked back towards the kitchen, her mother having just pulled a tray of blueberry muffins from the oven. The smell made Laura's stomach rumble.

"Yes?" She asked as she entered, her mum standing by the bench, as her dad sat behind the breakfast bar, both wearing serious expressions. "Who died?" Laura tried to joke, but neither her dad or her mum laughed, not even a smile.

"Where were you?" Her mum accused, her eyes cold and her expression harsh as she fiddled with the pearl bracelet on her wrist.

"I was at the hospital with Isabella. Savannah hurt herself and they needed a ride there," Laura clarified, still confused as to why she was being accosted.

"Why did you have to take her?" Her mother probed.

"Uh...because I'm her friend and I live nearby," Laura answered somewhat sarcastically.

"Andrea Diaz just called me, she was at the hospital today..." Astrid paused, waiting for a reaction from Laura, when she didn't get one, she continued. "She said she saw you kiss Isabella. Is that true Laura?"

If Laura's anxiety was piqued by her mother's tone, that was nothing compared to how she felt now. Her heart was hammering in her chest so forcefully she was almost certain her parents would be able to see it bouncing through her shirt. She actually had to physically stop her jaw from dropping at the question, she couldn't believe that this was how her parents were going to find out. She had only pecked Isabella once the entire time they were at the hospital to console her. Usually they were beyond careful, but the moment had called for affection.

"What? No!" Laura recoiled, fabricating a lie in her head. "I may have kissed her on the cheek to comfort her, but that was all." Laura's mum and dad both looked at her in disbelief.

"Andrea was very insistent Laura—"

"I don't care, it didn't happen," Laura raised her voice now, getting angry. "Your bloody Catholic spy ring doesn't always get it right!"

"Laura lower your voice and don't curse," Hugo scolded her as he got up off the stool to stand by her mother's side.

"Sorry," Laura apologised, feeling like a little kid again under her father's analysing gaze.

"I think it's best you and Isabella take some time apart." Her mother's tone was final as she smoothed down her pink pastel cardigan. She always had to present as perfect and she had very specific ideas of what that looked like for her family. "I don't want any sort of rumours spreading around town, whether they hold any truth or not, about my daughter being...gay."

"Would that really be so terrible?" Laura shot back, before her rational mind could catch up with her mouth.

"You know our beliefs Laura, God made men and women for each other. Think of the consequences of what this looks like. You could get expelled from school," her father warned sternly.

"Nothing's happening," Laura tried to reassure them.

"Even so," her mother jumped in. "I still think a break from Isabella is needed."

Laura looked up at her parents' determined expressions and she nodded her head in defeat, her shoulders slumping forward.

"That's all that we will say on this Laura. I don't want to hear any reports of this kind of behaviour again," her father ordered. Laura just nodded her head once again and turned to leave the kitchen, slowly dragging her feet up the stairs. When she was halfway up, she noticed Alex sitting on the landing, having been *listening to their conversation.*

"Mrs Diaz is an asshole," he tried to console her, his Nintendo discarded on the floor beside him. "And so are our parents. Don't worry Laur, just a few more months and you'll be moving to New York, they won't have a say in anything."

"Thanks Alex," Laura smiled weakly, ruffling her brother's messy hair.

"Yeah, that's a pinky promise," he smirked, causing Laura's eyebrows to shoot up in alarm.

"Alexander...have you been reading my messages again?" Alex's smirk was all the confirmation Laura needed as she lunged towards him. He shot up off the stairs and barrelled towards his bedroom, slamming the door shut before Laura could grab him.

"I hate you," Laura whispered through his door.

"You love me," Alex whispered back.

Laura just shook her head and walked back towards her room. "Little shit," she mumbled under her breath.

* * *

"Go on," Cate urged her. She and Parker had been nothing but supportive since they discovered the girls relationship.

Isabella looked back at Laura who was staring at the floor despondently. "Ok, I'm going..." She lingered for a moment looking at Laura, but she refused to meet her eyes. Her friends watched on as Isabella walked from their spot behind the music studio, to the oval where Mitch and his friends sat.

"This is so stupid," Parker groaned shaking her head.

"Parker," Cate warned her.

"No Cate, I'm allowed to have an opinion and I think this is stupid," Parker huffed folding her arms.

"It's not our relationship, you know what Laura's parents said."

For the last week Laura and Isabella had only seen one another at school in the halls, casting each other longing glances. Laura had even had to stop sitting with the girls at lunchtime as her mother's friends got their kids to spy on her and report back.

Every lunchtime Parker and Laura had gone to sit on the oval, whilst Cate sat with Isabella in their usual spot. After school her parents had insisted, she be home as soon as she finished soccer and basketball practice and they had kept her house bound on the weekend after her games. They had even taken away her phone and banned her from the internet for the time being until they were satisfied Laura wasn't engaging in 'homosexual activity'.

"I just don't understand why you suggested this, Laura?" Parker asked. "This is only going to hurt you." Laura finally raised her eyes to meet Parker's.

"No what would hurt me is not being able to see Isabella every day. What would hurt me is her or I getting expelled for having a relationship. What would hurt would be if my parents found out we do in fact have a relationship and they kicked me out. This," Laura pointed towards Isabella and Mitch in the distance, without actually looking their way. "Is temporary pain for long term gain. If this allows us to finally be together in New York in a few months, like properly be together, then it will be worth it."

"If you say so..." Parker said doubtfully as she watched Mitch wrap Isabella up in a tight hug. Laura finally looked up and watched the embrace, her eyes growing dark.

"I've um, got a free period and I promised I'd pick Ellie up from school, I'll see you guys later," Laura lied weakly as she picked her backpack up from the floor and began walking towards the carpark.

"Laura!" Cate called after her.

"Laura, you have Bio with us after lunch!" Parker called as they watched Laura speed up.

* * *

As they walked onto the court for the third quarter, Laura's eyes scanned the stands. Isabella and Mitch were sitting beside their friends, a large grin plastered on his face. Mitch's arm was slung loosely around Isabella's shoulders. Laura rolled her eyes and looked back towards her teammate who was waiting to inbound the ball. Laura received the ball and set up a perfect offensive play that allowed her power forward to get a basket.

"Go Laura!" She heard Isabella cheer loudly from her stands, her cheeks flushing.

"Nice play back there," the opposing point guard smiled.

Laura raised her eyebrows in confusion. She wasn't used to chatter on the court between teams unless it was trash talk.

"Uh...thanks," Laura said as she stepped closer to defend her. The girl had olive skin and light brown hair with stunning hazel eyes, and all game Laura had been impressed by her skills. She could almost predict every move her players would make and was able to set up shots perfectly because of this. She was one of the best point guards that Laura had come across in the league, she just wasn't as good as Laura.

The girl's teammate threw her the ball and she caught it, raising it to her chest between her two palms. Laura stepped closer and raised her arms, her knees bent in expectation for a move. The girl smiled mischievously as she began dribbling, passing the ball back and forth between her hands in a steady rhythm, trying to confuse Laura before she made her move towards the basket. But almost as if Laura could read her mind, as soon as the girl shifted her weight to her left foot to go for the layup, Laura manoeuvred her hand to block the move and got the intercept. Laura was fast, she left the other point guard behind as she barrelled down the other end and scored her own layup.

When Laura ran back in defence again the girl smiled at her and shook her head, "Nice shot."

"Nice dribbling," Laura smiled back. Encouraged by Laura's banter the girl winked at her as she got the ball and dropped her eyes, running them up the length of Laura's body.

"Do they normally talk this much?" Isabella leant over towards Parker who was sitting on her other side. "I don't remember Laura talking this much to the opposite team before," she said insecurely.

"It's probably just trash talk Bella. Happens all the time in team sports," Parker reassured her, her eyes fixed firmly on the court as she took another handful of popcorn from the bucket Cate was holding.

The rest of the game continued in the same fashion, with Laura and the opposing point guard exchanging friendly banter throughout. Laura's team won *seventy five points to fifty one.*

"Hey three!" *A voice called from behind Laura as she shook the hand of one of the opposing players and said 'good game'. As she turned around, she saw the opposing point guard smiling at her and offering her, her hand.* "Good game."

"You too, bit more dribbling practice and you'll be better next time," *Laura teased playfully, the brunette feigning a stab to the heart.*

"Ouch. You talk a big game," *the girl poked her tongue out, Laura's hand still secured in her own.*

"I'm only joking," *Laura blushed.*

"Well your basketball skills are definitely better than your jokes. Bit more practice and you'll be better next time," *she smirked, finally relinquishing Laura's hand. Laura grinned at the girl's brazenness.* "So what's your name superstar?"

"Laura, yours?"

"Naomi Murray. Is there a last name that goes with that or are you like the Madonna of basketball?" *Laura chuckled at her joke and shook her head.*

"It's Carlsson."

"Well Laura, gorgeous eyes, Carlsson, expect some serious social media stalking later on, now that you've offered up your deets. Hopefully we'll see you guys again in the finals."

"Maybe," *Laura shrugged playfully.* "Depends how your dribbling practice pans out." *Naomi leant forward and slapped Laura's shoulder playfully, giving her one last wide smile before she moved off towards the locker room, waving at Laura as she went.*

"Told you it wasn't trash talk," *Isabella whispered into Parker's ear as they stood waiting for Laura. Parker offered a shrug as an apology.*

"You were amazing Laur! Best game this year I reckon," *Cate smiled proudly at her friend as she drew back from their hug.*

"Thanks Cate."

"Seriously impressive stuff Carlsson, you thought about going pro?" *Parker smirked and Laura looked up at the ceiling for a moment and rocked her head from side to side as if she was weighing it up.*

"Good game Laura," *Mitch smiled, as he went to place his arm around Isabella's shoulders, she shrugged him off before he could.*

"Thanks Mitch," Laura tried as hard as she could but the words still came out through gritted teeth.

"You were so good Laur," Isabella said energetically. "Best player by far!" Laura smiled briefly and looked back to the stadium doors, she was still struggling seeing Mitch and Isabella together.

"Thanks. Anyways, I should go, Dad's waiting out front. Thanks for coming guys," Laura smiled, directing her comment mostly at Parker and Cate.

"Of course!" Cate replied.

"Wouldn't have missed it," Parker asserted.

"We'll walk you out," Isabella suggested, motioning towards the door. Not wanting to say anything in front of Mitch, Laura just nodded and began walking out ahead of them.

"Hey Mr Carlsson," Isabella smiled as they approached Hugo's car.

"Hi Isabella," he said sternly, shooting Laura a look and staring at the boy Isabella was holding hands with.

"Hey Dad," Laura said quietly, as she opened up the passenger door and clambered into the front seat.

"This is my boyfriend Mitch," Isabella introduced happily. Hugo looked slightly taken aback by the title, but he reached his hand out of the window politely and shook the boy's hand.

"Nice to meet you. You two have a good night."

"We will," Isabella smiled, waving to them as they drove off.

Laura wasn't terribly surprised to find her internet privileges and her phone returned to her when she had arrived home from the game. Clearly Isabella's little show had been a success and her dad had bought it. She should be happy about the whole thing, but she couldn't help the nagging jealousy inside at having to see Isabella and Mitch together.

When she got out of the shower, she heard the vibrating sound of her phone ringing on her bed. She threw herself down onto the soft mattress, a towel wrapped around her wet hear. Isabella's name appeared on the screen as a Facetime call, after a second's hesitation she picked up the video chat.

"Hey."

"Hey," Isabella replied happily. "Parker said your parents gave you your phone *back."*

"Yeah they did," Laura admitted, leaning back against her bedhead.

"Why didn't you text me?" Isabella accused. Laura just shrugged. This was the first time in a few weeks they were able to have a proper conversation, but for once she didn't feel like it. "Why are you being weird, what's the problem?"

"Nothing," Laura lied unconvincingly.

"Laura, you've barely spoken to me the last few weeks or even looked at me—"

"I wasn't allowed to," Laura interrupted her and Isabella just glared at her in response, her own anger flaring up.

"That's bullshit Laura. We've had chances to talk, but you haven't taken them. I had to find out from Parker that you even got your phone back, if it were me, I would've called you straight away."

"Are you sure?" Laura asked sarcastically, "I thought your boyfriend would be your first call."

Isabella sighed and looked down at her sheets running her fingers along the smooth fabric. "Laura..." She shook her head, her words failing her. "I don't have feelings for Mitch, he's just a friend and that's it. I wouldn't even be pretending to date him if you hadn't suggested it. I want to be with you. Ok?"

"Why? Things with him would be so much easier," Laura said defeated, her eyes still fixed on her hands.

"Easier, maybe. But better? Not a chance." Laura finally looked up to meet Isabella's eyes and she gave her a warm smile. "I haven't ever met someone so intelligent, so patient, so kind and loyal as you. When I'm not with you I want to be and when I am, I never want to leave. No one could ever come between that ok?"

"Ok," Laura grinned back. "Who knew you were so eloquent," Laura teased, Isabella rolling her eyes.

"After everything I just said, that's all you have to say?" Isabella asked feigning offence.

"No," Laura smiled. "I just want to be with you."

"Good," Isabella smiled.

"Can I just say not talking for the last few weeks has been the worst thing ever," Laura pouted, making Isabella smile.

"*I'm going to add not touching to that too.*" *Laura flashed Isabella a mischievous smile before continuing.*

"*I feel like I need to stay up all night just to catch up on your life for the past few weeks.*"

"*You seriously don't. It's been majorly uninteresting without you.*"

Isabella sighed dramatically, making Laura chuckle. "*But I have a question...?*" *Isabella trailed off, looking down nervously.*

"*Yes?*" *Laura asked somewhat apprehensively.*

"*Who's Naomi Murray?*"

"*Oh,*" *Laura was taken aback by the question.* "*She's the point guard from the team we played tonight.*" *Isabella just nodded her head in response as if she wasn't surprised.* "*Why?*"

"*I saw her pop up on your Facebook and I was just curious. I thought that's who it might be.*"

"*Yeah, she was really friendly on the court which is a rarity and she added me,*" *Laura explained shrugging.*

"*I wouldn't say friendly, more...flirtatious.*"

Laura raised an eyebrow. "*How do you even know, you weren't on the court?*"

"*I can read body language Laura. The girl was screaming 'I want to fuck you' with her eyes.*"

"*Issi!*" *Laura said surprised by her use of profanities.* "*She was just being friendly.*"

"*You're so naïve Laura, everyone in that stadium could see she was flirting with you.*"

"*Are you jealous?*" *Laura smiled, endeared by Isabella's sudden irritability.*

"*Um...yes! You haven't spoken to me in weeks and tonight I see you flirting with some other girl.*"

"*Ok now for the record I don't think she was flirting with me. But I one hundred percent wasn't flirting with her. Hello! Did we not just have a discussion about my jealous rage over Mitch?*" *Laura joked lightly.* "*You literally consume my every thought, I wouldn't know how, nor would I want to flirt with anyone who isn't you.*"

"*Good answer,*" *she smiled.*

* * *

"Go on, do it at the same time," Parker urged. Laura and Parker had already received their acceptance letters for Columbia University the week before. Their New York hopes now rested with Cate and Isabella.

"I'm too nervous," Cate complained, the NYU University letter visibly shaking in her hand. "It seriously is true, ignorance is bliss. Like I could open this letter and my whole world could shatter."

"Or you could open that letter and have all your dreams come true," Parker countered. Cate pondered this thought for a minute before nodding.

"True. Ok, I'll do it." Cate ripped open the letter and pulled it out, reading it slowly.

"What does it say?" Laura asked apprehensively.

"I got in," Cate said bewildered, her eyes not leaving the letter.

"Cate!" Parker squealed, clapping her hands.

"Cate that's amazing!" Isabella smiled, her voice laced with nerves.

"We're going to be roomies!" Parker tackled Cate into a tight hug causing her to drop the letter.

"I'm going to NYU!"

"Damn straight you are! Our best friend is going to be a nurse," Laura smiled, jumping in on the hug after Parker and Isabella.

"Get off, you great big lumps. It's your turn Bella," Cate smiled confidently.

"I'm so nervous," she said, her face as white as paper.

"You'll be fine, you're gonna get in," Parker reassured her.

"What if I don't?" Isabella asked anxiously, turning to look at Laura.

"You will," she reassured her. "But for some crazy reason if Columbia don't want you, somewhere else will."

"Yeah and what if that somewhere else isn't in New York?" Isabella asked hesitantly.

"Then I'll kill you for ruining our plans and you won't have to worry about College," Parker smirked, eliciting a small smile from Isabella.

"If you don't, I'll follow you wherever you get into," Laura smiled, making Isabella smile widely. "But you're going to get in Issi. I believe in you."

"You're such a sap," Parker laughed, Laura glaring back.

Isabella sighed and slowly ran her finger between the glue and paper, ripping open the envelope. She pulled out the letter with just as much apprehension, drawing out the time she took to open it. When her eyes fell on the word 'accepted', she looked up at Laura.

"I got in!" She yelled, as she sprung from the coffee table and leapt into Laura's lap.

"I told you, you would you goof," Laura laughed, squeezing Isabella tightly. She didn't tell her she had been holding her breath ever since they had arrived at Cate's or that she had struggled to sleep for weeks worrying about it. Everything had worked out, so Isabella need know none of that.

"We're going to New York," Isabella smiled adoringly down at Laura, her arms wrapped tightly around her neck.

"We're going to New York," Laura agreed.

"Uh hello," Parker interrupted, pointing at herself and Cate. "We're going to New York," she emphasised, making sure Laura and Isabella realised it wasn't purely the two of them.

"Oh man, we're going to be living with these love birds," Cate frowned, looking like she was rethinking her decision to move to New York altogether.

"Oh shut up," Isabella rolled her eyes. "It's going to be fun."

16

Chapter 16

Laura stood out on the balcony, drinking in the cold night air and listening to the sounds of music humming through the buildings. She pulled her coat tighter around her, her breath appearing like puffs of cloud in the early morning air. Parker, Cate, Kevin, Kyle and Isabella were all asleep inside. They had enjoyed their usual New Year's Eve routine of board games and wine. Only this year they had the extra addition of Isabella. It still felt very surreal to Laura, she could hardly sleep.

Rachel had called her a little while ago to wish her a Happy New Year. She was spending the holiday with her family in California. Her stomach swirled with anxiety often now when Rachel's name flashed on her phone, she felt conflicted when it came to her girlfriend. Rachel made her feel confident and loved, but they also valued different things in life and Laura often felt the ME didn't quite understand her. Then there was the resurgence in feelings she had when she was around Isabella, they rattled her with guilt.

She pulled out her phone and scrolled through her speed dial, finding her brother's number at the bottom. The phone began ringing as she heard the door behind her click open. She hung up and tucked the phone away in her pocket, squinting through the darkness at the figure approaching.

"Morning." The familiar raspy voice caused butterflies to stir in her stomach.

"Morning," Laura smiled as Isabella sidled up beside her, rubbing her hands together to try and create some warmth. Her hair was poking out every which way, her eyes had dark shadows beneath them. Laura couldn't help but think how adorable she looked in her flannelette pyjamas and puffy black coat.

"What are you doing up?" Laura asked surprised. They had all only gone to bed a few hours earlier, she wasn't expecting anyone to be up until mid-morning.

"Nightmares," Isabella shrugged, Laura nodding. Her phone buzzed in her hand.

Ellie (3.00am): HAPPY NEW YEAR LAUR!!! Love ya xx

Laura pulled a face, it was a mix between a frown and a smirk. Scrolling down Ellie had attached a photo of herself wearing a 'Happy New Year' crown and chugging a glass of champagne as fireworks went off in the background.

"Everything alright?"

"Yeah it's just Ellie wishing me a Happy New Year," Laura shook her head smirking. "I haven't seen this Ellie in a long time, it's like I've got my little sister back again. Definitely a much rowdier, more rambunctious version, but she's there," Laura smiled affectionately as she tucked her phone back away.

"I'm happy for you," Isabella smiled back at her, Laura staring deeply into her eyes.

"I know I have you to thank for that. Ellie told me about the court ruling and all the meetings you went to with her and Martin. After everything she said about you..." Laura shook her head in disbelief. "That's, that's really amazing of you Issi. Thank you."

Isabella shrugged and looked out over the city. "Honestly it was nothing. You would do the same for me." A look of recognition crossed Isabella's face. "Actually, you already have...only on a ten times larger scale."

Laura picked up on the inference and shook her head smiling. She turned away from Isabella to look out towards Times Square, drinking in the stunning views around them. The tension and anguish that was bottled up inside her only moments ago, completely dissipating.

"Ten years ago I never would have dreamt we'd end up here." Laura said, still not quite believing it.

Isabella sighed and turned to study Laura's side profile as she watched the city moving around them. "Ten years ago all I dreamt for was a moment like this...with you," Isabella almost whispered it, her warm breath tickling Laura's neck as she moved in close. Laura turned to face her, her eyebrows raised slightly as the familiar chocolate eyes sparkled up at her. She saw the image of the girl she had loved and the woman now standing before her.

"Laura, I..."

Laura's phone vibrated again in her pocket, Alex's name lighting up the screen. Isabella grabbed the phone out of her hand and tucked it into the pocket of her coat.

"What are you doing?"

"No more interruptions," Isabella shook her head. "I can't take this anymore."

Laura raised her eyebrows and turned her body towards Isabella, letting her know she had her full attention. Isabella's teeth were chattering as she tried to gather her thoughts. She took a deep breath and looked up into Laura's emerald eyes, grabbing a hold of her hands.

"I love you Laura. I've loved you for over a decade and I should've told you that back then. I was just so scared of my feelings I ran away from them. But I'm not now, I know what I want and that's you. For the past ten years it's you I have thought about before I go to sleep and it's your eyes I see when I wake up."

* * *

It had been a few weeks now since the accident and Laura had barely seen Isabella. She had called and called her, but Isabella kept dodging her calls. She had even turned up to Isabella's house a few times, but no one ever answered the door when she did. Attendance wasn't mandatory in the last few weeks of school, so Isabella had barely shown up.

After they received their diplomas, Isabella had quickly retreated towards the carpark before Laura could catch up with her. It wasn't only Laura she had been avoiding, but Parker and Cate as well.

"Issi!" Laura yelled as she chased after her, Isabella only increasing her pace. Isabella reached her car, but not before Laura caught up to her, both girls puffing and holding onto their caps. Laura's fingers closed around Isabella's wrist and she pulled her around, her heart pounding. Isabella looked beautiful as always, her hair out in long waves, a pair of gold hoop earrings just visible.

"Hey," Laura's tone was soft as she looked into the chocolate eyes. Laura was fighting the tears. Her eyes were almost permanently glassy and red these past weeks. Not only was she grieving, she was hurt, she couldn't understand why Isabella wasn't there for her. "What's going on? Why are you avoiding me?"

Isabella shrugged nervously, "I'm not."

Fury simmered away in Laura's chest as Isabella lied to her, the brunette purposefully avoiding her eyes. Something was obviously going on and she couldn't understand why Isabella wasn't confiding in her. Isabella was the most caring and comforting person Laura knew and after everything that had happened, they both needed each other more than ever. The fact that Isabella was lying to her on top of everything made her blood boil.

"Yes, you are," Laura spat, her pain and sadness flowing out of her as a rage. Isabella continued looking at the bitumen. Laura sighed, her breath rattling in her throat as she tried to contain her emotions.

"I needed you. Everything's a mess. You just left all of us." A tear ran down Laura's cheek, her voice growing more and more weary. "I still need you." She whispered again, her voice breaking. She could see Isabella's hands shaking.

"I'm sorry. I...I can't be there for you anymore Laura." Isabella's voice came out robotic, but firm.

"Why?" Laura's lips trembled.

"This thing between us, whatever it is. It's not normal Laura. It's got to stop."

Laura's jaw dropped, she had struggled with her sexuality, particularly con-sidering their upbringing, but she never felt that from Isabella. She had noticed in the last few weeks that whenever she had seen Isabella, Mitch wasn't too far behind. Something had clearly changed; she just didn't know why.

"I've been offered a scholarship to Berkley and I've accepted it. It's time to move on Laura." Isabella's voice wavered slightly. Laura grabbed her chin and

forced her to stare into her green eyes.

"I love you Isabella." *Laura pleaded, admitting for the first time just how much Isabella meant to her. She was surprised when the words didn't elicit any emotion from Isabella. Her stare remained cold.* "I don't know what's going on, but whatever it is I know we can get through it together. This is just a rough patch," *Laura tried to reassure her, her eyes becoming more and more glassy as Isabella remained seemingly unfazed.* "I can't let go. I'll come with you to Berkley," *she was pleading with Isabella, grabbing a hold of one of her slender hands.*

Isabella took a deep breath, glancing at the ground for a moment before she met Laura's gaze once more.

"I don't love you Laura. I can't love you."

Laura felt stabbing pains in her chest, her mind racing as she turned over all of their interactions in her head, searching for the possibility that Isabella never felt the same way.

"Mitch has asked me to marry him and I said yes. He's coming with me to Berkley." *Laura dropped Isabella's hand, her jaw trembled as she tried stifling a sob.*

"Hey babe," *Mitch approached Isabella from behind Laura and she brushed the tears from her cheeks.*

"Oh, hey Laura," *Mitch smiled warmly. Laura looked at the floor and didn't say anything.* "Did Isabella tell you about Berkley? We're so excited. We fly out tonight. I couldn't wait any longer, everything's going to be perfect." *He kissed Isabella's head and waved at Laura before getting into the driver's side of the car. Laura looked up as she noticed Isabella taking a step backwards towards the car, her brain was telling her to let Isabella go, but her heart refused.*

"Issi..." *she pleaded as tears cascaded down her cheeks, her fingers reaching out for Isabella's wrist. Isabella just took another step back and shook her head.*

"Bye Laura."

Isabella climbed into the passenger's seat; Laura watched as they drove out of the parking lot. A pair of beautiful brown eyes staring at her in the side mirror as they disappeared. Tears streamed relentlessly down her cheeks and she wasn't sure if they would ever stop.

* * *

Laura sucked in a sharp breath as she tried to let go of the memories from the last time she had seen Isabella, ten years earlier. That day had changed her whole world for the second time in just a few weeks and she hadn't been the same since. Isabella's confession simultaneously made her heart soar and stiffen at the same time. After all these years she was overjoyed to hear those three words finally leaving her mouth, but after everything they had been through, she wasn't sure she could believe her.

Isabella paused for a moment, gathering her thoughts, "When I saw you again that first day in the precinct, my heart leapt in my chest. I was so enchanted once again by your presence and those damn tantalising green eyes of yours, that my breath caught in my throat." Laura's heart was racing as she listened to every word she had ever dreamt of hearing.

"It made me realise that even after ten years, no one had the ability to send my heart into a complete tail spin quite like you do. As soon as we locked eyes I knew that nothing had changed for me. It was like I was seventeen again." Laura smiled, similar feelings having coursed through her body that day too.

"I don't ever want to lose you again and I promise I will prove to you that things will be different this time." Isabella stepped forward and secured Laura's hands within her own. "I love you Laur. I've always loved you. I'm sorry it's taken me so long to tell you."

Laura stared back into Isabella's chocolate eyes, her mind ticking over with a million different thoughts. She was stiff, frozen to the spot. Isabella was looking at her concerned, her eyes darting back and forth between Laura's clearly trying to gauge her reaction. After a few more seconds of uncomfortable silence, Isabella finally let go of her hands defeated.

"I'm sorry. It was selfish of me—"

Laura stepped forward, cutting Isabella off as she grabbed a hold of her neck, pulling her in to a deep kiss. Their lips locked in perfect unity an electricity pulsating through Laura's body, all the way to her finger tips. A tear slipped down her cheek as she held on tightly, unwilling this time to let

Isabella go.

Laura probed at Isabella's bottom lip with her tongue, she opened her lips to allow Laura to deepen the kiss. This kiss wasn't rough or desperate, but slow and deliberate, Laura was taking her time to become fully re-acquainted with the kiss. Both of her hands stayed put in Isabella's hair, as Isabella clung to her hips tightly.

When Laura finally detached their lips and pulled back, attempting to catch her breath, her eyes were still fixed on the sparkling chocolate eyes. She couldn't tear her gaze away, certain she was in a state of Déjà vu, the woman before her transforming into the girl she had known. Her heart concurrently leapt and wrenched all at once, caught in a state of elation and grief and unable to rectify the correct emotion.

"Laura, are you ok?" Isabella asked concerned. Laura didn't answer her. After a few moments, she stepped forward, running her thumbs across Isabella's cheeks.

"What are you doing?" Isabella whispered, Laura merely inches from her face.

"Checking that you're real," Laura answered, continuing to stare penetratingly into Isabella's eyes.

"Why wouldn't I be real?"

"Because I've heard this all before from a different girl," Laura answered cryptically. Isabella's eyes dropped to the floor in response. "Oh," her voice cracked.

"The girl is seventeen, she has the same chocolate brown eyes and perfect smile, only she's totally carefree. When I approach her at graduation she doesn't run, she takes me in her arms and tells me she loves me. She agrees to come to New York with me and start a life together." Tears silently streamed down Isabella's cheeks, Laura's tone full of melancholy. "I don't want to wake up and realise none of this was real."

"I can't go back in time and change what happened," Isabella replied sorrowfully, placing her hands on top of Laura's as they caressed her tear-stained cheeks. "But I promise you Laura, if you let me, this time around I'm holding on to your heart and I'm never letting go."

Laura sighed deeply and looked back up into Isabella's eyes, trying to decide whether or not she was ready to open herself up to the potential heartbreak all over again. She knew full well that there was only one person that could ever hold her heart, because that one person had taken it from her a long time ago and she had never gotten it back.

"Promise?" Laura's voice came out soft and vulnerable, a sweet smile appearing on Isabella's face.

"Pinky promise."

Laura stepped closer once again and pulled Isabella into a deep and slow kiss, savouring the way her lips connected perfectly with her own. If it were even possible this kiss was far better than Laura ever remembered it to be or ever dreamt of it being. Laura removed her lips and planted three sweet kisses on Isabella's cheeks and one on her cold red nose.

"So, what do we do now?" Isabella asked tentatively.

"We start again. We put everything in the past behind us and we move forward."

"That sounds amazing," Isabella smiled briefly and then frowned. "Before we do, I kind of wanted to talk to you about something..." Isabella trailed off nervously.

"Can it wait?" Laura asked, looking down into the sparkling chocolate eyes. "I want to enjoy this moment for a minute." Isabella smiled as Laura pulled her in close so that her back was against Laura's chest, her arms wrapped around Isabella's body. The two of them looked out on the colourful lights of the city, the only noise present in Laura's ears was the strong hum of her heartbeat and Isabella's familiar steady breath.

Isabella sighed contentedly as she slumped back further into Laura's body, "Yeah, it can wait."

Laura pulled Isabella over toward the lounge, her body resting on top of Laura's as they gazed up at the stars. Laura leant her nose against Isabella's hair as she drank in the moment.

"Ah, I love your smell." Laura nuzzled her face into Isabella's neck and took a deep breath.

"My smell?" Isabella laughed, turning to look at Laura.

"Yeah, your perfume. It's the same daisy perfume you wore to the junior prom that night we had our first kiss."

"That's still one of the best nights of my entire life," Isabella confessed.

"I can't believe Savannah saw us kissing," Laura laughed lightly, glossing over Isabella's confession. Her heart was still struggling to take in the gravity of Isabella's feelings for her. "I nearly died when she admitted that, that day at the coffee house."

Isabella laughed. "You did look like a deer in headlights when she brought it up."

"I was just shocked. I didn't think Savannah would know about us," Laura admitted.

"Why not?" Isabella asked, turning around on the lounge chair to look at Laura. She shifted uncomfortably in her seat before meeting Isabella's eyes.

"I didn't really think I mattered to you," Laura shrugged.

"You do, more than anyone ever has. Savannah hasn't stopped hearing about you for ten years."

"I'm sure she loved that," Laura joked, again ignoring the weight of Isabella's words.

"She did actually. She loves you too, you're family."

"I like that," Laura smiled. The sun slowly beginning to rise above the buildings around them.

"The sun's rising," Isabella commented, as she looked up at dawning day. "What do we do now?"

"Well, I have some things to sort out," Laura sighed, thinking about her girlfriend sleeping soundly in a house in California. She felt insanely guilty that it had come to this. She had never wanted to hurt her and she never would have. But this was Isabella, the girl who had stolen her heart years ago. "I need to talk to Rachel before anything else."

Isabella nodded her head sadly, "Ok."

"I'll see you at the precinct later today though?" Laura asked, Isabella nodding her head, not wanting this moment to end. "I don't want you to go."

"I don't want to go." Isabella climbed up off the lounge chair and held her hand out to Laura, pulling her up as well.

"I'll see you soon ok," Laura reassured her.

"See you soon," Isabella smiled as Laura pulled her in for one last hug.

* * *

A nervous excitement filled her chest as she thought about seeing Isabella again in under an hour. She knew what had happened between them early this morning couldn't happen again until after she told Rachel. She felt guilty for being swept up in the moment and kissing Isabella, but she couldn't help it. Ten years of pining had built up to the point where her will power was non-existent. As soon as Isabella had confessed that she loved her, all logic went out the window.

She was desperate to talk to someone about what had happened the night before, she thought about calling Parker, but she didn't want her friends to know before she had spoken to Rachel. She knew that if she told Parker there was no way her friend would keep it to herself and her close friendship with Rachel made the situation all the more awkward.

She reached for her phone to check the time and saw the message from Alex. Before she could overthink it, she was dialling his number, the phone ringing out before it eventually went to voicemail.

"Yo this is Alex Carlsson! Leave me a message after the beep and I'll definitely, probably, actually it's not likely but I might get back to you." His lame message tone made her smile everytime.

"Happy New Year little brother. I swear time is going by at an alarming rate. No one ever tells you when you're a kid about that. One day you're eighteen and the next you're twenty eight. When did I get this old?" Laura laughed. "So...I need to tell you something. I know I told you about what happened between me and Issi in Atlantic City, and how I thought she was getting swept up in the obvious chemistry between us. But things escalated last night. Alex..." Laura hesitated.

"She, she told me she loved me. Ten years I've been waiting for her to say it back and she did." Laura shook her head as she held the phone to her ear, not quite believing the gravity of that moment herself. "I know we need to talk things through, this whole thing isn't easy. She broke my heart once and I just can't forget that. But I couldn't stop myself Alex, I kissed her."

"I don't know if I should be feeling this way after all this time and after everything that happened. I might be completely naive. But I know I never really stopped loving her. And if it's possible, I think I love this version of her even more now. I might be taking the biggest risk of my life and setting myself up for complete heartbreak, but I have to take the chance Alex. I've been missing a huge part of me all of these years and now there's this feeling in my chest that's been gone since the accident. She brought that back."

"I love her Alex and I've decided I'm going to give us another chance. I wanted you to be the first to know."

* * *

"She completely stole my idea for the debate and claimed it as her own in front of the entire class. I swear Nancy Fanning is the biggest cun—"

"Ellie!" Alex and Laura both yelled at once form the front seat, Alex turned around to glare at his sister, as Laura followed suit through the rear-view mirror.

"Don't use that word Ellie, it's disgusting and terrible," Laura scolded her.

"It's just a word..." Ellie defended shyly.

"No, it's not Ellie. It's trashy. You're no better than Nancy when you say stuff like that. No one will respect you if you talk like that," Alex reprimanded, Laura smiling from the front seat at her brother's maturity, he had grown up so much.

"Ok, I'm sorry," Ellie frowned, playing with her dress, clearly embarrassed to have been scolded by both her siblings.

"It's fine Ells. We're just looking out for you," Laura reassured her.

"I'll never say it again, I promise!" The resoluteness of Ellie's tone made Laura and Alex laugh as they pulled up out the front of her school.

"Good," Alex smiled warmly, ruffling his younger sister's hair playfully. She simply rolled her eyes at him and smoothed it back down.

"Mario Kart later?" Ellie asked excitedly.

"Sure," Alex smiled, Ellie reciprocating warmly as she hugged Laura and then

Alex over their seats.

"See you Ellie!" Laura shouted out the window, her sister turning at the gate to wave to her and Alex once more before disappearing into the crowd.

"When did you become all mature?" Laura asked, disguising her admiration for her brother with her teasing tone.

"Probably when I realised our parents weren't, so someone needed to step up," Alex smirked.

"Can't argue with that."

"How's mission 411 'Isabella's fake boyfriend' working out for you?"

"It's ok, I mean Mum and Dad have relaxed a little now that they think Mitch and Isabella are dating. But it's still hard to actually get any alone time with her. God, I am counting down the days to New York!"

"Well, I for one am very happy I won't be sharing a bedroom wall with you and Isabella in New York," Alex laughed, causing Laura to take a hand off the wheel for a second to smack him.

"HA, HA!"

"In the meantime though, you should invite her over this afternoon. Mum and Dad are working so you'll have the house to yourself."

"Don't you need a ride from baseball training?" Laura asked, astounded by her brother's generosity.

"It's all good, I can walk home. It's not far."

"I swear you're like the teenage brother anomaly," Laura laughed. "Like seriously, aside from the dirty jokes and insinuations, no guys our age are as cool as you."

"Well of course you've written off guys our age," Alex teased. "You're gay."

"I can revoke the compliment..." Laura threatened.

"You wouldn't. You're too nice. You're the teenage sister anomaly," Alex smiled. "But if you tell anyone I said that, I'll have to kill you."

Laura laughed. "Secret's safe with me, wouldn't want to ruin your street cred," she bantered back. "But seriously, thanks. You've made being me so much easier with our parents and school..." Laura trailed off. "But if you tell anyone I said that, I'll have to kill you."

Alex just laughed as they pulled into their school's carpark. "No biggie. The ignorance in this place astounds me, but New York will be different. No one will even bat an eyelid when you and Isabella make out in public."

"I'm nervous, it's going to be completely different in New York. We're going to have all these adult responsibilities and we'll be living together. I just don't want to ruin it," Laura sighed.

"You won't," Alex reassured her.

"How do you know?"

"You and Isabella are end game. No matter what happens, you'll get through it."

"Thanks for the vote of confidence, I hope you're right" Laura laughed, masking how touched she felt by her brother's confidence.

"I am right. The two of you love each other. Neither of you are stupid enough to let that go."

"I don't know that she loves me, we haven't said that yet," Laura shrugged, doubting Alex's absolute faith.

"She does, it's clear as day. So just follow your goddamn heart and hurry up and tell her."

"Ok," Laura nodded, a small smile on her lips. "And you'll be fine here with Mum and Dad, and Ellie once we're gone?"

Alex just nodded. "And if I'm not, my super smart, soon to be Doctor of a sister will fly me out to visit her."

"You better visit!"

"It's a done deal, couple of weeks and I'll get Laura withdrawals..." Laura smiled endearingly at her little brother. "You know me, I can't go two weeks without some sort of dirty Isabella joke," Alex winked as he got out of the car.

Laura leant out the window and yelled after him. "Loser!"

Alex just spun around and ran backwards a few steps as he gave his sister a devilish smile and waved goodbye as he sped off to his classes.

That afternoon Isabella was laying on top of Laura on the living room couch at the Carlsson house. Isabella's body firmly pressed against Laura's so not an inch of their skin wasn't touching. Both of them had a free period on Thursday afternoons so they had snuck back to Laura's place before Alex came home from baseball training.

Laura bent her chin down, searching for Isabella's perfect lips. They crashed into Laura's forcefully. Laura's heart was beating erratically as her hands trailed up and down Isabella's back. Laura broke off the kiss and began kissing Isabella's neck, the brunette giggling.

"What?" Laura smiled, their lips only a fraction apart.

"You know it makes me crazy when you do that." Isabella bit her lip, avoiding Laura's gaze.

"Oh really?" Isabella blushed and tried kissing Laura, but she pulled back. "You just can't handle how irresistible I am."

Laura stuck out her tongue and pulled an ugly face, Isabella bursting into laughter. Laura pulled her back in again and desperately kissed her lips, stifling her laughter. Laura's phone began ringing on the coffee table and she groaned in frustration.

"Don't answer it," Isabella urged, kissing Laura's neck.

Laura thought about getting up, but she couldn't when Isabella started sucking on her neck. It felt like electricity was being funnelled through her veins. The phone stopped buzzing for a second and then immediately began ringing again. This time Laura groaned and pushed Isabella off her as she reached for the phone.

Her mum's number flashing on the screen, the time reading 5.30pm. "Shit." She normally would've been to pick up Alex at practice an hour ago. She was sure her mother had somehow found out and was ringing to scold her seeing as he still wasn't home.

"Mum, I'm sorry—" Laura abruptly stopped speaking, Isabella watching her full of concern. Laura's face dropped, her skin turning ghostly pale as she listened to her mother's frantic voice. Tears began streaming from her eyes.

"Laura?" Isabella asked, grabbing a hold of Laura's shoulder. The phone dropped out of Laura's hand and she ran towards the bathroom. Isabella didn't hesitate and immediately ran after her. Laura grabbed the toilet lid and threw it open before she doubled over and began throwing up inside. Isabella ran to her side and pulled her hair out of her face. Laura wiped her mouth with some toilet paper as more tears continued to stream down her face.

"What happened?"

"Alex is dead," she choked.

* * *

Laura hung up the phone after bearing her soul, getting out all the emotions she was holding onto for so long and finally admitting what she was feeling. As she put the phone down the screen lit up with a message from Alex. Laura opened the text.

Alex (7.31am): Voicemail Full.

She sighed and deleted the message. The familiar pain in her chest still just as prominent as it had been ten years ago on the day her brother had died. No matter what people told her, the grief never got easier, she had just learnt how to manage it better. Even though Alex wasn't able to answer her when she spoke to him, she felt that he was listening to every word. As she looked out her window, the city moving around her, she felt the morning sunlight warm her face. She closed her eyes and saw her brother's blue eyes and bright smile as he gave her a reassuring nod. A nod that said 'follow your goddamn heart'.

17

Chapter 17

"Morning," Isabella smiled shyly as she held up Laura's coffee. Laura smiled warmly in response and took the coffee from her, their fingers brushing slightly in the exchange. She could feel the electricity travelling between them. As she took a sip, her piercing eyes refused to leave Isabella's for one second.

"Morning again," Laura's raspy voice replied, the tension that was rolling between them was palpable.

"Good morning Detectives," the Captain's deep voice echoed as he stepped out of his office and into the hall. "Any updates from Reynolds and Foster yet?"

"No Sir," Laura answered, standing up straighter to meet their superior. "They should have arrived at the address at 0900 hours."

"If they get any leads, I want the two of you to follow up on it immediately. The Mayor's already called me again this morning asking about the case."

"Yes sir."

"Excellent. Let me know as soon as there is an update."

"Will do Sir," Isabella answered as the Captain nodded and retreated back into his office.

"I guess this wasn't the best day to come to work with no sleep," Laura chuckled to try and break the tension. Isabella smiled lightly, but as Laura looked up, she sensed her nerves. Though it wasn't the place to address personal issues, she knew neither of them would be able to concentrate today if she didn't. By the sounds of it, they would need to be focused. "It was definitely worth it though," Laura added, eliciting a wide grin from Isabella.

"It was," she agreed, her cheeks blushing slightly. "How did things go this morning?"

"They didn't," Laura answered, running a hand through her hair.

"Oh," Isabella said, looking dismayed.

"I'm going to talk to her," Laura tried to reassure her. "She doesn't fly in to New York until later today. I'm going to tell her this afternoon. I just want to get it right..." Laura sighed gloomily. "I never wanted to hurt her, I care about her."

"It's ok. I understand wanting to be delicate with it. I'll wait for as long as you need," Isabella smiled genuinely, her eyes had that irresistible sparkle that made Laura go weak in the knees.

"There it is," Laura smiled warmly.

"What?"

"That massive heart of yours you try to hide away."

Isabella blushed as her mouth curved up at the sides. "God you're making this hard," she shook her head as her fingers trailed lovingly up and down Laura's arm, she took a furtive glance towards the Captain's door to make sure he wasn't looking.

"What?" Laura asked.

"You're making it hard for me not to kiss you right now."

Laura knew she shouldn't, not until she talked to Rachel, but after ten long years of pining after the woman, her willpower was gone. She stood up suddenly, causing Isabella to crinkle her eyebrows as she grabbed her hand and dragged her to the break room. Being New Year's Day, the precinct was quieter than usual, giving Laura the confidence to be bold. Laura closed the blinds and pushed Isabella up against the wall, her lips so close to Isabella's she could feel her breath tickling the skin.

The door swung open and the pair of them jolted apart, their eyes darting towards the door. Laura was surprised, albeit somewhat relieved to see Cate standing in the doorway open mouthed, practically gaping at the pair of them. When her jaw finally closed, she wore a stupid grin on her face as her eyes flittered in between the two of them.

"Either the elevator's a time machine or...this just became the best New Years I've had in a long time." Laura and Isabella both laughed, their cheeks turning pink.

"Don't mind me," Cate waved her hands at them as she perched herself on the break room bench, placing Laura's badge down. "Do carry on."

Laura shook her head, a guilty smile on her lips as she reached for her badge. "Thanks Cate, didn't even realise I'd left that on the bench."

Cate waved her off and looked towards Isabella. "I'm glad you took my advice and finally told her." Isabella went ghostly white as the words left her mouth.

Laura looked towards Isabella confused, "Told me what?"

Isabella looked frightened, her eyes turning glassy. Cate's face dropped as she realised what she had done.

"It's ok, you can talk to me," Laura urged, her voice soft and affectionate. Isabella shook her head in response.

"It's about the accident."

* * *

"We have all come here today to say goodbye to our son and our brother Alexander Carlsson. But today isn't just for us to gather in our grief, but to celebrate the life of a marvellous young man. While Alexander is no longer here with us, we can take comfort in the fact that he is with our eternal father in heaven and we will see each other again in our rest."

A sob escaped Laura's lips, her body shaking furiously as she tried to stop the onslaught of grief that was threatening to escape her throat. Her father was cradling her mother in his arms as she sobbed and cried. In between them Ellie sat, tears streaming down her face as she blew her nose into her handkerchief. Laura had tried to take Ellie's hand as they had walked into the church, but she had refused, her parents having poisoned Ellie against her.

Just a week before, Alex' body had been discovered by the side of the road, not far from the baseball field. It was clear he had been hit by a car whilst he was walking home as there were tyre marks in the dirt surrounding his body and his injuries were visibly extensive. The only comfort that Laura took from it all, was the coroner's pronouncement that he had died on impact and therefore hadn't suffered. The driver had yet to be found and the police still had no leads. How someone could hit a child and drive away as if nothing had happened was beyond Laura. She couldn't comprehend that kind of evil, it made her blood boil.

Her family had blamed her for Alex's death almost immediately. Her parents screamed and yelled at her, telling her that her brother would still be here if she had have picked him up from the field like she was supposed to, instead of spending time with Isabella. They had called her a dyke, a whore, an abomination, even going as far as referring to her as the devil incarnate for her sinful behaviour. But Laura could take the abuse, in fact she welcomed it. The combination of grief and guilt she felt over Alex's death was so overpowering that she felt she deserved her parents' abuse. She couldn't help but also blame herself.

Laura felt more alone than ever as she sat on the cold hard bench alongside her fractured family. Knowing full well that they could never be whole again without her brother, he had been the chain-link holding them all together. Now that he was gone, she would be all alone. She stared up at the large bouquets of white lilies positioned over Alex's coffin. They were both beautiful and devastating.

"I would now like to invite Alexander's sister Laura to deliver the eulogy," the Pastor announced, motioning to Laura.

She stood up mechanically and walked towards the lectern, her hands fumbling with the piece of paper that held her speech. Her parents had agreed that their Pastor would deliver the eulogy, but Laura refused. Begging and begging for them to allow her to deliver it, until they finally agreed, just wanting to be rid of their daughter's presence. In the past week her parents had barely even looked at her and she was sure after graduation, when she moved to New York, that she wouldn't hear from them.

As she stepped onto the stage she walked over to Alex's closed casket and placed a gentle kiss on the wood above where his head would be. The smell of the lilies was overpowering, she knew it was a scent she would never again be able to stomach. Tears streamed down her face as she took a deep breath and turned back towards their friends and family.

She looked down at her speech as her tears splashed onto the paper, causing the ink to run. "A-Alex," Laura choked out, before wiping her eyes rapidly, trying to maintain her composure. "Al-ex w-was," she tried again, but her sobs caught in her throat and stopped her from continuing.

As she took a deep breath, preparing herself for another attempt, she felt a comforting hand entwine with her own as someone joined her on the stage. She didn't need to turn around to know who it was, but she still glanced over her shoulder to give Isabella a grateful smile, the girl's sparkling eyes all the comfort she needed in that moment.

"Alex wasn't just my brother, he was my confidant, my adversary, my team mate, my partner in crime and most of all my best friend. Alex was wise beyond his years and despite being younger than me, it was always me who went to him for advice. He always knew just what to say to comfort me. Alex was like that with everyone, he was an open book and would happily talk to anyone about anything..."

Laura took a deep breath before she concluded her speech, her final earthly farewell to the one person that had always provided her with unconditional love, who believed in her when no one else did and wished for her happiness above his own. She wiped away some more tears as she prepared herself for her goodbye, a goodbye she would never be ready for.

"So my darling baby brother Alex — wherever you may journey, our hands may have let you go, but our hearts never will. Fly high my angel."

As Laura said the last words of her eulogy, the music faded in and photos and videos of Alex throughout his life began playing on the screen behind her.

"Let's dance in style, let's dance for a while," the music played heartbreakingly from the speakers.

Even though she wasn't facing the screen, she could see every picture and every video playing in her head. She had spent hours and hours trying to find the perfect imagery to sum up Alex, to one of their favourite songs. Unlike so many other people she knew, even herself, Alex had never hidden himself away, he was always himself.

"Let us die young or let us live forever..."

Three-year-old Alex's laughter erupted on the screen behind them and Laura's body began shaking as she silently sobbed. Isabella pulled her away from the lectern and into her arms. Holding her as tightly as she possibly could.

"Laaaauuuurrrraaaaa, stop it!" Alex's high-pitched baby voice giggled behind them as she tickled her baby brother mercilessly.

As Laura's sobs increased Isabella whispered into her ear, "I've got you Laura, I won't let go."

"Forever young, I want to be forever young, do you really want to live forever, forever and ever..."

* * *

Cate left once Isabella began her story, offering the women a sympathetic glance as she slipped out the door. Laura couldn't quite fathom the words leaving Isabella's mouth, she felt her body shutting down around her. The grief felt just as raw as it had done ten years ago. Tears glistened in her eyes but she refused to let them fall. She took another step back from Isabella, her hands balled into fists and her jaw rigid. Isabella tried to step forward, but Laura held out a hand.

"Don't come near me." Her voice had taken on a robotic quality.

"Please just let me explain everything," Isabella pleaded desperately.

"I don't want to hear anymore. You lied to me," Laura spat, the fury in her words obvious now as she became more lucid. "You lied to me about the most important thing in my life."

"I was worried that if I told you the truth you could never look at me the same way again," Isabella pleaded, her words laced with desperation.

"You were right. I could never look at you that way again."

* * *

Isabella felt completely and utterly drained as she turned the door handle to enter her house. She hadn't wanted to leave Laura's side, but she assured her she would be fine and Isabella promised to call her later that night so that they could fall asleep talking to one another. The funeral had been equally beautiful and heart-breaking, Laura's final tribute to Alex had been perfect. She could still see his infectious smile like it was glazed into her eyes.

"Bella!" Savannah squealed as she ran down the stairs and threw herself into Isabella's arms. She lifted her up and held onto Savanah for dear life, never appreciating her little sister more than she did in that moment. "You're wet Bella," Savannah laughed as she pulled away and looked up at her sister.

"It's raining outside," Isabella answered her sister softly, Savannah turned her head slightly and looked at Isabella. "Why are you sad?"

"I just said goodbye to our friend Alex," Isabella answered her, lightly stroking her sister's hair.

"Where did he go?" Savannah asked, Isabella having chosen not to tell her sister what had happened before now.

"He went to heaven Savannah, we're not going to see him again," Isabella whispered tenderly, deciding it was time to tell her the truth.

"Like Mum?" Savannah frowned, looking down at the floor. Isabella had decided against taking Savannah to the funeral. After her mother's funeral a few years ago, she wanted to protect her little sister from the overwhelming sadness. She didn't want to darken the already bleak world her sister was being forced to grow up in.

"Yeah like Mum."

"Do you think they'll find each other up there?" Savannah asked, forcing a small smile from Isabella.

"I'm sure they will."

"Can we watch Tarzan?" Savannah asked, again eliciting another small smile from Isabella at her abrupt change of conversation.

"Sure, let me put my umbrella away and I'll meet you in the living room."

Savannah smiled happily and ran off towards the living room to set up the DVD.

Isabella entered the dark garage and walked around to the side of the car to open up her umbrella and let it dry out. As she bent down to place her umbrella on the floor, she noticed the muddy tires of the car peeping out from underneath the car cover. They never normally covered the car. An ominous curiosity swept over her and she stepped towards it, slowly pulling at the grey cloth.

Her heart broke as she took in the sight before her. The bonnet of the grey sedan was completely crumpled, the windscreen smashed. Bile rose up in her throat as her eyes fell on the large blood stain in the centre of the smashed windscreen. Looking through the window she saw a half empty bottle of whiskey open in the centre console.

Isabella waited for Savannah to be picked up before she went up to Samuel's room to confront him. The whirlwind of emotions churning through her body were inconceivable. Heartbreak, fury, confusion, betrayal. She just couldn't understand how things could get to this point. Her father was a killer, whether it was intentional or not, the result was the same.

It was dark outside by the time Isabella had finished the conversation with her father. Hours and hours of yelling, screaming and crying had left her completely drained. It had already been an emotional day before she had found the car and now, she was unsure if she would ever be happy again. Anxiety and fear were bubbling in her chest as she left her front porch and headed towards the beach. Dry, muffled sobs escaped her lips as she walked towards the one place she felt at peace.

Her phone vibrated in her pocket and she looked down to see Laura calling her for the third time tonight. She had promised to talk to her later on, to calm her down after the funeral so that she would be able to sleep, but now seeing her name on the screen she just felt guilt and overwhelming sadness. There was no way she could face talking to Laura now. As much as she wanted to be there for her, she knew now that wasn't going to be an option.

As she finally reached the beach, she sat down on the sand dunes and closed her eyes, breathing in the fresh salty air and trying to block everything else from her mind. Letting the soothing sound of the crashing waves wash over her. With each deep breath she managed to slowly calm her racing heart. She wrapped her arms around her body and hugged herself, imagining she was sitting there with someone who loved her unconditionally, who would listen to her heart ache and help her through it.

"Why did you leave us Mum?" Isabella whispered to herself. "Everything's a *mess now. I need you," a sob escaped her lips after that last word. She couldn't help but think none of this would ever have happened if her mother were still here, then Alex would still be here too.*

"Isabella?" A voice asked, pulling her from her thoughts.

She looked up to see a shirtless Mitch standing above her, sweat was dripping down his chest, making his abs shine in the light of the moon. A worried look was etched across his face as he noticed the tears glistening on Isabella's cheeks and her puffy eyes. He dropped to his knees on the sand beside her and pulled her into a tight hug. The moment his arms wrapped around her body she let herself cry, her sobs being muffled against his skin as she tucked her face into his neck.

After a while, once Isabella's sobs had begun to slow down, Mitch pulled away slightly so that he could look into her eyes. "I'm sorry about Alex Isabella, I'm here for you."

Before Isabella could stop herself, the words flew out of her mouth like word vomit, "My father killed him. He killed Alex."

* * *

Laura's heart was hammering in her chest as she tried to process what Isabella had just told her. Once again Isabella had managed to give her whiplash with the contradicting emotions she forced upon her. Ten years ago, she had believed that Isabella had dumped her because she loved Mitch instead. Now she had found out that, that wasn't true at all, that Isabella had loved her all along. Instead, she had lied to her to hide the fact that Samuel had killed her brother. The truth hurt more than the lie.

Laura's phone rang, disturbing her from her tumultuous thoughts. "Carlsson." Laura scribbled down the address Jordan gave her in her notebook, her nerves now escalating again. "On my way," Laura said firmly as she hung up the phone and picked up her badge and keys, stalking towards the elevator. After a moment's hesitation, Isabella grabbed her own badge and ran after her partner, making it inside the lift just before the doors closed.

"Should I call for back up?" Isabella questioned carefully.

"No," Laura curtly replied as they entered the basement and made their way towards the cruiser.

Isabella began to protest "Laura—"

"It's Carlsson," Laura spat back as she rounded on Isabella. "Reynolds and Foster are meeting us there. That's all the back-up we need. Unless you feel you're too incompetent for the task? In that case, I'll go myself."

"No," Isabella spoke through gritted teeth. "I'm fine."

They drove the rest of the way in silence before pulling up in front of a very drab looking apartment building in Midtown. The surrounding street was littered with rubbish and gave off a pungent smell as they stepped outside of the cruiser. As they looked up at the apartment building there were scorch marks covering the third and fourth levels as if someone had thrown a petrol bomb at the building some time ago.

"This place actually makes my apartment look good," Isabella tried to joke, but Laura refused to acknowledge that she had spoken, instead walking straight into the foyer.

As they walked inside a middle-aged man was sitting in a small office at the base of the stairs. He had a box TV set up and was watching an NBA game as he smoked on a self-rolled cigarette. His eyes widened in disbelief as he took in the two attractive and well-dressed women standing in front of him. He dropped his feet from off his desk and poked his head out the window as he gave the Detectives a toothy smile.

"Can I help you ladies?" The man asked with his distinctive Bronx accent. He ran his hand through his greasy hair as he surveyed them, offering them a wink and gold tooth smile. Laura rolled her eyes and huffed. Isabella stepped forward and flipped open her badge, the man's cheesy smile quickly diapering behind a frown.

"Detective Medina, NYPD. Do you know the tenant living in room 401?"

"Know him? Not really. He pays his rent every week and that's all I need to know. Why? He in some sorta trouble?" The man asked curiously, his mouth slightly askew.

"Do you know if he's home?" Laura asked.

The man just shrugged and turned back to the TV, losing interest when he realised they weren't going to tell him anything. "How would I know lady, the Knicks are playing!" He scoffed as Laura headed for the stairs, deciding he wasn't going to be useful.

"Thank you," Isabella said politely as she trotted off after Laura, having to jog up the first few flights of stairs to keep up.

When they reached the fifth floor Laura placed a hand on her holster. She exuded confidence and a certain level of fierceness, but in reality she always got nervous in situations like this. After all of her years of takedowns of some of New York's worst criminals, she felt a sense of invincibility, that no crime or criminal was insurmountable.

Standing in front of door 501, she couldn't help but feel this could finally be it. She might finally be able to place cuffs on the wrists of a ruthless murderer and bring some justice to the families of his victims.

"This the NYPD open up!" Laura yelled, her voice projecting confidently. No answer.

There were no signs or sounds of movement on the other side. Laura pulled a blank white card from her back pocket and slid it in between the lock and the door, jimmying it open as Isabella covered her back, pointing her gun firmly at the door. Laura drew her gun and nodded, signalling to Isabella to take formation and move forward into the apartment.

The hardwood floors had been stripped and varnished recently, the walls had been given a new slick of paint and everything had been meticulously cleaned, the faint smell of bleach still present as they stepped further inside.

The lounge room and attached kitchenette were minimalistic. No items of décor, just clean, bare surfaces. As Laura's eyes scanned the scene, she couldn't help but feel this was the guy they were looking for. The meticulously clean and minimal apartment fit the profile for the Washington Killer to a T. He obviously lived the same way as he murdered, he wasn't a low IQ opportunistic killer, he was analytical.

"This is the NYPD come out with your hands up!" Laura yelled again as they checked around the room, the starkness making any sort of hiding spot extremely difficult.

She moved towards the bedroom door, feeling Isabella close on her heels. The door was slightly ajar, allowing Laura to keep both hands on her gun as she nudged the door open with her foot. Her heart was rattling in her chest just waiting for someone to leap out at her. But as they moved further into the room, they soon realised no one was going to. The apartment was empty.

Both women holstered their guns as they took in the room around them. It was a small bedroom with a single bed, a desk and a neatly kept clothes rack with a couple pairs of shoes. Laura headed straight for the desk, whilst Isabella began going through the clothes rack.

Laura opened the lid of the laptop, but that was as far as she was able to go. The computer was password protected and she was sure if it did in fact belong to the Washington Killer, it wouldn't be easy to crack. She began pulling open the drawers of the desk and rifling through papers and books. Whoever owned the apartment had a lot of books on computer science and hacking.

"His jeans and sneakers look to be a match to the CCTV," Isabella spoke over her shoulder, though Laura didn't acknowledge it as she continued to rifle through the desk. As she reached the bottom drawer, she found what she was looking for. Something that could definitely pin their suspect to the murders. Sitting at the bottom of the drawer, gleaming back up at her were the familiar dirty green bills with the face of the first US president, George Washington, staring back up at her.

She reached down and pulled them out of the drawer as she felt Isabella sidle up behind her. Just like the bills found on their victims, these too had no serial number. She brushed her thumb along the side of the bills, flicking through them to see exact carbon copies. They definitely had their man.

Thud.

The sound of a door thudding in its frame caused Laura's head to snap up. Her heart rate soared in her chest as she realised, they were no longer alone in the apartment. He was here.

His soft footsteps were moving across the freshly varnished floorboards as Laura and Isabella both quietly unholstered their guns. Laura looked at Isabella and held a finger to her lips as she moved to the side of the bedroom door, getting ready to exit. She held her gun closely to her chest, signalling to Isabella to wait for her lead as she listened carefully.

There was another sound mixed in with the footsteps, a sound harder to distinguish. As Laura strained to listen her ears and nose made the connection at the same time. He was putting down an accelerant and they couldn't afford to wait any longer.

Isabella pushed past Laura and flung open the door as Laura's eyes widened in shock. Standing a few metres in front of her was a man dressed all in black, a ski mask pulled over his face. In his hand was a drum full of paint thinner that was now dribbled across the hardwood floors. Isabella pointed her gun directly at his chest.

"NYPD drop the drum and put your hands up!" She yelled as Laura stepped out of the room behind her, her gun also pointed directly at the man's chest. The man stopped pouring and held the drum out from his body, his light eyes penetrating into Isabella's.

"Drop it!"

The man lifted the drum and threw it towards them, the paint thinner gushing out on the floor around them as his hand shot towards his pocket. Laura fired off a warning shot, the bullet coming within a few inches of his head.

"Hands up!" Laura yelled, as she stepped closer, the man finally raising his hands. "Turn around," Laura ordered. He turned slowly so that his back was facing them, his hands still raised above his head. "Take two steps back," she yelled again. He took two slow steps towards her as Laura holstered her gun and removed the handcuffs from her belt.

As she snapped the left handcuff onto his wrist, she noticed a dark bruise and her mind flashed back to her brother's bruised and lifeless body lying on the cold metal table of the morgue. His lifeless blue eyes had stared up at her, all of their depth lost in death. Another face was burned in her brother's eyes as she thought back now. Samuel's face. She wondered what it would feel like to handcuff him, to finally bring him to justice after all the heartache he had caused.

"Laura!"

The killer took advantage of Laura's loss of focus and shoved her to the floor, her hands and body immediately moistened by the strong chemical.

Isabella sprinted after the man as he bolted out the door, slipping on the wooden floors outside as he exited. She took advantage of his blunder as she dove and crash tackled the man to the ground.

As the two of them wrestled on the floor, the man kicked out at Isabella's chest sending her backwards into the opposite wall with a thud. She groaned in pain and grabbed at her ribs. The man scurried to his feet just as Laura ran out of the apartment, her eyes shot first to Isabella seeing the pained expression on her face and then towards the killer. She ran full force down the hallway ready to tackle the killer to the floor.

As Laura dove towards the man, she saw him pull something shiny from his pocket. As her eyes focused in on the object, she recognised the sharp hunting knife that had been used to kill so many innocent victims. He pointed it towards her abdomen as she heard Isabella scream behind her. It was too late for her to pull back, she had too much momentum.

It all happened in a series of flashes, her body collided with the killer as he swung the knife. She felt a fiery pain in her stomach as she crashed to the floor. Isabella fumbled to her knees and crawled frantically towards her. The killer bolted out the fire escape, still brandishing the bloody knife. Isabella couldn't do anything but watch him run away.

Isabella rolled Laura onto her back and saw the blood oozing from her abdomen, quickly soaking her white blouse in vivid red. Laura's eyes were fluttering open and closed as she grimaced in pain, a throaty groan escaping her mouth. The blood was flowing steadily, the colour draining from her face.

"Laura it's going to be ok, just breathe ok. I'm looking after you," Isabella reassured her as she ripped off her coat and pressed it down on Laura's abdomen.

Laura was struggling to remain focused on what was going around her, the throbbing pain in her abdomen had quickly increased to a point where it felt like she was being repeatedly stabbed by a scorching blade. As the seconds passed by the heat began turning cold as more and more blood seeped from the wound. Her eyelids felt heavy as she forced them open to look up into the sparkling chocolate eyes that were glistening with tears.

"Stay with me Laura, keep your eyes open." Laura's eyes fluttered closed again at the sound of her voice, her body relaxing. "Laura! Keep your eyes open!"

Isabella pressed on the wound with one hand as she fumbled to dial 911, yelling the address at the operator and urging them to hurry. Heavy footsteps were ascending the stairs, Isabella instinctively grabbed for her gun, positioning her body in front of Laura's. Laura's eyes fluttered open and she saw Kyle running towards them, his eyes widening in panic as he took in the scene.

"Isabella, what happened?" He yelled as he came running over, causing more tears to spill down Isabella's cheeks.

"He stabbed her," she answered, a soft sob coming out of her mouth.

"Laura, can you hear me? Open your eyes," Kyle ordered, as he knelt down beside her head. Laura's eyelids fluttered slightly.

"Here," Isabella passed Kyle the phone. "Take this and go back downstairs. I need you to flag down the ambulance when it gets close," she ordered.

"Are you sure?" Kyle asked concerned, as Isabella gave him a firm nod.

"Hang in there Laura," Kyle uttered as he stroked Laura's hair. "Help is coming." He turned and sprinted back down the stairs, his heavy footsteps rattling the floor.

"Laura please, I need you to open your eyes."

Laura felt as if she were floating in darkness, her mind and body somehow detached. Everything felt distant as if she was listening to the world around her from deep underwater, the pain was dull now, she could barely feel it. She could only feel the cold clinging to her tightly, pulling her further and further away from the voices. The more she let herself drift into darkness, the less she could feel the pain. It was nice, peaceful.

"Laura, please! Please don't leave me," Isabella cried, Laura's skin becoming colder and colder beneath her fingers.

As she felt her body becoming more and more weightless, the pain nothing more than a dull ache, a voice erupted through the depths. Her ears pricked up at the sound and she began fighting against the darkness, desperate to hear what the voice was saying, it was calling to her, she was sure. She could feel it. The darkness began dissipating around her as the pain crept back and shot through her body in devastating spasms.

"Laura please..." she heard Isabella plead with her, the desperation in the woman's voice shot another stab of pain through her chest. Her eyelids felt heavy, she tried blinking rapidly to open them, desperate to look into those sparkling eyes. "I love you." The darkness was persistent and she felt herself fading.

18

Chapter 18

As the paramedics lifted Laura onto the stretcher, they pulled a grim face at the already blood-soaked coat Isabella had used to try and stop the bleeding.

"It's going to be alright Isabella," Kyle tried to comfort her with a supportive hug, his own face betraying the confidence of his voice. Isabella couldn't reciprocate the hug, nor did she take in what Kyle was saying, she was too busy watching the paramedics work on the woman she loved.

As they began to close the doors of the truck Isabella pushed past Kyle, "No wait! I'm coming." She held her arm out and stopped the paramedic from closing the doors.

"Are you family Ma'am?" The man asked, provoking a deathly stare from Isabella

She opened up her badge and flashed it in the man's face, "I'm a New York City Detective and I said I'm coming," she spoke firmly. The paramedic gave her a nod and opened the door wider for her to enter. She turned and threw Kyle her keys as she stepped up into the truck.

"I'm right behind you," Kyle yelled as he turned and sprinted towards the cruiser.

Isabella's hands were shaking as she sat down inside the truck and grabbed a hold of Laura's hand. Her skin was ice cold. The anxiety that she may never feel warm again, pressed on her heavily. Tears were still streaming down her cheeks as the paramedic added more gauze to Laura's wound, the bandages quickly turning red. She stroked the back of Laura's hand soothingly with her thumb, willing Laura with all her love to be alright, to open her beautiful emerald eyes once more.

A rapid beeping began emanating from one of the machines as the paramedic began moving quickly around the truck. "What's happening?" Isabella asked panicked.

"Her heart rate's dropping," he answered as he picked up the paddles for the defibrillator, awaiting the moment Laura would flatline and he would have to shock her heart back to life.

Isabella squeezed Laura's hand tightly, her eyes widening in horror as she watched the heart rate monitor dropping steadily until she heard the sound she had dreaded since the moment Laura had been stabbed. The cruel beep that signalled the big heart she loved so much had stopped.

"Stay back Ma'am," the paramedic warned her as he started rubbing the paddles together. "You're going to have to let go of her hand."

Isabella reluctantly let go of the cold fingers that just hours ago had returned pressure on her hand, but now were rigid. As soon as the paramedic administered the shock to Laura's heart, Isabella grabbed a hold of her hand again, squeezing as tightly as she could. The man began chest compressions as the truck began to slow.

The doors were pulled open, a handful of nurses and a few trauma surgeons were waiting to take Laura to surgery. Two nurses stepped up into the truck to get the stretcher out as the paramedic continued the chest compressions, Laura's heart beat still remaining flat lined. As they rolled the stretcher inside the emergency doors of the hospital, the nurses began a fast jog towards theatre, Isabella trotting alongside of them. Her eyes were casting desperate glances between the heart rate monitor and Laura's face, begging the universe to save her.

"You'll have to let go now Detective," the nurse spoke gently to Isabella, giving her a sympathetic smile as more tears spilled from the chocolate eyes. "We'll take care of her," she promised, her reassuring words finally allowing Isabella to let go as the stretcher rolled away from her and into theatre. Isabella didn't want to contemplate the idea that this was where it all ended. After all this time, this surely couldn't be it.

* * *

"So, I told him if he wasn't going to tell the police what he had done, then I would have to," Isabella practically whispered as she wiped the tears from her eyes.

"Did he accept that?"

Isabella shook her head and reached for the box of tissues on Martin Davis' desk. It was a large mahogany desk with a sage leather top. His office was what Isabella imagined a lawyer's office to look like, full of leather-bound books and gold trinkets.

"He said if I told anyone and they arrested him that the State would take Savannah and I away. I don't turn eighteen for several more months so legally I'm still a child and we don't have any family in America. He said that foster homes never take siblings, that most of the time they're split up," another sob escaped Isabella's mouth at the thought of losing her sister. Savannah was the only family she had left and losing her was not an option.

"I'm sorry to say he's right," Martin sighed, as Mitch picked up Isabella's hand and gave it a squeeze to comfort her. "Even though your eighteenth birthday isn't that far away, if they arrest him now, they will put you into the system. Paperwork for these sorts of things becomes so backlogged it could be months after your birthday before you were given custody of Savannah. And even then, you will have to prove that you can support her."

"I don't know what to do," Isabella sobbed, her whole body convulsing with the effort.

"What I would advise, with our foster system as it is, would be to say nothing," Martin stated with a serious expression.

"I can't say nothing. Laura's my best friend, my father killed her brother. I can't see her every day and not say something," Isabella protested. She was beginning to question her decision to confide in Martin.

"Well then it's Laura or your sister. Do you really want to be responsible for Savannah ending up in foster care? I apologise for being blunt, but the gravity of the situation requires it. Without going into detail, in my experience with foster

care, more families are bad than good."

"What am I supposed to do then?"

"Go to college. Take Savannah with you and leave your life in Miami behind. Leave Laura behind."

"I don't think I can do that," Isabella shook her head.

"If you're worried about finances don't be," Martin added, "Mitch mentioned you both received scholarships to Berkley?" Isabella nodded, still trying to process everything Martin had told her.

"Mitch will be moving into our family owned apartment near Berkley, you could move in too," Martin suggested. Isabella's heart raced at the suggestion and not in a good way.

"Dad..." Mitch protested awkwardly from over by the study door, he had remained tight lipped up until then.

"I was actually planning on going to Columbia," Isabella interrupted, still holding onto the reality she had created before the accident.

"New York?" Martin questioned and Isabella nodded. "Why Columbia?"

"My friends and I are getting an apartment together." Was the answer she gave Martin, but in her head she thought, that's where Laura's going to be.

"Do these 'friends' include Laura?"

"Well yeah," Isabella admitted sheepishly.

"Isabella by not going to the police now you become an accessory after the fact, any slip could land you in serious trouble and then Savannah ends up in foster care anyway. You've already said you can't lie to Laura." Martin leaned forward on his elbows and fixed Isabella with a serious stare.

"But I can't not have her in my life," Isabella whispered completely dejected.

"I'm sorry, that's your only option," he said matter-of-factly.

* * *

When Kyle found her she was a sobbing mess, frozen in place outside the doors to theatre. She was completely and utterly broken, her eyes puffy and red. Her white blouse was covered in Laura's dried blood, so were her hands.

"Isabella," Kyle spoke softly as he placed a hand on her shoulder. "We can't stay here. We have to go and sit in the waiting room."

"I don't want t-to leave..." Isabella sobbed, trying to calm herself down with some deep breaths. "I need to k-know. I need to know she's going to be alright."

"She will be, they're looking after her," Kyle reassured her once again.

"Her...heart...stopped...Kyle, she...flatlined," Isabella informed him as she took some deep breaths.

"What?" Kyle seemed shocked as he looked back towards the closed doors.

"I-t, it just stop-ped in the truck."

"They'll get her back," Kyle said firmly. He pulled her in for another hug and they just stood in the hallway embracing one another for a long time whilst Isabella calmed down. Eventually she spoke up and broke the silence. Her voice now even, but lifeless.

"I just let him go..."

"Who?" Kyle asked confused.

"The Washington Killer. I just watched him run away," Isabella shook her head in disgust.

"If you had gone after him, Laura probably wouldn't stand a chance right now. You saved her life," he reassured her, squeezing her arms.

"I could kill him," Isabella seethed, her grief turning to anger. "I was supposed to protect her."

"You did Bella! No one can stop that woman when she has her mind set on something, you of all people should know that." Kyle took hold of Isabella's arm and began guiding her towards the waiting room.

"Exactly, I should have seen it coming and tackled him myself."

"We're going to get this guy. I radioed the station from the car, CSU are at his place now. We'll get him." Another stretcher went barrelling past the pair, causing them to break apart quickly. Isabella winced in pain as she stepped back against the wall, the movement aggravating her bruised ribs. "You ok?" Kyle asked, noticing the pained expression on her face.

"Yeah, I got kicked in the ribs. It's just a bit of a bruise that's all," Isabella brushed him off.

"Have you been checked out?"

"No," Isabella responded as she took a seat in the private waiting room, dropping down into one of the blue plastic chairs. She pulled out her phone from her pocket and began dialling Ellie and then Rachel's numbers to let them know what had happened. They both grilled her with a million questions that she had to try and answer as unemotionally as she could, whilst also offering them comforting words. Both women were reluctant to hang up, wanting to hear any news as it happened, whilst they made their way to the hospital. When she got off the phone from a hysterical Rachel, Kyle came back into the waiting room accompanied by a nurse.

"Lift up your shirt," Kyle ordered as the nurse bent down to examine her. Isabella rolled her eyes and lifted her shirt.

"It looks like you might have a fractured rib," the nurse said, though Isabella didn't bother acknowledging her. "We should do an X-ray to make sure."

"If it is a fractured rib, there's nothing that can be done anyway. What you can do is go into that operating room," Isabella exclaimed as she pointed down the hall to the closed theatre doors. "And either help save my partner's life, or come back out to us with an update."

The nurse simply nodded and turned on her heel, walking down the hallway and disappearing behind the closed doors. Isabella's legs were tapping furiously up and down as the minutes ticked over. She chewed on her fingernails, barely blinking as she waited for the doors to open.

"I can see why Laura says you're such a great interrogator," Kyle smiled, trying to lighten the mood. "You're tenacious that's for sure."

"Laura said that?" Isabella asked surprised, Laura never really let on much what she thought of her professionally.

"Yeah," Kyle nodded. "She's a pretty private person, she doesn't reveal much. But god she loves to talk about you."

"Really?" Isabella asked, even more surprised now.

"Let's just say if I were Rachel, I'd definitely be worried," Kyle smiled, as Isabella sat deep in thought. As she was considering what Kyle had said she heard the sound of the doors at the end of the hall opening and closing and she immediately stood up from her seat. The nurse she had ordered away was walking towards them accompanied by one of the surgeons.

"How is she?" Isabella asked as they got closer. Her question was interrupted as a door swung open on the other side of the room, a tear-stricken Ellie and Rachel both rushing inside. Both women's eyes widened in horror as they took in the amount of blood on Isabella's blouse.

"Isabella," Ellie sobbed as she fell into her arms, her chest heaving with heavy breaths. Isabella squeezed her tight as she kept her eyes on the surgeon.

"How's Laura?" Rachel asked the surgeon desperately as another sob escaped Ellie's throat, her body shaking vigorously in Isabella's arms.

"Are you family?" The surgeon asked the room.

"I'm her partner," Isabella and Rachel both said at once, the two women's eyes then meeting awkwardly. The surgeon raised his eyebrows as he looked at them both.

"I'm...h-her sister," Ellie responded as she turned around, still clinging onto Isabella's waist.

"Are you happy for me to talk freely?" Ellie nodded as she wiped away more tears.

"Laura experienced cardiac arrest shortly before arriving at the hospital," tears spilled from Rachel's eyes as another sob escaped Ellie's mouth. "We were able to revive her once we got her into surgery, but we still faced a lot of complications. She had lost a lot of blood so we had to begin blood transfusions right away.

"When we opened up her abdomen it took us some time to determine where the bleeding was coming from. The knife had punctured one of her kidneys and she was losing a lot of blood from that area. Once we removed the kidney, we were able to stop the rapid blood loss. She is far from being out of the woods yet. Right now, she is in a serious but stable condition, but she still needs more blood. I'm afraid we're running low on O negative. Are any of you that blood type?"

"I am," Isabella responded immediately.

"Come with me Ma'am," the nurse asked, motioning her forward.

"I'll be back with more updates soon," the surgeon smiled sympathetically before making his way back to theatre.

Isabella stepped forward to follow the nurse as the doors behind them slammed open once again, this time Parker, Cate, Jordan and Bri all entered, all looking terribly worried. Cate was wearing her pink hospital scrubs, a handkerchief clutched firmly in her hand as she clung onto Parker's wrist.

"Bella, what's going on?" Parker asked worriedly, only having received a quick text from Isabella letting them know Laura was in the hospital. The group's eyes all fell on Isabella's blouse and the tension amongst them increased instantly.

"I'm sorry I have to go," Isabella responded. "Kyle can fill you in."

"Is she going to be alright?" Parker asked as a single tear slipped down her cheek.

"I don't know," Isabella whispered as she looked down at the hand intertwined with Ellie's. Without looking back at her anxious friends, she reluctantly let go of Ellie's hand and followed the nurse down the hall.

19

Chapter 19

The transfusion bandage felt scratchy on her skin, the caning in her ribs made it hard to breathe, but all she could think about was Laura. Hours later she was still in surgery, with no further updates on her condition. More eyes had begun fluttering closed in the waiting room. Ellie's head lolled restlessly on her lap as she slept. Cate and Kevin were also asleep, her head resting comfortably in his lap. He had gotten to the hospital as fast as he could after his shift at the fire station had ended and he was clearly exhausted. His snores echoed throughout the quiet waiting room, sometimes muffled by one of Kyle's soft whines.

Bri had reluctantly gone home to take over from the babysitter, but had asked Jordan to call her as soon as they had any news. Kyle and Jordan were two of the first to drift off to sleep, Kyle's head resting on Jordan's shoulder and Jordan's head resting on Kyle's. It would have been a comical sight given any other circumstance, but in that moment, Isabella wasn't able to see the humour in anything. Parker had disappeared a while ago to get everyone coffees. The only two awake were herself and Rachel, both sitting silently except for the incessant tapping of her nervous foot.

"I knew something like this was going to happen," Rachel mumbled, distracting Isabella from her nervous thoughts. Rachel hadn't said a word to her for hours so she was startled by the sudden outburst.

"What?"

"I knew one day she was going to get hurt. She's too head strong, I swear she acts sometimes before she thinks," Rachel shook her head and sighed, the stress of the last few hours beginning to take an obvious toll.

"I don't think she acts before she thinks. If Laura is anything, she's an over thinker. She reacts quickly to protect others around her," Isabella whispered back as Rachel just stared at her, analysing her. Isabella knew Laura had reacted so drastically in order to protect her. No matter what had happened that morning, Laura couldn't help but protect those she cared about.

"She should've been a doctor," Rachel stated, ignoring Isabella's comment. "She's so smart, her terrific brain could have helped save so many people."

"What do you think she does now?" Isabella asked perturbed. "She's the best detective in New York, she's closed more cases than any other her age. She's saved hundreds of lives. Once upon a time she might have dreamt of being a doctor, but I think what she does now suits her so much better. She's a brilliant detective."

After a few silent moments of thought, Rachel spoke up. "You're the girl, aren't you?"

"What?"

"Don't play dumb Isabella, we've been there before," Rachel's tone was irritable and demanding and her blue eyes conveyed the same distaste, causing Isabella to shift uncomfortably in her seat. "You're the girl that broke her heart all those years ago?"

Isabella met Rachel's blue eyes and she knew the ME already knew the answer. She could see the pain reflected in them, that same pain she felt when she saw Laura and Rachel together. Rachel simply nodded having gotten her answer from a simple look.

* * *

"What's this?" Mitch asked as his father slid a small black box across his desk.

"It's an engagement ring," Martin smiled.

"Are you crazy?" Mitch practically yelled, before checking that Isabella wasn't at the door. He lowered his voice, but kept the same tone. "Isabella has already

agreed to move in with me at Berkley, that's a big enough step as it is. She's not even eighteen yet Dad."

"Don't you love her?"

"Of course, I do. I adore her."

"Then what's the problem?" Martin countered as he leant back in his leather wingback armchair and placed his hands firmly on his mahogany desk.

"What's the rush?"

"What do you think will happen if the police come knocking at her door asking questions? You as her boyfriend could be brought up on accessory charges. As husband and wife, neither of you can be forced to testify against each other in court."

"You're acting like Isabella herself murdered someone Dad, it's not like withholding information is some big crime," Mitch shrugged.

"One charge on your record and your life is ruined Mitch. Whether you go to prison or not. You will never be able to practice law."

"Dad, I told you...I don't know that I want to study law. I want to do Sports Science," Mitch lowered his voice, his eyes dropping to the floor under the intense scrutiny of his father.

"Mitch, we've talked about this. You're my only son. I singlehandedly built the largest legal practice in Miami and I will be damned if it doesn't remain in the family once I'm gone."

"Dad..." Mitch began to protest, but Martin held up a hand to silence him, instead placing a ring box in Mitch's hand.

"Do this now and I'll give you access to your trust fund early." Mitch shook his head in a weak protest. "Your future is important to me Mitch. Now go and secure it."

When Isabella woke up in Mitch's spare bedroom her body felt exhausted from all of the tension and lack of sleep. She had tossed and turned all night taking in what Martin had told her.

She checked the clock on the nightstand, 8am. She had an hour before she had to pick Savannah up from her friend's house. She had arranged for the pair of them to stay at her Auntie Susie's house for the next few weeks until graduation. She wasn't really her auntie, but her mother's best friend. She hadn't told her exactly why they needed to stay with her, she just vaguely mentioned something about renovations at their own house, but Susie hadn't pressed her on it.

Isabella rolled out of bed and took a shower in the guest bathroom. Mitch had offered for her to stay in his room, but she had told him she didn't feel comfortable sharing a bed with him at this point in their relationship. To his credit he had been more than accommodating and didn't press the issue. Once she was dressed, she wandered into his room and when she didn't find him there, she went downstairs.

Their kitchen and living room were nearly the size of Isabella's whole house combined. The marble floors and benchtops screamed decadence. The smell of bacon had permeated right to the second floor, though it wasn't Mitch she found cooking, it was Martin. As the bacon sizzled on the pan her stomach grumbled, she realised she hadn't eaten dinner the night before. Martin turned around and smiled, he was wearing a regal apron with blue and white stripes.

"Morning Isabella."

"Morning Mr Davis," Isabella returned.

"Please, call me Martin. Would you like some breakfast?" He offered, placing two eggs and a couple of pieces of bacon on a plate.

"No thank you. I've got to pick up my sister soon, so I should probably leave," Isabella answered as she fidgeted with the hem of her top. It pained her to say no when her stomach was practically eating itself, but her anxiety wanted to get moving.

"What time are you picking her up?"

"9am."

"Plenty of time for breakfast then," Martin said as he motioned for her to take a seat at the bench. Isabella defeatedly decided not to protest and gave in to her stomach grumbles. She took a seat as Martin placed the plate of fried eggs and bacon in front of her.

"Thank you." She picked up a piece of bacon and began chewing. The crispy bacon cracked delectably on her tongue. "Where's Mitch?"

"He went for a swim and a run down the beach." Isabella nodded and continued eating. "It will be good you two both attending Berkley together, you can keep him motivated."

Isabella raised her eyebrows confused as she sprinkled some salt over her eggs.

"I don't think Mitch needs me for motivation." That was clearly evident as she dug into breakfast whilst he trained.

"No, I mean with his studies. Mitch isn't as driven as you are." Isabella didn't think herself particularly driven in that area either. She had only managed to do so well because Laura had tutored her in so many of her subjects. *"Did he tell you he wants to study Sports Science?"* Isabella shook her head.

"I see. Well, Sports Science isn't going to support his family. Law is a guaranteed path for him, I will give him my practice when I retire. It's the best option...don't you agree?"

Isabella looked at Martin confused, unsure of why he thought she had an opinion as to what Mitch would study. Sure, she had sort of agreed to move in with him at Berkley, but that was simply so that Savannah and her would have a safe place to stay before she was able to afford her own place and be able to financially support both of them on her own.

"I guess," Isabella replied in order to break the awkward silence that had fallen over them.

"This affects your future too Isabella," Martin spoke sternly. *"Being married to a lawyer offers a lot of protection,"* Martin stated bluntly. Isabella began choking on a piece of bacon, coughing frantically to try and clear her throat.

"What?" She rasped. Completely bewildered for the millionth time in the last twenty-four hours. It was like as soon as she took a second to breathe, she was hit with something else.

"Marriage. You and Mitch. It's the only safe way to traverse these waters we find ourselves in," Martin said simply, continuing to flip the eggs as if this was the most normal conversation one could be having at 8am on a Saturday morning.

"What do you mean?"

"Say a policeman comes knocking and wants to ask you and Mitch some questions. If you're married, neither of you can testify against the other in court, meaning there is no evidence to support accessory charges. Those sorts of charges would ruin both of your lives, and Savannah's," Martin emphasised significantly. *"Is that what you want?"*

"No," Isabella spoke dejectedly, her voice barely audible as she tried to take in what he was saying. He was a smart man, a lawyer, and he seemed to care about

her. She felt like she should take his advice, but she didn't want to. She didn't know what the right thing to do was. It was all far too much for her to process.

"Smart girl. So, when he asks, you have your answer," Martin spoke firmly, as a significant lump formed in Isabella's throat. The walls were beginning to close in around her and she couldn't see a way out. "As for Mitch studying law, I hope that you will be persuasive? It's what's best for both of your futures."

Isabella didn't answer, she was so close to tears, she couldn't believe the reality she now found herself in. Her dreams of studying at Columbia, of living in New York and starting a life with Laura. They had all been forced so far away from her, it was impossible to see them. All she could see swirling in her head were images of herself in a white dress, holding back tears of heartbreak as she walked down the aisle towards Mitch.

"Isabella?" Martin prompted.

"I understand," she finally answered dismally. "Mitch would make a great lawyer."

"Excellent," Martin smiled, as he flipped over another egg on the stove. "I want you to know Isabella as long as you are family, I'll always be here if you ever need legal help. If you follow my advice, I won't let them separate you and Savannah."

"Thank you, Martin," Isabella spoke softly as she produced a contrived smile.

* * *

Her eyes flittered as exhaustion threatened to take over. Her resistance had been broken down after hours and hours of waiting, her body and mind worn down by the heightened anxiety and adrenaline. But each time her eyes closed she forced them back open, refusing to be taken away from the waiting room. She needed to be awake, she needed to hear news of Laura. She needed to be there for her.

The sound of a door opening and closing forced her eyelids open once again. The trauma surgeon from earlier was walking towards her again and she stood up out of her seat, steadying herself on the armrest as everything around her spun. Ellie's head slipped off her lap and slammed against the hard plastic of the waiting room chairs.

"Ow," Ellie grumbled, rubbing her eyes as other eyes in the waiting room began to shoot open.

"Ms Carlsson?" The Doctor asked as Ellie slowly sat up.

"Yes," she answered, frantically rubbing at her eyes to make herself more alert for the news she was about to receive. Rachel had also stood up from her seat, her arms folded tightly against her chest. "Your sister is out of surgery now—"

"She's alive?" Isabella interrupted, a sob escaping her throat.

"She's alive," the Doctor confirmed. Ellie stood up and grabbed a hold of Isabella's arm, tears spilling down her cheeks. Cate began sobbing loudly as Kevin held onto her, Kyle and Jordan both sighing in relief as tears silently ran down Parker's cheeks. "She's in an induced coma in the ICU—"

"A coma?" Ellie interrupted.

"Yes, we have put her in a coma in order for her body to recover from the trauma."

"How long will she be in the coma?" Jordan interrupted.

"We will monitor her over the coming days and discern when to slowly bring her back out of it," the Doctor answered, giving up on finishing his update before the next question was asked.

"Is she going to make a full recovery?" Rachel asked as she dabbed at her eyes with a tissue.

"The surgery was very successful. Scar tissue never goes away, but after some rehabilitation, I'm quite confident she will make a full recovery."

"Can we see her?" Ellie asked as she wiped the tears from her cheeks.

"Not all of you," the Doctor shook his head. "Maybe one or two for tonight and only one at a time. She's very weak." Isabella's heart sank. She knew she wouldn't be able to rest until she saw Laura. But if only two of them were allowed there was no way she would be given priority over Rachel.

"I'm sorry Doctor," Isabella spoke up, an idea coming to her head. "The man that attacked Laura is still out there somewhere. She needs to be under police guard 24/7 until she leaves this hospital, in case he tries to finish the job." The surgeon appeared pensive for a moment before he spoke up.

"Do you have an officer available now?" Isabella pulled her badge from her pocket and showed it to the man. "I do."

"Very well," the man agreed. "Ladies, if you follow me, I'll take you to her room."

"Thank you, Doctor," Ellie smiled, as she turned around to the rest of the group. "I'll be back with an update soon," she said, the group offering her a thankful smile.

"Isabella," Jordan spoke, stopping Isabella in her tracks. "You're exhausted, we can call in another officer, let you get some rest." Isabella shook her head firmly.

"I'm not leaving her. If the Captain asks, this is where I'll be." Isabella turned on her heel and jogged after the surgeon.

She was sat outside the door to Laura's room. The frosted glass window prevented her from seeing what was going on inside. Ellie had been inside for a quarter of an hour before a nurse knocked on the door and told her it was time for the next visitor, allowing Rachel to enter the room. Ellie exited and rushed off to the waiting room to update all the others, Isabella assuring her that she would stay with Laura all day until visiting hours were allowed again later that night.

Time had never felt slower as she fidgeted anxiously with her watch, watching the seconds go by in what felt like hours. She needed to be in that room, she needed to make sure Laura was ok. She only hadn't broken down the door and barged in because she didn't want to do anything to disturb Laura's recovery or get herself removed from the hospital. Once she was allowed entrance to that room, she was intent on not leaving. The proviso of Laura's protection was her excuse and she was going to be adamant in enforcing it.

She heard the rattle of the door knob next to her and she shot out of her seat as Rachel exited, her eyes still glassy, but her cheeks finally dry. "She's all yours," Rachel uttered as Isabella reached for the door knob. "Just not how you might want her to be."

Isabella ignored the stabbing comment and pushed past her to enter the room, the door closing firmly behind her. When her eyes fell on Laura, laying motionless and pale on the bed, her tears insisted on falling once again. She looked so peaceful and fragile at the same time. Her usual larger than life aura gone, for once she looked small and vulnerable. There were tubes and wires running all over her body. She had an intravenous cannula in her hand and a nasal cannula that pumped extra oxygen through her body.

Isabella moved closer to the bed and picked up Laura's free hand, feeling more warmth radiating from her fingers than she had in the ambulance. She leant forward and placed a soft kiss on Laura's forehead, as she drew circles on the back of her hand.

"You're going to be ok Laura. I'm going to make sure of it."

20

Chapter 20

"Do you mind giving us some privacy?" Rachel demanded as she sat by Laura's bedside, stroking her hand. Isabella stood up, reluctantly letting go of Laura's other hand as she walked to the door.

"I'll be right outside." Rachel ignored the statement as she caressed Laura's face with her fingers. She had mainly said it for Laura's benefit. She wanted her to know she wasn't leaving her, even though she knew Laura couldn't hear her. For three days she had been right by her side, catching a few hours sleep here and there, in the armchair by her bed.

As she stood watch outside, she tried smoothing the kinks that had built up in her neck, flexing it from side to side to try and stretch the muscles out. She hated waiting in the hall, the anxious tension that reverberated there was unbearable. There were never enough staff for the number of patients and the poor nurses looked stretched to their limit. Anxious families wandered in and out of the halls, sometimes crying, sometimes yelling and very occasionally smiling. Isabella could only hope she might be one of the latter soon.

The elevator rattled to a stop down the hall. The opening chime having woken her countless times over the last few nights. Her caretaker stepped out and walked towards her, holding the desired care package. Savannah handed over a steaming cup of coffee and placed an overnight bag over Isabella's shoulder. "How's she doing?"

"No change," Isabella's voice was almost robotic as she delivered the same news as yesterday.

"What have the doctor's said?"

"Not much. They've said she's still too weak to come out of it," Isabella's face fell into her hands.

"Hey," Savannah spoke softly as she pulled Isabella into a hug. "She's going to be ok. The worst is over now."

"I know, I'm just worried about her."

"You love her," Savannah stated as she stroked Isabella's back. She forgot sometimes that Savannah knew her maybe even better than she knew herself. "Is deluded girlfriend inside?"

Isabella chuckled lightly. "Savannah..."

"What? She is!" Isabella just shook her head and looked to the ground. "I'm telling you Bella, Laura's going to wake up from that coma having nearly died, with a whole new perspective on life. She's not going to let the fact that you lied to her stop her from getting what she really wants," Savannah stroked her forearm, forcing Isabella to look up. "You Isabella. She loves you."

"I just want her to open her eyes, that's all I care about."

"She will," Savannah nodded, offering her sister a confident smile.

"Thanks Sav. You've honestly been a godsend these last few days." Isabella looked up as yet another teary-eyed family left the ICU without their loved one. She tried to compartmentalise everything that was going on around them and just focus on Laura, but it was hard not to let the anxiety overtake her when people were dying all around them.

"Have you been talking to her?"

"Who? Rachel?"

"No!" Savannah rolled her eyes like that was the most ridiculous concept. "Laura, stupid."

"Ah...Sav, she's in a coma," Isabella replied sarcastically, taking another sip of her coffee.

"I saw a video on YouTube with this dude talking about how he could hear everything going on around him while he was in a coma. It was like torture because he could hear people talking about him, but he couldn't respond."

"Really?" Isabella asked surprised, having not even considered that possibility at all these last three days.

"Yah huh, YouTube it," Savannah responded as she pulled out her phone to reply to a text.

"What would I even talk to her about?" Isabella asked as Savannah continued typing, completely ignoring the question. "Sav?" Isabella asked again. "Savannah Medina!" Isabella raised her voice. "Who are you texting that causes you to ignore me?"

"Sorry, just my friend Andy." Savannah tucked her phone back into her back pocket. "What was the question?"

"I said, what should I talk to Laura about?"

"Seriously?" Savannah asked bewildered as she crossed her arms over her chest and shook her head. "For someone supposedly smart, you can be awfully stupid sometimes."

"Says the girl that stuffed a Barbie stiletto up her nose and had to be taken to emergency."

"Examples of stupidity from fifteen years ago do not count!" Savannah pouted. "Obviously you need to talk to her about why you lied to her. Explain things from your side. Then that way, she's even more likely to wake up willing to forgive you," Savannah winked.

A nurse approached Laura's room and smiled at Isabella and Savannah as she knocked on the door. "Visiting hours are over sweetie," she called through the door. "Say your goodbye's please." The nurse then turned back to Isabella and gave her another warm smile. "You look exhausted Detective, you need to go home and get some sleep."

"I'm fine Carol, and we spoke about this...please call me Isabella." Carol smiled again and gave Isabella a nod, she knew no matter her insistence Carol would still call her Detective later on that evening.

Rachel stepped out of Laura's room, looking particularly withered. Not at all her usually well-kept self. "Carol, her sheets don't look like they've been turned down today. There's an ink stain on her sheet that was there yesterday. Can you have someone get right onto that please?"

"I assure you they were Ma'am. I turned them down myself this morning,"

Carol smiled politely.

"Well why is that ink stain still there then?" Rachel questioned rather abruptly.

"Carol changed the sheets Rachel. I watched her do it this morning." Isabella's interruption only seemed to annoy Rachel more.

"Well, changing the sheets twice a day wouldn't hurt either. I know the kind of bacteria that can breed in a hospital."

"I'll do my best Ma'am," Carol answered as Rachel gave her a firm nod and began walking away from them towards the elevators. No goodbye to Carol, Isabella or Savannah, just like all the days prior.

"Laura's taste in women concerns me," Savannah smirked as she watched the tall brunette disappearing down the hall. Isabella smacked her across the arm to shut her up.

"I'll bring you round some soup later tonight dear. The kitchen's making pumpkin and ginger!" Carol clapped, as she smiled at the women once more and went tottering off towards the nurse's station.

"See Bella. Literally everyone loves you. There's no way Laura doesn't. I'm going home for pasta," Savannah wiggled her eyebrows excitedly as Isabella groaned.

"Don't dangle real food in front of me like that, it's not fair!"

"Bye Felicia," Savannah smiled as she turned on her heel and headed towards the elevators, blowing Isabella a kiss before she stepped inside the doors.

Isabella took a deep breath as she turned back towards Laura's door and grasped the handle in her hand. The room was exactly how she left it, the blinds closed and lights dimmed to a soft golden light. The only noise was the continuous beeping of Laura's heart monitor. Though it was annoying, it was more of a comfort to Isabella than anything. She sat down next to Laura's bed and picked up her hand once again, her other fingers caressing the baseball tattoo on Laura's wrist.

"Savannah says I should be talking to you, telling you stories," Isabella spoke softly into the room, glancing over at Laura's face to see if her words were registering. It was naïve, but she felt slightly embarrassed talking to an unconscious person. "She said you might be able to hear me. I hope you can, I really want to explain some things..." Isabella trailed off as she gave Laura's hand a comforting squeeze.

She sat pensive for a moment considering where to start. She figured right after the funeral would be best. She recounted the moment she had entered the garage and found her father's damaged car and realised what it had meant. It wasn't a memory she liked to visit, she tried never to think about it, so telling Laura instantly brought out her tears. She moved on to that night at Mitch's and the advice she had received from Martin. She realised all of these years later that it hadn't necessarily been good advice. It was advice that suited him and his son.

"I was so scared Laura, you've got to understand. I couldn't lose Savannah. I was terrified of us being split up after everything that had happened. She was so traumatised from our mother's death, then our father's alcoholism and then she didn't really understand what happened with Alex and why we were moving. I just wanted her to be safe." Isabella looked towards a motionless Laura, pleading with her to understand. She hoped she did.

The text messages and the voicemails were some of the hardest to recall. She had cried every time she read or listened to one of Laura's desperate messages. Until graduation. She knew her words in the carpark had done it. The texts and the voicemails stopped that day. And she was sure why. She had broken Laura's heart alongside her own. And she confessed now just how hard that was. The hardest thing she had ever done, maybe only eclipsed now by their goodbye in front of theatre. At least she had known ten years ago Laura was alive, even if that meant never seeing her again.

"I had promised myself before graduation that I was going to get in and out without seeing or talking to you. So when I heard you running after me in the carpark, I wasn't sure I was going to be able to go through with it. I wanted nothing more than to take you in my arms and kiss you and tell you everything was going to be ok. It's just that, I never thought things would be again. I used to have these recurring nightmares where I watched your eyes in the mirror as I drove away. And every single time I woke up, I initially felt relief, thinking it was just a dream. Then the realisation that it wasn't, was a new heartbreak each time."

It was difficult casting her mind back, she didn't like to think too much about the last ten years. She had achieved some great things in her career, sure. She had watched Savannah grow up into a young woman. But she preferred to dwell in the times before, the times that featured Laura front and centre. Savannah was right though, Laura needed to know. So she pressed on, recounting her early days at Berkley, her short-lived marriage to Mitch and its subsequent breakdown.

"I always pictured it being you, you know," Isabella smiled, looking over at a peaceful Laura. "Ever since that first kiss, anytime I've thought about marriage, it was you walking towards me in a white dress," she chuckled thinking about the scandalous looks on their friends and relatives faces had they got married in Miami. "It almost killed me getting to the end of that aisle and seeing Mitch there. For some reason I'd had this nervous anticipation all morning that maybe I would get there and it would be you."

The marriage breakdown had been one of the hardest times. Not in the way one might expect, not emotionally as such, more logistically. She was then solely financially responsible for herself, a full-time student and part-time worker and her ten-year-old sister. They got by for years just barely surviving on credit limits. Still now she was repaying those debts.

She was surprised when the laughter came, when she was telling Laura about her days as a beat cop in West Hollywood. She had been the smallest officer in her class and that had presented its challenges. But putting on the badge had given her, her purpose. As she knew it had for Laura. It was an attempt to claw back the injustices that had been levelled upon them, she thought. It was an incredible motivator.

West Hollywood had its challenges, but the move to narcotics in Miami had been far more difficult. The work was long and arduous and the criminals were far more intelligent. Not only that, she was raising a teenager in the same place she had been a teenager. The setting brought back far too many memories. Far from bringing familiarity, Miami had brought back the trauma she had fought to suppress. So when Savannah had brought up colleges in New York, the prospect had been exciting. For one reason in particular.

* * *

It had been a full twenty-four hours since the doctors had stopped the sedation medication, meaning Laura could wake up at any time. After visiting hours had once again ended, Ellie and Rachel both left the hospital, asking Isabella to call them as soon as Laura woke up. She had received multiple text messages throughout the course of the day and another evening of visitation passed with no movement.

She was beginning to become fidgety with each passing hour. Panicked that Laura may never wake up from this. Carol had tried to calm her down and told her it was perfectly normal for patients to take up to seventy-two hours to wake up from an induced coma and not to worry. Isabella however couldn't help herself but worry, she was exhausted and anxious after spending the last five days by Laura's bedside.

The extra time spent with an unconscious Laura had allowed her to be the most honest with the detective, that she had been in ten years. It felt like some of the weight she was carrying had lifted off her shoulders, though she knew she would have to have these conversations again with a conscious Laura. She looked to Laura's eyes, seeing a slight flutter in her eyelashes. She blinked rapidly to test whether or not her tired eyes were causing her to see things. But the long eyelashes continued to flutter as slowly her green eyes began to appear.

Isabella grabbed a hold of Laura's hand and squeezed comfortingly as she grinned down at her partner. "Laura? Laura can you hear me?" She leant to the side of Laura's bed and pressed the button to call the nurse.

"Alex," Laura whispered, her eyes fluttering between consciousness.

"It's me, Issi. You're in the hospital, everything's alright," Isabella smiled, completely elated.

Laura's eyes flittered briefly around the room before falling on Isabella, looking slightly clouded and confused. "Get out."

"Laura?" Isabella stammered, completely bewildered by Laura's words.

"Get out," Laura repeated firmly, her eyes clear and resolute.

21

Chapter 21

"The Knicks beat the Cavaliers 102 to 90, yay Knicks!" Isabella read off her phone, her cheery tone echoing loudly around Laura's hospital room. "That teen Mum couple, you know the one always breaking up and getting back together again? Well, they broke up again. Supposedly for good this time." Isabella looked up towards Laura, but she continued to eat her yoghurt in silence as she stared at the door.

"The weather today is a brisk 35 degrees Fahrenheit...not that, that will impact you *much*," Isabella added sarcastically as she glanced again at Laura, still not getting a reaction. After she had refused to leave the room the night before, Laura had simply ignored her.

"Though despite the radiator, I have to say it's definitely bitter in here," she jabbed, again looking up to an expressionless Laura. The woman licking away at her yoghurt as if the attack had taken her hearing as well.

"You know, I'm glad the Bachelor didn't choose Mary Beth." Isabella held up her phone so that both her and Laura could see the screen, the latter completely ignoring it and instead fiddling with her hospital band. "I really don't think she was genuine. Another one after her fifteen minutes of fame."

Isabella pulled a moisturiser out of her bag and began applying it to her face. "How young is too young do you think to start thinking about anti-aging measures? Because I saw this infomercial the other night about this new organic type of botox and I don't know...it was pretty convincing..."

Isabella trailed off, this time her statement elicited an almost imperceptible sigh from Laura as she took a sip from her water bottle.

"Baby shark, doo doo doo doo doo doo," Isabella sang loudly as she pumped the volume up on her phone to the maximum. "Baby shark, doo doo doo doo doo doo." She could see Laura's eyelids squeezing tighter in annoyance as she stole glances between the screen and Laura's eyes, just waiting for the woman to finally snap and talk to her. "Baby shark, doo doo doo doo doo doo. Baby shark!" Isabella shouted the last line and Laura's eyes flung open and connected with Isabella's in pure annoyance.

"I swear to God Medina!"

The door swung open as they glared at one another, "Good Morning Detectives! How is our patient feeling this morning?"

"About ready to go back into a coma..." Laura trailed off softly as Isabella rolled her eyes, the Doctor shooting her a warm smile.

"Sorry?" He asked, moving closer to check her blood pressure.

"Sore," Laura answered. "When can I leave the hospital?" She asked, as she tried to lift herself up into a sitting position, the effort causing a pained expression to materialise across her features. Isabella stood to help Laura up, but she only swatted away her hand at the attempt.

"It will be another few days yet Laura and then there will be an extensive rehab period," he said as he read over her charts.

"Great," Laura groaned.

"We'll get into all of the specifics later, for now I just want you to rest," he smiled as Laura rolled her eyes.

"In that case, can you force the living and breathing jack in the box to leave?" Laura asked, her thumb jerking towards Isabella. The Doctor chuckled, clearly believing it to be a joke. He assured her he would be back later to check on her as he closed the door.

"Seriously Laura?" Isabella's tone was sharp, the sudden movement casting her toiletries bag and the items inside all over the floor. "Will you please just listen to me? I need to explain some things."

"Why? Why should I? Every time I open myself up to you, you—"

"Laur!" The door burst open and an excited Ellie rushed inside, throwing her arms around Laura in a tight embrace. Laura groaned in pain. "Don't do that to me again," Ellie uttered, "I can't lose you too."

"You won't. Unless you do end up in gaol one day, then I might disown you," Laura teased as she stroked her sister's back, her eyes wandering to the door to see Rachel staring back at her worriedly. Laura gave Rachel a small smile, Isabella noticed her eyes flicker towards her and then return to her girlfriend.

"Hey Rach," Laura greeted her girlfriend softly.

"Hi baby," Rachel smiled uneasily as she leant down and captured Laura's lips in a soft kiss.

Isabella couldn't just sit there and watch them kissing. For the first time in the last week, she felt out of place. As discreetly as she could she stood up from her chair and nodded towards Ellie, signalling to her that she would be outside. Ellie offered her a warm smile and nodded in response. Rachel pulled away from the kiss, caressing Laura's cheek adoringly.

"What are you doing out here?" Savannah asked as she stepped into Isabella's line of sight, pulling her sister away from her thoughts. She had been going over everything in her head for hours and her body was stiff and sore from standing still for so long.

"Just giving them some privacy," Isabella sighed.

"Bella, we talked about this...persistence!"

"Laura asked me to get out," Isabella answered. Savannah looked shocked at the admission. "I didn't leave. I tried to get her to talk to me but she won't, she's practically ignoring me."

"She's still recovering, things will calm down—"

"When?" Isabella asked defiantly. "It took months for her to open up to me again and now...she hates me more than ever." Savannah placed a hand on Isabella's shoulder.

"Hi Medinas."

Isabella forced a smile onto her face as she looked up to greet Jordan, he was carrying a smiley Andre in his arms as Bri stepped forward to wrap her in a hug. "How are you doing sweetie?" She asked in a nurturing voice, Isabella sinking into the embrace. She had been so strong all week, it felt nice to be held and comforted.

"I'm okay...better now that she's awake," she answered honestly as Bri pulled back from the hug, a concerned look on her face.

"You need to go home and get some rest Isabella."

"Mhmm," Savannah agreed, nodding vehemently.

"Bri," Jordan reproached.

"I will, I just want to make sure she's ok first," Isabella promised, Jordan and Bri both nodding sympathetically.

"Is she free?" Jordan asked, signalling to the closed door behind them.

"Rachel and Ellie are in there at the moment."

"Well how about I go grab some coffees for everyone and come back. Then we might be able to duck in and say a quick hello?" Jordan nodded in agreement as his wife walked off towards the cafeteria.

When Isabella looked up at Jordan this time, she really looked at him. She noticed the dark circles under his eyes and his unkept stubble, that was usually always so well groomed. Something was going on; her detective sixth sense was screaming at her.

"What's wrong?"

Jordan paused for a brief second as if considering whether or not to tell her. "Another girl was murdered."

Isabella shook her head in shock. "When?"

"Two days ago," Jordan answered gravely. "We would've told you sooner but we didn't want to cause any more stress. It's been crazy trying to keep this whole thing under wraps from the media."

"Where was she found?" Isabella asked, her mind racing with the images of his bloody knife.

"Inside her dorm room at NYU."

"Oh joy," Savannah remarked, Isabella knew her paranoia was already high since the shooting.

"Jesus," Isabella sighed as Andre began blowing raspberries in his dad's arms. Jordan bounced him up and down to try and settle him. "Did you find anything at his apartment?"

"Forensics are still sorting through the evidence. There was no laptop at the apartment like you mentioned. He clearly doubled back after the attack and retrieved it before our boys in blue arrived. Nothing came up on the apartment either, landlord had a cash in hand deal with him."

"God, I feel sick," Isabella slid down into one of the chairs bordering the wall.

"We could really use your help when you're ready to come back."

"Yeah of course, I just don't know when that will be. I'm staying here until Laura gets out." Jordan nodded in understanding as Bri returned with coffees for the four of them, Savannah eagerly grabbing hers and taking a swig. The door to Laura's room opened a moment later and Ellie and Rachel stepped outside.

"You guys can go in now, we're going to grab some dinner," Ellie smiled at Jordan and Bri, Rachel not uttering a word as the two women began walking to the elevators.

"Go ahead," Isabella motioned towards the door. "We'll wait out here." They didn't speak, just sat, too many thoughts swirling in both of their heads as they drank their coffees.

"Medina!" Isabella looked up to see Kyle sauntering over towards them in a slick leather jacket with his well-kept hair and cleanly shaven jaw. He didn't look stressed or dishevelled like Jordan had, he seemed to be coping far better than his counterpart. "How's she doing?"

"Good as far as I can tell. She's tired and still in a lot of pain, but I think she's excited to see everyone," Kyle nodded and looked at the frosted glass behind which, his friend lay. "How are you coping? Jordan told me about the other murder?"

"Yeah it's terrible. We're still struggling for clues on this guy, female, blonde and young isn't much of an MO to go off."

"Well aside from Atlanta, that murder seems to have been more opportunistic than methodical, that's three girls from NYU," Isabella deduced, having been pondering that fact for the last few minutes.

"That could just be a coincidence," Kyle suggested apathetically.

"Two is a coincidence, three is a pattern," Isabella insisted.

"Maybe," Kyle shrugged. "Is Jordan in there?"

"Yes. Go on in." The door closed again and Isabella rested her head back against the wall, the effects of the caffeine beginning to slip away.

"Is Kyle in grad school?" Savannah questioned.

"Not that I know of, why?"

"I just see him around the Steam Bar a bit," Savannah shrugged, dropping the name of the coffee shop she, Isabella and Laura had gone to when they were at NYU. "Maybe he just lives nearby."

"He doesn't. Though I wouldn't be surprised if it were one of his stomping grounds for picking up girls."

"He's a player? Huh, I guess he looks the type," Savannah shrugged and Isabella nodded.

"He's definitely the type," she agreed, thinking of the many occasions he had flirted with both her and Laura.

"Good evening Detective," Carol smiled cheerily at her. "I was hoping to do Detective Carlsson's obs in a moment when she's free."

"No worries Carol," Isabella smiled as she stood up from her seat. "I'll just let her visitors know."

Carol smiled and waddled back over to the nurse's station as Isabella entered Laura's room. She was looking tired, slumped up against her pillow, her eyes were more glazed than glowing.

"Sorry to interrupt, but Laura's nurse wants to do her nightly obs."

"Not a problem," Bri smiled, "We should probably get this little guy home." She stroked Andre's hand, now blissfully asleep in Jordan's arms.

"Good to see you Carlsson, get better soon. The precinct isn't the same without you," Jordan leant down and kissed Laura's forehead before the small family engulfed Isabella in a hug and made their way out of the room.

"Seriously Carlsson, we need you back. Our attractive rating as a precinct has seriously dropped without you. I'm having to hold us up all on my own," Laura chuckled and Isabella rolled her eyes as Kyle leant in to kiss Laura's cheek. He grabbed her neck with his left hand as his lips touched her skin, Laura's eyes falling on his discoloured wrist as his leather jacket rode up. Isabella watched Laura's body stiffen and her face grow pale as Kyle planted a kiss on her cheek.

"What happened to your wrist?" Laura's tone was blunt and there was something in her eyes Isabella couldn't put her finger on. It seemed almost like fear.

"Oh..." Kyle was obviously surprised by the question as he stood back up and pulled his sleeve back down. "Just a gym injury," he shrugged, his smile now seeming forced and uncertain. "I'll leave you ladies to it." He smiled one last time and then headed for the door, his demeanour and Laura's having both noticeably shifted with the question. The tension radiating from Laura was palpable as the door closed.

"What's wrong?" Isabella didn't miss a beat, she could see Laura was nervous, scared even.

"Did you see his wrist?" Isabella nodded. "The Washington Killer had bruises in the exact same spot. You said Kyle was the first on the scene?"

"Yes, but Laura what you're implying—"

"It makes sense Isabella! Why he leaves no trace, he's methodical, always one step ahead of us."

"This is Kyle, Laura," Isabella emphasised, not wanting to believe their colleague and close friend could be capable of such a thing. Though as she was defending him, she couldn't help but remember what Savannah had told her earlier. She had seen him regularly at NYU. Though there was surely a logical reason for that she thought. A far more rational reason than him being the killer. "He's not capable."

"Then why did he tense up when I asked him about the bruises?" Laura asked, her hands noticeably shaking.

"I don't know, that could've been for any number of reasons."

"I need you to look into him for me at the precinct," Laura stated firmly, she looked so tired and vulnerable in her hospital bed, but still she had retained her authoritative tone.

"Laura," Isabella shook her head. "I can't do that. I could get suspended for an accusation like that."

"Typical," Laura pouted, folding her arms across her chest.

"What?" Isabella asked, annoyed.

"Whenever I need you, you're not there to help."

"Laur—"

"Hi darling," Carol interrupted as she stepped into the room and picked up Laura's chart smiling, she was completely oblivious to the evident tension engulfing them. She waddled around the room checking numbers on the various machines and taking Laura's temperature and blood pressure. Isabella cast anxious glances at Laura who was once again ignoring her. "You've got more visitors outside. You're a popular lady," Carol smiled, prompting Laura to give her a small smile back. "Should I tell your friends to come in?" She asked as she headed for the door.

"Could you ask them to give us a minute and then come in?" Isabella asked.

"Of course, dear," she smiled and let herself out.

"What are you still doing here Isabella?" Laura asked, her hands once again crossed over her chest as she sunk back against her pillow. It was clear she was beginning to lose the energy to have these conversations. "How many times do I need to ask you to leave? I don't want you here."

"And I told you Laura," Isabella spat back, her tone becoming less patient after so many hours of trying to get Laura to listen. "I'm not going to leave you again."

"This time I want you to!" Laura shouted as the door swung open and Savannah stepped inside, a bright smile stretched across her face.

"Now, now you two. We can hear you in the hall," Savannah spoke through her teeth, keeping the smile on her face. She walked over to the bed and wrapped her arms around Laura, the detective returning her embrace affectionately. "You scared us Laur."

"I'm sorry," Laura said softly, her tone returning back to normal.

"You need to take better care of yourself, I'm not ready to lose you." Savannah planted a kiss on Laura's forehead and straightened up. "Now I have to go, I just wanted to say a quick hello before I left. If you kids can agree to play nice, Cate and Parker are waiting outside."

"Bring them in," Laura smiled tiredly.

"Alright. I'll see you later Laur. I'm glad you're ok."

"I swear to god you better not die on me!" Parker announced as she squished past Savannah into the room, Cate trailing closely behind.

"I'm trying not to," Laura smiled back.

"I love you, I love you, I love you, I love you," Cate announced as she buried her face in the side of Laura's neck, clinging on to her best friend.

"Not dying Cate, I'm actually on the mend," Laura chuckled, only then to grimace from the pain.

"You *did* die," Cate corrected as she pulled away and Parker went in for her hug. "And now I've vowed to tell everyone I love, how much I love them, while I have the chance."

"That's sweet Cate, I think we should all do that," Isabella chimed in purposefully, causing Laura to roll her eyes. Parker picked up on it and looked between the two women suspiciously.

"What's up with you two?"

"Cate didn't tell you?" Laura asked surprised as Isabella and Cate both became increasingly more uncomfortable.

"Tell me what?" An awkward silence fell within the room as Cate avoided eye contact with everyone, Isabella stared Laura down, Laura seemed to be pondering her next move and Parker looked at them all confused.

"Laur?" Parker asked, unnerved by everyone's behaviour.

"Samuel killed Alex, Isabella knew about it and instead of telling me she dumped me, ran off to California and married Mitch Davis." Parker's mouth fell practically agape as her eyes zeroed in on Isabella. She then turned to look at Cate who seemed captivated with the cord on Laura's blinds.

"You knew Cate?" Cate glanced up slowly and met Parker's eyes.

"Yes," she answered sheepishly, looking extremely guilty under the intense gaze of her friend.

"How long have you known?"

"Just a few weeks, I didn't think it was my place." Cate was hunched, cowering in on herself. Isabella regretted having told her now, she didn't want Cate to pay for her mistakes too.

"And you had the audacity to come back?" Parker shouted, turning on Isabella this time.

"There's more to it than that Parker, Laura won't let me explain—"

"I've told you I don't want to hear it, I want you to leave!" Laura attempted to shout, but she ended up doubled over in pain instead. Isabella stepped forward to help her, but Parker held up a hand to stop her as she moved in closer to Laura.

"You need to leave," Parker said firmly, grabbing a hold of Laura's hand. "Both of you," she asserted, this time looking towards Cate. "Laura's been through enough."

"Parker please, you don't understand—" Cate spoke up this time, her words choked with emotion.

"Get out Cate, I don't want to see you either," Parker ordered, Isabella looking over at a devastated Cate. Her head dropped as she walked towards the door, tapping Isabella's shoulder as she went.

"Come on Bella."

"I'll be right outside," Isabella called as she followed Cate out into the hall.

They waited outside for ages, the hour becoming later and later with no sign of movement inside. Cate's phone was going off with messages from Kevin, eventually she had to give up and offered Isabella an apology as she sulked off into the night.

"You're not inside?" Ellie asked surprised as she entered the hallway, placing her hand on the door.

"I got kicked out."

"Sounds like Laura," Ellie chuckled. "Stubborn as ever that woman. Come on," she motioned for Isabella to get up as her hand fell on the door handle, "I'm giving you permission to come in."

As Parker's eyes fell on Isabella, she shot her the biggest death stare she could conjure up. Ellie ignored the tension and threw herself down in the armchair by the bed. "I've got to go Laur," Parker said as she leant down and kissed Laura's cheek. "I'll be back tomorrow."

"Thanks for coming Parks," Laura smiled at her best friend. "Do us a favour? Don't be mad at Cate, it's not *her* fault." Laura said pointedly, shooting another glare at Isabella.

"You don't have to be, but I am. Get some rest ok?" Laura nodded and Parker waved goodbye to Ellie before walking out the door. Making Isabella feel every bit of the pariah she felt when she first turned up in New York.

"What was that all about?" Ellie asked confused as Laura glared back towards Isabella.

"I'll tell you later," Laura sighed as Ellie looked between the two women.

"Is this about Alex?"

"What?" Laura asked shocked. "Why would you think that?"

"I know about Samuel," Ellie answered, a look of guilt washing over her features.

"Excuse me?" Laura's voice shot up a few octaves as she said it.

"Why do you think I gave Isabella such a hard time when I got to New York?" Ellie shrugged. "She's the one that reported him to the police." Laura looked shocked again as Isabella shifted uncomfortably on the spot. She had told Laura all of this while she was sleeping, but that was far less intimidating when she couldn't respond.

"How long have you known?"

"Nearly ten years." Laura shook her head and closed her eyes. "You weren't talking to Mum and Dad and they told me not to tell you," Ellie tried to reason. "But after my court case I sat down with Isabella and she told me her side of the story. I think you need to hear her out Laur."

"Maybe I'm not ready to hear her out! Why do I have to do things on other people's terms. This is about me and what I want, and right now, I don't want to see her!" Laura shot back, causing Isabella to retreat further into the corner of the room struggling with being talked about as if she wasn't present.

"Isabella said you said Alex's name when you woke up?" Ellie asked, changing the subject. "Were you dreaming about him?"

"I—" Laura appeared pensive. "I might have been."

"Do you believe in guardian angels?" Ellie asked seriously.

"I don't know."

"I always thought when Alex died that he became ours. I still feel him around sometimes. I still talk to him," Ellie sighed, her eyes becoming glassy with tears.

"You called him on New Years Eve."

"What?" Ellie asked shocked. "How do you know that?"

"I merged our accounts when he died. How do you think he still has a voicemail if no one's paying the bill?"

"I don't know, I never really thought about it," Ellie shrugged.

"I call him too. I just need to hear his voice sometimes. I feel like when I leave a message, he hears it. I know it's stupid." Isabella's heart was aching at the confessions, she felt like she was intruding on a private moment.

"It's not stupid Laur," Ellie assured her as she wrapped Laura's hand in her own. "I think he would be happy you know, to see us back together again. If this attack proves anything, it's that life's too short."

"I didn't know you got sentimental Ellie," Laura mocked.

"Shut up," Ellie rolled her eyes. "As I was saying, life's too short to hold onto anger. Case in point, you need to hear Isabella out." Laura cast her eyes over to Isabella, a warm blush appearing on her cheeks, but she refused to leave.

"I'm not ready for that. I need space." Isabella could tell this time it was a genuine plea and her heart sank. "Please Isabella, just leave."

The door opened and Rachel returned, this time carrying a bag of fresh clothes for Laura. Ellie got up from her seat and offered Rachel her chair. Isabella considered what to do, maybe her act of defying Laura's wishes wasn't really what Laura wanted deep down. She thought she needed to prove her love, to prove to Laura she wasn't going to leave this time. But she was becoming increasingly doubtful.

"Hi baby," Rachel smiled as she placed a tender kiss on Laura's lips.

"Ok now I'm leaving," Ellie raised her hands, poking her tongue out at Laura as she ducked out the door.

"I'm just dropping these clothes off quickly and then I'm heading back home," Rachel said as she stroked Laura's hair.

"Stay," Laura spoke softly, staring deeply into Rachel's eyes.

"I've got to work in the morning," Rachel protested.

"Stay," Laura urged more firmly this time. "Please." Isabella's heart ached as she watched Laura pleading with Rachel to stay with her when she had just moments ago begged her to leave.

"Laura—" Rachel went to protest again.

"I love you," Laura whispered, loud enough that it still carried across the room. Rachel looked completely taken aback as Isabella's heart sank. After a second's pause, Rachel's lips connected with Laura's tenderly. The door opened and closed, leaving them alone for the first time.

22

Chapter 22

As she put the car into drive the target she was after exited his apartment building. Just like all of the other mornings she had watched him he turned left and began walking towards the subway. He tucked his hands into his pocket and began a brisk walk down the sidewalk, Isabella giving him a fair amount of time to gain some distance before she followed carefully behind him.

As she put her indicator on to pull out from the curb, someone else leaving the same apartment complex caught her eye. They stepped onto the sidewalk and began walking in the opposite direction. Isabella looked both ways before pulling out, deciding to tail the second figure instead.

* * *

Laura groaned as her alarm went off to wake her up for her first day back at work. Her mind was swimming with Alex's cheeky smile, visions of court cases and car accidents blurring away as she became cognisant. She had never been the type of person to dread going to work, she had always loved and been passionate about what she did, but today was different for so many reasons. The most obvious being that she hadn't seen or spoken to Isabella in nearly six weeks and she wasn't sure if she was ready to see her.

The second reason she was dreading going back to work was the festering paranoia that had been chipping away at her all this time. She knew she would have to confront Kyle and get to the bottom of those bruises. Savannah had also casually mentioned to her, in one of their many bedside conversations, that she had seen Kyle a few times at NYU. Now that she had caught up on all of the case notes she believed NYU was indeed the Washington Killer's hunting ground.

She had warned both Savannah and Ellie to keep their wits about them on campus, not to go out alone after dark and if they were out and about, never to let their drink out of their hands. Ellie had successfully begun a bridging course at the university a few weeks before, if her course went successfully, she would be able to apply to study an undergraduate degree at NYU. Between the course and her community service hours Ellie had barely been at the apartment in the last six weeks. Laura was certain that's why the two sisters were getting along so well currently, if they saw each other too much, their fiery personalities often collided in an explosive way.

With Ellie constantly out and about, Jordan and Kyle busy with the case, Cate seemingly avoiding her and her avoiding Isabella, only Parker knew exactly what had happened to her in the last six weeks. She regularly checked in on Laura at her apartment, chauffeuring her to rehab, doctor's appointments and therapy sessions. She was also smart enough to bite her tongue on the topic of Rachel.

* * *

Laura had initially been relieved when she had been discharged, that was until she realised, she was now bed bound at home instead. For two weeks she had occupied herself going over and over the Washington Killer case files, trying to prove or disprove one way or the other whether Kyle was in fact the culprit. She had barely slept, barely ate, and had hardly spoken to anyone in days aside from her usual appointments.

Rachel had been busy at work, but her girlfriend still checked in on her every now and then. Despite Laura having told her she loved her, there was a definite tension between the two women that had been there since Christmas and Laura was honestly relieved that Rachel was being distant. The doorbell rang and she delicately lifted herself up off the couch to answer it.

"Hey I brought you lunch," Rachel smiled, but Laura sensed some tension in her tone.

"Thanks, that's really sweet. Come on in." Even the way they spoke to each other these last few weeks had shifted. It was awkward and uncomfortable and not the easy going and affectionate way it had been in months past. Rachel sat down on the lounge across from Laura and her blue eyes pierced into her own, the look in them told her she wanted to talk. Laura almost sighed sensing after these last few weeks what might be coming. "Something on your mind?"

Rachel shifted uncomfortably in her seat and smiled lightly back, Laura could tell she was nervous. "I've been holding off having this conversation because you're still hurt and I don't want to upset you, but...honestly, I'm upsetting myself by continuing to ignore this." Laura raised an eyebrow and waited for Rachel to continue. "You don't love me Laura, at least not in the way I love you." Laura felt the sting of Rachel's honest truth deep within her chest.

"Before you say anything let me just finish what I have to say," Rachel spoke as Laura went to open her mouth, instead nodding her head in acknowledgement. "Ever since I met you I have always felt you were holding back. I tried so hard for so long to get you to open up to me, but no matter how hard I tried there was always a part of you, you wouldn't relinquish. Then when Isabella showed up, I noticed a change in you, you were happier and more relaxed. I thought maybe after struggling with the stress of incompetent partners for so long, having a friend in the position would allow you to give yourself fully to me." Laura took a deep breath, knowing what would be coming next.

"But instead over the last few months I've watched you slip further and further away. At first, I didn't completely understand it. But then I remembered the girl. The girl Parker had told me about that broke your heart so many years ago. I realised before my eyes the pieces were being put back together...only not by me, by her.

"When you told me you loved me in the hospital I was overjoyed, the love of my life loved me back. But then when I stepped away and looked into those dazzling green eyes of yours, you were looking at the door with an undeniable sadness. I

don't know what is going on between the two of you, but I know you didn't mean those words for me when they clearly belong to her. I can't stand by and watch the love of my life pine after the love of hers." Laura shook her head as the first tears began running down her cheeks.

"I love you Laura and that's why I have to let you go."

Laura brushed a few stray tears from her cheeks, mustering up the courage to look Rachel in the eye. "I'm sorry Rach, I never meant for you to get hurt. I do love you, so, so much." She took hold of Rachel's hands. "But I'm sorry, I'm not in love with you. I wish I was." Rachel offered her a small smile back as she nodded her head.

"You're truly one of the most amazing people I've ever met Rach. The truth is, I've been hurting for a really long time. I should have told you about Isabella. I was just so angry, upset and overwhelmed by everything I didn't know how to act and I've ended up hurting you in the process, something I never ever wanted to do." Laura took a deep breath, it was one of the hardest conversations she had ever had. "I hope that maybe one day down the track you could forgive me and that maybe we could still be in one another's life." Laura looked into Rachel's blue eyes as a few tears spilled over her cheeks.

"Maybe one day," she smiled sadly, standing up off Laura's couch. She bent down and placed a soft kiss on the top of Laura's head. "Bye Laur."

* * *

That had been the hardest day since she had left the hospital. Rachel had been so good for her, had done so much for her and yet she couldn't simply return her same love. The six weeks since the accident had given her plenty of time to think. Her heart and head were in a deathly struggle. She knew she loved Isabella, her heart had always loved Isabella. Her head though was angry. Angry that she had lied, that she had left her. Her head wanted to hold onto that anger because it felt that Isabella didn't deserve another chance, but her heart was never ready to let go.

Swirling thoughts and feelings aside Laura forced herself into the shower and got ready for work, donning her favourite grey pantsuit. She perfected her makeup, wanting to look her absolute best before seeing everyone, or rather one particular someone, after so many weeks. Pushing her nerves aside she climbed into her car and made her way to the 34th precinct.

"Well, well, well. Look who finally decided to turn up to work," Jordan smirked, earning him an eye roll from Laura and a slight upwards pull in her lips as she stepped out of the lift.

"Shut up Foster, I've been through that case file so many times in the last six weeks, I can pretty much guarantee I know the case better than you."

"Is that so? Tell me then...who's our main suspect?"

Right on cue, the clatter of the break room door closing, drew her attention to said suspect. In walked Kyle in his custom-tailored suit and usual confident swagger, a cheeky smirk forming across his face as his eyes landed on Laura. "Aye, the cripple's back!"

Jordan laughed, but Laura didn't so much as crack a smile. Her eyes were piercing and her jaw set. Kyle seemed to notice the heavy gaze as she noticed him gulp.

"Just the man I was looking for," Laura said, Jordan quirking an eyebrow. "I've got a few questions for you."

Kyle opened up his palms to Laura, signifying that he was an open book, "Hit me."

"I think it's best to do this in private." Laura motioned to the interrogation rooms down the hall. Kyle looked nervous as his eyes flittered to the doors and back to Laura.

"Carlsson...you can't be serious," Jordan protested.

"I'm one hundred percent serious. You can wait outside," Laura ordered, her tone signifying that Jordan shouldn't dare protest. Jordan still looked in utter shock as he turned back to face his best friend and partner. The unnerving part for Laura was that Kyle didn't look surprised or outraged at all, he seemed to know what she was angling at.

Laura began walking down the hall towards the interrogation room as Kyle followed behind first and then Jordan. Laura entered the room and sat down in a chair at the table, leaving the other one open for Kyle as Jordan entered the adjacent room and began watching through the glass.

"Kyle Reynolds, I'm going to ask you a few questions. As you are aware you have the right to remain silent. Anything you say can be used against you in court. You have the right to talk to a lawyer for advice before I ask you any questions. You have the right to have a lawyer with you during questioning. If you cannot afford a lawyer, one will be appointed for you before any questioning if you wish. If you decide to answer questions now without a lawyer present, you have the right to stop answering at any time."

"Jesus Carlsson, this whole charade is a bit much don't you think?" Kyle asked, perspiration beginning to form on his forehead.

Laura ignored him and decided to launch straight into things. She had to try and hold her nerve and move fast or she knew she would crumble. "Where did you get the bruises that I pointed out on your wrists when I was in the hospital?"

"I told you I hurt myself at the gym." Kyle rubbed his wrist subconsciously and looked down, Laura could tell once again he was lying.

"How?"

"Um...I dropped a dumbbell on my wrist." Laura rolled her eyes as Kyle took a deep breath.

"The night of the NYU murder, where were you?" Laura placed a CCTV camera photo on the table showing Kyle's car leaving his apartment building that same night.

"What?" Kyle asked, completely bewildered this time as if he suddenly didn't understand why he was in the interrogation room.

"Where were you going this night?" Laura pointed to the photo.

"I don't know, maybe going to my Mum's place or something or out with a girl. How is that relevant?" He asked, his voice becoming higher pitched.

"I think it's completely relevant," Laura countered, shuffling through some papers in her folder. "The day of my stabbing, your cruiser was in an accident. Jordan said you left him at approximately ten am. That would mean you would definitely have made the ten past ten subway. Why did it take you forty minutes to do a twenty-minute trip?"

"Wait a minute, wait a minute," Kyle began to look panicked as he looked at the folder of papers sitting on the desk. "What the hell are you inferring

Laura?"

"I'll ask the questions Mr Reynolds."

"Mr Reynolds? What the actual fuck!" Kyle slammed his hands down on the table and Laura looked up and glared at him, her teeth clenched.

"Calm down or I'll be forced to restrain you." Kyle just scoffed and threw his head back as if he couldn't quite believe what was happening. "You've been seen on countless occasions lurking around NYU despite the fact that you don't attend the school or live anywhere close. Why is that?"

"The campus has good coffee," Kyle shrugged, causing Laura to roll her eyes again.

"Don't bullshit me Kyle! Why are there so many signs pointing to you in this case?" Kyle was shifting uncomfortably in his chair, his cheeks growing redder. "Tell me the truth!"

"I'm not the Washington Killer Laura! Jesus. You know me, how could you even insinuate such a thing?" Kyle looked genuinely hurt as he spat back at Laura. She hesitated for a second, her friendship with the other detective clouding her ability to properly interrogate him.

"Because I know when you're lying to me Kyle. If you're not the killer, then just explain all of these things."

"I already have, I'm innocent! And I'll be waiting for my apology when you realise it." He sat back in his chair, his eyes cold with anger.

"If that's the case, explain the bruises," Laura pressed again as Kyle shook his head

"I told you—"

"I don't believe you!" Laura shot up out of her seat, her anger projecting her voice to a yell. The door burst open and in stepped a concerned Isabella and an even more panicked Ellie behind her. "Medina? What the hell are you doing!"

"Calm down Laura, it's not what it looks like. He's innocent." Laura shook her head, waiting for an answer. Ellie stepped forward and Laura looked even more confused.

"What are you doing here?"

"Making sure you don't either arrest or kill one of your best friends," Ellie answered, looking nervous and uncomfortable under her sister's gaze.

"Can someone please explain what the hell is going on?" Laura demanded, looking first to Isabella and then to Ellie. Isabella placed a reassuring hand on Ellie's shoulder and squeezed.

"Kyle and I... have sort of been seeing each other," Ellie's voice came out in almost a whisper as she looked up at her sister, clearly terrified of her reaction. Kyle too was sheepishly looking up. Laura turned to look at Kyle and then back to Ellie, still not saying anything. "It started at Christmas and we've been hanging out ever since."

Laura took a minute to process what she was being told before she answered, "Define 'hanging out'?"

"Casually seeing one another," Ellie replied bluntly. Laura now glared back at Kyle and he stood up from his seat, backing up a few steps as Jordan entered the room. She was so sure she had been right about Kyle; this news was completely bewildering.

"But the bruises?" Laura asked, sure that they couldn't simply be a coincidence.

"Handcuffs," Ellie shrugged as Kyle turned bright red and Jordan slapped a hand across his face.

"Dear lord," Jordan mumbled. "That's just embarrassing dude." Kyle ignored him and instead turned to Laura.

"Laura," Kyle spoke softly, but the detective refused to meet his eye. "Laura?" She looked up this time, her jaw still set in anger. "It's not just sex ok? I care about her."

Laura began walking around the table to stand in front of Kyle, Isabella following, holding her hand up to keep Laura from getting too close. Laura sighed and looked up into Kyle's eyes, pushing Isabella's hand away. "Well, I'm glad you're not the killer." The room all let out a collective sigh. "But if I ever hear anything about the ins and outs of you and my sister's sex life again, or if you hurt her in any way, I will kill you."

"I don't doubt it," Kyle smiled, prompting a chuckle from Jordan. "Good to have you back Carlsson."

"Good to be back."

CHAPTER 22

* * *

Laura's head was throbbing with information already as she read through the coroner's reports for each of the Washington Killer murders. It was far too early in the morning to be functioning without coffee, but she had decided to come into the precinct early and get a head start on things after she skipped out early yesterday.

"Morning Carlsson," Jordan smiled as he dropped his gym bag to the floor and took a seat at his desk.

"Mhmm."

"Someone's chipper this morning," Jordan chuckled.

"Coffee."

"Want me to make you one?" Laura shook her head and looked down at her watch, Isabella should be arriving sometime soon with hers. She felt guilty at the thought, but she just wasn't ready to deal with the whole Isabella thing right now. She needed to get back into work and finish up her last week of rehab without any complications.

"Morning," Laura looked up as Kyle approached his desk, a tentative smile on his face. She could tell he was nervous as to what her reaction would be today, she did have a tendency to be hot and cold. Attempting to rid herself of her Isabella nerves, she decided to have a bit of fun with him.

"Reynolds. Have fun fucking my sister last night?" Both Kyle and Jordan's jaws dropped at the question and she had to try her hardest to keep her smirk at bay.

"Wh-what?" Kyle asked, completely dumbfounded.

"I mean, I know you've always had a thing for me," Laura said, as she stood up and approached Kyle, drawing out her words in the huskiest and sexiest voice she could muster. "Why settle for second best?" She practically purred as she grabbed a hold of Kyle's tie and pulled him closer.

"I-I," Kyle stuttered nervously, his eyes flittering to Jordan's in a desperate plea for help. "I really like Ellie."

"Good answer," Laura smirked, dropping his tie and stepping away from him as Jordan burst into a fit of laughter. Laura was mildly disgusted with

259

herself as she wiped down her blouse like it had been infected after touching Kyle. Kyle on the other hand looked like he was ready to collapse from the nerves. "Imagine if you two get married, I'll have a life time to mess with you!" Laura laughed as Jordan high-fived her and Kyle took a deep breath, trying to compose himself.

"Fuck you Carlsson," Kyle pouted.

"You wish," Laura smirked, sitting back down at her desk. The lift doors opened and Isabella stepped out and began walking towards them.

"Morning," her voice came out robotically as she placed her purse and coffee on her desk. As Laura's eyes fell on the singular coffee, she couldn't help but feel hurt. She had wanted to hurt Isabella when she told Rachel she loved her, just like she was hurting, but now she realised it might have been a step too far.

"Morning sunshine," Jordan smiled.

"Morning," Isabella replied as she took a quick glance at Laura and then slumped down in her chair. Kyle raised an eyebrow to Laura as if to ask 'what's up with her', but she just shook her head. She couldn't help but feel maybe Isabella's mood had something to do with her presence back at work.

"Before we begin hashing out any more personal dramas, can we go over these case notes please?" Jordan asked. As if right on cue, the Captain's door opened and he popped his head out.

"Carlsson," the Captain's voice came out gruff and stern.

"Yes sir?"

"There's been another murder in the East Village, looks like Washington Killer MO," he walked over to Laura's desk and placed her gun and badge down. Laura couldn't help the smile that spread across her face, after so many weeks of being bored to death on her couch, it felt good to be back. "You'll be needing these."

"Thank you, Sir." Laura stood up and motioned for Isabella, Kyle and Jordan to accompany her.

"And Carlsson?"

"Yes sir?"

"Try not to get stabbed this time." Kyle chuckled and the Captain glared at him as he attempted to stifle his laughter.

"I'll do my best Captain."

They pulled up at an address in a popular nightlife area of the East Village. CSU had already set up in an alleyway beside a trendy cocktail bar, Laura had even frequented the bar on occasion. As they approached the scene Laura noticed the light brown hair peeping out from behind the dumpster and a feeling of trepidation took over her.

"Rach!" Kyle called, capturing the ME's attention as she stood up from behind the bin.

"Hey stranger, haven't seen you in a while," Jordan smiled and Rachel gave him a warm smile back, her eyes flickering up to Laura's nervously. "Laura been keeping you busy?" Laura internally kicked herself for not having told the other detectives about their break up before now. It just made this whole scenario all the more awkward.

"Just been busy with work I guess," Rachel played it off, not acknowledging the statement about Laura. She always let Laura go about things in her own time.

"What do we have here?" Laura asked, trying to take control of the situation before things could get more uncomfortable.

Rachel began explaining the apparent cause of death of the woman lying in the pool of blood before them, a note atop her chest. From her initial examination it looked like the same cause of death as every other case, a hunting knife to the kidney. They thanked Rachel before turning towards the cocktail bar to inquire with the owners about the CCTV cameras.

"I sensed tension Laura, something up with you two?" Jordan asked, as Kyle and Isabella walked close by.

"We broke up."

"What?" Kyle asked, completely astounded by the revelation. "When?"

"About a month ago."

"Who broke up with who?" He inquired again, as Laura's eyes flittered to Isabella's for a reaction. The detective however still looked completely out of it, as if the news of Laura's break up meant absolutely nothing to her. Laura felt a surge of anger flare up inside her.

"She dumped me."

"Ouch, that's rough," Kyle pulled a pained face.

"Sorry to hear that Laura," Jordan offered, eliciting a small smile from the detective.

"Thanks Foster, it was probably for the best." Laura looked to Isabella one last time, but was again dismayed to see her eyes trained on the bar, not even the slightest acknowledgement of their conversation was present on her face.

They headed back to the precinct with no CCTV and few witnesses to come by. It was becoming increasingly frustrating that he seemed to continually allude them without leaving any evidence behind. Laura ran her hands through her hair, squeezing her eyes closed as she tried to push away the tiredness and hopelessness she felt.

"Do I have the best news of the day for you," Parker clapped as she exited the lift. The four detectives stared up at her dismally, all exhausted from the ongoing investigation. "Who's ready to catch the Washington Killer?"

"What?" The four detectives asked in shocked synchronicity.

"You all spend way too much time together, that's just freaky!" Kyle and Jordan laughed as Parker placed a piece of paper down on Laura's desk.

"What is it?" Laura asked as she leant forward to examine the paper.

"DNA results. I've got a match to your killer."

"Seriously? They're already in the system? Are they from New York?" Kyle asked excitedly.

"They were from New York…"

"They're dead?" Jordan guessed, his tone once again dispirited.

"Unfortunately, yes. The DNA was matched to an unsolved homicide from six years ago. Victim's name is Elin Herman. She was murdered by strangulation and there has never been any strong leads in the case."

"Until now," Kyle quipped.

"According to our database she was a 31-year-old Dutch national living in America illegally. She worked as a sex worker and her body was found beaten and lifeless by the side of a dumpster in Harlem. Police were never able to locate the victim's family."

"Well I guess that clears up the mystery of the dollar bills." Jordan, Kyle and Laura all nodded at Isabella's deduction.

"Do you have a photo?" Jordan asked and Parker pulled out a picture of a young blonde woman, her eyes closed, her skin a pale white as her body lay lifeless on a metal table.

"Does the coroner's report mention any signs on the victim's body that show that she had given birth?" Laura asked.

"Actually, she does. They found a C-section scar on her stomach. The scar was well healed and barely visible indicating that she likely gave birth during her growth years, potentially between the ages of fourteen to eighteen."

"So, in that case it's highly likely she has a late teen or young adult son running around out there murdering girls." Kyle shook his head.

"That would be a reasonable assumption, though digital forensics ran a trace and being that she was an illegal immigrant, there is no mention of a child anywhere on our systems."

"So the kid's a ghost?" Jordan asked, frustrated.

"Essentially." Kyle and Jordan both groaned.

"Well it's more than we knew yesterday, thank you Parker," Laura smiled. "At least now we are beginning to paint a picture of our killer. We know what motivates him. That can only propel our case forward."

"Agreed," Jordan nodded as Parker waved goodbye on her way back to the morgue.

"Start seeing what you can dig up on Elin Herman." Laura ordered the detectives. "I'm going to grab a coffee, anyone want one?" Laura asked as she made her way to the lift. Kyle and Jordan shook their heads, Isabella not bothering to acknowledge her question, too consumed by something on her phone. Laura simply rolled her eyes and walked away.

She rode in the lift back up to their level, sipping on her black coffee with one sugar from the shop just down the street. Seeing as Isabella was no longer getting her coffees, she wasn't about to make her own. The doors opened and her eyes were drawn to a man standing by her desk, beside Isabella. His tousled brown hair and the way he stood were all so familiar. A terrible sense of foreboding took over Laura as she got closer.

"I'm Mitch Davis," the man introduced himself to Kyle who took his hand reluctantly. The name sent a shiver up Laura's spine and she had to compose herself enough to even walk straight.

"Kyle Reynolds."

"Jordan Foster. How do you know Isabella?" Jordan asked, his eyes falling on Laura as she approached.

"I'm her husband," he smiled as Kyle's jaw dropped.

"Ex-husband," Laura corrected, drawing everyone's attention to her. Isabella's eyes connected with hers for a split second before they dropped to the floor, she looked extremely uncomfortable.

"Laura, good to see you," Mitch smiled falsely as he placed his hand on Isabella's lower back. Laura's cheeks flushed with anger. Unlike Laura, he didn't seem completely shocked to see his old schoolmate. "But no, we are still married."

"What?" The question came out of Laura's mouth before she could stop it, a venom in her tone she couldn't control.

"Exactly what you heard Carlsson," Mitch spat back, Kyle and Jordan glaring at him. Laura couldn't believe what she was hearing, yet another lie, and Isabella wasn't correcting him. "Now if you'll excuse me detectives, I'm here to take my wife to lunch."

Mitch motioned towards the lifts and Isabella picked up her purse and began walking ahead of him, leaving behind three completely bewildered detectives. Laura watched as Isabella stepped inside the lift, the reality of the situation hit her like a ton of bricks, she had waited too long.

23

Chapter 23

"Carlsson," Laura picked up her phone as she walked hurriedly to her appointment, the cool air whipping up her coat as her boots trod purposefully on the damp pavement.

"Hey, Reynolds tracked down an old neighbour of Elin Herman, she's living in Chicago now and she's about 85-years old, but she's got a good memory." Jordan sounded excited.

"And? Did she have a son?"

"She did, the old lady lived next door to them when he was just a toddler. Said he looked just like his Mum, light blonde hair and blue eyes. So, based on that timeline, that should mean he's about twenty-one now."

"Did she say anything else?" Laura asked as she trotted up the marble stairs to her doctor's office.

"She thinks she remembers he had some sort of injury; she said his mother was really protective."

"Does she remember what kind?" Laura asked urgently, looking down at her watch.

"Unfortunately not."

"It's a start." Laura sighed, slightly frustrated that the investigation wasn't moving quicker. "Have you got a list of Herman's around those birth years," Laura asked.

"Yeah, there's thousands though," Jordan answered, his tone beginning to sound just as exasperated.

"See if you can narrow the list down to Manhattan born only."

"Can do."

"And Jordan, good work," Laura complimented, she knew her team needed the morale boost, everyone was working overtime to try and get this guy. She hung up the phone and pushed the office door open just as the secretary came out to call her name. She took a deep breath and walked towards the door, entering and taking a seat in her usual leather armchair.

"So Laura, how has your recovery been going?" The psychologist asked, her voice soft and drawn out.

"Good, I'm still going to physical therapy, but they've started easing me off all pain killers as of this week."

"That's great news." The woman smiled warmly and Laura nodded in agreement. It had been a hard few months in therapy initially for her, but over time she slowly began to open up and trust her psychologist. She allowed her to see that it was ok to be vulnerable sometimes.

"How have things been going at work?"

"Fine. We're still struggling for leads on our major investigation at the moment, but apart from that it's been fine."

"And how have you been coping since the break up? Have you spoken to Rachel since?" She enquired, scribbling down some notes.

"Here and there we text, but I think we're both just trying to move on. I had to work alongside her on a case last week, but it was all pretty amicable." Rachel was too professional to act any differently at work, but they also had a mutual respect Laura was sure wasn't just going to disappear now they had broken up.

"That's good," she smiled, pausing and giving Laura a long penetrating look. The detective knew what was coming next. She was easing her into their session with some small talk and a few easy questions before she would hit her where it hurt. "How are things with Isabella?"

Laura shrugged, "We have a working relationship and right now, that seems that's all it's ever going to be."

"Why do you say that?" She probed.

"I pushed her away, I told her I didn't love her and made her believe I was in love with Rachel and now it's all over," Laura sighed, it was hard to say the words.

"That doesn't mean it's all over Laura, give it time. You need to sit down and talk to Isabella about all of this." Laura shook her head and stood up, beginning to pace around the room. She was too antsy to sit down any longer.

"No, there isn't time." The psychologist looked up at Laura confused, before she could open her mouth to speak once more Laura answered. "Mitch is back."

"He's back? As in back together with Isabella?" The psychologist seemed shocked by the admission, almost as bewildered as Laura felt.

"It looks that way."

"It looks that way or it is that way?"

"I don't know."

The psychologist began scribbling something in her notepad as Laura stared absentmindedly at one of the pictures on the wall that read 'every day starts with a new dawn'. Laura just rolled her eyes.

"How are things with Ellie?"

"Good. She's been busy with college and she spends a lot of time with Kyle. But I feel like we're the closest we've ever been." They had never really been close as kids, she and Alex had always been the closest. The falling out after he died had prevented them from building a relationship, until now.

"So you have forgiven her for the past? For lying to you and for taking your parents side for all those years?"

"She was young, it wasn't her fault. The important thing is that she has forgiven me."

"If you can forgive Ellie, why can't you forgive Isabella?" Laura stared at her confused. The two things weren't the same at all and she couldn't reconcile how this woman could even compare them.

"It's not the same thing," she argued, Ellie had sided with her parents sure, but she had been so young. Isabella had lied to her and broken her trust.

"It is the same thing Laura," the woman urged, as the green eyes stared penetratingly back at her. "You know what I think?"

"It sounds like you're about to tell me," Laura grumbled.

"I think you have forgiven Isabella for lying. I think you're withholding your forgiveness in order to protect your heart because you haven't fully forgiven yourself yet." There was a long moment of silence as Laura and the psychologist stared back at one another, refusing to break eye contact.

"I'd say you have some wild theories Doc." The woman let out a deep sigh.

"Have you still been experiencing the same sort of dreams each night?" Laura nodded.

"Yes. The same ones over and over again with Alex. Though lately there's been another voice, I think it might be Isabella's." The doctor asked Laura to keep a journal of her dreams to discuss at their next appointment as she let herself back outside and headed home.

She had just sat down on the lounge when she heard two sharp knocks at her door and reluctantly stood back up to answer it. She was in a considerable amount of pain since she had begun weaning herself off the painkillers and her body was exhausted. When she opened the door, she was surprised to see Parker on her doorstep.

"Parker, what's up?"

"Good to see you too Laur," Parker smiled as she pushed her way past Laura and into the apartment. "You look like shit by the way," she called over her shoulder as she marched into the living room and took up residence on Laura's large white couch.

"I'm in pain and I'm really feeling a nap, so if you're here to hang out I'm going to have to reschedule," Laura winced as she sat back down on the lounge, her stomach really giving her grief.

"I'm not here to hang out."

"Oh," Laura raised an eyebrow as she adjusted the pillow behind her back. "Then what do you want?"

"A touch of hospitality wouldn't go astray, but that seems doubtful in your current state, so instead I'll go with some freaking common sense," her tone was aggressive and demanding, catching Laura off guard.

"What?" Laura asked, confused by Parker's sudden outburst and in too much pain to try and decipher her riddles.

"Look, I talked to Isabella. She told me everything. I can admit when I'm wrong and I was wrong to judge her so quickly without hearing her whole story. You know that Martin Davis basically tricked her into marrying his son. You really need to hear her out." Laura sighed and looked up into the eyes of her best friend.

"Ok. When she comes back to work, we'll sit down and talk."

"That might be too late. Do you know who I saw her having lunch with today?"

"Let me guess, Mitch?"

"Mitch, Laura! Freaking Mitch Davis." A look of complete and utter revulsion took over Parker's face at the mention of him. "Are you seriously going to give her up again to that complete tosser?"

"They're separated. Isabella wouldn't get back together with him," Laura said doubtfully, pretending her mind hadn't been plagued the last week with thoughts to the contrary. Parker raised her eyebrows and shot Laura a look of complete disbelief.

"From what I could see, I wouldn't be surprised if he was here to win her back. And seeing as you so brutally turned her down, I'd say she's open to the idea. I mean the boy's only gotten more attractive." Laura rolled her eyes and groaned.

"Good for Isabella," she stood up from the couch and pulled Parker up with her. "Now if you wouldn't mind, I have a throbbing headache, my stomach is killing me and sleep is calling. Bye Parks." Laura opened the door and guided her best friend out, closing it in her face before she could say another word. She made her way back over to the lounge and within minutes she was fast asleep.

The next morning Laura headed towards the NYU campus to collect a few more witness statements from the victim's friends. After she collected the statements, she headed to the Steam Bar and sat down, ordering an Iced Caramel Macchiato and black coffee for herself. She looked around at all the students sitting around her, textbooks piled up on tables, laptops stained with coffee rings. She was glad she no longer had to cram for exams. Savannah bustled her way through the door, past the huge line to order coffees, waving at Laura as she approached.

"Hey, sorry I'm late." Savannah dumped her backpack on the floor, her scarf falling to the ground alongside it as she dropped into the opposite chair. Her hair was messy as if she had just woken up.

"No problems."

"How did you go with your statements?" Savannah asked as she smiled a thanks and picked up her coffee.

"Good. Had a few new witnesses come forward and hand over written statements. Now it's just a case of trawling through them to see if we can find anything new."

Savannah leant forward and lowered her voice, "So do you think maybe it might be a student here?"

"We're not sure," Laura answered vaguely and looked around the café uncomfortably. "How are things with you?"

"They're good, finally feeling like I'm settling into the college life you know. It was all really overwhelming at first, but I think I've got the rhythm now."

"That's great."

"How about you, how are things with you?"

"Good. Been working through some of my PTSD from everything with the psych and I'm making progress. I still have the nightmares, but they're getting less and less."

"That's great Laur, I'm proud of you." Laura smiled, her cheeks blushing slightly from the compliment. "I don't know about Rachel, but I'm banned from staying at Bella's at the moment, the two of us yell out so much in our sleep neither of us get a good night's sleep." Laura shifted uncomfortably again, staring at Savannah confused. She was sure Isabella would have told her about the breakup by now. "What? Why do you look weird?" Savannah asked, staring at Laura's bewilderment.

"Rachel and I broke up," Savannah stared back confused. "I just assumed Isabella would have told you."

"No, she didn't. I'm pretty sure she still thinks you're together. Did you tell her you broke up?"

"No, but it came up at work."

"She's been pretty distracted lately," Savannah trailed off, Laura's mind wandered to Mitch.

"Yes Mitch came to the precinct the other day," Laura left it open for Savannah to comment, but she only nodded, looking down awkwardly.

"She's doing it tough at the moment. She misses you," Savannah said, dodging the statement about Mitch. "It's our father's anniversary today." Laura's blood boiled at the mention of Samuel, but she didn't want to upset Savannah by letting on that was the case. "Isabella always takes this day off."

"Anniversary?"

"Yeah," Savannah nodded sadly. "It's nine years since he passed away. It was right before the trial."

"Oh," Laura didn't know what to say. For someone whose job it was to know the details, it was clear she was missing a lot of them from her own life.

"I don't think he wanted to put us through that," Savannah said sadly, looking out the window. "I don't think he could've gone through that. I only saw him once after he was charged, he was so frail, so lost in grief." Savannah's eyes were glassy with tears and Laura herself felt sad at the thought of a grief-stricken Samuel. She had pictured him only in anger since she had found out about the accident, not as vulnerable, sad. "I've seen two people I love lose the person they love most in the world and it's awful. I don't even know if I want to meet mine."

Laura smiled sadly and looked at Savannah, "Of course you do, there's nothing better." Savannah looked down and picked up her coffee. "Are you dating anyone at the moment?"

"No, not really. My friend Andy asked me out a few months back but he's really not my type. We're just good friends now. I'm happy being single right now, I just want to focus on me."

"That's a good attitude," Laura added, knowing it was her own for now.

After she said goodbye to Savannah she headed back to the precinct, she was antsy, nervous. The murders were continuing and they still had no strong leads to point them to their suspect. The strongest lead they did have was now in prison himself, the Mayor having to pull strings to get him transferred from Texas to New York for their interrogation.

Laura stepped out of the lift and stalked down the hall, Kyle and Jordan were standing in front of the murder board discussing tactics. "Is he in there?" Laura asked, her head nodding towards the interrogation room.

"Oh he's in there," Kyle said, raising his eyebrows. "And he's pissed."

"Yeah seems he figured out it was my tip off to the D's that got him incarcerated," Jordan said. They had discovered his involvement in multiple phishing scams whilst they had been checking into his background. A few words to their friends at criminal enterprise and he was incarcerated shortly thereafter.

Greg Blant sat in the interrogation room in an orange jumpsuit and handcuffs, a deep scowl written across his pretentious hipster face. Laura matched his glare as Kyle sat beside her, Jordan watching on from behind the glass.

"Thank you for coming Mr Blant—"

"You say that like I had a choice," he huffed as he moved his hands up to his face and pushed his glasses further up on his nose. Laura's jaw became more rigid at the interruption, she couldn't stand disrespect.

"We have some more questions for you about the man you know as Mason," Greg rolled his eyes as Laura looked at him penetratingly.

"No comment." Greg said as he lounged back in the chair. He appeared bored as his eyes searched around the room, looking anywhere but Laura's.

"Where is Mason now?"

"No comment."

"What is Mason's last name?" Laura shot back, stronger this time.

"No comment."

"Look Greg, if you talk to us and we're satisfied with your answers I have friends down at the prison, I could get you your own cell," Kyle tried to reason, playing good cop. "A good-looking guy like you, it won't be long until someone comes along and tries to make you, their bitch." Greg looked horrified. Laura was surprised, the vulgar approach was definitely not one she had ever tried, but the horrified look in the young man's eyes told her it had been somewhat effective.

"I can handle myself." There was a slight quiver in Greg's voice and Laura was certain he would stand little chance next to some of the thugs at Lincoln Correctional Facility.

"Sure you can," Kyle smiled sarcastically. "That offer expires in the next five minutes."

"You know Rikers makes Lincoln look like a five-star resort," Laura watched as a shiver passed up Greg's spine at just the mention of the infamous New York prison, she smiled smugly. "If you don't answer our questions, I will be forced to indict you for obstruction of justice and Rikers would be my recommendation to the board," Laura's voice was assertive and authoritative and Greg crumbled under her gaze.

"I don't know his last name ok; we were never that close. We hung out a few times, worked out sometimes together, that was it. To me he was Mason, but I sort of got the impression that wasn't his real name."

"How come?" Kyle inquired and Greg shrugged.

"Just a feeling...honestly the guy was a bit of a nerd trying to play tough and it wouldn't surprise me if the name was part of that."

"Did he have an accent at all? Maybe European sounding?" Laura enquired, as she tried to dig for a connection between Mason and his potential dead mother.

"Mmm nah, had more of a Queens tang honestly."

"Did he ever mention his family?" Greg quirked his eyebrow and pulled his lip to the side as though he was thinking.

"Think he said he didn't have any. Not too sure, we didn't really get into the personal details."

"What *did* you to talk about then?" Laura asked, getting frustrated by the lack of useful information their witness was offering up.

"Gaming, sport, girls, hacking. Guys stuff," he shrugged. "Honestly nothing ever seemed too far out of the ordinary. He was a bit shy and socially awkward, but overall, a nice enough guy."

"Did he ever mention a girlfriend?"

"Nah, no girlfriend, he didn't seem to have a hell of a lot of respect for woman tbh," Greg fiddled with the cuffs on his wrists, "He talked a big game, but I'm not sure I believed most of it. It's hard enough these days for a good-looking guy like me, an average, nerdy guy like him?" Greg scoffed. "Not exactly a lady magnet."

"You're right, a white-collar criminal is far more attractive," Laura jabbed, earning a head shake from Greg.

"You said you discussed hacking, what exactly did you guys talk about?"

"I don't know, he was interested in it, he was more of a novice. Wanted to know more about geo tracking."

"Geo tracking?" Laura asked alarmed, wondering if maybe that meant the killer had tracked his victims.

"Yeah, not exactly my area of expertise, so I couldn't help the guy."

"Ok...is there anything else about him that could be an identifying feature, tattoos, deformities, different coloured eyes, a stutter maybe? What about any scars?" Kyle leant forward, enclosing the space between him and Greg, as the man pondered his question.

"Yeah actually. He does have a big scar down his chest. He said he had, had heart surgery as a kid. That's all I know though."

"We'll be in touch if we have any further questions." Laura picked up the file and motioned for Jordan to send the patrol officers down to pick up the prisoner.

"What about my cell?" Greg asked urgently as the two detectives made their way to the door.

"I'll talk to my boys at Lincoln," Kyle answered, "No promises though."

"This is bullshit—"

Laura closed the door behind them before having to listen to the rest of the man's rant. The two detectives walked back to their desks and were met by Jordan.

"Well, at least we got some useful information I guess," Jordan sighed as he looked at a dejected Laura and Kyle. They had been hoping for something a bit more concrete, a last name, another known address, something more immediate.

"Yeah, it's something," Laura shrugged, "Can the both of you begin cross checking the names on that list with any criminal charges. A guy like this surely has a past record."

"You got it," Jordan nodded.

"And also track down a list of names for heart surgeries during that time period."

"I mean we can try, but it's probably going to be a long list, maybe hundreds or even thousands of names." Jordan didn't look optimistic.

"True, but if we get those names and cross check them in our system for past criminal charges it might narrow things down a bit. This type of killer doesn't just go from civilian to serial killer, he has to have a past."

"We'll try," Kyle nodded.

"How are my favourite detectives doing?" Parked asked as she walked towards them from the lift, her black wedge heels tapping on the floors.

"Hey Parker, you look nice," Kyle commented, Laura looking at him pointedly. "What, I'm just saying she looks nice," he held up his hands. "Can't a guy give compliments anymore."

"A guy can, you don't give compliments, you flirt," Laura bit back.

"So, what brings you up here?" Jordan asked, refocusing the conversation.

"I just wanted to hear how the interrogation went...well that and coffee," she wiggled her eyebrows in excitement.

"Yeah it went alright. We found out the killer likely had heart surgery when he was a baby, judging by the neighbour's comments. We believe he is around twenty, twenty-one, and grew up in New York."

"Do you have a mug I could borrow?" Parker asked. Laura looked around her desk not seeing any mugs. She looked at Isabella's desk, but thankfully, unlike her last partner, she wasn't one to leave mugs out either. She opened her desk drawer and spotted a mug inside. She reached inside to grab it, as something else caught her eye. Her own name, jutting out from a news clipping tucked inside a folder.

She grabbed the mug and handed it to Parker, the ME thanking her briefly before continuing her conversation with Kyle and Jordan. Laura reached inside and pulled the folder out. Resting on top, the first article read

'Young Officer Cracks the Case of Missing Boy'. She knew what case it was immediately. She had only been a constable, barely finished her probationary year, and that case had been a big part of the reason she was accepted into the detective's program so early.

She flicked past the article to the next one, 'New York's Youngest Detective Hits the Beat'. In the centre of the article was a picture of her accepting her graduation award from the Detective's Commander. She looked so young in the photo, so excited.

The next article read 'Midnight Madman Caught', the next 'Manhattan's Elite Detectives', and there were half a dozen more like them. All newspaper clippings from Laura's biggest cases and achievements as a police officer. She was taken aback, her throat dry and her stomach jittering. She found it hard to believe Isabella when she said she had loved her all this time, she didn't think it possible. And yet here in her drawer, was more proof, she had been keeping tabs on her all this time.

"Hi guys," Cate's voice pulled Laura from her pondering. Laura looked up and smiled as Jordan and Kyle greeted her, Parker offering a cold 'hey' back.

"What are you doing here?" Laura asked, standing up to greet her friend.

"I thought I'd come and check in and see how you guys are doing." Cate held up the plastic container in her arms. "I baked you all some muffins."

"I love muffins!" Jordan said excitedly. "Bri never lets me have them."

"Thanks Cate," Kyle smiled.

"That's really sweet of you," Laura smiled back, looking towards Parker who was still giving Cate the cold shoulder. Cate's eyes kept flittering across to her nervously. It was clear to Laura this was her idea of a peace offering. "Jordan, did you want to take Cate to the break room and make her a coffee?"

"Sure," Jordan nodded and led her towards the break room. Once the door closed Laura turned to Parker.

"Come on Parks, time to let it go."

"She should've told us," Parker defended as Kyle watched on, arms crossed and pensive.

"No, she was being a good friend to Isabella and a good friend to us. This is Cate, she puts all of her friends before herself. You need to get over it."

Parker looked at Laura uncertainly.

"Does that mean you're over what Isabella did?"

"I'm working on it." The breakroom door opened and Jordan and Cate reappeared, the nurse looking nervously at Parker.

"Hey Cate, there's this art show happening downtown tonight if you want to go?" Parker offered nervously. Cate's face lit up like a child at Christmas and Laura smiled brightly.

"I'd love to!" The pair disappeared down the hall discussing details for the art show as Jordan and Kyle packed up for the evening. Laura sat back down at her desk, the events of the day pressing down on her as she fought her eyelids.

"See you tomorrow Carlsson," Kyle waved as he got into the lift. She waved back and opened up the folder of statements, filtering through them again to see if there was anything she might have missed.

Two coffees and several hours later, her table lamp was the only light illuminating the darkness that surrounded her, pressing in through each window. She rubbed her eyes and yawned as she got ready to leave, her eyes flickering to something within one of the statements. It was a name, Andrew. One of the witnesses had mentioned a young man the victim had recently befriended by that name. It wasn't much to go on, but given what Greg had said about the geo targeting, she found any new male friends suspicious.

She left herself a note to follow up with the witness in the morning and turned off her lamp, making her way to the lift. As she pulled out of the precinct carpark and into the dark night, she caught a glimpse of blue eyes and brown floppy hair out the side of her window. Alex's face whooshed into her mind as she sped the rest of the way home.

24

Chapter 24

Laura slumped down into her chair at the precinct, the folder of witness statements landing on her desk with a thud. She was barely keeping her eyes open. It had only been a few short hours since she had left the same chair and her body was aching, her stomach felt as though someone was repeatedly shocking it with a branding iron.

She looked across to Isabella's empty desk, butterflies swarming in her stomach as she thought about the articles, she knew were in her desk drawer. Her eyes wandered to the elevator, she felt excited, anxious for Isabella to step out those doors. Isabella's eyes had been occupying her dreams more often than not of late. She kept finding herself going back to moments in their past with a whole new perspective. The anger she felt had mostly ebbed away, instead replaced with a deep longing. She missed her, present and past version. The doors opened, her heart raced, she looked over her shoulder.

"Morning Carlsson," Kyle waved, Jordan also waving as they stepped out of the elevator. "You're going to love me," he smiled widely as he waved a wad of paper.

"Oh yeah, why's that?" Laura asked, slightly disappointed she wasn't looking into the sparkling brown eyes she was desperate to see.

"Because, I called in a favour," he smiled devilishly. "You know John in digital forensics? Well I set him up with Mel in support services—"

"Didn't you sleep with her?" Jordan asked.

"Years ago," Kyle scoffed. "Anyways, point being, they've been happily dating now for like three months, he's definitely punching—"

"Was that the point?" Laura jabbed, yawning.

"Getting there," Kyle was practically breathless he was talking so quickly. "Anyway because of that he owed me a favour, so I got him to cross check all the names of registered heart surgeries during our predicted birth years, across any names with criminal charges or warnings. No Herman's on the list, so guess she didn't give him her last name. But..." Kyle dropped the wad of paper in front of Laura. "We're down to twenty names." Kyle and Jordan both looked at her excited.

"Wow," Laura breathed, flicking through the pile of names and records in front of her. "This is amazing work Kyle."

"It was bound to happen sometime," he joked.

"This really gives us a solid chance, we need to start working through these records straight away and narrowing things down further."

"You got it," Kyle agreed and dropped into his chair with his own wad of paperwork.

"Medina in this morning?" Jordan asked, looking over to Isabella's empty desk. Laura looked at her watch, it was eight o'clock now. Isabella was generally in by this time.

"She should be, I haven't spoken to her."

"Hmm...weird. Because I'm pretty sure I saw her ex-husband downstairs in the lobby," Jordan gave her a pitying smile. She liked that he called him that despite knowing the truth. It was his way of showing support.

"Who Mitch?" Laura asked, knowing what the answer would be. Jordan nodded and her heart rate accelerated. It felt like it had the last time, Isabella was distant and Mitch was around all the time.

In her head she was right back in that parking lot, she could see Isabella's brown eyes staring at her in the side mirror as her and Mitch drove away together. Her eyes fell on the baseball on her desk, she could almost hear Alex whispering to her, 'don't let her go this time'. She picked up her phone and dialled Isabella's number, her throat going dry as she heard it ring multiple times, no answer. She hung up the phone and picked up her keys and the wad of suspect profiles. "Guys I just need to—"

"Go," Jordan said smiling at her.

"Yeah we've got this," Kyle smiled. "Go get your girl." Laura smiled and took off at a run towards the elevator doors, her heart felt like it was going to leap out of her chest.

* * *

It had been an emotional few days and Isabella felt exhausted as she got off the subway and began walking toward Savannah's dorm. When she looked back on the last ten plus years, it often felt like she was in a constant state of grief. Grieving her mother, Alex, her father, her relationship with Laura. None of it got easier with time, she just learnt how to manage it. But today she was feeling overwhelmed by the grief and so she needed her sister's support.

She knocked on the door to Savannah's dorm, her younger sister answering with a warm smile. "Hey Bella," Savannah wrapped her arms around her and pulled her close. Isabella relaxed into the embrace, her body decompressing as she felt the warmth traveling from her chest right down to her fingertips. Savannah's dorm room smelt like pizza, there was an empty box on one of her roommate's beds, the sheets unmade and books strewn across it.

Her other roommate's bed was in complete contrast, it was perfectly made, the sheets folded and pressed so there were no wrinkles in sight. The desk next to the bed perfectly in order with books colour ordered and laptop and pens lined up in perfect right angles.

Savannah's corner was a mix of the two, she had at least pulled the covers up on her bed, most of her textbooks had made it to her desk, only a few were spread across her covers. It was a decent sized room seeing as there were three of them, they even had their own bathroom.

"How are you doing?"

"Good, I'm meeting up with Mitch later this morning and there's a lot going on with work right now. After yesterday I just felt like I needed a hug from my little sister."

"I would've come with you, if you asked," Savannah said, Isabella shaking her head. She had flown down to Miami and back yesterday to lay flowers on her parents and Alex's graves. She liked to spend that time on her own, reflecting in her own emotions. It was one of the only days she allowed her grief in.

"No, you're busy with school. You have more important things to do," Isabella waved her off.

"No I don't. I'm always here if you need me." Isabella smiled and squeezed her sister's hand.

"I know."

"I caught up with Laura yesterday," Savannah said slyly as she packed a textbook into her backpack.

"How was she?" Isabella asked, slightly scared of the answer. She had tried to give Laura her space ever since she had told Rachel she loved her at the hospital. She wanted Laura to be happy.

"She and Rachel broke up." She looked at Savannah confused; she had only just seen Rachel the other day.

"What? When?"

"Weeks ago. Apparently, she brought it up at work the other day and you didn't even flinch," Savannah gave her a quizzical look.

"Because I didn't hear her," Isabella said, astounded with herself. "I've just been so stressed with Mitch being back and working out everything there, I had no idea."

"Yeah she was quite surprised to hear you didn't know."

"Well like I said, I've been preoccupied." Isabella ran a hand through her hair, her mind racing with this new information. "How about a coffee, do you have time?" Savannah looked down at her phone.

"Actually, I don't sorry. My friend Andy is coming by any minute." Isabella's phone began ringing in her pocket, she pulled it out to see Laura's name flashing on the screen. She silenced it and slid it back into her pocket, Savannah looking at her questioningly.

"Who is this Andy guy you keep talking about? You're not dating him are you Sav?" Isabella teased.

"God no, he wishes." Savannah chuckled. "He's just a friend, he's studying art as well."

"Well I'd like to meet your friends, all three of us could go and get coffee?" Isabella suggested, feeling like she wanted to delay her day getting started with everything she had on her plate.

"Oh, Andy doesn't drink coffee."

"What kind of person doesn't drink coffee?" Isabella asked surprised.

"I don't know, he said he's got some heart thing and it doesn't help with that." Isabella's mouth went dry as she looked at Savannah, her mind ticking over with the possibility.

"What?" A knock reverberated against Savannah's door, she gave Isabella a quizzical look and went to answer it. Isabella's eyes flittered to the door as it opened, a young man stood behind it wearing jeans and a warm jacket. She could see the top of his light brown hair as they chatted, his black vans tapping on the floor.

"Andy, this is my sister Isabella," Savannah opened the door wider so that she could see his full frame. He had piercing blue eyes, the kind you weren't quick to forget. He seemed nervous as her brown eyes fell on his, they were so familiar, the hair on the back of her arms raised. She watched his face intently as he surveyed her, his lip quivering slightly.

"Nice to meet you," he offered, his eyes travelling straight to the floor.

"Come in," Savannah ushered Andy into the room and closed the door. Isabella felt the space around her shrinking with his presence, she was very aware of the gun strapped to her hip. Her sister again gave her a look as she pointed to the bathroom. "I'm just going to go to the toilet quickly and I'm ready to go." Andy gave her a nod, his eyes then travelling back to Isabella.

"So you're an arts student?" Isabella asked, trying to keep a hold of her voice as she surveyed him closer. She wasn't sure if she were being overly paranoid, or if her instincts might be right.

"Uh yeah, mostly," he said vaguely, his eyes looking around the room. He came across awkward and nervous, appearing uncomfortable in his skin. He was of medium height and build, definitely not unattractive, though his demeanour made him appear unapproachable.

"Did you move to New York to study or?"

"Mmm...no I grew up here," he replied, hesitating for a moment before answering." His accent gave him away anyway, when she listened carefully, she could hear what she thought might be a Queen's twang.

"Big family?" She pried again.

"Not especially." Isabella heard the toilet flush and the tap going, Andy turned around as Isabella exited the bathroom. As he turned around her eyes fell on the centre of his backpack, the Shred Fitness logo couldn't be more distinct against the black fabric. She was filled with dread as she began reaching for her gun. As she did Andy's eyes met hers in Savannah's mirror, those dead blue eyes fixed on the hip that held her gun as her fingers closed around it.

His hand flew to his back pocket, disappearing inside and pulling out the hunting knife she had watched him stab Laura with. At that same moment Savannah exited from the bathroom and he grabbed her around the neck, pulling her into his body as he held the knife to her throat. Isabella's gun was trained on his head, but he was too close to Savannah for comfort. She looked petrified and confused.

"What gave me away?" He asked, his eyes now fixed on hers rather than flittering across the room. His tone was strong, he no longer looked awkward and shy, he looked powerful, angry.

"Your backpack." Isabella told him, her arms outstretched ready to shoot at the first sign of movement. She could see Savannah was trembling, she was looking at her sister full of fear.

"Greg?" He asked, already knowing the answer. "I knew that would come back to haunt me."

"Then why befriend him?" She asked, her mind ticking over with ideas on what to do next. Knowing she needed more time to come up with a plan.

"Thought he could be useful, turns out he wasn't."

"But you found help somewhere, you tracked Helena all the way to Atlantic City after you met her in Manhattan." It was purely a hunch as Helena was in fact from Atlantic City, but they knew she had been in Manhattan in the days prior to her murder. She didn't feel the Washington Killer would leave his stomping grounds so easily. Savannah looked to have comprehended exactly what was happening as she let out a small whimper.

"She looked too familiar, I couldn't let her go." Isabella cast her mind back to the photo of Elin Herman and the body of Helena. They had looked particularly alike.

"She did have very similar features to your mother." Andy's eyes flickered with rage and he loosened his grip on Savannah for a split moment. Isabella's phone began ringing in her pocket once again and Andy tightened his grip at the sound.

"Someone looking for you?" He asked, staring at her pocket.

"No," she replied, keeping her focus on his head. The two stared at each other as Isabella's phone rang out and went silent. A few seconds later it began ringing again.

"Who's calling?" He raised the knife further up Savannah's neck as he said it. Isabella slid the phone out of her pocket, being careful to keep one eye on Andy as she did. Laura's name appeared flashing on the screen.

"My partner."

"Get rid of her," he ordered, it was clear from his use of 'her' that he knew exactly who her partner was. In fact, she was sure he had been using Savannah to stay close to the investigation. "But you tell her anything and I cut Savannah's neck." Savannah looked as though she might pass out, she was deathly white, her eyes glassy with tears.

"Hello."

"Hey, where are you? How come you're not at work?" Laura asked on the other end, her voice breathless.

"I had some personal things to deal with."

"I really need to speak with you, where are you? I'll come to you," Laura offered.

"I can't do this right now Laura." Isabella said, her eyes trained on Andy to ensure he wasn't going to do anything rash.

"But I really want to talk to you. I'm remembering things from the hospital, things you told me. I'm ready to talk us." Isabella's heart began racing, knowing what she had to do.

"There is no us Laura, it's over." She paused. "I'm with Mitch now. There's too many scars between us."

"Isabella—" Andy motioned for her to hang up the phone, she ended it before she could hear Laura's next words. Her eyes stung as she tucked the phone away, ten years later and it still hurt just the same.

"Now that was brutal," Andy chuckled. "And here I thought you two didn't get along...my, my, was I wrong."

"Relationships obviously aren't your strong suit."

"I won't disagree there," he smirked.

"What was it about your mother do you think?" Isabella asked, trying to take control of the situation again, edging slightly forward. "Was it that she was a sex worker?" Andy's nostrils flared, but he didn't say anything. "That she was a single mother? Or was it the fact that she never wanted you and because of that she resented you every single day?" Andy's dead eyes looked more black than blue as he glared back at her, full of rage. She could see the ruthless killer behind those dark eyes, she knew first-hand what he was capable of.

"Do you resent your murderous father every day?" Isabella tried to keep the reaction from her face, but it was difficult. She hadn't expected him to know that level of detail about her life. But seeing how he had always been one step ahead of them this whole time, it made sense.

"Don't you dare talk about our father," Savannah spat, summoning all her courage as he breathed against her neck. She recoiled each time his breath touched her skin.

"You never had an issue before. You told me everything about your family." Savannah tried to pull away but Andy held on tighter. "So much tragedy. And today there's about to be more." A knock at the door startled all three of them, Andy's eyes flickered with what looked like panic as he focused on the door.

"Isabella open up!" Laura called from the other side, Isabella's heart racing at the sound of her voice. "I know you're in there."

Andy glared at Isabella, angling the knife so that it was now pressing against Savannah's skin, creating a small bloody cut. "Put the gun down," he ordered in a whisper. "And get rid of her."

"Isabella," Laura called again. Isabella looked into Andy's eyes as she slowly bent down and placed the gun on the floor. She backed away towards the door with careful steps, watching Andy closely until she was forced to turn her back and answer the door. She opened it slowly, just enough to show her body, concealing Andy and Savannah behind the door. Laura looked tired and windswept, her face looked pained and she was clutching her side.

"What do you want Laura?" She asked, her tone blank and robotic.

"To talk to you, to work things out." Her eyes were nervous and pleading.

"Like I said, there's nothing to talk about," Isabella repeated, her eyes piercing into Laura's.

"Yes there is. I need to know."

"Need to know what?"

"If you could go back to ten years ago, to that carpark where you left me, would you still leave?" Laura grabbed her wrist, her piercing green eyes the same ones she watched in the mirror as she drove away.

"Laura I have to go," Isabella began closing the door but Laura grabbed a hold of her coat and pulled herself into the room after her. Laura looked shocked as the door swung closed behind them and her eyes fell on Andy and Savannah.

"Hello Detective."

25

Chapter 25

Laura examined the man in front of her. Light brown shaggy hair, an angular jawline and bright blue eyes that looked so familiar, yet a total contrast. Initially she half expected to see the toothy smile, but instead her eyes had fallen on the hunting knife he was holding, the same hunting knife he had used to stab her. It was unfair how much he looked like her little brother.

"Hello Drew."

"So you remember me then?" He asked smugly, Savannah staring at her with terrified eyes. It was like they were back in arts room once again, though this time it was a knife instead of a gun and he wasn't a victim.

"I never forget a face, particularly not yours." She could see Isabella beside her looking between Andy and herself, trying to put together the pieces.

"Yes, Savannah mentioned that after the shooting. She said I looked like your dead little brother. I guess that's why you saved me then?"

"I saved you because it was the right thing to do." Laura said, though now knowing what he was, it was hard to reconcile.

"Bet you regret that now," he sneered, moving forward a step with Savannah.

"It's not up to us to play God, to decide who lives and dies," her tone was strong, but her stomach was in knots. She was petrified what he might do if she didn't make the right move.

"Who says it's not?" He asked, pushing Savannah forward another step so he was just metres from them now. Laura's eyes flickered to the knife and she felt a stabbing pain in her stomach, she was sweating profusely. She could feel that knife cutting through her skin, feel the blood draining from her body. She fought to keep her voice steady as beads of sweat began forming on her forehead.

"The law, justice, common human decency." Andy moved them forward a step, Laura had to hold her nerve not to reach straight for her gun. She didn't want to spook him, she needed to catch him off guard.

"All societal fabrications," he scoffed, Isabella's gun now at his feet. "Bend down and pick up that gun," he ordered Savannah. As she bent down, her hands trembling, Laura noticed an opportunity. Savannah was no longer shielding his chest, she had a free shot. She didn't hesitate.

Laura grabbed at her hip and removed her gun, her heart beating frantically, she knew she had mere seconds. Andy caught the movement right away and as she lifted her gun he struck out. She watched with horror as the knife sliced at Savannah's arm, blood oozing from a long incision. Savannah screamed as Andy pulled her to her feet, again using her as a shield. Laura had lost her opportunity.

"Savannah!" Isabella yelled, not daring to move from her spot, her arms reaching out hopelessly. Laura felt a stabbing pain in her chest, one wrong move down already.

"Dammit Detective!" He yelled, wiping at his brow with his free hand. He was sweating more now too, his eyes flittering and less focused. He grabbed the gun from Savannah's hand and tucked it into his pocket. "You make a move, I make a move. Doesn't matter to me if I kill her, but clearly it matters to you." Savannah's lip trembled, Laura could feel the tension and stress radiating from the sisters.

"Just calm down," she said softly, keeping her gun trained on his head. "We can work something out here." Tears were streaming as steadily from Savannah's eyes as the blood was from her arm. The wound didn't look too deep, but Laura knew it had to be dealt with soon.

"You're not in charge of this situation Detective, I'm running this show. I say what happens next," he yelled, spit flying from his mouth.

"What do you want to happen?" Isabella asked in a level tone, her fists balled by her sides.

"I want to have a redo of my morning, but clearly, that's not going to happen," Andy said through gritted teeth, as Laura inched forward, grimacing slightly as another shock of pain travelled through her stomach. "Your injury still hurting you?" He sneered, twisting the knife around in his hand. "An inch lower and it would have been lights out for you."

"Pity for you it wasn't, it won't be the same this time."

"You're right, this time I'll finish the job." Isabella took a step forward beside her, Andy missing the movement as his eyes were focused on Laura.

"No, you won't," Isabella said, her voice angry and strained. His dark blue eyes landed on her with fury. Laura didn't like that look. It was the same look he had given them when they had confronted him in his apartment. She decided to pull the attention back to her.

"Why leave the dollar bills?" Laura asked. "Why connect the dots for us?" Andy stared back at her tight lipped.

"You want to be famous don't you Andy? After always being a fly on the wall, an annoyance to your mother, a nobody at school, you want to be remembered." Isabella concluded, Laura taking a small step forward.

"And I will be. Look at the fear, the paranoia already. They're talking about me everywhere, the Washington Killer," he sneered, a look of great pride swimming in his eyes.

"For now, maybe. But all that notoriety disappears in a day, a week. The next headline comes and no one remembers you." Laura said firmly.

"It won't after today, I'll be in the papers bigger than ever. 'The Washington Killer escapes New York's Finest'. I'll be a ghost." Andy smirked devilishly as he took another step closer to the door. "Now Detective, you're going to put that gun down or I slit Savannah's throat."

Laura knew it wasn't an empty threat, the look in his eyes told her that he would do just about anything to get out of there. She slowly lowered her gun and placed it on the hardwood floor in front of her, her heart felt like it was going to beat right through her chest. She could hear it thudding in her ears.

"Kick it this way," he ordered. She gave it a light kick and it spun the short distance across the wooden floors to land at his feet. This time he pushed Savannah down to the floor with him to pick it up. He began tucking it into his back pocket as Laura gave Isabella a small nod. The two women dove at him at the same time. Isabella grabbing a hold of Savannah as Laura dove for the arm with the knife.

She felt something connect strongly with her head, she thought it might have been an elbow, her vision blurring. She could hear Savannah and Isabella yelling as limbs flailed around them. She had managed to grab at Andy's right arm and was wrestling with him for the knife. He was kicking madly at her, she raised her knees to try and deflect the blows as she struck back at him. She heard a door open and briefly saw Isabella shove Savannah into the bathroom. Andy launched a strong kick at her stomach that connected with her scar, she screamed in agony and fell back, releasing her grip on the knife.

She saw a tangle of dark brown hair dive across her and heard the scuffling as Andy and Isabella wrestled. She rolled onto her side, clutching her stomach as she tried to catch her breath, the pain felt just as bad now as it had when she was stabbed. "You've been through far worse pain than this," she heard his calming voice in her head." She slowed down her breathing, her eyes still squeezed shut. "You need to get up now Laura, you need to fight." She could see his blue eyes and warm smile, the complete opposite now she realised to Andy's. She heard a loud thud behind her and Isabella scream. She pulled herself up onto her knees and opened her eyes.

Isabella was bleeding from a cut on her temple, her arms were raised above her head as Andy straddled her, trying to force the knife into her chest. Isabella's arms were buckling, he was slightly stronger than she was and had the added advantage of downward pressure. Laura took a deep breath and gritted her teeth. She took a dive and crashed into Andy, the two of them colliding hard with the dorm door, forcing it off its hinges as they landed in the hallway. The knife had dislodged from Andy's hand in the scuffle, both of them desperately trying to secure it.

"Your pocket," Laura yelled over her shoulder, hoping Isabella would get the message. Andy got a hold of the knife and raised it up above his head, pointing it at her neck. This was it, she thought. It was over.

Memories flashed through her mind, Parker and Cate smiling at her as they clinked their drinks, Ellie hugging her after years of no contact, Kyle and Jordan laughing at an inappropriate joke, Alex's cheeky smile as he went sprinting away from the car and Isabella's sparkling brown eyes right before she leant in and kissed her for the first time. She felt calm, peaceful as she looked back into his dead eyes.

"Love story ends here Detective," he said menacingly, the knife thrusting towards her neck. A gun shot rung out behind her, the noise reverberated across the walls. A bullet flew past her head, colliding with Andy's chest. His body whipped back against the wall from the force, the knife clattering to the floor, his mouth agape in shock.

Laura looked behind her, Isabella was on her knees holding her spare gun. Blood was dripping down her face. Laura scrambled to her knees and crawled over to Isabella, her hand cupping Isabella's cheek. "Are you ok?" She asked softly. Isabella's eyes widened at something behind her, she started to raise her gun again, Laura's heart racing once more with dread. There was a sudden crash behind them, followed by a series of yells.

Laura turned around to see Kyle in a bulletproof vest, laying on top of Andy, her gun on the floor beside him, having just been knocked from Andy's hand. Jordan moved forward, his own gun raised and picked Laura's weapon up off the floor. Kyle forced Andy onto his stomach, the killer yelling in pain as Kyle straddled him and forced handcuffs onto his wrists.

"Andrew Kordel, you are under arrest under the suspicion of multiple murders in the Washington Killer case." Kyle began reading Andy his rights as Jordan ushered the paramedics in. The door to the bathroom clambered open and Savannah rushed out, sobbing, and fell into Isabella's arms.

Laura smiled as the two sisters embraced, she stood up slowly, clutching her stomach. The pain was unbearable, she thought she might even pass out as she made her way out of the dorm. She followed Kyle and Jordan outside into the carpark, passing multiple officers in the hallway of the dormitory. The building had been cordoned off with multiple patrol officers stationed at each end. As they exited, the SWAT team were just arriving, now no longer needed. Kyle lead Andy over to the back of an ambulance as Jordan began walking towards her.

"You should get checked out Carlsson," he said concerned, noticing the hand on her stomach and her pained expression. "You don't look good."

"I've been through far worse pain," she said, repeating Alex's voice back to Jordan.

"You're a badass, I can't believe you figured it out," Jordan shook his head in disbelief.

"Wasn't me, it was all Medina," Laura said proudly, looking back towards the building as Isabella and Savannah exited. She saw a man begin approaching them, she squinted and looked closer, seeing Mitch's tall frame as he wrapped Isabella up in a hug.

"You know this area is cordoned off from the public, I can have him escorted away," Jordan suggested, watching the interaction himself. Laura laughed and turned her back on them, looking back at Jordan.

"Tempting," she smiled. "Thanks for backing me up," she said genuinely.

"Anytime, that's what we're here for. I mean that and boosting the attractiveness quota," he wiggled his eyebrows and smiled.

"Oh god, not you too." Laura laughed as Jordan pat her on the shoulder.

"Make sure you get checked out," he ordered, looking over her shoulder and smiling at something as he turned and walked off towards Kyle. Laura turned around, Isabella was standing just behind her, a small smile on her lips.

"We did it," she smiled, the cut on her temple now shining with mostly dry blood.

"You did it, thanks for the heads up," Laura smiled back, thinking back to their phone call. The scar hint alongside all of the other information she had gathered had tipped her off.

"I was hoping you would pick up on that, I wasn't sure that you would though. How did you?" Isabella asked intrigued.

"It was just lucky Savannah had mentioned being friends with a guy named Andy to me just the other day, then the same name popped up in one of the witness statements and then again there was an Andrew in the list of suspects Kyle put together. Plus, you being late and with Savannah, too many coincidences."

"You really are the best Detective in New York," Isabella complimented.

"I don't know," Laura shrugged, "After this I might have some competition for that title." Isabella smiled shyly. Laura's eyes drifted to Mitch and Savannah chatting behind them. Isabella looked over her shoulder, then turned back to Laura.

"It's not what you think," Isabella began to reassure her.

"You're getting a divorce," Laura answered.

"Yes," Isabella looked surprised. "Those detective skills." She shook her head and Laura chuckled.

"No, I ran into Mitch at the station on my way here." Isabella nodded.

"So you and Rachel broke up?" Isabella asked, as Laura nodded. "What was it you were wanting to speak to me about."

"I've been having these weird dreams lately," Laura said, thinking of Alex and Isabella, visions swarming in her head. "And I think I understand it all now, why you did what you did." Isabella nodded, her eyes sad. "So I have to ask, if you could go back to that carpark, would you still leave?"

"Yes." Laura was taken aback by the answer, she looked at Isabella confused. "If it means I get to be standing in this carpark now across from you, then I would." Laura looked at the floor, tears streaming from her eyes.

"Do we at least get to leave this carpark together?" Laura asked, smiling.

"I'm not going anywhere without you again partner," Isabella smiled, grabbing a hold of Laura's hand and running her thumb lovingly over Laura's tattoo.

"I'm going to hold you to that."

"Of course, it's a promise," Isabella held out her pinky, a warm smile stretching across her face as Laura interlaced their fingers. She smiled and drew her hand up to Isabella's cheek.

"God I've been dying to kiss you."

"You have no idea," Isabella smiled as she slammed her lips into Laura's. It was electrifying. Her skin raised with goose bumps as butterflies replaced the painful throbbing in her stomach. She could only ever have dreamed of this moment. Both women were smiling so much it was hard to keep the kiss going. Isabella pulled back, a wide smile across her face as she looked into Laura's eyes, "I love you Laura." She had been waiting ten years to hear those words and this time, she knew she could believe them. It was always her.

"I love you Issi." Isabella blushed, becoming bashful all of a sudden.

"I've missed you calling me that."

"You don't like Medina?" Laura smirked. "I think it's kind of hot." She winked at Isabella seductively. Isabella bit her lip and shook her head, her eyes running over Laura's body. Laura wondered if Isabella was undressing her with her eyes.

"That damn Carlsson charm."

Sirens sounded behind them. Kyle was standing at her cruiser, pointing discreetly towards the Captain, who had just pulled up at the scene. "Come on," Laura ushered, holding Isabella's hand and pulling her towards him.

"But wait, Laura. Do you think we should?" She asked, her eyes looking down at their hands.

"Definitely. I'm not hiding this again," she smiled, Isabella's grin stretching even wider. They walked over to the Captain, only dropping their hands when they were right in front of him.

"Detectives," he said firmly, his arms folded. Laura was concerned with what might come next, the arrest hadn't exactly followed proper protocols and intimate relationships were also against protocol. But she knew she didn't care, she wasn't hiding anything this time around. "Fantastic work," he smiled. "The Mayor wants to have a press conference, he's elated."

"That's great Sir," Laura smiled.

"Very impressive, I'd like a debrief when we get back to the station on how you cracked this one. You two make an excellent partnership," he said, a knowing look in his eye. "I thought as much the very first day you walked into the station Medina."

"Thanks Sir," she smiled back, looking at Laura bashfully.

"It was a team effort, we couldn't have done it without Reynolds and Foster." Laura said, looking at her teammates standing either side of the cruiser. The Captain turned around to look at them.

"Reynolds, Foster, excellent work!" He congratulated before walking off to talk to the SWAT commander. Kyle and Jordan walked over, large grins on both of their faces.

"You know you cost me fifty bucks Medina," Jordan said with a falsely grumpy countenance.

"And how did I do that?" Isabella asked.

"He bet you wouldn't last a week partnered with this one." Kyle pointed towards her and she rolled her eyes.

"And what was your bet?" Laura asked folding her arms.

"I bet you'd last. I even guessed Laura would fall in love with you," he smirked.

"Bit of an unfair bet now we know the history," Jordan huffed.

"You know it's funny, I had the same bet," Laura smiled, looking at Isabella. The detective wrapped her arm around Laura and they began walking back to the cruiser.

"You did?" Isabella asked, not quite believing it. Laura nodded.

"Never stopped," Laura whispered to her, Isabella leant up and placed a kiss on her cheek.

"Ugh are we gonna have to deal with all this PDA on a day-to-day basis now?" Kyle groaned. "I think I preferred the hostile sexual tension." Laura and Isabella both chuckled.

"I still can't believe the Captain watched you two make out and didn't say anything," Jordan said amazed.

"Please, as if he would. Carlsson's his favourite. You wait, she'll be in the papers again tomorrow." Kyle stretched out his hands in an arc. "Washington Killer nabbed by lesbian crime fighting duo."

"Correction, crime fighting foursome," Jordan corrected.

"Correct," Kyle agreed, Laura unlocking the car. "I call shotgun!"

"Nope I'm shotgun," Isabella informed them. "Partner gets automatic shotgun."

"So it's going to be like that now?" Jordan asked with an exasperated smile.

"Yep," Laura smiled.

Epilogue

"You're sure it's not too soon?" Isabella asked nervously as Laura taped up the last of the boxes. It had only been a few weeks since they had officially started dating, but when Isabella's lease came up for renewal, Laura couldn't stomach the idea of her staying in that tiny, dingy apartment any longer.

"Of course I'm sure babe, I think we've waited long enough," Laura smiled, thinking back on the last ten years.

"Me too," Isabella smiled and wrapped an arm around Laura as they looked around at all the boxes. There really weren't that many Laura thought thankfully. She had become a bit of a hoarder over the years. It had been incredibly difficult for her to even clear one quarter of her wardrobe for Isabella. "We're officially going to be roomies, you're stuck with me now," Isabella joked.

Laura shrugged, "It comes with its perks."

"Oh yeah? And what would those be?" Isabella asked, running her index finger down Laura's neck to the top of her chest.

"The cooking definitely, I won't be surviving on takeaway alone now. The chirpiness in the morning for sure, I hate mornings. And other things..." Laura finished seductively, her own finger now trailing the top of Isabella's blouse.

"Ohh those perks." Laura leant down and placed a series of soft kisses along Isabella's neck, slowly backing her towards the bed. Isabella held on tightly to her waist as she pulled Laura down on top of her. "We have soooo much unpacking to do," Isabella smiled mischievously.

"That's why we have movers," Laura argued, smiling back as she leant down and began kissing Isabella's lips. Her lips were so soft, Laura deepened the kiss, tracing her tongue alongside Isabella's. They had waited until now while Laura recovered, but she didn't want to wait any longer.

"Mmmmk," Isabella mumbled. "Whatever you say." Isabella grabbed Laura's neck and pulled her closer, kissing her with fever. She wrapped her legs around Laura's hips and rolled them over so that she was now on top. Laura chuckled at her assertiveness, it only made her more excited.

Isabella's fingers trailed down Laura's linen shirt, stopping at the top button as she snapped it undone, leaning in to place a kiss at the top of Laura's breast, her brown eyes looking up at her seductively. Button, by button she made her way down, kissing every new part of exposed skin, causing goose bumps to form, adrenaline was coursing through her veins as she struggled to contain her excitement.

She popped open the final button and opened Laura's shirt, revealing her angry red scar. Laura looked down self-consciously as she realised what Isabella was looking at, she grabbed at her shirt to try and cover it, but Isabella held her hand. Her sparkling brown eyes bore into Laura's a warm smile stretching across her face. "You're so beautiful." She leant down and placed a kiss on top of the scar. Laura let go of the breath she had been holding and looked back up at Isabella.

"I've been waiting for this for such a long time."

"Me too," Isabella smiled.

"What if I don't live up to the memory?" She asked, her insecurities again bubbling to the surface. Isabella chuckled and shook her head, causing Laura to pout glumly.

"You're Laura Carlsson," Isabella smiled. "From what I've heard, you've got nothing to worry about. Me on the other hand, I'm a little out of practice." Isabella looked down awkwardly.

"You? Not possible." Laura shook her head. "I've never felt more connected to someone than I do with you."

"Really?" Isabella asked excitedly, Laura nodded.

"Plus add the ten years of pent-up tension and you don't have anything to worry about," she laughed lightly.

"Always the charmer," Isabella smiled, staring into her green eyes.

Laura smirked, rolling them back over so that she was once again on top.

She removed the rest of her shirt and looked down at the perfect woman laying beneath her, she couldn't quite believe they were really here. "I didn't think I'd ever get back here after the accident."

"Back where?"

"To the happiest I've ever been," Laura smiled and leant down enveloping Isabella in a passionate kiss.

* * *

Laura paused at the door and pulled out a key from her purse, holding it up to Isabella excitedly. "Here's your key, you want to do the honours?" She asked as a smile lit up Isabella's face.

"I just can't believe we're going to be living together." She took hold of the key and began unlocking the door. Laura smiled happily as Isabella pushed it open and her friends jumped out from the lounge.

"Happy moving day!" They yelled in synchronicity. "Happy moving day," Kyle added, half a second behind the rest. Bri had her hands over Andre's ears, shielding him from the noise. Parker was the first to step forward and envelope Isabella in a hug, she had completely let go of any of her previous animosity and was quite obviously trying to prove that.

Laura was impressed as she looked around the room to see Ellie and Savannah had followed mostly all of her instructions when it came to decorating. There were silver and rose gold balloons dotted around the living space, a large 'Welcome Home' sign hung up above the dining table. Isabella teared up when she saw the sign. She looked over to Laura and gave her a wide smile, Laura's chest swelled with happiness as she smiled back.

Savannah wrapped her sister in a hug and squeezed tightly, "I'm just so happy to never be going back to that awful apartment again," she said gleefully, "but seriously this is so exciting for you guys!"

"Hey roomie," Ellie smiled and pulled Isabella in for a hug.

"Yeah, about that, you know I was thinking...we wouldn't want to cramp your style, maybe you would want to get your own place," Laura suggested lightly, as Ellie rolled her eyes.

"You won't cramp my style," she said, looking down at Laura's mismatched buttons and dishevelled hair. "We're just going to have to have a system." She reached down and rebuttoned Laura's blouse. "No one wants to walk in on that," she pointed between the two of them, Isabella blushing as she smoothed down her hair.

"I suppose you'll be busy at college now anyway Ellie, Laura told me, so exciting!" Ellie had only received her full-time acceptance letter two days earlier. Laura was relieved to say the least, for the first time in a long time, her sister seemed to be moving in a positive direction.

"Even more so now I don't have to worry about getting murdered on my way to class," Ellie joked.

"Because everyone knows you've got a burly detective boyfriend?" Kyle asked, stepping up behind Ellie and wrapping his arms around her. The display of affection still making Laura somewhat uncomfortable.

"Um no," Ellie looked sideways at Kyle. "Because the Washington Killer is behind bars."

"Oh yeah," Kyle shrugged awkwardly, letting go of Ellie. "That too." He cleared his throat and pulled Isabella into a hug, Laura next. "I'm so happy for you guys."

They received more hugs from their friends as they made their way further into the apartment, Cate was of course crying as she enveloped them both. She kept saying over and over again, "I just never thought this would ever happen, ever." Kevin pulled his wife away before her tears completely soaked through their blouses. Laura's eyes continually searched for Isabella's as she was pulled into different conversations with each of their friends.

"Big day," Jordan commented as he placed a hand on her shoulder, both of them watching as Isabella was regaled with tales from Kyle's patrol days. Laura nodded, chuckling to herself as she watched Isabella and Ellie become increasingly more disinterested as Kyle became even more animated. "I wasn't sure I'd ever see this day."

"What day?" Laura asked, turning her attention back to Jordan.

"The day Laura Carlsson settled down," he smiled.

"Never?" Laura asked disbelieving. "I was in a serious relationship just a few months ago."

"Yeah," he shrugged. "And we did really like Rachel, but we knew she wasn't the one."

"We?"

"Oh yeah, Kyle and I talked about it all the time," he smiled, as Laura shook her head.

"And now?" Laura asked incredulous.

"Now I'm not worried."

"And why's that?" Laura asked, trying not to sound too intrigued.

"Because you're with the one, it might have taken me longer than Kyle to put it together, but I see it now." Laura's stomach fluttered with butterflies hearing that. "It's good to see you happy."

"Thanks," Laura smiled, looking across at Bri who had handed Andre over to Cate for a nurse. "You too."

"So when are we seeing rings? Babies?" Jordan probed.

"Hey hold on, one thing at a time," Laura laughed, though the image of Isabella holding a little baby in her arms excited Laura more than she would presently like to admit.

"See old Carlsson would have shot down a comment like that completely."

"That's because I wasn't sure I wanted those things before."

"And now?" Laura looked over at Isabella, her sparkling eyes once again flittering over to look at Laura, offering her a warm smile.

"Now I know I do." Jordan squeezed her shoulders as there was a clinking of glass, drawing their attention to Savannah who was standing at the end of the dining table.

"I'd just like to propose a toast," Savannah raised her glass towards Isabella, "to my big sister," she then turned towards Laura, "and to the one that got away...for all our sakes, please let this be it, I don't think any of us can handle another break up." Everyone in the room laughed, Kyle for a little bit too long, but Laura suspected he had, had a few too many champagnes before they had arrived.

"But seriously, things happen and you can't change the past, but you can rely on true love prevailing and we're all really happy for you." She smiled, her eyes turning glassy with tears.

"To Laura and Bella," Ellie echoed, raising her glass.

"To Laura and Bella," they all echoed and began clinking their glasses. Laura didn't hesitate and walked over to Isabella, wrapping her arms around her waist as she enveloped her in a kiss. Their friends all cheering around them, Isabella kept smiling through the kiss.

"I want to show you something," Laura whispered into her ear, pulling her away from their friends and down the hall.

"What is it?" Isabella asked excitedly as Laura opened the door to their bedroom. She had been very conscious of the fact that it had been a long time since Isabella had felt at home anywhere. Savannah had told her Isabella hadn't felt at home since Miami and she knew she had to change that.

Isabella stepped into their bedroom, her eyes wandering to the wall above their bed, now filled with photo frames. She pulled Laura up onto the bed with her to take a closer look. In the middle was a photograph of the two of them from when they were teenagers. Laura's arm was wrapped around Isabella as they sat on the sand at their favourite beach spot.

"Is that from the polaroid?" Isabella asked, Laura nodding.

"Yep. I've had it in my drawer all these years." Isabella's smile widened and she wrapped an arm around Laura.

"So you didn't really hate me?" She smiled.

"Mmm..." Laura hesitated and then chuckled, Isabella rolled her eyes and turned back to the wall.

Next to their photo was a photo of Cate, Parker and the two of them sitting outside the dance studios at school. Above it a more recent photo of the four of them from one of their dinner dates. She had side by side photos of Savannah and Isabella from ten years earlier to a few weeks prior.

Isabella reached out to touch the photo of Alex and Laura, his cheeky smile radiated out of the frame, Laura always felt like he was right there with her whenever she looked at it.

"He gave me his permission you know."

"What?" Laura asked surprised, unsure exactly what Isabella was saying.

"He told me that when I was ready to come chat to him, I would have his blessing," Isabella smiled fondly.

"Is that so?" Laura shook her head and smiled, it sounded just like Alex.

"Well you know I am officially divorced..."

"I'll take that under advisement," Laura smiled and placed a kiss on Isabella's forehead. Just the thought of Isabella in a white dress making her pulse rush.

Isabella gave her an adoring smile as she turned back, noticing the photo of the four detectives from the Washington Killer press conference. The hype was only just beginning to die down, the Mayor had even taken the four of them to lunch to celebrate. It was her biggest career achievement to date and she did it with Isabella right by her side.

Isabella's body stiffened as her eyes moved to the last photo. It had taken Laura some time to consider this one, but she knew it belonged up there just as much as all the others. Savannah looked so small cradled in her mother's arms, next to her Isabella looked elated sitting on top of her father's shoulders, the man smiling widely as his daughter clung tightly to his neck.

"Laur," Isabella choked on a sob as tears ran down her cheeks. Laura pulled her tightly into her chest as they stared at all of the photographs, a lifetime of memories. "This is incredible." She managed to choke out, her fingers trailing her family photograph.

"I just wanted this to feel like home," Laura said, squeezing her tightly.

"It does," Isabella smiled, her eyes sparkling as she tapped Laura's chest. "Right here."

"I love you Laur, I'm so excited to live with you."

"I love you too Issi," Laura leant down and placed a soft kiss on her lips, wiping away the remaining tears before they climbed down off the bed. The sound of glass shattering in the kitchen made both of them jump. Laura stalked towards the kitchen. Ellie was bent down sweeping up glass as Kyle stood sheepishly beside her, the stalk of one of her champagne glasses remaining in his hand.

"Right Kyle, I'm cutting you off," Laura announced, removing the glass stalk from his hand as he muttered complaints. "I know you, if I don't cut you off now, the rest of my crystal will go the same way."

"Ugh fine," he rolled his eyes as Isabella passed him a cup of water, he sighed before taking a big sip.

"Let's eat!" Cate called from the dining table, Parker carrying over the last of the salad bowls. They sat down side by side at the table, Laura placing her hand on Isabella's knee as they ate. Stories being passed from one end of the table to the next, Laura couldn't feel more grateful for everyone sitting at that table.

Her phone began ringing and conversation around the table died down, all of her friends looking towards her. She sighed and picked up the phone.

"Carlsson," she answered, watching as Kyle shovelled a large piece of ham into his mouth. All eyes were on her as she nodded and hung up the phone.

"There's been a murder downtown."

About the Author

Nicole Taylor is a queer romance writer and producer from inner Sydney where she lives with her partner.

She loves the powerful blend of the romance and crime genres, inciting high stakes drama and intense passion.

Nicole also enjoys being outdoors; travelling to new and exciting places, going on hikes and trying but failing to surf.

Printed in Great Britain
by Amazon

42309583R00175